Gunpowder Percy

Gunpowder Percy

Grace Tiffany

Tempe, Arizona
2016

Published by Bagwyn Books, an imprint of the Arizona Center for Medieval and Renaissance Studies (ACMRS), Tempe, Arizona.

I am afraid of this gunpowder Percy,
though he be dead. How if he should . . . . rise?
—*Shakespeare,* Henry IV, part 1

Prologue

August, 1597. Yorkshire, Northumbria. A Sabbath Evening.

The Scotsman lay hidden behind a low stone wall, his musket trained on his enemy.

It had been two weeks since Thomas Percy, rent-collector, had wounded the Scotsman Douglas with his heavy sword. Leaning from his high horse, the English rogue had cut an inch into the flesh of the Scotsman's thigh. Then, with a gruff warning shouted over his shoulder, he'd ridden back in the direction of York, leaving Douglas bleeding in the dust. The gash was half-healed now, but when his anger rose at the memory, his skin burned and the wound seeped.

He shifted position behind the wall as his target rode closer. *There.* Thomas Percy again. A big bravo on a proud roan horse, traveling the old Roman way beside his master and kinsman, Henry Percy, the Earl of Northumberland. Thomas, younger of the two Percys, wore a stubborn frown. His lord was preoccupied in face, and clad in some slipshod elegance. Douglas noted the details. His eyes were sharp — once with an arquebus he'd shot a sparrow, high in the air above the thistle-flecked moor — and even from twenty yards away he could detect the earl's look of irritation. He was unhappy with his servant, was the master.

They rode closer. Douglas held his musket steady. *To blow his black heart apart with powder and shot.* He imagined the *boom!* and the smoke. Squinting, he mouthed a gospel verse about hard masters who gathered crops they had not sown. Scripture came easily to his lips. Trained in the strict Scottish kirk, north of Hadrian's Wall, he'd had the parables by memory before age eight. Here in Northumbria, where land-need had brought him, he'd seen parables come to life in the harsh light of an English day. He'd met with hard masters in the flesh. Or rather, with their proxies. For the earl did not visit his tenants' farms, but sent his servant, the big-handed, fine-gloved, sneering Goliath. Last month Douglas could not pay his rent; his harvest yield was not in. To justify himself, he'd quoted St. Luke, and gotten stabbed by the man, for his godliness.

The court of assizes had heard Douglas's case. The jury, twelve Yorkshire sheep farmers and growers of oats, had approved his cause to a man. Yet the conclusion was foregone. Thomas Percy was, after all, a valued retainer and a cousin to mighty Northumberland. The earl had visited the judge, and within the space of an hour he'd had his servant back.

That was three quarters of an hour past, in the town. Time enough for the Scotsman to race through the city gates and back over the fields for his gun, and then out again, to this low-walled stretch of road, down which the pair now came astride their high horses, here fifteen, here ten yards away.

And yet.

The Scotsman hesitated, finger on trigger. Thomas Percy was the target. But if the ball went wide, it could hit the earl. It was death to slay a lord, but, more, it might be damnable. For the earl *was* the master of harvests. And even if the ball hit the bad servant — still, the gospel was troubling on this point. For though the Word seemed to condemn the cruelty of landlords, it also threatened destruction to any husbandman who harmed the landlord's messenger. What said the verse? That a stone falling on such a husbandman would *grind him to powder.*

Douglas thought of the powderbag at his belt, and of hell-smoke and fire.

Perhaps the earl's servant should be spared until he rode his way into into a less confusing parable.

The enemy was now directly in front of Douglas, trotting on the right hand of the earl, who was chiding him in a querulous tone. "More *restraint*, Thomas. You must spare me the enmity of the countryside at large."

The voices and hoofbeats moved past and grew fainter. Douglas watched the men still, and the eye of his gun also watched as the pair disappeared down the road.

He had waited for many a late harvest.

He knew how to wait.

Chapter 1

Thomas Percy of Yorkshire was ill at ease on the street.

He walked brooding and starting, jarred by the patter of saucy tradesmen and the press of wheeled and foot traffic. Immigrants were everywhere. Near the Royal Exchange a flock of dark-clad Dutchmen passed him, gabbling in their harsh tongue. To his left, in a courtyard, an Italian fencing master yelled "*Stoccata!*" at a jumping, sweating, foil-waving student. Thomas rounded Old Street corner, and heard, from unshuttered windows, the voices of Huguenot weavers singing French psalms as they worked. He wrinkled his nose.

On Lower Thames Street he got spattered by mud when a carriage rolled by him, too fast for him to identify the crest painted on its side. But he glimpsed, through the coach's small window, the delicate features of a wastrel earl he'd noted now and then at a city entertainment. Thomas curled his lip. Of all city annoyances, such dainty gentlemen irked him the most.

How he despised them! These ladyish noblemen proved that though London had grown like a canker, England's honor had shrunk in its more-than-century of peace, since the day the first Tudor king put a bloody end to the Wars of the Roses, killing hunchbacked Richard the Third at Bosworth Field. Not for five score and seventeen years had the realm's great men acted as true lords, keeping armies of pike-wielding soldiers to defend their rights and their borders, leading those men in battle. Such militias were long dissolved, such heroism vanished from the earth. And the barons? The last duke had been beheaded in 1584, for too closely befriending the Catholic Queen of Scots. Now the highest form of nobleman was, indeed, earls such as that one in the carriage.

Butterfly earls! Those of Oxford and Southampton and Derby went gaily, dressed in orange tawny and peacock blue. Southampton's golden hair reached his waist. These lords bought houses in the Strand, where they played cards and danced the *volta*. They built new manors with ponds instead of moats, and stocked those with goldfish. The old battle-broadswords hung rusting from thick castle walls in the provinces. The new men preferred the Italian rapier, flexible and supple, easily drawn in disputes over tavern reckonings or games of dice, and as easily sheathed.

Such was this brave new world.

It was no world for Thomas. With a mixture of anger and mute longing, he pined for an England he thought he remembered. His native country had passed into history before he was born, and he was heavy with homesickness.

"Pardon." He squeezed himself through a press of women at a fishwife's stall. London Bridge was his destination, and it lay straight ahead. "By your leave, make way." Women eyed him with humor or frank interest. Thomas was a big man, possessed of a certain grace when astride a galloping horse or engaged in tasks of heavy lifting, though awkward in crowds, where nimbleness was called for. He was slow in the quicksilver modes of speech that currently reigned, devoid of the sharp wit in which even menials and tradesmen seemed perfect nowadays. Most of the time he chose not to talk.

He was handsome, though he did not know it. His face was angular, his nose beaked and Roman, his brown eyes fine. At six foot four inches in flat-heeled boots, he towered over other pedestrians on the busy bridge where now he walked. "Pardon. Pray, *pardon*." He edged past, heading south, toward the one thing in this town that could ease his discontent.

Hotspur.

He lay dead on the stage, but he wasn't. Thomas could see him breathing. True, the great knight's body lay motionless, but the yellow scarf his foe had draped over his face was gently moving up and down. There was life in Hotspur, plainly. No matter that this champion of the family Percy two centuries past had lately been sliced through the guts by his enemy's broadsword. No matter that the man playing his part in this history play had collapsed on the scaffold, groaned forth his last, truncated lines in fits and starts, and then stopped moving, to all but the keenest eye. No matter, either, that the actor had copiously leaked great amounts of red liquid, privately squeezing the bladderful of pigs' blood lodged inside his stage-armor. None of that mattered. *Hotspur lived.*

As though to prove it, the counterfeit corpse's mailed foot suddenly twitched.

The thought of undead Hotspur absorbed Thomas Percy as he left the Globe theater's yard after the close of the play. Its scenes had heartened him, though he still felt alone with his thoughts, separate from the crowd that streamed toward the exits, dense with idling apprentices and gamesome lords, law students, a score of wives, and some two dozen whores.

Thomas put a hand to his heavy purse, which he'd kept hidden under his doublet this day, having met with cutpurses in the playhouses before. Good! Its leather strings were still tied tight.

He paused briefly to adjust his sagging sword belt. By law, three feet of blade only were allowed in the city and suburbs, but his rapier's six extra inches were generally winked at by officers of the peace. During Thomas's twenty visits to London since he'd transplanted himself to Northumbria over ten years before, he'd not once been challenged to change his weapon. Perhaps the peacekeepers were fooled by the length of his legs, which kept his sword-tip at mid-calf, like those of other armed men. But Thomas thought otherwise. No, the officers let him pass because they saw it: the aura of honor that clung to him, the *noblesse* and implicit privilege that flowered naturally in a son of the house of Percy.

Now, as he emerged from the theater's shadowy entryway into day, a shaft of reddish afternoon sunlight caught the hilt of his rapier. *So late already!* He stopped, blinking against the glare from the haft, and frowned in disapproval of the hour. He fished in a hidden pocket of his doublet, not for a watch — for Thomas had none — but for his rosary. Finding it, he touched the beads briefly, then rested his hand on the shining pommel of his sword. *Can it be so late?*

He pondered the lateness of the day, of the year, of the century, a quarter-hour later, seated before a tankard of nut-brown ale in the Tabard Inn. This old Southwark establishment stood four streets from the Globe. Set off from the lane by an arched entryway, it boasted a stone floor laid in Chaucer's time. Thomas liked the place.

Why? he thought, gazing blankly through the half-open tavern window into the courtyard, and beyond that, into the street. He smacked his lips over his foamy draught, dabbed his beard absently with a handkerchief, and drank again. *Why could 1602 not be 1403? Why could now not be then?* And he was off, once more indulging the fantasy that he'd been born in the fourteenth century. He knew it was folly, but still, he loved to picture himself grown to manhood at a great battlefield like Shrewsbury in the north, clad in shining greaves and a metal beaver, seated on a horse under a fluttering gold banner and awaiting his lord's signal to charge.

His brain was awash with such images, having been steeped in English history since he was a puny. His education couldn't be blamed for this. His tutors at St. Peter's of York had fed him the regular schoolboy fare of Plutarch and Pliny, and he still recalled snatches of lore concerning Cato and Aristotle and such ancient fellows as that. The lads at St. Peter's were all from Catholic recusant families, and so their schoolmasters — priests in hiding, every one — had also covertly taught them the Roman catechism, which Thomas could still say in his sleep. But other topics and subjects, more colorful ones, had sparked his waking fancy. His spare moments, and some that weren't spare but stolen from Latin declensions, he'd spent reading the penny ballads and historical romances he'd bought or begged from peddlers passing through York.

Thus, better than the lives of the Ancients, he knew English tales of the heyday time of his ancestor Percys. On the instant, if asked, he could tell anything about the Percy who'd become the first Earl of Northumberland in 1377, and about that first earl's son, the fiery warrior whom history called Hotspur. And Thomas had by heart the Ballad of Chevy Chase, which told of Hotspur's tragic fall at the Battle of Shrewsbury, near Wales, at the dawn of a new century. This was, indeed, the event he'd just seen enacted today at this town's newest playhouse. Many in the London audience didn't know the tale before they saw the play, but everyone knew it in the north country. Up there, everyone sang the Ballad of Chevy Chase, though few besides Thomas had memorized its thirty-seven stanzas of iambic trimeter before the age of seven.

He softly sang a stanza now, beating rhythmically on the table top.

The Percy out of Northumberland
An' a vow to God made he
That he would hunt in the mountains
Of Cheviot within days three
In the maugre of doughty Douglas
And all that e'er with him be!

A man dicing at a corner table cocked an eye at Thomas and smirked. "A Yorkshireman, he!" He winked at his companion. "Come, sing 'Bonny Cock Robin' and we'll all join."

Abashed, Thomas looked down into his ale. He'd barely known he was singing aloud.

"Or this!" called the smirking man. "You've heard this one." He launched a new song, mockingly rapping a hand on the table wood as Thomas had done.

You north country noddies, why be ye so brag
To rise and raise honor to Romish renown?
Our queen is the daughter of Henry th'eight,
Who brought every altar and imagery down.

As soon as he recognized the hated old London tune Thomas lunged forward, a hand to his sword. He started to rise, but a shout of "No brawling!" from the host brought the song to a halt, and Thomas, disgruntled, sat back. He stroked his beard and glared at the man, who, laughing, returned to his game. After a few more moments of fixed scowling, Thomas relaxed his brow and lapsed back into fancy.

He had grown in this fitful dreaminess while a youth at Cambridge, scanting his lectures in logic and Greek to haunt the bookstalls like an eager ghost, pouncing on new copies of the English historical chronicles. Lolling in his ill-kept Cambridge room, his patchy new beard already starting to grow wild, Thomas would avidly turn pages, as ink from the fresh type blackened his hands, and his nose when he scratched it. He'd read much of Shrewsbury, where the valorous Hotspur had taken a stand against a hard English king. A treacherous king, who'd betrayed the Percys, his faithful northern nobles. Every version of the tale made Thomas's blood tingle.

This notwithstanding the fact that his own Percyness was not, to be sure, in the direct line of descent from Hotspur. A study of the musty

Northumbrian historical register would have shown him a mere collateral seventh cousin to the present and ninth earl of Northumberland. And that ninth earl had never heard of Thomas Percy until the day he'd received Thomas's letter begging any kind of employment, some twelve years before Thomas's present sojourn in the Tabard Inn with a tankard of nut-brown ale.

Thomas's letter to that puzzled earl had been written and sent after several trials and knocks, when he was no longer a new-bearded student but a full-grown man. Having tumbled from York to Cambridge, he'd bounced more heavily to London, after his year of dubious scholarship. His object in the great city was work. His brawn and a certain untamed look in his eye had garnered him a soldier-adventurer's berth on several ships, last on a westbound vessel, on which he sailed to the Azores in 1589 to fight the Spaniards there. His ship had robbed richly freighted Spanish galleons that bore silver freshly plundered from Indian mines, a sort of English secondary piracy much applauded by Queen Elizabeth, who knighted Thomas's captain on the ship's return to home shores. The captain alone was so honored, but all the sailors had ended enriched. Thomas himself owned a bar of gold when he landed in Portsmouth. In a quick reverse alchemy, he'd reduced the gold to a large pile of silver coin at the shop of a dockside money-changer. That silver pile had decreased by a tenth by the time he'd got back to London, and by a fifth after his three days spent drunkenly weaving through the muddy lanes of the capital city with a band of soldier friends, singing sea catches, waving swords at lawyers, and shaking off the slops poured on their heads by angry housewives in Shoreditch and Eastcheap. The band of bravos had finally landed in Southwark, on the far side of Thames. For twenty-four hours they'd careened in and out of a brothel there.

Thomas had grown shy in the brothel and set forth on his own, still finding his land legs, holding his head from the effects of strong ale, squinting to see in a pale English sun. How much fainter was that orb than the yellow fireball that had blazed over the seaboard of the Spanish main, browning his skin as its light winked at him from the waves! He'd been away at sea so long that land sounds and sights were strange. His brain ached at the roars of the bears and the snarling of dogs in a bear-baiting pit one street to the south. He bought bread and a cabbage from a greengrocer, but felt too queasy to eat them. On Rotherhithe Street he was accosted by a beggar, legless, the fellow claimed, after fighting with

Sir Francis Drake against the Armada off the Dorset coast two years before. This, he was learning, was what all scarred or crippled men said in London, but the fellow had lost his legs somewhere, and Thomas was a Percy, so he gave him the food and a shilling for his lack.

He'd wandered farther, still dizzy, until he found himself carried by the current of a motley crowd. He drifted with their thickening press as they flowed into a tall polygonal house with a thatched half-roof topped by a curious, fluttering flag. He overpaid his passage into the place with a silver coin whose weight stunned the gatherer. Then, halted by the blast of a trumpet, he came to a stop in a wide, dusty yard. And there for three hours he stood stock still and amazed, as for the first time in his life he watched a thing he'd almost forgotten he was seeking.

It was England's own past, the England of his dreams, lived and breathed before him on the wooden planks of a stage.

That had been twelve years before, in the Rose playhouse, which had since been abandoned, replaced in Southwark by the Globe. Now, here on the Bankside for the hundredth time since, he sipped his brown ale, reflecting. These days he lived in Northumbria, where he'd gone back after a year or so more in London. There, in the north, his second wife, Martha, waited for him in their fine stone house, the dwelling a gift of the ninth earl. But since that first day in Southwark a dozen years past, the theaters of London had been a home to Thomas in a way no other place could match. Having discovered the playhouses after his hard seafaring, he'd never long stayed away from them. Now his work for the ninth earl brought him down-country on occasion, but even if it hadn't he'd have come on his own, to see played on scaffolds the glorious time of two centuries before.

The last rays of the sun lit the street outside the Tabard Inn. But Thomas wasn't looking at the street. Sipping his ale, with hooded gaze he peered inward and muttered, "Fourteen-naught-three!"

"Is that the reckoning for your ale?" called the gamester at the other table, the same man who'd sung the rude tune about Harry Eight. The rogue rattled a handful of dice while his partner smiled. "Fourteen naught three! A grand sum. How many months since you paid it?"

Thomas glared at them. "'Tis a *year!*"

"What! And still they serve you!"

No brawling. Thomas turned fully toward the man and said, slowly and proudly, "Fourteen naught three is a year. A year in the era when barons had might to match their wealth. When their liegemen banded in armies to fight for the honor of their lords."

"I thought so." The dicer smiled at his companion. "He's been idling at the plays. *What mean ye to follow the man in the moon –*"

"Thou churl!" Thomas half-rose, hand on sword-hilt. But his word of insult, so far from rousing the gamesters to the challenge, sent the pair awash on a new tide of merriment. "*Churl!*" said the first man, as he flicked drops of ale at his table-mate. "Thou poxy *caitiff!*"

"*Out* on you!" Shielding himself with one hand, the companion drew a deck of cards from a pocket with the other and threw it on the table. "There. Take up my glove, *if* thou darest. St. Geronimy be my speed, thou *varlet!*"

Thomas reseated himself in disgust. The men lacked honor as well as brains. By the *rood!* To call *him* idler! As though the playhouses were a mere carnival ground, while the taverns were universities! He thought he would pause at these dicers' table on his exit, to tell them in a low voice that in the theaters, at least, the Church was Catholic and whole, not false and fractured, and that once, in the Curtain, up in Shoreditch, he'd seen soldiers in a history play shriven before they went into battle, taking the sacrament right there on the scaffold. No trivial piece of symbolic wafer-cake such as the new "priests" offered, but the holy Host, the body and blood of Christ! Where else was such a blessing to be found in England nowadays?

But he saw the host peeping at him from the scullery door with an intrusive sort of interest, and he knew he wouldn't do it.

Moody, he stared into his tankard. His zeal, suppressed, began to fester. He wished more ale, and looked up, but the host had gone. Glancing about, he marked and summoned a boy whose stained cloth apron marked him a drawer. "What's this brew, lad?"

The boy slouched before him, scratching at a head-louse. "Today we serve Huffcap."

"'Tis good. I'll another. And a loaf of manchet bread, my young Trojan."

"We've no more manchet," the boy replied, without as much as a *so please you* or a *begging your pardon*, let alone a bow. He disappeared into the back of the house.

Thomas stared after him in disappointment. The manners of apprentices had gotten depraved enough in the north, but here in London they were worse. All things seemed bent on decline. Instance this tavern! The place should have been crowded with pilgrims, men and women from all parts, ready to embark on blessed journeys to Canterbury or Compostela or, indeed, to Jerusalem. Instead, what did he see? The pair in the corner had grown to a foursome, playing cards, now, and starting to quarrel. And outside? He looked through the latticed window and spotted a ragged, limping beggar being shouldered onto the paving stones by a robed, officious lawyer, proud under his white skullcap. The brisk man of law walked clutching no finely lettered scroll, but a printed book. Fie! That beggar should have been a mendicant friar with a bowl, succored by passersby. But the city harbored no such men now. West of the old walls, once-solemn Whitefriars was a stable for horses, and in Blackfriars, north of Thames, pimply boy players staged raucous comedies that depicted not the old days, but the very scandals and vices of the present year.

Fie. Fie on all. And the outrageous young churl with the beer-blotched apron showed no sign of returning with Thomas's Huffcap.

Suddenly angrier than he could bear sitting still, Thomas jumped to his feet, dropped a coin on the table for his single ale, and banged through the doors of the tavern to the street, fingering his hidden rosary in wrath rather than piety, glaring at the darkening city as though the force of his gaze alone could restore it to its ancient health. He heard the peal of a bell from the church on the corner, and it angered him, since it marked the ordinary hour of the clock, not the hour of vespers. He walked faster, not noticing that instead of progressing toward the bridge and his temporary Eastcheap lodging he was going backwards, retracing his steps to the playhouse.

England! This country was infected at the wellspring, its cathedrals shrunk to headless churches. On its throne sat no crusading king bound for Jerusalem, but an aged queen, denounced by the pope for embracing the renegade church of Martin Luther. A queen whose chief guard dog, a counselor named Cecil, ferreted out Jesuit priests, then tortured and banished them. A queen who disdained to join all virtuous Europe to fight the Muslim infidels who even now threatened Christendom, swallowing Greece, menacing Austria. A damned queen, who forbade masses, and with her last breath sustained a faltering war with Holy Catholic Spain!

It still pained him to think of the service he'd done Queen Elizabeth in the Azores, fighting men who were true Christians like him, for all that their names ended in *a*s and *zed*s.

He stopped short, seeing the blank, circular mass of the playhouse towering before him. He'd completed a circuit, and was back where he'd begun. All was dark in this building now. Only a few lights shone through the small apertures in the whitewashed walls. The lights came from sweepers with lanterns, no doubt, as they culled the ground for the afternoon's relics, garbage and coins and jewelry drawn from the ashes and hazelnut shells. Thomas was here to no purpose. There'd be no play again until the morrow.

Chapter 2

But the next day it rained and London was a sea of mud. The famous Lord Chamberlain's Men had promised a play at the Globe that afternoon, but from the northern bankside Thomas could see that no playhouse flags were flying.

He had business with the ninth earl at his manor just west of London, but had come south two days ahead of the appointment to allow himself time for entertainments. Now a gray afternoon loomed before him. He knew men with houses in London, Catholic men, whose company he could seek for wine-heated discourse concerning their present situation in the realm. Still, he found himself inclining to solitude.

He knew where he would go.

It was a twenty-minute walk from Lower Thames Street to Hart Street corner. From thence he turned down the narrow lane called Crutched Friars. He stopped in the shadow of an apple cart. *There.*

And suddenly, he was.

"Thomas! Old bird!"

The dormer window was half-open, and smells from the bakery downstairs drifted into their two rooms. Sweet scent of warm pastry, sweet sound of a warm voice.

"Sit, husband!" She patted the windowseat.

He joined her obediently, pulling on his shirt. She was tying back her hair as she looked into the street. Closing her eyes, she breathed in, in pleasure. "I smell bread rising."

"Will we guess occupations, Mary?"

She opened her eyes. "Aye." She pointed. "There. Some mechanical. A hooper's apprentice –"

"Scanting work, and off to the plays."

"One like thou." She laughed.

"And thou! Whenever you can, you go with me." His gaze fell on a youth in the street, a stripling some eighteen years of age, his hand on the new-looking hilt of his sword. He was rebuking one of his spot-faced fellows, standing with his legs braced before the apothecary's shop across the lane. Thomas gestured. "That one, then. The roaring boy who pretends he'll pull his sword, though he doesn't know how to do it without cutting himself. A servant, all puffed up with the grandeur of his master —"

"He is like thee as well."

"Ah, but I have no master, and am no servant." He spoke with a note of bitterness. "Would I were! Twenty-four, and no place. As yet." He brooded, idly following the progress of a new arrival to the street-scene, a silk-clad fellow with a feathered cap who led his proud steed down the thin, crowded lane, horse and man both stepping carefully, then disappearing around the corner just as the horse shat. Thomas gave a bark of a laugh. "No post I, and no horse to shit in the street."

She leaned to kiss him. "This will change, Thomas."

"Let us pray it changes soon. I've only two pieces left of my Azores silver."

"You have that, and the goodwill of friends who will place you. Strong friends."

"Huh. Catholic friends."

"There are Catholics at court."

"There are no Catholics who *say* they are Catholics, at court."

Mary did not reply. After a moment she took his heavy hand and kissed the narrow gold band on its third finger. She turned the paw over as though she would study his palm. Then, turning it back, she used his forefinger to point at the lane. "Look there."

"What is't?"

"There, there. Coming from the apothecary. Now just out the door."

He narrowed his eyes, trying to follow the track of her gaze. He saw a white-bearded man pause in the shop entrance, holding a bottled potion up to the light and nodding with satisfaction.

"What of him?"

"What *of* him? But that is Merlin! He knows of our troubles. That is why he's come to London. He'll cast a spell over the queen's privy counselors, to blind them to our holy masses. And you *will* gain your post at court."

"I have read that Merlin was no Catholic, but a Druid. And I'd be glad of a post in *Wales*." But Thomas smiled in spite of himself.

A water drop fell on his hand from his hat-brim, jerking him back to the present rainy day. His smile vanished abruptly. He shook his head, then tapped his heavy purse instinctively. Memory was hurtful magic, and that was all it was. He felt a twinge of guilt. His present wife, Martha, would not like his walking here.

Yet he lingered still, watching the dormer window. As he did so a woman spoke sharply from within the house to a boy capering in the street. The boy darted inside. Thomas followed the lad's back with his eyes. *How old, he? Eight, nine?*

What would it have been, to have had a son with Mary? Or to have a son now? Though his, were Martha to give him one, would be no muddy Protestant street rat like that, but a well-clad young man in fine woolen weave, attending a school where he might be taught true piety, such as his own St. Peter's in York. In the holier country of the north.

Thomas left Crutched Friars Lane and headed for the Strand, thinking not of his newer wife Martha but of the other one, the first one, with whom he had dwelt in London for ten happy months, ten years before. Gentle Mary would not have yelled into the street.

The next day was fine, and Thomas went back to the playhouse. The players were staging the Shrewsbury play again, which was well, since it allowed Thomas once more to see Hotspur fighting. Most particularly, it gave him the chance to examine his idol's death scene with more care. This time, when Hotspur collapsed spurting pig's blood, Thomas pressed through the thick of the crowd toward the edge of the scaffold, again closely eyeing the man's breathing corpse. "Pardon," he whispered repeatedly as he pushed himself forward. "Pardon." Despite his courtesy, and despite his formidable stature, complaints burst from the spectators he elbowed past. "Rudesby!" snapped a saucy redhead who stood arm in arm with her scowling husband. "Marry, you block the view." "Take off your head!" a man jested, lamely, though those around the fellow laughed. The mockery angered Thomas, and he turned to confront the impertinent, hand to sword. But he saw only a mass of faces, most with eyes still trained on the play. He turned and plowed forward again. "Pardon. Pardon." At last he arrived at the front.

Today marked his eighth witness of this great play. Though the ending never changed, the breathing of Hotspur's corpse at the close had begun powerfully to haunt him. Against all reason, he found himself thinking that one day the actor would find himself so overcharged by his part that he'd leap to his feet again, crowing the motto of the Percy crest in expectation of final victory. *Esperance!*

Yet this disciplined actor lay quiet.

The other player on the scaffold was fat. He wobbled mock-drunkenly four paces from the great fallen knight. With a keen eye he scanned the audience, appraising the folk, waiting for the laughter he'd provoked in them to subside. Probably because Thomas was half a head taller than most in the crowd and stood so very close to the stage, the fat man's eye caught his, hooked it, and held. "To counterfeit dying when a man thereby liveth, is to be no counterfeit, but the true and perfect image of life indeed," the fat player said thoughtfully, conversationally, as though proposing to Thomas a point for debate. He then took a stance and cocked a quizzical eyebrow.

Thomas felt uncomfortably visible. Already infamous among the yardlings after his unpopular pilgrimage to stage-edge, he now heard laughter rippling through the crowd, saw folk in the galleries looking back and forth between him and the fat player. The player was still challenging him with his saucy look, raising his eyebrows higher and higher until it looked as though they might disappear into his powdered hair. More laughter came from the audience, waves of laughter, until Thomas felt compelled to nod as though he agreed with what the man had just said — *Most true!* — though he hadn't followed its logic. *Counterfeit living? Counterfeit dying?* He even smiled gamely, though to be sure, the question of whether Hotspur was alive was not a light one. No matter for jest.

Now the fat man was shaking, feigning the feigning of fear. He pointed at Hotspur's corpse while still looking at Thomas. "Zounds, I am afraid of this gunpowder Percy, though he be dead!" Freeing Thomas from his stare at last, he strolled in his insolence about the knight's body and poked it rudely with the tip of his sword. Thomas flinched. The fat player must have seen the movement, for instantly his eye was up and hooked to Thomas's again. His smile was more mocking, his stare shrewder than before. Now he seemed so directly to be posing a question to Thomas Percy that watchers from everywhere in the playhouse, and not just the yard, fell silent and stared at Thomas as well.

"How," said the fat man, tapping Hotspur again on the thigh, "if he should counterfeit too, and rise?"

Yes, that is the point. How if he should? Thomas mused, treading the well-beaten path from the playhouse to the south shore of Thames and the river-stairs. *And did that man know me for a Percy? Players affect to know all, but their knowledge . . . mere seeming, perhaps, like the rest of it.* Still, when he next came to the plays he would hang back from view. He would come to the theater once more before going north, he knew, drawn like a coin to a magnet. Perhaps he would purchase a seat in one of the curtained rooms where lords sat. He could pay.

Now there were truly things he must do, but, arrested by what he'd seen and heard, he stayed still for a moment, allowing the river-bound crowd to eddy around him. *Gunpowder Percy,* he thought. *That is clever. I'd not noted that jest before. Hotspur only plays dead. If he would, he could jump up in a trice like flaming powder. Back on a sudden, like a jack-of-the-clock.* He chewed his lower lip, thinking. *Has the ninth earl seen this play of his forebears? 'Tis doubtful.*

Thomas's master the earl took little time for the playhouses when he was in London. Unlike the distant kinsman he'd hired to collect his rents, he especially shunned entertainments that sported with the reputations of his ancestors. Thomas was eternally baffled by his lord's reluctance. Surely all Percys *should* see this play, and every other play in which a Northumberland was mentioned. And there was opportunity now. The Lord Chamberlain's Men would proceed with the cycle, performing the next play, and then the next, and then all of it again from the first. They'd be at it till All Souls' Day. So, at the play's close, had said the bowing fat man, whose girth, after all, had been quilted padding. He'd stripped it from his frame and brandished it for the audience's laughter in the epilogue.

Near the quay, a bony dog came sniffing about Thomas's legs. Thomas raised a booted foot to push it away, then lowered the foot, remembering the half-eaten apple he'd stuck in his sword belt during the entertainment. He plucked the browning fruit from its lodging and threw it to one side of the lane. The dog bounded to it, sniffed, and gobbled. Thomas took a step, slipped in the mud of the street, swore, caught himself, touched the rosary in his secret pocket. *Mea culpa.* Only three days in London and he was cursing like the sailor he once had been! It was the time he spent in the alehouses here, especially in Southwark. This swearing was a fault, to be amended. Certainly fairground terms would displease the ninth earl, should they become Thomas's ordinary speech.

Crossing the river, he reached Lower Thames Street and the mews where he'd stabled his horse. A groom held the bridle, jesting with two gallants who were also there for their mounts. "Sure this be a great man, see the size of him, and it will do you no harm to wait!" Abashed by the raillery, Thomas ignored it, and stepped into a stirrup. As he swung his long right leg up over the roan's saddle, reaching at the same time into his purse for a penny, he dislodged his rosary, which fell in the dirt.

He froze in the saddle. Had they seen? The groom was patting the horse's nose, still bantering with the gallants, who were pretending to draw their rapiers on him and yelling mock threats. No, none of them had seen anything. Should he dismount, stoop, pick up the beads? In the end he let them lie. He handed the groom the penny and turned his horse's head toward the street. The roan trod on the rosary as it moved toward the gate. Thomas cursed himself for his cowardice, and cursed the times that made cowardice necessary.

Mea maxima culpa.

Chapter 3

A hundred miles north of London, on the grounds of a stone Warwickshire house, a man in a farmer's straw hat sat on the bank of a small lake. The day was windless, and the lake was as still as his face. Beside him stood a woman of middle age, peering intently at a stone now skimming over the surface of the water.

"There. Three times." Anne smiled triumphantly.

The man picked up a flat stone, leaned to the right, cocked his own arm, and let fly. His stone skipped once on the water, then sank.

"You see, Henry?" she said smugly. "I am better than you."

He laughed. "I do not doubt it, Mistress Vaux. But your reason? Because you waste time throwing pieces of flint in a moat, you are better than me?"

"For that, and other reasons." Her tone was teasing and warm.

He squinted at the low, westering sun, and pulled down his hat to shade his eyes. "Name thy reasons."

"One. I pray daily for thy welfare."

"As I do for thine."

"Ah, but 'tis thy occupation so to do. In me it is an act of charity."

"O, charitable Anne Vaux! Thy second reason?"

"I . . . hmm. I will find one."

"So I thought. No second reason. Here, sit by me."

Carefully, she smoothed her skirts and lowered herself to the bank. At her slowness, he turned and looked at her. "All's well?"

"Yes, yes."

He leaned back on his elbows. "Do you know, on this beach, I must stop myself from whistling for old Dash. I am so used to seeing him tear down the grass and run in circles around us. Or splash in the drink for a stick. Would he were here!"

Anne frowned and picked at a blade of grass. "You know why he is not."

"I know. I can still wish him — "

"A good house *should* have dogs. But dogs love you, and so we may keep no dogs."

Henry said nothing.

"Human love can be hidden, but a dog –"

"I know, I *know*, Anne. Pray, let's not always speak of our . . . predicament. Be *content*." Instantly remorseful at his tone, he reached for her hand, but did not find it. She was suddenly clutching her side, feeling an inward pinch. *Agenbite,* in the Saxon tongue. An old word for an old pain.

In a moment the pain loosened its grip, and so did she. She touched his palm, which was still lying open on the sand, as though he'd forgotten he'd left it there. He was gazing past the shore, and had not seen her quick movement, or her wincing. His eyes were filled with the dying sun.

Still, feeling her touch, he held her hand to his lips and whispered, "Hush, Nan. Hush."

Chapter 4

By six Thomas Percy was at Syon House, the earl's great palace west of the city on Thames. Night was falling, and though the house's white walls still glimmered as he approached the gate, all but a few of its windows were dark. He'd expected a light, at the least, in the highest tower, where the ninth earl liked to sit with his books and experiments. But none shone. Was Lord Henry at supper?

In ill humor — it had begun to rain during his ride, and he was cold and wet — he dismounted, felt unconsciously for the absent rosary, and grimaced. He pushed past a groom who (offensively) did not recognize him as belonging to the house, crossed the broad stone-floored entryway into the first chamber, and found himself suddenly faced with the earl's wife. The lady sat in the large presence room, dressed according to the fashion of the year in a low-necked brocade gown and, around her neck, a starched yellow ruff which lay stiff and bright against the freckled whiteness of her exposed bosom. Thomas tried not to stare. The lady's dress was blue, her wide sleeves jeweled and hanging. She sat placidly listening to madrigals sung by four liveried servants. Obliged to wait for her acknowledgment, Thomas stepped to the side, masking his impatience, treading on rushes, and noting with dismay that a shoulder of his muddy cape had soiled the rose-colored Turkish tapestry that hung on the wall. He chafed, waiting for the song to end. Apart from his penchant for ballads, he was not a musical man.

At last the singers bowed, receiving the lady's polite applause. She turned to Thomas, who, like the singers, bowed, having removed his hat. He shifted his position, placing his bulk before the mud stain on the hanging rug. Before he could speak, she said coolly, "You are welcome, Thomas, but my husband is not here."

Thomas was vexed, though not amazed, since the lady's presence generally argued the absence of her spouse. But where was the earl? "Lady, I am sure he requested a meeting at Syon House at this hour."

A brittle smile. "Doubtless he did. But finding me present, he suddenly bethought himself of business at Petworth. If I go there, he will come here. But I will not go there. So at Petworth he will stay all this week, until he returns north. A merry rout of thinkers attend him. Master Thomas Harriot, the mathematician, has called on him there, and Sir Walter Raleigh." Her voice was sour ice. "Men of science."

Thomas struggled to master his irritation. The earl's wife saw his effort, and seemed to find it comical. When she spoke again, her voice was kinder. "He's not forgotten you, Thomas. Above all, he's not forgotten the rents you bring. The estate tax is due the Crown, and he needs money for three *exceedingly rare books* he has found." She raised her penciled brows and dropped her jaw as though transported by awe. Amusement tempered Thomas's anger. But he knew better than to laugh.

The lady went on. "Yes, he remembers you are to visit him. 'Tis *my* words he cannot keep in his mind. I'd told him I would be in residence here through September, until Michaelmas. He wasn't listening, so occupied was he in examining the wing of a dead jackdaw through a magnifying glass. He arrived here two weeks ago, thinking I'd been in London lodgings since the end of August." She paused. When she spoke again, her voice was guarded. "You are welcome to stay the night, though my lord the earl did state his expectation that . . ."

Thomas bowed once more. "Then duty calls me to Petworth." Back on with the hat.

The earl's second southern estate lay in Sussex, twenty miles to the south. Rain fell in scatterings, on and off, as Thomas rode, and he did his best to stay under the cover of the tall elms that lined the southwestern road. His horse splashed through puddles and kicked up more high-flying mud to stain his boots. No moon shone.

His thoughts returned to the play he'd seen that day. He'd had a thought to mention it to the earl's wife before he departed, knowing she enjoyed the London entertainments. He was glad, now, that in his vexation he'd forgotten to do so. Churlish, it would have seemed, in light of her family's recent disgrace. The lady's brother, General Essex, had been executed eighteen months before, found guilty of a plot to thrust Queen Elizabeth from the throne. The conviction had been unjust, Thomas thought, and many others thought the same. Unjust, and all the more painful for that. To speak to the lady of a play that her brother Essex had loved, had talked of and seen more often even than Thomas had (if that were possible) — the topic would have displeased her. Why allude, however indirectly, to her brother's ruined hopes and her family's shame? This should not be Thomas Percy's way. Always he sought to increase his welcome in the fractured Percy household, though at times, in his eagerness, he stepped wrong. He offered thanks to God, and to Saint Winifred, his chosen patron, that he'd not loosed his tongue on this occasion.

Yes, the plays were a fraught subject, because the plays Essex loved had been linked with his too-bold enterprise. At least, the queen's principal investigator, Cecil, had tried so to link them, and not without reason. For some of General Essex's friends had also been fond of plays. Those friends had paid the Globe's actors to present the English history play *King Richard the Second* on the eve of what became the Essex disaster. Like Thomas Percy, Essex's companions had lineage to boast of. More than one of them had seen an ancestor counterfeited in the play they'd hired, a famous forebear or two who spoke glorious poetry like no man on earth spoke outside the theater. Those modern gentlemen had thrilled to the verse as they shivered and sat. The sound of the poetry had heightened their ambition and their valor, reminding them who they were — or wanted to be.

The next day had come the debacle. General Essex hadn't planned to go forth into London, but some of the queen's privy counselors had closed on him, bearing down on his house to arrest him, and in the end he'd had no choice. He left his house in the Strand and galloped through the streets, making his way toward the court. At his back rode those friends — two of them Thomas's friends as well — who'd sat the day before in the cold Globe heartening themselves for such an effort, cheering what they saw on stage, warmed by their passion in the near-empty place in the snowy month of February, when only lunatics, lovers, or well-paid actors would even think of spending time in an open-roofed playhouse. Now, the next morning, *they* were the actors, with fine leather gloves clutching bright sword-hafts, arms and voices strong and ringing in the chill London air. Their leader Essex meant to seek his childless sovereign in her very throne room, or wherever she could be found; to press his claims for her regard, perhaps even for the succession. Beset by court enemies who hated him for making peace with the Irish rebels he'd been sent to vanquish, enemies who plotted to destroy him — threatened by chief counselor Cecil, above all — Essex craved only an audience with Queen Elizabeth. Confident in her fair-mindedness, in her own regal concern for England's future, he meant only to kneel before her, to hand her his sword (that was why he had raised it!), to state his just case. But he never reached her. Her guard blocked his passage and chased him back to his own house, where they arrested him. They dragged him forth, stowed him in the Tower, and beheaded him a month later.

That is what honor and a high-held blade brought in this brave new world of statecraft, of politicians like dwarfish Cecil (such a short man!), who only worked behind the scenes.

And the shadowy playwright who'd authored the soul-changing play the friends of Essex had paid to see, on the eve of the ride? *He* could work behind-scenes as well. After Essex's scandal, that player-playwright and the others of his company had taken care to bring out *all* their history plays, to mingle the more dangerous with the less, to trumpet forth even the oldest works, the ones that had caused no clamor on their first appearances, a bit dusty now, to be sure, but polished anew, and serviceable. *Look you now, milord privy counselor, these plots were taken from the chronicles!* They had argued that mere players could not be blamed for what messages modern men took from a few moldy plays of old England. The actors had merely given what was paid for, and strove only to please (a deep bow, a leg, a cap held to the side). *General Essex, say you? O, he of the Ireland campaign? We know little of him.* All innocence were those actors — because they were actors! — and whether the queen and her guard dog Cecil believed them or not, both saw that Londoners did, and so had not troubled their playing.

Thomas shifted in his saddle, lightly touching his sword. He knew he was lucky not to have been with the men who'd drawn their weapons in the street, who'd seen that play and run with Essex that day by the frigid Thames eighteen months before. He knew his good fortune.

Yet all he could feel was resentment that he wasn't invited.

He rode on under black sky, smelling damp earth and rotting leaves. An owl hooted distantly in the trees by the side of the road. He nodded, jerked himself awake in the saddle, nodded again.

More than half the night was gone and Thomas was hungry when he reached Petworth. At this hour that house was darker than Syon had been. After some minutes, a sleepy servant answered his knock. The earl? He'd left suddenly for his estate in Northumbria five hours before. He required a book about planetary orbits from his northern castle's library, and had not been willing to wait. Thomas was to attend him up there, within the week. Less courteous than the earl's wife, the servant closed the door.

Northumbria! And this wet western ride for nothing! Now Thomas must head back north to the place from whence he'd started the week before, all to deliver his rents and receive butter money for an impatient wife.

Under cover of darkness, he picked up a stone and threw it heavily against the bricks. *Men of science.*

Chapter 5

This question of wives.

For him, no matter how often he tried to flee her ghost, there remained only the one. All other wives, including his present Martha, were her distorted reflection, her image in a dim glass.

He'd first seen Mary in the company of gentry. He'd been in London for four months, after the Azores expedition, at the turn of a decade, in 1590. He'd met one day in the Rose playhouse with some acquaintances from York, a pair of wealthy Catholic brothers whose family owned a London house as well as a manor in the north, and who liked Thomas Percy not only for his name but because his accents reminded them of home. Those youths had begun to include him at their gatherings in the Strand. When he first caught sight of Mary at one of those meetings, Thomas thought her a friend of the house. She seemed a noblewoman, so dignified was her bearing, so quiet and well-tended the hands she kept carefully folded before her. She wore a blue muslin dress, a collar of lace, a cross of gold. Was she the men's sister? But no. She'd not eaten with the family, and from a casual remark made at table he'd come to know she was a servant, a teacher of a young lady of the place, charged especially with the girl-child's religious instruction. Ill at ease in the fine surroundings, Thomas was glad he'd not addressed her as an equal and so called attention to his own lack of breeding. He had the name of Percy, his grandest collateral. But he'd no title to go with that name, and was striving his mightiest to act as though he had. His father — a younger son of a younger son of a son of the Percy house — had lacked any income beyond what he'd earned or skimmed as a collector of taxes in rural Northumberland. He'd mustered enough money to send his son to Cambridge for the one year, but not to keep him there or find him any grander place, and all in all Thomas was barely a gentleman. This was a fault he meant to rectify. Marriage with a gentlewoman was his prospect and aim, though in truth, he was shy, and had tarried long years in studying the graces that might earn him such a match. At twenty-four he was still a bachelor.

And then *she*.

Leaving the house that day, he saw her seated with her pupil in the parlor, instructing the little girl in her catechism. He glanced at Mary furtively, and both he and she blushed. He would never forget the flame of her cheeks in that moment, their fusion of red and white. The next day he returned and, himself again pink-faced, requested an audience with this lady — for a lady she'd seemed. Given leave by her employer, she received him. He found, to his joy, that it mattered little to her whether he could write fair, or deliver courtly words of admiration, or bow with any grace. For her, proof of his love was his joy when he discovered she'd no more money than he, and hence no higher prospects.

When he pondered the thing closely, he was still amazed that Mary's heart had chosen him before he uttered a word. That was a kind of miracle. Afterward, once her warm regard had freed his tongue, there emerged between them secret correspondences that began to bind them tightly. She was a dreamy maiden, and though she did not partake of Thomas's brusque vigor, both their minds were awash in the past. Mary's thoughts, like her reading, drifted through old myths of dragons and giants and questing knights; tales of Launcelot and the Lily Maid of Astolat. Thomas's own notions galloped apace through three prior centuries, always circling back to stop at the Battle of Shrewsbury, as though to rest a horse.

The two of them found much to talk about.

They married within weeks, and settled in Crutched Friars Lane, under a slanted ceiling in two rooms at the top of a stairway. From such a home he considered what next to do.

In the mornings and evenings they prayed. For Mary had not only stoked his interest in old legends, but inflamed his piety. While the blue muslin dress and lace collar had been gifts from her employers, the gold cross, he soon found, was not. She wore always this pendant, which had been given to her by a fiercely Catholic mother at a hushed confirmation ceremony when she was twelve. Most of the Percys were also recusants or, at the least, Catholic sympathizers, and famous for it. He himself had been raised a Catholic, in the haphazard fashion of so many in the north. With his parents he'd stood at masses held at irregular times, not in churches but in neighbors' houses, usually in rooms that lay far from front windows. Sometimes the rites were inexplicably interrupted, and he and whatever other children were present were hurriedly shoved into hallways, told to go and play. He'd been six before he'd understood that not everyone in the world was a Catholic, and that he should not say certain words, like "pope" or "chalice," outside the house or the walls of St. Peter's school. Maturing, though he'd not lost his ardor for tales of old Catholic times in England, he'd let his personal religious observances slip.

But that changed with Mary. She was devout, and at her side he became keenly aware that for years he'd not given religion the place in his life it demanded. He knew why he hadn't, of course. Cambridge had been especially hostile to Catholics, full of masters and students who mocked any Romish gesture, like making the sign of the cross, or bowing to the Host, or kneeling in church. And after Cambridge he'd come south to a London full of hot talk of war with Catholic Spain. At that time honor had seemed to consist in putting England first, despite its lamentable breach of faith with Rome. So Thomas had spent some of his own blood at sea in 1589, proving his English mettle. Up and down the Atlantic he'd sailed, with shipmates who'd called Spaniards papist dogs — he'd done it himself! — and themselves true Christians, though they broke nine of the ten commandments every day and kept the sixth whole only because no women were aboard. These sailors were not Catholic, therefore they were good. Inwardly Thomas had sneered at such folly, but it had seemed then that Protestantism such as theirs was a necessary evil to be embraced by a man who wished friends or aspired to rise in Elizabeth's kingdom. And so, once back in London, he'd refrained from proclaiming himself an official recusant, a Catholic willing to pay fines rather than attend Protestant services.

But no real benefit had come from this restraint. He'd not risen in the world. No great post had been awarded him, no knighthood conferred, despite his good service in the Azores. A place in a noble house refused, a secretaryship denied, and then he was half through his twenties and sprouting early white hairs in his beard like his father had done. Doors were quickly shut against suspected Catholics not already born to lordly office, such as an earldom, which no sane king or queen would attempt to take away. Or so Thomas had told himself, though in his darkest moods he'd wondered whether the sticking point was deeper and more personal: whether, Catholic or no Catholic, there was simply something wrong with him, and people knew it.

But then came Mary. Mary loved him. She would give him a child, and the child would love him too, and honor him. He felt his value proven by the shining regard of his wife and imagined babe. He believed, again, that the world's doors would open to Thomas Percy.

One day she came to him with her hair loose, her blue gown open at the neck. He was reclining shirtless on the bolster, watching her glide in a ghostly way between their rooms, smiling like an image of Saint Claire of Assisi. He held out his hand as she approached, and she caught and kissed it. She sat next to him then, and put a hand at the base of his broad back, touching the curious thatch of hair that grew there, the patch that Thomas himself had never noticed until she'd touched his own hand to it months before. Now, with a meaningful look, she took his large hand and placed it on her belly.

He went still.

Mary's smile widened by a fraction.

There was no need, then, for words.

Chapter 6

September 28, 1602. Michaelmas Morning

Thomas saw his horse walked and stabled. He spent the night at Petworth, despite the surly servant. He slept late and was served a mid-morning breakfast of venison, eggs, milk, and butter, which put him in a better frame of mind.

Where the gate met the London road he sat his horse and pondered. Within the week, the earl had said. A se'nnight, he must have meant. It was Wednesday now, and Thomas's roan would need to sprout the wings of Pegasus to reach Alnwick Castle by Sunday. The earl himself would not have reached it, unless he'd said magic words and flown. The ancient seat of the Percys lay in the northernmost part of England, just south of Scotland's border. Six days' hard ride. But Thomas always rode hard, so that left, at the least, a day to spare. If he left London at dawn on the morrow, by Friday he'd be in the midlands. He knew there was now a priest in Warwickshire, at Baddesley Clinton, a safe house rented by friends. He'd stop there and be shriven. Perhaps there'd be a mass.

And today? He squinted at the sun, which was just now breaking from behind the clouds. There'd be playing today. He could spend one more afternoon in Southwark.

Watching that day, Thomas took careful note of the players' manners, the modes of courteous speech they used to enact their betters, the noblemen. "My lord" at every other word, and "My honest noble friends," with a bow not too deep, merely a duck of the head. "Sirrah," of course, to the inferiors.

The play today was the promised next of the history cycle. Most of the characters were the same. There again was the annoying fat one, Sir John Falstaff. He sent the crowd into gales of laughter whenever he appeared. But Thomas fidgeted through the fat knight's scenes, waiting for more talk of battles. He knew battles would only be talked of in this play and not staged, since he had seen all these plays before. Today the players would show how the honor of swordsmen could be defeated by the treachery of politicians: by the Cecils of two centuries past, dogs already coming into their day (clever playwright!). This serious thing was what Thomas wanted to see and hear.

While the other playgoers laughed at fat Falstaff, Thomas Percy yawned, peering from behind a half-drawn curtain in a lord's box. He'd paid a shilling for the seat today, and gotten not only room to stretch his legs but near-privacy for his money. The box's only other occupants were a bejeweled gallant and his painted, overdressed ganymede, a youth clad in women's skirts and a wig. Neither paid any attention to Thomas, much less to the play, as they conducted their own scene of murmured denial and furtive groping in a corner of the box. This was well. Thomas scorned their depravities, but at least he could listen to the verse undisturbed by loud laughter or card play or drifting, chokesome tobacco smoke. And with the box-curtain half-drawn and his seat set far back from the lip of the stage, he could remain shielded from the actors. Today saucy Falstaff would not seek his eye, noting his height and broad beard, and his eagerness, especially when Hotspur was spoken of.

Hotspur had died in the last play, brave victim of his own valiant effort to install a just English monarch. But no matter, taken all in all. Though no breathing corpse now lay on the stage, the Hotspur of the earlier play was still alive to memory, recalled most eloquently by his widow, who praised her dead lord and reproached Hotspur's sluggish father, the first Earl of Northumberland, whom she blamed.

The chronicles had told Thomas the story. The first earl had feigned sickness on the day of the great battle at Shrewsbury in 1403. He'd betrayed his gallant son, who'd looked for and not found his father's forces when he needed them. How could the old man so have forsaken his blood? How could he have stayed so preoccupied, so absent in heart and mind, as to hide in his northern castle and allow his noble sprig to fail? *Esperance!* Hotspur had cried alone, bold on the field of endeavor. That was the Percy motto: *Hope!* Fired by hope and just grievance, Hotspur, the pearl of chivalry, had then challenged a prince of the royal house to single combat at Shrewsbury. Though he had lost and died, still, *that* was honor! And where had Hotspur's father's honor been?

So asked Hotspur's widow, speaking tartly on the scaffold. She was, in truth, only a mock lady, an adolescent boy in a jeweled head-dress and a yellow peruke. But the stage and the story redeemed the youth, changed him from an ordinary Southwark lad to a holy thing. *This* was no ganymede-for-hire, but a noble he-she who lent spirit to the players' enterprise, declaiming words that conjured great Hotspur straight back into being. The knight might have been standing there, his glory *stuck upon him as the sun in the gray vault of heaven. For by his light did all the chivalry of England move to do brave acts!*

All wished to be like him.

He was the mark and glass, copy and book, that fashioned others. O wondrous him! O miracle of men!

Gone now, gone forever.

But might he not rise?

Thomas left the theater halfway through the scene that followed the young widow's speech. For that next, inferior patch of dialogue seemed to go on forever, raveling forth a low quarrel among sodden wretches in an alehouse, wherein honor, no longer a high theme, was simply mocked in the blustery knavishness of a character called Pistol. Thomas was sure this Pistol had never truly existed. An explosive fellow was he, with that name that marked him a modern, gun-bearing soldier, though he spoke in an old-fashioned style, snatches of bad stage poetry stuffed with allusions to the Trojan War. And such a fool!

The worst horror of it was that Pistol was played by the man who'd played Hotspur the day before. This was almost blasphemy. It angered Thomas to see how the players' miraculous trade could turn so suddenly false, letting an actor swiftly decline from a high part to a low one, from the mold of chivalry to an outrageous brawler. Yesterday a bright sword of battle, now a cowardly sneaking gun, fired from behind a wall! What were these players playing at? They truly should think harder about who was given which part.

Later Thomas brooded, seated at a small table in a tavern called the Irish Boy, in the Strand. He'd just exchanged fiery words with the tavern host about the sad state of the cod he'd been brought for supper. He'd called the man villain, mocked his effete and presumptuous crystal buttons, come near to brandishing his sword, and now felt himself sliding back into the black mood of two evenings before. Ill thoughts, an old enemy. He groped for his missing rosary and, disappointed, flattened his empty hand on the scarred wooden table. Briefly he prayed to Christ and Saint Winifred. *Lighten my spirit. Light my thoughts.*

Melancholy could lead to madness. This was a well-known medical truth, and furthermore the theme of another play that man had written, wherein a vengeful son spoke to his father's kingly ghost. Thomas had heard that play twice, and knew that, like the histories, it was Catholic. For the angry ghost had stood under the stage, in a place that must have been Purgatory, since his cause was so just that it couldn't have been Hell. He spoke from the middle-realm of the afterworld, the temporary dwelling of the Heaven-bound dead, the place which the Protestant prelates mocked and whose existence they denied. But no matter what the English Church said, the writer had put Purgatory in his play. He dared. Add to this that he'd written a play for Essex, or staged a play for Essex, or allowed himself and his company to be paid to stage it for Essex's friends, which was almost the same thing as joining Essex in the street, waving a sword. (Which Thomas too would have done, had he been in London that day, and invited.) And Essex, while not a Catholic, had been notably sympathetic to the downtrodden Catholics' cause, which was why Thomas's own good friends, Robert Catesby and Thomas's own brother-in-law Jack Wright, had rallied behind Essex in the street.

Thomas's mind turned its slow wheels, and finally the thought came clear. It all fit together. A play about Purgatory. Essex, a playgoer, a friend to the Irish in Ireland so green, and to Catholics at home. Fiery Hotspur, bold challenger of monarchs, whom the fat Falstaff pleased to call Gunpowder Percy, a corpse that might rise. Did these strands not combine in a tapestry depicting one truth? And that truth was that this playwright was one of the secret faithful, holding to the old religion of Hotspur's time, two hundred years before! Now, like the rest of them, he was biding his time.

Thomas stood up abruptly, his cod only half-finished. He straightened his sword and bowed to the host, who was rolling a barrel of ale toward the tapster. "Forgive harsh words. I withdraw 'villain.' Belike the fish was well."

The host looked oddly at the big, well-dressed man with the broad beard who spoke like a man out of *Tales of King Arthur.* He thought Thomas looked sad, in his black garb and his Hamlet hat, with a youngish face belied by his white-flecked hair. Aged prematurely? Some grief in youth? The host saw the scabbard that hung from the man's swordbelt almost to the floor, clearly half a foot farther than the law allowed. He'd not noticed that sword when the man had come in. Now the sight of it inspired the host to stop, prop the ale-barrel with his toe, and bow graciously to the burly fellow in return for his courtesies. "'Twas no matter, good sir," the host said pleasantly. Lord or knight? The big man might be neither, but was doubtless employed by such a one. In cases like this, deference was wise, as was scrutiny. The host noted the look of his customer. All such intelligence might prove profitable, later, to someone or other.

Thomas strode out into the Strand. It had been dangerous, perhaps, to come to the Irish Boy for his ale. The place stood near Essex House where Essex had lived, and had furthermore been Essex's favorite public meeting place. The Irish Boy was still known as a haunt of the disaffected, though a year and a half had passed since the general's disgrace. It followed that it was also a house of spies.

But I did nothing wrong, he thought. *Now. What?* Having allotted himself a full day and night more in London, he cast about for activity. Where to go? Not back to the play, which would have ended.

He'd again stalled his horse in the mews. He walked, aimlessly at first, then up Godliman Street with a purpose, to Paul's Yard. In the shadow of the great cathedral he passed the bookstalls. Books, he knew, were the dark seeds of each malicious innovation to beset this realm in the past century. But the strawberry grew underneath the nettle, and good fruit could be found among the weeds.

Following that thought, perhaps he might find a pious book among the trash of Paul's Yard. So he walked, scanning the ware. Among the numerous printers' stalls he saw mostly comic and serious handbooks, offering to teach the buyer how to spot thieves or to cut purses, how to tame a shrew, how to grow delphiniums, three infallible methods of unmasking an adulterous wife. From stretched cords, drying, hung English translations of Latin odes, comic and tragic playbooks, and treatises on architecture. Stacked on the counters below all these lay Bibles. Protestant Bibles.

He walked, looking for a tradesman bold enough to sell a Latin bre-
viary. For his was frayed. But his questions earned him nothing but eva-
sive replies, and, in one case, an incredulous look.

He saw a high-browed man in a plain cloak thumbing thoughtfully
through an edition of Foxe's Book of Martyrs. A papal agent? No. The
man was smiling at something in the book, though it was full of Protestant heroes and Protestant lies. Thomas had heard of Foxe's book. It
slandered the good, dead queen Mary, first daughter of Henry the Eighth,
called Bloody Mary now, though she'd been a pious Catholic who wanted
only to repair the damage her father had done, to restore her country to
the arms of God, and had known only radical measures would serve. Yes,
she'd burned a few heretics! But had she been worse than her successor, her Protestant younger sister, Elizabeth, who winked at the tortur-
ing of Jesuits? Who stood denounced by the pope? Elizabeth, now an old
woman who thought she would never die and hence refused to name a
successor, but who had best look to the state of her bitch-stubborn soul,
mark you, now that rumor's tongue ran busily among the houses of the
great saying *The queen is not well, Queen Elizabeth is not well at all,* and
well it was that she was not well. Truly the hand of God struck the enemies of the faithful and –

"Sir?"

Thomas glanced at the high-browed man, who now stood with his
thumb in Foxe's book, regarding him quizzically.

"What is't, sirrah?" Thomas asked.

The man's eyebrows rose, but he made no complaint. "You spoke,
good sir. Of the hand of God. Do you speak to me?"

Thomas dropped his eyes to the man's book, casting upon it a full
righteous glare. "*Readst* thou that?" he asked loftily.

"You can see that I do." The man's voice was mild.

"I mean dost thou read that in *particular?*"

"I read nothing in particular."

"So I see. For 'tis a very nothingness thou readst."

"Ah!" The man smiled. "Then may I return to my nothing?"

"Yes," Thomas said coldly, turning away. "Back to thy vomit."

"I thank you," said the man. But he did not return to his vomit.
Glancing at the sun, he replaced the book, then melted into the crowd of
purchasers and cut-purses. Thomas felt he had scored a point.

Bloody Mary, he thought with energy. Why bloody? That queen should have been made a saint.

He looked again at Foxe's book, now back on its stack of like paper heresies. He gave it a fierce final frown, glaring down his beaked nose. Then his eye wandered idly over the stall's other offerings. *Strange Birds of Africa, Discovered by Dutch Sailors.* And another. *Monstrous Birth in Kent Signals Division of Christendom.* Under that title was stamped a crude woodblock print of a two-headed infant, from which a midwife recoiled in gape-mouthed horror.

Bloody Mary.

He winced, and turned away, trying not to remember.

Chapter 7

At mid-term Mary's pregnancy had turned difficult. She'd begun to bleed.

In their rooms over the bakery in Crutched Friars Lane, the two of them prayed again and again to Saint Winifred, who blessed women in matters of childbearing. Thomas spent hours on his knees invoking that holy woman's name, and endured nights with no sleep, until his vision doubled.

And one day, in his exhaustion, the saint came to him. She shimmered in the air. Her voice was a music. Thomas saw and heard Winifred saying Mary would be healed of the bleeding and the child born whole if they did pilgrimage to her shrine at Holywell, in Wales. They must arrive on Saint Winifred's feast day, November the third.

He repeated the instruction aloud as he heard it. Afterwards, when he looked up, stunned from the radiance of the fading vision, Mary was looking at him from the bed where she lay with eyes as wide as his. When he told her of Winifred's promise, she said she believed she had heard it as well.

So they took steps to join a pilgrimage that was already being planned, with stealth and hope, by the small Catholic community in London to which they belonged. The group was made mostly of women: young matrons anxious to conceive, and women in their thirties and forties, years married, who'd almost given up hope of motherhood. But men would accompany them for protection, because husbands honored Winifred, too. Oft told among the congregants was the story of how old King Henry the Eighth himself had journeyed to Holywell to pray for a son half a century before. That was before he'd turned against the Church and dismantled the blessed shrines, which had vexed Winifred. The wealth of Winifred's holy site had been ravaged, stolen decades and decades ago by the Crown, but the chapel remained, it was said. It lay far from London, Parliament, and the queen's spies. And of course the place was still blessed. Nothing could change that.

The Londoners would go.

The group laid plans for the journey before the masses they secretly observed at the city house of a rich recusant. Their guide would be the young, ascetic-looking Jesuit priest who ministered to them, a man named Quindle.

Mary was still bleeding intermittently, but she felt the child move in her belly, and now knew herself blessed, or soon to be blessed, by Winifred. She was calm. Thomas spent a precious portion of his remaining silver on a horse for her to ride. They prayed and he fasted, though he insisted that she eat, for the sake of her own health and the baby's. They would be traveling for more than a week there and back, and needed strength.

Then, on the eve of the day chosen for the group's departure, word came that the pilgrimage must be postponed. Pursuivants had arrived at the house that shielded Father Quindle. His host had barely had time to whisk him into the priest-hole, a hiding place built behind a false wall in an attic.

The queen's searchers looked for three days, as the friends of Father Quindle anxiously and covertly watched the house. The searchers came out empty-handed on the fourth day, leaving only a harsh warning to the place's owner. It was the feast day of St. Matthew.

That evening the congregants gathered in the house, entering one by one and through different entrances. They met a wan Father Quindle, who was starving but determined not to profane his stomach with stew and ordinary bread before celebrating mass. He must give thanks, with particular gratitude to St. Matthew. He donned his massing clothes and began.

As they all stood, heads bowed, in a windowless room at the house's center, they heard boots on the stairs. An instant later the pursuivants burst back in. They'd been watching, of course, from a church across the street.

Father Quindle was holding the Host to Heaven in consecration when they seized him. He dropped it, looking more aggrieved at the falling of the Eucharist than at the rough hands about his body. Thomas, who stood nearest Quindle, caught the Host as it tumbled. He stood appalled, holding Christ in his hands, begging God's forgiveness for so rudely handling Him with unconsecrated fingers. But to have let it touch the *floor!* He looked around desperately, seeking Mary in the flurry of persons running helter-skelter from the room. The pursuivants were not chasing them. It was the priest they'd wanted. There! Thomas saw his wife standing by the door with a face full of fear. Dashing to her, he caught her hand and held the Host to her mouth. "Eat!" he said, pushing the Body between her lips. She swallowed.

Then they ran.

Once they were safely home, Mary looked at him whitely. "We cannot go to Holywell." She held up a hand at his protest. "Without Father Quindle's knowledge of the roads, we'd not get there now by the Feast Day, and I fear going. They will stop any group of us leaving London. You saw those men. There was no mercy in those faces."

He pled with her, racking his brain for arguments. They should go. They could do no more here than pray for the father's release. And how could they forswear their pledge to Saint Winifred? Thomas was Mary's husband, and could and would protect her. Besides, she need fear no more pursuivants, since it was clear that these officers wanted only to trap the Jesuits. Hard men the priest-catchers were, but they cared little which citizens did ambling pilgrimage to a well in Wales. They were watching for the fathers, and for men with the means to support them, nobles of known Catholic houses –

"And your name is Percy!" she cried.

He could not change her mind, so at last he relented. They would not go.

For a week her slight bleeding persisted, at the same worrisome rate as it had since it started. Missing in Mary now was the calm hope of deliverance. And it seemed to her that the child's movements were weaker.

She carried the babe nearly to term, well past the date when they could have walked to Winifred's well and back again. Then came a night when she woke him, crying. It was hemorrhage. Desperate to stanch the blood, afraid if he left in search of a surgeon she'd be dead when he returned, he wrapped her in sheets, in her clothes, then in his.

In the morning two neighbors approached the door, cautious and wide-eyed, armed with pitchfork, pole, and net. They feared a wild dog was loose in the room. They found something worse: a naked, bloody man, crouched howling in a corner, his arms covering his head.

Pale white on a red-drenched pallet, by the wall farthest from the window, lay a woman, lifeless, her belly nine months swollen with a still child.

Chapter 8

September 28, 1602. Michaelmas Night.

Thomas left Paul's Yard and went to reclaim his horse. Half an hour later he was riding northward, back to Northumbria on the old Roman road. The roan had been well rested and fed at the mews, and it trotted so well that by sundown Thomas could see the spire of the church at St. Alban's. He stopped only briefly at the small grave where he'd seen Mary buried ten years before, with his child still in her body, at Hartford, near her birthplace. He laid a hand on the stone and said a prayer for her soul's swift passage to Heaven. That her time in the vale of Purgatory might be lessened.

He did not know how to pray for the child.

He remounted and turned his horse's nose north. His own must be turned north as well, his mind framed to thoughts of a newer wife, who was jealous of the dead.

Not that he'd go to Martha straight away once he entered Northumbria. The earl's command was paramount. Thomas patted the bag that hung inside his shirt. There were rents to deliver, and he'd not see his own pay and Martha's household cash before this silver was safely transferred to Lord Henry Percy's coffers at Alnwick.

And yet there was time for a mass.

Each time it seemed a miracle. He'd be riding, shrouded by woods, hearing nothing but birdsong, the earth-muffled thud of his horse's hooves, and wind in the branches. Then suddenly he'd burst from shade into light, and the big stone house would be standing before him like a fairy castle, a vision risen from a green lake decked with lily-pads.

There was magic in the midlands manor called Baddesley Clinton. Three of the house's strong walls were surrounded by water which gave the appearance of a moat, though not the function, since the bridge that led from the bank straight up to the high front door was of solid stone, not hinged planks. Regarding it, Thomas felt his joy at the first vision of the house sour slightly. Gone were the days of the old nobility, who protected their rights and holdings with drawn bridges and open defiance. The new century was, by necessity, the age of the sneak.

He dismounted, reminding himself that there could, after all, be boldness in subterfuge, and great skill. He knew that the placid house before him was a case in point. It was owned by an old Catholic country gentleman, and leased by a brave spinster named Anne Vaux. Like White Webbs, Anne Vaux's other house, near London, Baddesley Clinton had been artfully riddled with warrens, with trapdoors in turrets and hidden stairways and dens that could conceal as many as twelve priests at a time when pursuivants came to call. Queen Elizabeth's black intelligencer Cecil knew of White Webbs and Baddesley Clinton, and sent agents on surprise visits to both locations several times a year. But they'd not snatched a priest yet, though once five Jesuits had been present together at Baddesley Clinton, conducting their semi-annual convocation. Warned, they'd spent a day in priest-holes, and the next morning were gone, dispersed to five different parts of the country. *Ha! Let the churlish pursuers rage and rail, the virtuous shall elude them, though they—*

"Thomas! Stop waving thy sword in the air and striking poses! Thou'lt frighten my chickens!"

Thomas looked to the right. Tall, spare Anne Vaux was leaning from the house's window, watching him with amusement. She cupped her hands and called again. "Give thy horse to my groom! A walk in the field and some oats will suit him better than grass. And you'll like a pheasant wing better than air. Come in! We're at supper."

Loud laughter pealed from the large dining room. Thomas hung his sword in the entryway, wiped his boots with the cloth a servant handed him, and went in.

Ravenous, he first marked the board, which was heavily laden and richly dressed with damask cloth, silver spoons, and Venetian glass. His gaze passed quickly over this fine household stuff and settled on the offerings: sweetmeats, half-filled wineglasses and half-filled bottles, three kinds of fine white bread, green sallets, prawns in wine sauce, and there in the middle, the remains of a partly eaten pheasant which looked cooked to perfection. *Ah!* Yet to display one's hunger was less than genteel. Swallowing, he forced his eyes from the feast and took in the company.

The size of the gathering made him blink. As he'd expected, there sat his brothers-in-law, Kit and Jack Wright, who'd told him weeks before of their purpose to meet with their priest, Father Garnet, in Warwickshire. And there was Henry Garnet, a humbly dressed man of middle age, murmuring something to Anne Vaux, his most devoted communicant. Across from that interesting pair sat two northern brothers, Bors and Gawain Wintour. Also expected. Next to Bors, on a high seat, perched the dwarf.

There was nothing amazing in the fact of the dwarf's presence, but Thomas stared at him nonetheless, thrilled, as he always was, by the man's very smallness. Two of him stacked could not have reached Thomas's crown. Nearly a year had passed since he'd been in a room with tiny Nicholas Owen, and he wondered now whether during that time the little carpenter had shrunk even smaller than before, self-compressed by the fervent exercise of his calling. Perhaps, at times, Owen prayed to disappear. Invisibility would have helped him in his vocation. The dwarf had spent his adulthood creeping into small spaces in large houses, carving hundreds of tunnels into dwellings of the Catholic gentry in the midlands and farther north, crouching and crawling as he dug. At least a dozen of his hidden passageways snaked through Baddesley Clinton. The scrape on his cheek tonight looked fresh. He must today have been repairing one of Anne Vaux's hiding places. He looked tired from his labor, but content, as always, salting his roasted fowl next to Eliza Vaux, Anne's cheerful widowed sister-in-law, who watched Owen protectively and patted his shoulder. Eliza's own plump face was rosy with the heat of exertion. Doubtless she'd been helping Anne's servants carry dishes in from the kitchen. Thomas felt the comfort of knowing these people and the likely occupations and cares of each.

Except for one. Thomas frowned. Who was the richly dressed gentleman on the other side of Eliza, so impeccably dressed, point device in a brocaded doublet and a most effeminate pearl pendant earring?

It was, in fact, this trim gallant who first noticed Thomas standing in the entryway. Catching his eye, the man rose and held out a hand. "Thomas Percy. *Salutem in Christo.*"

Jesu! Before he recognized the face, Thomas knew the voice. He'd last heard it raised in a reverent Latin chant: *Agnus Dei, ecce qui tollit peccata mundi.* His own face changed completely, and tears sprang to his eyes. Flooded with shame and contrition, he barely resisted the impulse to fall to his knees. "You, father," he said in a strangled voice. "Father Quindle!"

The other men of the table had risen when the priest did. Father Quindle chuckled. "Gentlemen and sweet ladies, I hold this man to be the savior of the Host."

"Thomas! There you are, my strange old bird." Coming from behind his shoulder, the rich, warm voice made Thomas turn. He saw the sparkling green eyes of Robin Catesby, who had strolled in from another room, bearing a wineglass. "Here." Catesby raised the glass like a chalice. "Drink with us."

Thomas took the goblet a bit too abruptly, and the wine sloshed over the rim. He placed a hand over it, as though that might cover the gaffe, and ducked his head. A slight bow to the fine company, not too deep, signifying that his breeding might be thought to match all of theirs. A bow learned from the players, though how could anyone know that but he? "My honest noble friends!" he said, and drank.

"It was my father's religion before me. And *shall I seem crestfallen in my father's sight,* as the poet says?"

His hunger appeased, Thomas listened with a mixture of envy and admiration to the laughter that greeted Robin Catesby's sally.

"What we profess is, quite simply, the natural religion of a gentleman." Catesby raised both hands and eyebrows in a questioning way, in mock protest of the merriment.

"'Tis your good fortune still to *have* a gentleman's crest, after last year's Essex interlude," Eliza Vaux said tartly, to more laughter and some comic hisses.

Silent servants had cleared most of the crumbs, bones, and plates from the cloth. A few of the guests had retired from the room. Through the leaded windowpane Thomas could just see Father Garnet and Anne Vaux seated on a stone bench in the garden that backed the stately house. Nicholas Owen had gone to rest above stairs, spent as he was from working all morning with his tools, as he'd confessed, to enlarge the hidden cellar that stretched underneath the garden. Catesby, Eliza Vaux, Father Quindle, and the Wintour and Wright brothers still sat with Thomas at table.

As always, Robin Catesby was the leader of their dialogue. He held out an arm and shook it, revealing a ripped seam. "But look you," he said. "Eliza, I will need you or your seamstress to patch the holes in my garments, or none will *know* I'm a gentleman. I'm a poor one, in fact, after the three thousand pounds the queen's faithful beagle made me pay for the Essex matter. A good business for Cecil! He saw that the Crown made a profit, and gave himself some gold as well, I've no doubt. You all know in the end I had to sell Chastleton."

"Which left thee with only *one* house, cousin Robin." Eliza sniffed as she bent to refill Robin's wineglass. "One house should be enough for any man."

"Ah, but the sleeve!" Robin pointed to it once more, with the corners of his mouth turned down clownishly.

"Thou'lt need to sell thy crucifix for another shirt." Kit Wright spoke quietly from down the table.

Catesby touched the gold cross that hung about his neck. "Never. Not for two score made of the finest Holland."

Eliza Vaux laughed. "Then tell thy sisters-in-law to patch thy sleeve, for the love of St. Paul the Hermit!"

"They have denied and disclaimed me for returning to my father's faith after we buried my poor Catherine."

"Disclaimed, yes. Was that not for selling the house they'd hoped would be theirs?" Eliza looked shrewdly at Robin. "Their mother's house?"

Robin waved an airy hand. "That may have had its effect, I confess. Whatever the reason, I am a widower, and my sisters-in-law are turned Protestant and will do nothing for the love of St. Paul the Hermit."

"Then go ragged." Eliza sniffed. "I'm busy enough keeping Father Quindle in clothes."

"But that is charity, with a purpose beyond vainglory." Father Quindle winked at the company in general, and tapped his pearl earring. "Disguise, for the glory of God."

"And hawking on Thursdays, for the glory of God." Eliza laughed.

"And mass on Sundays, for the glory of God," Thomas said fiercely. It was almost the first thing he'd said since entering the room an hour before. "Masses. On Sundays. For the which, if they take him, he'll be killed."

He might as well have dropped an anvil on the table. In the silence he reddened and cursed himself. *Blurting fool!* Had he not lately learned that the widow Vaux was risking her own safety, sheltering Father Quindle at her estate at nearby Harrowden? She'd lodged him since the priest's covert return from France, to whence he'd been deported after his two years' harsh imprisonment in London. What needed Eliza Vaux his reminder of her priest's bravery and worth?

Robin eased the tension. "God prevent such a happening," he said softly. He looked at Thomas. "You are right. The shepherds fare worse than the sheep, in the Tower."

"If the sheep's fleece is golden, Cecil's content with a mere shearing," quipped Jack Wright. "That happened to the best of us."

"As well as to Robin Catesby." The dry words came from one of two new gentlemen whom a servant was just then ushering into the far end of the room, taking from them their capes and gold-hilted swords. Thomas recognized the one who had spoken. Francis Tresham, a cousin of Catesby and Eliza Vaux. A counterfeit Protestant from one of the wealthiest recusant families in the north, and a man who'd also ridden with Essex. Yes, he knew Tresham. But the other?

"Welcome, Francis! I'd not thought to see you here." Robin's voice sounded gay, unoffended by his cousin's comment. He turned to the group at large, who'd all risen in honor of the newcomers. Eliza Vaux called to the kitchen for more glasses.

"Gentlemen, and Lady Eliza, know William Parker, Lord Monteagle." The newcomer Tresham gestured toward his friend, who bowed.

"I know him well." Catesby's voice was a grade cooler than usual.

Monteagle. Ah. Thomas ducked his head, trying valiantly to keep from sneering. He'd heard of him. The man was a church papist, more elaborate in his feigning than any of the rest of them. He went to Protestant services and took Protestant communion and had his children baptized by the Protestant rite. Monteagle was the most artful of the double dealers, hiding his Catholicism so as to keep all doors open at court and escape the fines imposed for recusant stayings-at-home a'Sundays. Cautious! Dishonorable!

Though perhaps, Thomas conceded, Monteagle would have proved a braver man at this date had he not been so brave earlier. For like Catesby,

Francis Tresham, and Kit Wright, Monteagle had made one in the Essex rebellion, had been captured, and barely escaped with his life. Like the others, he'd paid heavily for his freedom, in cash, to Cecil. His subsequent conversion to Protestantism had been ostentatious, though everyone knew his true leanings.

"Here." Robin rose and bowed in Francis Tresham's direction. "Take my chair."

"I do not wish thy chair, cousin Robin." A servant had entered with a stool, and Francis seated himself across from Catesby. "I wish the return of the money my father lent thee to pay thy paltry fine. In the end it comes from my estate, remember."

"Talk of money at table!" Robin raised his eyebrows mockingly, as though money had not been their subject for an hour.

"If the fine was paltry, then why is the loan missed?" said Father Quindle. "Our Lord counseled us to give to the poor."

"Which brings us full circle back to my ragged sleeve!" Robin waved his arm in the air again. Even Thomas, shaken from his brooding, laughed at him.

"Now." Catesby turned to Thomas, beaming like the sun. "Tell us, Percy, what you hear in London of the succession. For since Essex's failure, our hopes lie in that. God send us a Catholic monarch! What says the great earl of the state of things at court? Doth he know?"

"I heard a thousand rumors. The Duchess of Parma—"

"She is spoken of, truly?" Eliza looked at him with excitement.

"Not by many," Thomas said. "A wild hope, I fear. Peace with Spain is spoken of—"

"Of that we know," said Bors Wintour. "Before you entered, my brother was telling us of his audience with Philip of Spain earlier this year."

Masking his stupefaction, Thomas said, "This was, yes...." He let his voice trail off vaguely.

"Gawain solicited peace on behalf of the Crown, though he did double duty, unbeknownst to our queen." Bors clapped his brother on the shoulder. "Duty most perilous. Privately, he spoke to King Philip of the desperate needs of we English faithful. You knew of this?"

Thomas hadn't, but he nodded sagely. He knew the younger Wintour brother, Gawain, had lately counterfeited conversion to Protestantism, for the honorable reason—as Thomas Percy saw it, granting Gawain this indulgence — to achieve a diplomatic post which would send him to Spain, where he might appeal to some grandee for the help of English Catholics. But no one had told him that young Wintour had already been to Spain and back, and that instead of a grandee, he'd besought the Spanish king himself. Thomas proceeded from amazement to envious admiration, which he also tried not to show. He wished he himself had met with someone in London, the ninth earl or anyone great, and been gifted with some fresh tidbit of intelligence concerning the state of the realm. "Peace with Catholics is one thing," he said gruffly, seizing the moment. "A Catholic ruler is another. The queen will never bestow her throne on a Catholic. We cannot look for rescue that way. No, the word on most London lips is 'James.' This though Elizabeth hated his mother and approved her martyrdom."

A brief but reverent silence greeted the reference to Scottish Mary, Elizabeth's old rival, the northern queen now eighteen years dead.

"James Stuart, then." Catesby nodded, breaking the spell. "And this King James hath a Catholic wife. This is to the good. What did your earl say of the Scotsman?" He grinned. "Rumor tells us he's cast James's horoscope."

"I did not see my earl." Thomas glowered, then brightened slightly. "I saw some entertainments that celebrated the name of his house." He told the rapt company of the history plays at the Globe.

"Then they're still playing them!" Jack Wright slapped the table.

"To be sure. Your only London pastime."

Wright looked fondly at Thomas, remembering the day he and his brother had met the big fellow northerner in the Rose theater more than a decade before, and, amused by his speech, had invited him to their London house. "Those plays must be six years old or more. How are they received? Do the folk still applaud them, now that Essex's head sits on a pike on London bridge?"

"I visited that head." Thomas laughed, feeling on surer ground, speaking of things he had seen. "'Tis scant more than a skull now. But Essex may rise! That is, his spirit may. The Londoners clap and cheer for Hotspur. 'Gunpowder Percy,' Falstaff calls him. He brings to mind pious Essex and his cause, and — "

"Essex was not of the faith," said Bors Wintour abruptly. The pheasant had been returned to the table for the two newcomers, and Wintour was nibbling a wing.

"Not a Catholic, no." Kit Wright had been quiet thus far, but now he spoke firmly. Like Thomas Percy, Kit had played no role in Essex's gallant ride the year before, but felt keenly the misfortunes of his brother Jack, who had. "Not a Catholic, but a *friend* of Catholics. What else but friendship with Catholics could have been meant by the peace he forged in Ireland?"

"The peace which earned *her* enmity." Wintour sucked the wingbone's marrow, then threw the bone back onto the platter before him. "Not a wise peace."

"Well, it's done now, and he's paid with his life," Robin Catesby said smoothly. "At least they did not torture him. They would not torture a gentleman."

Father Quindle shifted slightly. Thomas glanced at him, and caught sight of his damaged hands. Quindle's wrists bore scars of the strappado, the straps from which they'd hung him. They'd racked him as well, no doubt. No, they would not torture a gentleman. Unless the gentleman were a Jesuit priest.

"Elizabeth's flame flickers." Catesby smiled. "We can look to a time when we need no longer sneak and hide and *pay* to worship truly. That is, if the right sovereign may be brought to the throne."

"May be *brought?*" Eliza Vaux looked in surprise at Robin, her eyes half-laughing, half-calculating. "And you, a shunned Catholic gentleman with a ragged sleeve, will be the one to bring this Catholic sovereign to the English throne?"

"I did not say so." Catesby looked meaningfully at Thomas.

"Ah, then, Thomas will." Father Quindle chuckled. His voice betrayed no distress, but Thomas saw he'd hidden his hands beneath the table. "Good my Thomas Percy, savior of the Host."

Thomas could not speak. The words brought back too clearly the image of the wafer he had caught, the blessed Eucharist he'd pressed to the lips of his wife as they'd fled that upper London room on the night of their priest's capture. Terrified for his wife's safety, then frightened for her health, he'd made no attempt in the ensuing weeks to petition authorities on Quindle's behalf. That omission haunted him now.

"Pardon, Father," he croaked, a little too loudly. Quindle looked puzzled. Again Thomas felt discomfort descend on the table, and knew it was his fault.

As before, Catesby set things right. "You may make a full confession to the father later, Percy, of all the sins you committed in London yesterday," he said lightly. "Presently, there's business in hand. You say you did not see the earl?"

"I did not." *The earl, the earl.* Thomas was important to Robin, to this host in general, because he was a conduit to the ninth Earl of Northumberland. But this was not bad. It confirmed his membership in the House of Percy. "I did not see him, but I *will* see him," he amended importantly. "I travel north on the morrow." He concealed the humiliating story of his reception at Syon House and Petworth. No need to admit that he'd trotted the length of the country only to be ordered back to the place from whence he'd started. Perhaps Catesby and the rest of them would imagine he'd ridden to London only to see the plays.

"You travel north. Good, then." Catesby leaned forward. "You can bring our request to the wizard earl."

What request? But quicksilver Catesby was changing the subject again, launching a new jest about Kit Wright's extravagant boasts to Tresham and Monteagle about his new-bought stallion. "Write a sonnet to it, friend," Catesby proposed. "Begin it thus: *O lovely horse, with eyes the hue of night —* "

"*You kicked me low and now I walk not right!*" Jack Wright raised his glass to toast his own wit.

Thomas rose and made his way to Father Quindle, who amid general hoots was adding his own lines to the poem. "*I'faith, my mistress' blows are not so cruel. Kick higher, lest you harm a family jewel!*"

"This is too bawdy for a priest!" chided Eliza, laughing.

"I must perfect my disguise as an English gallant." Quindle beamed as he sipped his wine. "The costume's the least of it. Rude jests and pretended knowledge of horses are also necessary, if I am to be taken for one of you."

"For one of *us?*" Catesby said. "But no one of any importance likes us."

"Hold, hold. Speak for thyself," said Gawain Wintour. "Queen Elizabeth likes me."

A mock scowl from Catesby. "Only because you paid a great fine and then kissed her golden shoe, and likely her —"

"I deny the shoe-kissing."

Thomas bowed low to speak in Quindle's ear. Under cover of the table's merriment, he whispered, "Father, I must confess."

Instantly serious, Quindle looked at him with concern. "Thy need is urgent?" he said in a low voice.

"I have borne a particular sin for many years, and can only confess to thee. I can brook no further delay."

The priest looked at him searchingly for a moment. Then he said, "Come. Rise." The two left the room. Busy with their bawdy, the men took no note. But Eliza Vaux saw, and watched after the pair of them with sympathy.

In the parlor Thomas knelt. "Bless me, Father, for I have sinned. I . . . " He suddenly could not speak for fear of weeping.

Quindle wished to touch the big man on the shoulder, but knew if he did the tears would flow indeed, and that Thomas was struggling manfully to prevent this. So he stood and waited patiently. After a moment Thomas spoke again. "I . . . let my Mary die."

Now the priest knelt with Thomas and looked at him hard. "Let her die, Thomas?" Resisting the role of confessor, he spoke as a family friend. He knew this story already, from Eliza Vaux. "Many women die in childbirth," he said gently.

Thomas wiped his eyes, unable, after all, to contain his tears. "I . . . could not save her. And the child perished within her, with no baptism, no last rites!"

"These are hard things. Yet they were not your fault." Quindle took Thomas's hand.

Thomas plowed on. "And I did not visit you in prison."

"This was also not . . . ." Quindle stopped. As a friend, he found Thomas blameless, a mere victim of the Catholic-hunting temper of the land. But as a priest, he could see that Thomas was tormented by guilt.

He absolved him and gave him a penance, and was glad to see some relief enter the big man's face. And now Thomas let himself weep fully, burying his face against the elegant peacock-blue sleeves Quindle wore in place of a cope and chausable. Laughter and the sounds of continuing raillery drifted in from the dining room, as Thomas wept and snorted.

"Please you not to use my disguise for a handkerchief," Quindle said affably, patting Thomas on the head as though the man were a mastiff. "It cost three pounds ten-pence."

Chapter 9

"There are too many swords in the hall," Anne Vaux said softly. She bent her narrow face in a smile, then touched a hand to smooth the thick hair she kept piled neatly on her head. Chestnut brown, and only a few threads of grey. *My married head,* she thought. *Worn by a spinster.*

"All men must bear swords these days, it seems," said Henry Garnet, watching her soberly. "A shame."

Anne gazed at the darkening sky. Henry regarded her profile, appreciating for the thousandth time her quiet thoughtfulness. A restful counterpoint to her sister-in-law Eliza's boisterous wit.

"Well, 'tis the entertainment of men in their prime," Anne said at length. She turned to look him in the face. His was sunworn and handsome. He had the brown skin of a gardener or a shepherd. She wrinkled her nose. "Hypocrite. I saw *thee* admiring their swordplay this morning."

He shrugged. "It was admirable."

Grudgingly, she nodded. "Yes. Jack Wright is justly celebrated."

"He moves with grace. And who can but be pleased by the speeches they use to deck their contests? *The Spanish blade is subtle and prudent, it moves with my very thought!*" Henry laughed. "I'truth, Jack is in love with his sword. And to hear the controversy over the most honorable hilt, the noblest pass, the fittest length for a rapier!"

"The prize for length we must grant to wide-bearded Thomas." Anne laughed herself, then winced.

"What is it, Anne?"

"Nothing." She touched her abdomen. "This old pain again. I know not what ails me, but 'tis nothing to fear you. It never gets any worse or better; it only comes and goes. For years now."

"Ah, but you will outlive *me*," Garnet said gently. His hands, having nowhere to go, pressed themselves against the stone bench.

"'I would not wish to do that." Anne briefly kneaded her abdomen. "There. Better now."

"You will outlive *all* —"

"Henry, don't say such things, or think them. "

"Right. You are in the right. *Sufficit diei malitia sua.* "

She smiled. "Let us think, instead, on whether any one of us will survive Thomas Percy of the long sword. Would that you'd seen *him*, fighting shadows in the yard when he arrived today! Like the mad old knight in the new Spanish romance."

"That book's not a romance. But yes." Garnet nodded. "Fighting shadows indeed! He seeks a target for his wrath. I would he'd confess and govern it, instead."

"He confesses every time he sees a priest. He chases them down. He's pious enough."

"That's true, too." Garnet frowned in perplexity. "Dost know, Anne, despite the man's constant activity, I think he would make a good monk."

"Giant Thomas, who would quarrel for an eggshell!"

"Yes, I know it. But hotheads are not the best soldiers. Marry, I think battle is not his true element. For one thing, he lacks the grace of the rest in swording. I do not say he lacks valor, but skill? I've heard he suffered humiliation last year on the field, with the earl's command in the Low Countries."

"Yes," Anne said, and gave a disdainful snort. "Let's not speak of that, either. If that story's true, I count Thomas's indifferent performance to his credit. I think he had little heart to fight on the English side against true Catholic Spaniards and Flemish. He should have joined — "

"Ah, Nan." Father Garnet sighed. "You need a weapon yourself, my Joan of Arc. I cannot share your fierceness. The swording I find watchable in a . . . *gamesome* way. But I'faith! I would it might remain a fencing match."

"Well, there's fencing enough, between our queen and King Philip's diplomats."

"Or the Spaniard himself, with our Gawain as queen's knight."

"*Our* knight. Not hers."

"Right again! A hit. A very *palpable* hit." Garnet grabbed his side in feigned pain, then instantly folded his arms, chagrined. He hadn't meant to mock Anne's earlier gesture, and looked at her penitently. But her hazel eyes were smiling and full of warmth.

Their friendship was old. They had grown to adulthood in the same parish, neighbors, running together as children, in youth growing shy in each other's company, but always with the friendship bond between them, never broken. Not even on the day Henry had shared with her the glad, painful secret of his vocation, and watched the light fade from her eyes.

One of Henry's favorite games when a boy had been massing-play. He would belt an old, worn sheet around him for a chausable, though it made him look more ghost than priest. Eight-year-old Anne would kneel on his or her attic floor, head bowed, as little Henry, nearly tripping over his sheet-ends, walked solemnly back and forth chanting half-learned Latin, then enacted the transformation of his elements — barley bread on a cracked plate, and a cup of cider — into the body and blood of Christ. She would stick out her tongue to accept the bread, as he solemnly intoned, *"Hoc est enim corpus meum."* Once, when she'd tried to play the celebrant herself, and had joked as the Protestants did about Catholics, saying "Hocus pocus!" instead of the right words, Henry had flown into a rage and declared her excommunicate for her blasphemy. He'd not spoken to her for two days until she'd confessed and done the penance he'd given her. Neither of them was conscious, then or ever, of the slightest irony in their play: of the fact that, by merely imitating what a real priest did legitimately, they were behaving like Protestants. Had any of their parents caught them, they would have been beaten like carpets in April. Henry would not have understood why. He felt he was a priest, naturally, and that only the accident of his being nine prevented his formal recognition as such.

As he grew older, his faith grew fiercer and more passionate. Yet unlike Anne, and unlike most members of his devoutly Roman family, he gave only minimal ritual observance to holy saints, even to Saint Mary, the Mother of Christ. It was Jesus, founder of the Church, who claimed his whole heart; Jesus, whose fresh wounds he saw in dreams and ecstasies of prayer, whose heart he heard beating, whose eyes of love charged his soul. Jesus, whom he longed to emulate, to figure, to join.

Anne's faith was less ardent than Henry's, and more complex, once Catholicism began to reveal itself as a blight on the English marriage mart. She had grown into a handsome girl, tall, graceful, and reed-slim, and these qualities, along with her wit and her family's wealth, had garnered her suitors enough. But several early proposals of matrimony had not come to fruition because of the Catholic stigma. At first, hoping God had another match in mind for her, she did not much mind. Later, after Henry told her of his calling, she minded, but could not change. As a girl she'd once been warned, by a beloved aunt who had moved outside the family circle, that things would turn out thus. "If you want to bear children, you'd do best to convert, as I did," the aunt had written her. "Do it while there's time." Among her girlhood friends, first one, then another had sought confirmation in the English church. But Anne resisted, even after the night of Henry's revelation, which he'd proclaimed with a face ablaze with exaltation, sure that she would understand and approve of his choice.

His choice was not made easier for her by the fact that she did understand it, and, after seeing his face, did approve it. How could she not? All that lay unspoken between them, all that *she* had not said, seemed trivial in the light of that incandescent face.

And even after this, after Henry's departure to France to study for the priesthood — indeed, especially after that page was turned — lonely Anne could not understand those who forsook their religion in order to wed. There was, after all, God's love to be considered. Separation from Him? And from the family of the faithful? Sure damnation, in exchange for the earthly warmth of a man in bed? A temptation, yes. But one to be resisted. As for motherhood, well . . . there were children enough.

The truth was, even during her childbearing years — now fast waning — she'd suspected she'd never survive the birthing bed. Though this, and the reasons why, was a secret so intimate that she'd shared it with none but her sister-in-law Eliza, and Henry.

So she chose to complement Henry. If he had a vocation, she had one, too. So she'd passed into middle age doing reverent service to Father Garnet instead of becoming a wife. For who better to serve Henry? No one else knew him as she did. Once, they'd chased birds and thrown stones. In their youth, they'd sat for hours, content in each other's company, while they'd told and retold one another thrilling tales of miracles and saints' lives. Now that he was a man she fed and clothed him, and saw him well hidden in her house and the ample houses of her friends throughout the English midlands. And those friends had made him known to other friends, and these to others, so that for nearly three decades now, since his ordination in France, Henry Garnet had remained free, honored, loved, and able to serve the faithful.

It was Anne who'd rushed him and two fellow priests to the cellar of her house the month before, when the pursuivants came. The three Jesuits had stood knee-deep in water for twelve hours, praying silently, touching one another's arms for comfort, harrowed by fear and tortured by tedium, hearing the scraping of furniture and the steps pounding above, now distant, now horrifyingly close, now distant again. At intervals Anne had hastily fed them soup down a tube she'd pushed through a hole Nicholas Owen had drilled in the floor, months past. When would it end?

But all things pass. Eventually the searchers' footsteps had ceased to sound, and, distantly, blessedly, the two priests had heard horses on the bank as those were brought from the stable. Another hour for safety's sake. Then Anne had rapped, and she and her servants had pulled the men, stiff, cramped, and half-starved, from the water. "We need no bath, good Anne!" one of them had quipped, but she'd cleansed and anointed them, then fed them a meal.

Then or some other time Henry Garnet would have died if not for Anne. Or worse, he'd have forsaken his vocation from fear and discouragement, as the noose around Catholics tightened in England. Anne spent her unused marriage portion and her rents to make her house hospitable and as safe as it could be for the itinerant Jesuits — those whom Henry knew and could assure her were not spies. And her money also made possible the frequent meetings of the faithful with their priests. Friends said that in a blessed country she would have joined a nunnery, and been an abbess within the year.

Father Garnet doubted this was precisely true.

"May I confess to you here?" Anne asked in a low voice. "This hard bench may serve us for that."

"No. You may not."

"You do not know what I would say."

"There's a priest in the house. Confess to him."

"I know what penance any priest but you would impose. Would you wish for that?"

"If you know already, you may as well begin it."

"Ah. Father Garnet *is* a gamester. He calls my bluff at the hazard."

"Nan, you are my oldest and dearest friend. And you know I am married."

She had crossed a boundary with him, and knew it. Instantly she changed her bantering tone. "I am sorry, Henry. Forgive me."

"I forgive you instantly."

She regarded his serene face. How was it possible that his heart was never torn between flesh and spirit?

"I am attached to my body, and I don't crave its sacrifice," he said, as though she had spoken. "But I chose my spouse long ago. And I must counsel you. It is not wise for you to walk us onto dangerous ground, even in jest. You should not sport with a sacrament, and as for me, I cannot. Confession is no . . . bower."

At this she laughed. "*Bower!* That you even know the word! Father Garnet, I adore you."

"Nan –"

"Enough! You *have* heard my confession, despite your austere self. Now, come." She rose. "Who won this match, you or I?"

"What do *you* think?"

"Ah, Jesuit, he avoids the direct answer. Keep your counsel, then. Inside with both of us. You will rest, and tomorrow, we'll all meet before breakfast. The gentlemen have traveled far for a mass."

Chapter 10

From the distance, over the moor, Thomas could see puffs of smoke emerging from a loophole in the highest turret of Alnwick Castle. Seeing the earl would mean climbing, then. But at least the man was there.

He paused for a moment to admire a golden eagle circling high above the castle's crenellated battlements. When the majestic bird had disappeared from sight he spurred the roan once more. He passed over the drawbridge and under a raised portcullis, riding through the open gate into the bailey and from thence to the inner ward. In the smaller courtyard he dismounted and was met by a groom who, bowing, took his roan by the bridle and led it to be stabled. Thomas entered the castle proper. A hushed walk over fragrant rushes strewn on the cold floor of a gallery, three stone steps down, and then the great hall.

He stood for a moment, letting his eyes adjust to the dimness of the cavernous room. The hall's windows were not leaded but stained glass, wrought with beauty and skill, but not with an eye to the transmission of light. Jealous, the colored windows caught, held, and hoarded the rays of the setting sun. They glowed. Some of the panes had been bought by the last, eighth Earl of Northumberland from parish churches, decades earlier, when royal deputies had ridden north to enforce young Queen Elizabeth's edict commanding such vanities' removal and replacement by transparent glass, or by shutters, or by nothing. Now, in brilliant reds and purples and blues and yellows, the sacred images shone under the ninth earl's vaulted roof. There was Moses releasing water from the desert rock with his staff, and over there, the three Marys at the foot of the Cross, gazing in anguish at their dying Savior, whose hands and feet dripped scarlet blood. Roughly alternating with the Biblical pictures, and no less richly illuminated, were panes featuring scenes from British legend. A grey-bearded Merlin, clad in a wizard's cloak stained blue, standing behind a young Arthur as the secret king wrenched glittering Excalibur from a black anvil. Next to that pane, another: Sir Bors kneeling alongside Sir Percival, their four hands raised to a Grail that floated magically above them, gold against a rosy sky. The glass shone, luminous, next to the dark framing wall.

The lineaments of the room now visible, Thomas proceeded along the stony floor, past heavy oaken chairs, dusty tables topped with ornate brass flagons, and a hanging tapestry picturing great Hotspur's victory at Holmedon, when he'd beaten the Scots back over their borders one Holy Rood Day. In the tapestry Hotspur stood twice as tall as the blue-capped Scotsmen, who were shown sprawled and dead or from the back, fleeing. Near this and other woven scenes of battle, broadswords, poniards, maces, and axes were stapled by iron to the granite wall. Beneath one grim and dusty battle axe, an aged servant sat drowsing on a stool.

Thomas entered a passageway marked by the Percy crest, a rampant blue dragon with the motto etched brightly below. *Esperance!* Beyond this arched entrance stretched a long, dog-legged, torchlit corridor. He followed this, his sword clanking against the wall at the turns, until he came to the start of the narrow stairway that led up to the earl's tower.

He could smell cordite on the first stairwell, and the odor grew stronger as he climbed. The heavy door at the top of the spiral chain of steps opened to a familiar sight: books with stained pages that lay tumbled from their places onto the floor, odd-colored liquids bubbling in flasks over low flames in a brazier. Behind these, a man with an ink-stained cheek, hatless, and dressed well below his station. The ninth earl's usual oddnesses. Thomas doffed his cap and bowed. "My lord."

Henry Percy, Ninth Earl of Northumberland, looked at him with surprise. "Thomas! I had thought to see you in London. You bring the rents?"

"I do, my lord. From ten holdings." Thomas placed the heavy bag of coin on a table, glad to have evaded the highwaymen and be rid of it.

"No, not there," said the earl. "I will soon lay a dish of mercury on that surface. On the floor, perhaps, below. There. Only ten?"

"Christopher Baxter begs another se'nnight. By that time he'll be paid for his wool." Thomas shifted the bag, saying nothing of the sword he'd brandished a foot from four of the tenants' faces to make them yield the whole of what they owed for their land. He knew from past dialogues that the earl found such details unpleasant. As for the fifth soul, Baxter, the man had not quailed but claimed boldly that he'd be even less capable of paying with a split head, and that even now he was possessed of a great quantity of wool but no coin. Would Thomas like to buy his wares at market price? In truth, he'd made Thomas smile, though he wasn't inclined to levity at this present moment, after his hard pilgrimage south and back again and his climb up the earl's stony stairs. He was tired. And he'd a grave matter to discuss with Henry Percy. Robin Catesby's last words to him, the morning he'd left Baddesley Clinton, burned in his mind. *Ever to sneak, or to be damned? Tell him we can no more.*

"'Tis no matter, for the nonce," the earl said. "The London rents I have in hand. And this, which I bought in Oxford on my return." Reverently, the earl placed a heavy book on a stand before Thomas. Its text was not printed, but spidery manuscript on vellum, in Latin. *Palos Ferreos*, read the heading of one page. *Fire Sticks.* "The Book of Fires of Mark the Greek!" the earl said with satisfaction. "The world holds only two copies, and the other's in Constantinople. Sit, Thomas." He tapped a page spotted with fresh candlewax. "I find my challenge to Aristotle confirmed, here. Fire is not a single element, but many. It is, in truth, not a thing but the *doing* of a thing, an *exchange* among elements. It is in essence, that is to say *without* essence, a kind of appetite, which eats the very air! The late mage Cornelius Agrippa would agree. He called fire an 'insatiate hunger.' I myself would add that fire's ideal food is charcoal. Sulfur, now . . . ."

The earl droned on, while Thomas attempted to doze with eyes open. He'd stayed longer at Baddesley Clinton than he'd intended, not only for mass but for a lingering breakfast, at which had been discussed the particulars of the message he was now charged to bear for the whole company. Everyone had taken part save Nicholas Owen, who'd departed after two bites of toast to sand the floorboards over a hiding place.

The night before the breakfast, Thomas, Robin Catesby, the Wrights, the Wintours, William Monteagle, and Francis Tresham had retired to a room, drawn curtains, and spoken long in private. When the candles began to burn low Eliza and Anne Vaux had entered on the frail pretext of replenishing the wax. Then, as Anne was fiddling with the candlesticks, Eliza had insisted on their being told what the men plotted. Thomas thought it foolish to include women in their counsels, and had earned sharp looks from both ladies for saying so. Then Eliza had sat herself down and proved her shrewdness by accurately guessing the plan the men had been fumbling toward. She'd demanded full intelligence, reminding them of the risks she and her sister-in-law took daily to house the priests. After all that, the men had felt compelled to recount their whole discussion, and this had kept the ten of them awake well past midnight.

At breakfast, after the mass, at Anne's insistence, the whole group, men and women, had taken counsel with Father Quindle and Father Garnet to obtain their shared blessing. Then they'd sat and fleshed the plan whose bones they'd sketched in the midnight house. After, to compensate for the delay, Thomas had ridden nearly eighteen hours for two consecutive days to reach Alnwick Castle.

"*Squwwkk!*"

Thomas started, and glanced toward the room's dusty corner. A pair of beady eyes gazed at him from the shadowy interior of a cage, dark and steadfast over a long, hooked bill.

The earl interrupted his monologue to laugh. "Yes, I had to move your friend inside. He's from Mauritania, and doesn't like a damp English stable. I'faith, he was pining."

Thomas crossed the room and knelt before the cage. The large bird filled nearly all of it. It gazed stoically outward, nodding its bill as though in greeting to Thomas, and flapped its short, useless wings.

"I barely saw him in there," Thomas said, tapping the wire with a finger. "His plumage is as grey as the walls."

"Grey and black. A few white flecks."

The bird was larger than a pheasant, though its tail was less grand. It pecked at the dried fruits in its feeder, then half-turned on its stumpy legs. Thomas could see the odd patch of hair at the base of its spine. The bird tried to preen the patch with its bill, but lacked space to do so. It ceased the effort, and stood, stolid.

"He should be in an aviary," Thomas said sadly.

"What would he do there? He can't fly. The Dutchman I bought him from was right about that, though he was wrong about every other thing, including the bird's diet. Said the feathery boy would eat worms! Ah, but this is not a carnivore. He's a relic from the Garden of Eden."

"Ha," said Thomas, absently and without humor. He gazed at the dodo's dark eyes.

"Let him out, then. He'll only stroll and shit on the floor. It's swept every night by my servant, anyway, because of the ashes."

Thomas unhooked the cage door, but the dodo stood blinking stupidly, and wouldn't move. Thomas touched it above the tail, and it stepped forward a few paces, then stopped again. It craned its neck backward to clean its feathers and fur.

"*Do-daars.* 'Knot-arse.' That's what it means," the earl said thoughtfully. "Named for that patch it's preening. But enough, Thomas. Come look at this. Tell me your thought." The earl was tapping a finger on another open book, this one a well-thumbed printed tome that lay on the table next to the bookstand. "Roger Bacon, the mage."

With a small sigh, Thomas rose and approached the bookstand.

"I have shared with you Roger Bacon's anagram," the earl said. "I have told you that he knew the makings of gunpowder in the thirteenth century; was the first in all Europe to find it. But this anagram, this secret he places in the formula, has never been solved. Here, I have underlined it, as I told you I would."

Thomas had no memory of this discussion, but no doubt that it had occurred. He peered at the page the earl was tapping with a stained nail. "Saltpeter, sulfur, and *Luru Vopo Vir Can Utriet,*" he read aloud. "That is not Latin. It means nothing."

"*Not* nothing." The earl's voice was peevish. "Dost attend me, Thomas? It means something. Though it cannot be made to mean charcoal, which *should* be written there. That is the third element in what some think a diabolical trinity." He pulled the lobe of his left ear, a nervous habit that dated from the day he'd lost half his hearing in an explosive experiment with sulfur and dried honey. The hearing had partly returned, but the ear-pulling persisted. "I *will* make sense of it," he murmured. "*Vir* is 'man.' *Man can* . . . Man can what?"

Thomas could not fathom what the earl hoped to gain from solving the riddles of crazed old Friar Bacon. He decided, in any case, that now was as good a time as another to broach the subject of his mission. "My lord, I bring a message from the aggrieved faithful whom I met at Baddesley Clinton," he said in a rush. "Francis Tresham, Christopher and John Wright, Bors and Gawain Wintour, one Lord Monteagle, Robin Catesby—"

The earl held up his hand. "Thomas, if 'tis money they want to pay their fines, they must see their own fathers. I was glad enough to have been in the Low Countries when Essex made his mad bid in London for the queen's ear. Even so I was suspected in the game, simply because I hold an old traitor's title. Cecil railing at me in Star Chamber!" Thomas knew this oft-told tale of the earl's, which had enthralled him at first hearing. Now he fidgeted, anxious to finish his plea, but the earl plowed on. "The little man hummed the tune of that old ballad against the Percys. *'Though popery wrought a great while ago, that Percy provoked King Harry to frown, yet who would have thought there were any more that would not yet be true to the crown?'* No doubt he has spies lurking in taverns where such trash is sung."

Thomas started to say the very same song had been sung rudely at him on his last London sojourn, but halted, thinking the earl would only ask him what he'd done to provoke the insult.

"And then the little man quoted to me from a play, do you know it? *'Treason will have a wild trick of his ancestors.'* As though a line of stage poetry proved every new Percy a knave!" He laughed scornfully. "Cecil, First Baron of Essendon and Viscount of Cranborne, gone to politicians' school at the Globe theater! Would you dream it?"

Thomas shifted uncomfortably.

"An insolent beagle, Cecil. I was able to tell him in all truth that I'd been directing English artillery for the queen's glory the day Essex waved his bright sword on the London Strand, and that I knew nothing of events." The earl paused and wagged his finger at Thomas. "And 'tis your luck you were with me, else with your hot head you would likely have been caught up in the scheme. Been taken, and acquired fines of your own, at best, which you'd have asked me to pay." He chuckled. "Though you cost me money in Flanders, anyway."

The dodo made a clicking sound. Both men fell silent at the black mention of Flanders. Memory locked the pair of them in a shared guilt whenever that place was named.

Thomas was no more proud of his service against the Spanish in Flanders than of his secondary freebooting in the Azores. Indeed, he wouldn't have gone to the Lowlands but that his duty to the earl had enforced him, two years before now, during his lord's brief Holland command. The earl himself had disliked being plucked by the queen from his private experiments and sent to that wet, boggy country to assist in cannon emplacements and use the knowledge of black powder he'd acquired over the years.

Thomas had been asked first to load cannon and then to shoulder a musket, both of which duties had shamed him. No bearing, no skill beyond mere aim, no valor was required to fire a cannon or smaller firing piece, except the foolish bravery of hoping the gun did not go off in your face. He'd seen that horror happen to more than one of his country-men; seen heads blown off or, worse yet, survivors with noseless or eye-less faces.

Yet it could not be denied that Thomas was perfectly framed for the bombards. He could breach-load twice as fast as any other soldier under the earl's command. He plucked roundshot from the stack as though the balls were stuffed leather instead of lead or iron, handing them to the gunner, or himself firing the weapon when stinging smoke sent the other man to plunge his eyes in a bucket of water. Ramming the powder charge down the bore, lighting the linstock, standing back, and then: the hell of the blaze, the dense cloud of enveloping smoke, and the deafening thun-derclap of the explosion that released the ball!

What he hated most about the work was that he loved it.

For it was devil's work, not the work of a man. Yes! So had said Ari-osto, the great author of romances, whom he and his Mary had read aloud to one another, in the faraway when. *How couldst thou, curst inven-tion, ever find reception in the brave, the generous mind?* Ariosto had writ-ten truly. The powder was heinous. *By thee the glorious war is turn'd to shame, by thee the trade of arms has lost its fame!* Poets knew. Like the famed London playwright, who in the first great Hotspur play spoke of the *villainous saltpeter* used for explosions at Holmedon, even as early as 1403 — though surely that was not possible, no, not in Hotspur's time, no weapon so ignoble in England. No, powder was a modern horror. And as with the powder-fired cannon, so with the heavy musket. All, all villainous!

Some days Thomas had been ordered to crouch, gun in hand, with a group of other face-blackened English demons behind a wall or a stand of elms, surprising the Spaniards on the field with a rain of lead that hit them from behind and sent them sprawling. And the Englishmen had laughed in a strange, strangled way, pitching forward to keep from chok-ing on the balls they kept in their mouths for wetting and quick loading. Laughing at the sight of the men they had missed looking wildly around, not able to see the artillers clearly because those were hidden by smoke. And he, Thomas, was an artiller. One of Satan's minions.

And yet . . . the feel of the trigger! The blast of the gun! The power the machine unleashed, with the men twenty yards away flopping like rag dolls, then lying still . . . . Thomas was drawn to it, was tempted to laugh with the rest. And he hated his own depravity, so much that one morning, though still possessed of a mound of shot, he'd thrown down his gun and advanced onto the wet field with his bared blade high, slipping in the mud and flailing.

Right away he'd sensed he did not belong there. Off the coast of the Azores, on shipboard, he'd helped his countrymen simply by flinging Spaniards overboard when they tried to gain the deck. There his bulk and the might of his back had served him well. Thomas the sea-giant! In the smoke of the Flanders field there flashed in his mind a memory of the dreamlike aftermath of one corsair's day-long attack, when, all gunfire spent, the surviving English and Spanish soldiers had lined the rails of their ships and jeered at one another. Then, suddenly, both sides had broken into mad and spontaneous laughter. They'd raced for the holds, raided barrels, and run back to the deck, pitching precious oranges and lemons at one another's heads. He could still see the bright fruits hurtling across the sea-stretch between the two bands of giddy sailors, over the salt span that was clogged with their shipmates' floating corpses. Thomas could throw as far as the guns had shot. It was like a game.

But swords on the field were something else again. The ground of Flanders was as soggy as bread drenched in stew. His bulk and strength availed him nothing against the warriors who hemmed him in on that sudden field; dark, lithe men whose quick swords defeated his ill-taught, clumsy thrusts. He was no Robin Catesby, no Jack Wright, none of those blades who could dazzle their friends with the beauty and grace of their swordplay. Wearing heavy old armor lent by the earl, he'd been easily captured, and gladly ransomed. The Spaniards had known there was money behind him. To the Percy crest emblazoned on his borrowed shield he owed his life. But he hadn't been proud of the crest, at that day's end. Not proud to have been captured, or ransomed, or to have fought Catholics at all, when a renegade English regiment of loyal Catholics, fighting for Spain, had been there in the country for the joining.

Dark images of Flanders lumbered through Thomas's mind now, as he sat glumly in Alwyn Castle, watching blankly as the ninth earl shuffled his bottles and tools and whispered to himself. The Lowlands service had been horrible. As he always did when recalling it — as he needed to do — Thomas told himself that his actions there had been dutiful. He was Henry Percy's liegeman, and though the ninth earl was no Hotspur, still, he owed the earl what place in the world he'd gained.

And that place was not to be sneezed at, when it accorded him the regard of a gentleman such as Robin Catesby. Regard, and the entrusting of the message he now bore inside his cloak. Thomas patted the document briefly, seeking the words to relaunch his theme, and to introduce the letter.

Henry Percy was indulging his own thoughts about his tie to Thomas, as he stood by the window, peering at the greyish-white contents of a glass flask. Clouds scudded through the sky outside, making the room intermittently dark. The earl squinted. He preferred to be alone in his cell, but he'd grown used to Thomas's presence and could tolerate it when his servant sat quietly as he did now, bearlike and brooding.

Henry Percy had not taken much note at the start when Thomas had begged employment of him a dozen years past, laying particular stress on their shared surname. There were many Percys in Northumbria, and Thomas had not been the first to claim kinship with the old house. The earl had ignored Thomas's several letters of request, filled as they were with florid references to the ballad of Chevy Chase, with names comically misspelled. He'd thought the writer some audacious clown. But when Thomas had come to him in person, he had taken stock. His size and a wild, explosive grief in his face had marked Thomas Percy a likely man to succeed in the collection of rents from the earl's extraordinarily tight-fisted tenants in the northern region. Henry Percy had lately discharged a man who habitually brought the moneys late and who he suspected — from the gradually escalating fineness of his wear — spent a significant portion of the Percy rents on his own estate. Thomas came in good time. He had dismissed the other and hired him.

In the years since, the earl had often applauded himself for his choice. There had been, of course, the bad business between Thomas Percy and that player in London four years before, and, closer to home, the unfortunate episode of his servant's violent thrashing of Douglas, that Scotsman, in which some blood had been shed. Douglas was a Presbyterian who (Thomas had claimed in defense) stank with the teachings of John Knox, had been bold enough to quote to Thomas Christ's words about hard landlords, and had scoffed at the medal of Saint Winifred Thomas wore around his neck. Thomas said he regretted slashing him, but only because the man was lowborn, "a villein too base to stain the temper of a knightly sword." The Northumbrian judge of assizes hadn't been awed by these and other references to Percy grandeur, in part because Thomas, who uttered them, was not actually a knight. But the judge had been moved by Percy gold. It had cost the earl a month's rents to redeem his money-collector from the prison in Durham where the authorities had lodged him when the Scotsman filed suit. Since that whole event, however, the earl's northern payments had come in astoundingly promptly. This was a blessing, since the London and Sussex properties were far away, and the woods along English country roads were thick with thieves.

Nodding with satisfaction, the earl returned to his experiment. Thomas watched as his master poured the hot, silvery contents of his flask into a flat dish on the table. Having doused the heating-flames, the earl replaced the flask on a metal grill and gazed intently at the liquid.

"'It concerns King James," Thomas blurted.

The earl looked at him in surprise. "What does?"

Thomas withdrew from his coat the letter of petition sealed with the signet of the Catesby family. Rising, he placed the paper in the earl's outstretched hand. "Only read, my lord."

The earl broke the wax seal and sank into his chair, frowning more and more deeply as his eyes traveled down the parchment. "Ah," he said, and "ah." At length he looked up with a grim expression and let the paper drop to the floor. "Do they know I am no longer Catholic? When I scant churchgoing in London or here in Northumbria, it is not because I abhor pastors with English Bibles and flat caps, even if I do not like them much. No. It is because . . . ." He smiled slightly. "Because I forget the day of the week. *I* pay no fixed fees for recusancy. Why should I — "

"Yet you are a Percy, and a Catholic in your heart," Percy said in a thunderous voice, leaping suddenly to his feet. He was mysteriously galvanized.

The earl raised his eyebrows. "Take care, you unruly . . . ." He stopped, and slowly nodded. "Well, yes. You are not all full of nonsense, Thomas. I am a Percy, and, at heart, a Catholic."

"You believe in the mystical body of Christ transformed from bread by God's holy substitute, the priest," Thomas said fiercely. He still stood, his hand on his sword, zeal in his eyes. "You honor the spiritual headship of our holy father the pope. You hold the blessed saints to be efficacious in our prayers for the dead in the vale of Purgatory."

"I believe in the mystical body of Christ transformed," the ninth earl said softly, gazing with a private passion at his cooling alchemical experiment. "The metamorphosis of elements. The process that joins earth to heaven. Look you, Thomas!" Rising, he approached a metal beaker that stood next to the plate of silvery liquid on his sturdy worktable. He lifted the beaker high, as a priest would a monstrance, though, unlike a priest with his burden, he was only assessing the metal for cracks. Then he poured a few colorless drops from the beaker into the liquid which Thomas had guessed was quicksilver. Immediately the mixture began to burn with a brisk blue flame. To Thomas's amazement, the hot puddle raised itself into a nest of climbing snakes, first one, then another, then another, the black serpents glowing with inward fire. They rose, twisted, then fell into ashy remnants on the table. The earl looked at Thomas in delight and caught his servant crossing himself. He laughed. "'The effect is wrought by ammonium on the mercury."

Thomas dropped his hand, embarrassed. "Wondrous, my lord." Now that the counterfeit snakes had crumbled into powder, they did not frighten. "Wondrous indeed. But the letter?"

"Yes, yes." With sudden impatience, the earl bent and snatched the document from the floor. "At the request of our — what was your word? 'Aggrieved'? — friends, I am to suspend all other business, journey north to the court of King James of Scotland, and humbly call his attention to our imperiled state. To request — "

"His promise, my lord," Thomas said urgently. "A promise of tolerance when he ascends the English throne. For all signs suggest that the crown *will* fall in his lap — will be tossed that way by Elizabeth, at the end."

"Tossed! Ha. Yes. I know it will. If not by Elizabeth, then by . . . someone."

"You know something, lord?" Thomas's voice was eager. "Has Walter Raleigh spoken? I know you conversed with —"

"No, no, Raleigh knows no more than anyone else, except Cecil, who knows all that is to be known in this world. I've cast his horoscope. King James's, not Wat Raleigh's. Or Cecil's." The earl gestured to a rolled, bound chart in the corner. "I could take it to the Scotsman as a gift. But I will not go."

"But thou must, lord! Do we not have thy sympathy?"

"Sympathy, aye. Your fine friend Robert Catesby knows well that I abhor the punishments of priests, and the secret masses — I mean, the *need* for secrecy. I know this is Catesby's idea. What gentleman, finding himself out of favor at court, would not use the tongue of an earl to speak to a king?"

"The tongue of *the* earl! The greatest of the English Catholics —"

"Catholic no longer," the earl interjected, raising a hand as though to defend himself from some charge in Star Chamber. "At least, not officially."

But Thomas plowed on. "The Earl of Northumberland may be said in his person to represent all the faithful of England, most particularly those in the north and midlands. And . . ." He paused. "And a mere letter from him to the Scottish king. . . ." A wild thought had jumped in his head. His heart beat fast as he said the next thing. "My lord, if your. . . ." He looked doubtfully at the remains of the magic snakes. "If your . . . work prevents your departure from Alnwick, a fervent message from you, describing our plight and making earnest argument for our succoring in the kingdom, which is to say in his kingdom, when he is made king, of the kingdom . . . ." Thomas's tongue began to falter. "Such a thing would stand in good stead of your presence. And *I* would deliver such a message," he concluded lamely.

"Ah. Ah! You to go." The earl looked relieved. He began to sweep ash from the worktable with the petition from Baddesley Clinton. "I think that the best course. You might compose — no. No, I will compose the letter to King James. I noted some fine phrases in this one, which I'll copy. Golden-tongued Robin Catesby's inventions, no doubt."

Thomas felt a stab of envy. *Ah, Catesby.* Covertly, he clenched a fist, and thought, *But I, not Catesby, not Gawain Wintour, nor any of them, will have audience with the King of Scotland.* He felt his good humor growing, and with humor came boldness. He said briskly, "Our case brooks no delay."

"Ah?" The earl stopped sweeping the table and looked at him with interest. "Doth the queen totter?"

"'Tis said she is not well."

"The tongues of rumor will say anything." The earl crossed the room and dumped the ash from the turret's high loophole. He watched as the spiraling wind took it away. "But she cannot live forever, and the horoscope . . . ." He glanced at the rolled chart in the corner, made a move as though to get it, then dropped his arm. "No. Perhaps it would not be prudent for you to share the horoscope with James. Horoscopes are good science, but they seem witchery to some."

"I will certainly speak of thy horoscope, my lord."

"Yes, you can do that." The earl returned to his bookstand and began again to turn the pages of Roger Bacon.

"And the letter?"

"Yes, yes, I'll write it. And I'll send to the court at Edinburgh before you, of course, so the king will expect your coming. See my exchequer for your money, Thomas."

That was the signal for Thomas to leave, and he bowed and did so, thinking, as usual, that the earl was sometimes frightening and sometimes dull. His speech was not predictable. He'd keep a man prisoner for hours listening to arcane explanations of the alchemical philosophies of Hermes Trismegistus, or the natural properties of aconite and sulfur, and then abruptly dismiss his audience with a word so as to get back to his games with the elements.

Still. He could be brought to serve the purpose of the faithful.

As Thomas rode from Alnwick Castle his hand closed on the new rosary he'd been given by Father Quindle at Baddesley Clinton. He began to recite in a low voice. "*Ave Maria, gratia plena. Dominus tecum.*" His fingers kneaded the beads. As he prayed in Latin, he thought in English. *An audience with a king!*

Chapter 11

But harvest time passed, and the Feast of all Saints, and All Souls, and then Saint Winifred's Day, which Thomas, now home in his fine stone house, observed with prayers his wife thought excessively fervent. Still he received no order from the earl to proceed to the court of King James in Edinburgh. He busied himself with his ordinary rounds of fee-collection, and within his own walls he idled and chafed. He spoke sharply to Martha and to his daughter, and made the houschold generally unhappy.

Martha was partly at fault. She had taken longer than usual to warm to Thomas after his latest return from London. She had often asked to accompany him thence, and was always refused. His constant argument was that his business there was too pressing and serious to admit of a woman's presence. She knew that for a lie. After her husband's returns from the south, she often heard him amusing eight-year-old Claire with tales of this or that play he'd seen in Southwark. And such plays!

As a girl Martha had once seen a forbidden play of the Nativity. Her father had brought her, Kit, and Jack — all the Wright children — to a great house in York, where with a body of the northern faithful they had watched its performance. This event had come just after the passage of Elizabeth's law banning the impersonation of Christ, Mary, Joseph, or any saint on stage, and so the gathering had been clandestine. There had been comic scenes, but holy ones too, when the audience had hushed, partly in reverence, partly in fear of being caught. The play was enacted by the tile-thatchers of York, who'd brought homespun costumes, two live sheep, and child's doll for the baby Christ.

That had been many years ago, and now the great midlands and northern families could not find anyone, even servants, to play such parts. The old tradesmen who knew them had forsaken the activity through fear of arrest, and — though Thomas would never believe it when Martha said so — those tradesmen's grown Protestant children no longer cared. And so Martha's own daughter had never seen such a show. Martha disliked overhearing Thomas's descriptions of the newer plays, the very different ones that all London was mad for, plays that showed men guzzling sack in alehouses and stabbing each other to death or reclining lewdly in ladies' chambers, speaking verse that did not rhyme. She'd spent time in London as a girl, but those playhouses had not been thought places for children. Her brothers Kit and Jack had visited them, though, and she'd overheard enough of their conversation to know there was nothing sacred about the London plays.

Thomas disagreed. But his besottedness with the theaters only led him into follies and mishaps unbecoming a grown man. The worst thus far had been the action of battery brought against him by a London player four years before. Thomas had claimed that while relieving himself near the trees behind the Rose theater, he had seen a fair lady most villain-ously bruited about by a savage assailant. He'd run to her aid and drawn his sword against her ruffian adversary in gallant rescue. How could he have known that the pair were players — the fair lady a wigged boy — in rehearsal of a rape scene for the morrow's performance? The pummeled actor had recovered, and the earl had intervened and lessened the fine, but fine there had been, for the judge had not believed Thomas's story.

Martha, however, believed it.

The Puritans were right to condemn play audiences to hellfire. Heaven needed no idiots.

It confused her, following the train of her own thoughts, to reach a point of agreement with Puritans. For Puritans were the hottest and worst of the Protestants, and Protestants caused Catholics nothing but trouble. Yet the Puritans' plight sparked some sympathy in Martha's breast. After all, though the queen hunted those of the old Roman faith, pursuing them with the nose of a beagle, she made herself almost as busy jailing those wild, black-cloaked Puritan zealots for their attacks on her bishops. Sometimes Puritans shared cells with Jesuits in prison, and all strove mightily to convert one another. She'd heard this from Father Quindle. The thought made Martha smile.

She dropped her smiles whenever Thomas entered the room. For his negligence, and for his quenchless flame for his old wife Mary of London, he deserved some frost.

She'd married Thomas nine years before at the behest of her brothers and parents, who'd foreseen family advantage in this tie with a Percy, a man the great Earl of Northumberland had lately seemed to claim as close kin. She herself had been moved by the glamour that clung eternally to the Percy name, and by the fine cloak, boots, and sword her taciturn suitor had worn when he came to court her at the Wrights' ancestral manor in York, where she'd lived after her brief time in their London house. Since she and Thomas had begun sharing a household, however, she'd often wished she'd looked more closely into Thomas's pedigree at the start. He was some sort of gentleman, she knew. One of her brothers had known him at Cambridge. But in the calendar of the gentry he seemed to occupy a low place. His fine clothes, she discovered, were recent gifts from his employer the earl, not habitual garments. And he lacked grace in the wearing of them, frequently snapping the laces of his trunk hose so they sagged. Then, his beard and hair, though clean, were frequently matted and wild. When once she'd suggested that she curl his locks with heated tongs, he'd roared in outrage. No speech — a roar, like a lion! He'd consented, growling, after she'd reminded him that his friend Robin Catesby applied the tongs to *his* golden locks. But Thomas had looked so absurd after the procedure, like an Iceland dog beautified for a family portrait, that after glancing in a glass he'd doused himself with water from the well. Afterwards, he'd shaken himself like a dog to dry off.

The curling operation had not been repeated.

Now Martha did not try to alter Thomas. She busied herself with her house, and endured her graceless husband's unkemptness, his heavy footfalls , his loud voice, his slow speech, his lack of training in the gentlemanly arts of dancing and music, his mad shadow-fighting in their courtyard with his absurdly heavy sword.

All this might have been well had Thomas treated her more warmly, made her his friend, and taken her into his counsels. She admired and envied Eliza Vaux, the brave widow, who participated in the heated discussions of the men of her circle as though such was her natural right. On several holidays when the faithful had gathered, Martha, inwardly grumbling, had withdrawn to the kitchen, speaking to the cooks of the planning of meals, while Eliza drank wine at table and shared her thoughts on the state of the kingdom. And was listened to! Though Martha thought her no better schooled than she herself.

What rankled most was that Thomas spoke to Eliza Vaux as well, though he spoke very little to Martha.

Their daughter adored her oft-absent father, and seemed, in her affections, to compensate him for her mother's disappointment in her spouse. But Claire was also the source of more friction between Martha and Thomas. Martha had agreed some years before to Claire's betrothal to the son of the much-admired Robin Catesby, a boy also eight years old. But that had been before the Essex horror. Martha thanked God, Mary, and all the English saints that Thomas had not been a party to Essex's scheme. Much safer, as it turned out, to have been caught by the Spanish in Flanders than by Cecil in London: Cecil, who would have sent Thomas to the Tower or a worse prison, or to be hanged, and taken most of their money. As it was, the lucky Percys remained unscathed by the Essex tragedy. But Catesby had been punished for his part in those events, his career at court ruined and his fortune depleted. Little Claire deserved, if not a better, at least a safer match than a Catesby match. In the past year Martha had argued fiercely for Thomas to break their tie with Robin. Spellbound by that man, Thomas had refused.

At length, Martha had laid by her argument like a spring cloak in winter. Perhaps, she thought, Robin Catesby would somehow redeem himself in the coming years, though it was hard to see how. He'd need, for a start, to decline into a mere church papist, attending English services, pretending no longer to be Catholic. Yet she could not imagine anything that would cause that young zealot with the gold crucifix to give up his ostentatious display of faith. It would take a miracle. She was skeptical of those. Still, without one, she would not allow her daughter to be saddled with the Catesby name. Of this she was sure. She would keep quiet for the present only because of the children's youth, and the time it allowed. She was quarrelsome and knew it; knew she could vie with her husband in anger and better him in logic, and she did not fear him. But she, unlike he, knew when a topic was out of season. She could bide.

Not until late November did Thomas tell Martha the cause of his anxiety, his nightly pacing as he awaited a message from the earl. When, at her probing, he finally did so, she clapped her hands to her mouth in amazement. *A petition from the Catholic families to the Scottish court!* She felt first delight, then fear. Would Thomas look a fool before the king—that king who, if rumor spoke true, might soon be sovereign o'er them all? The earl trusted her husband, but everyone knew that the wizard earl was not entirely wise in the ways of the world. Sending *her* husband! An impressive-looking emissary, to be sure (or one who could be made so. She'd see to that). Still, if at the royal court of Scotland Thomas indulged his choleric tendencies—if he thought himself slighted, perhaps; his accent mocked by a kilted nobleman, and if he *popped off*—Martha shuddered. Might he not make things worse for all of them?

But—a king! She buried her doubts. When the earl's letter to James came, accompanied by a message to Thomas, she begged to see both documents. She was held off at arm's substantial length by her husband, who eagerly scanned the papers, then hid them somewhere (she could *not* find where), and afterwards would only say that the earl wrote that the king had told him he was busy with plans for a hunt and could not welcome Henry Percy's servant until Christmas was past. And yet, Thomas's going was assured. His mood lightened in the next weeks, and Martha shared his glee.

A mass-in-a-corner, attended by all three Percys in a hidden room in York on the Day of Epiphany. Then, the day after, the journey north. Thomas set off over snowy ground, his hair and beard doctored and trimmed by his wife, himself clad in warm furs and new leather boots. These last were a Christmas gift from the earl, who seemed to have had some delayed concerns about the figure Thomas would cut at the court at Edinburgh.

"The devil confound all dabblers in oil!" He heard James's burred, rasping voice before he saw the king. He followed a servant past two helmeted guards into the drafty royal presence hall. Thomas's sword had been taken and his person thoroughly investigated before he'd been allowed to cross the doorsill. Now Thomas stopped short, thinking the king's sudden curse was directed at him as Henry Percy's representative, the issue being, perhaps, the odd liquids the shadowy ninth earl famously used in his experiments. But then he saw the nervous portrait-painter who stood by a canvas on an easel, twelve feet from the king. The painter's arms were raised defensively. James stood on a dais in the center of the room, his reddish hair neat beneath a cocked, jeweled velvet hat stitched with a royal crest. A green cape edged with ermine hung from one shoulder, presenting a rich background to white satin trunks, doublet, and hose. A chain was draped over James's chest, and his hand

clutched a ceremonial sword. The king was, however, completely barefoot, and standing in a bowl.

The painter stammered. "If. . . If your majesty would permit —"

"I wish to look as though I were about to mount a horse, not as if I
were a horse! God's death, man, the *face* you have given me!" James yelled.
He stopped out of the bowl, gave it a kick, and jumped from the dais
to the marbled floor. "And the water's gone ice-cold." A liveried servant
scurried to mop the spilt water and remove the clattering bowl, as James
sat heavily down in a chair near Thomas. Thomas stood paralyzed.

"This man was searched?" James eyed Thomas suspiciously.

"Most thoroughly, sovereign." The servant who had led Thomas in
bowed as he withdrew. "He bore a most threatening sword, but surren-
dered it willingly."

"All the English go armed. I have seen them. It is to be regretted. But
look at these feet, man!" The king waved a foot in Thomas's direction. Its
skin was rosy-red and puckered from the water. "*View* them, I say! Chilblains. Have you seen such feet? They are thus in winter. Even silk netherstocks chafe. Have you seen such?"

Tongue-tied, Thomas could only bow. He sank to one knee, and
mumbled, "I have — nay, your majesty. I am Thomas Percy from the court
of Henry Percy, Earl of Northumberland, and I have never seen such feet."

"Well, get up then," the king said peevishly. Thomas rose. "Now you
have. A message you bring me, from the mad earl?" James held out his
hand, emitting a high-pitched laugh that broke off abruptly. "God save
me from one of that man's horoscopes."

"Nay, lord, it is no —"

"Three years past your earl sent word to me that all my stars were
auspicious for the next five years, and yet in a very month, one of mine
own lairds had me locked in a linen closet in his house. Swords waving
outside; aye, the man would have had utterly done with me! I was lucky
to escape with my life. That told me what to think of English soothsay-
ers." He brooded for a moment. "'Tis a curse in the blood, to be plotted
against. Did not my own father, Lord Darnley, have his manor blown up
beneath him, by gunpowder? The poor man escaped in a chair lowered
out the window, but the jealous lairds caught him in the garden . . . ." The
king shook his head to clear his brain of the image of his father, Lord
Darnley, hanging lifeless from a tree, his gold raiment torn, his tongue
lolling blackly, his shape outlined against the orange flames of his

burning manor. James had not been there. He was still in the womb at
the time. But he'd heard lurid descriptions of the scene so often, from
various malicious servants and caretakers in the royal nursery, that the
vivid, macabre picture still haunted his dreams. He was personally convinced that his mother's horror at the sight of her husband's murder had
penetrated his own infant consciousness, and sunk into his very marrow.

James had grown up parentless, his father assassinated, his mother
Mary imprisoned shortly thereafter in retaliation for her own ambitious plottings. Then, the English queen's bestowal of his mother's Scottish throne on him, a fresh lad of thirteen months, had rendered him the
impotent pawn of any thane strong enough to kidnap him and convey
him to a thick-walled highland castle until this or that demand was met.
It had only twice come to that point, but James remembered both terri-
fying occasions as clearly as he remembered his father's hanging corpse,
which, though he had never really seen it, was there whenever he shut
his eyes. Nor could he shake from his spirit the nerve-wracking effect
of the sudden, spooky disappearances, throughout his youth, of various
beloved regents and tutors, all victims of jealous court rivals or of the
malice of his mother's supporters.

When James reached majority he cast off his frustrated impotence
for ostentatious grandeur and vigorous displays of authority, trying to
banish his own fear. But the fear was always with him. His congenital
nervousness led him to seek mastery over the source of all threats: to
vanquish, through tabulation and analysis, the devilish powers that
darkened minds, that roughly awakened and stole sleeping children
from their beds, that crept through thick castle walls and did their
wicked work in defiance of armed guards and royal privilege. Witchcraft
was his new subject.

A door shut loudly on the far side of the hall. The king started. He
looked behind him, but saw only the liveried servant returning with a
steaming bowl. The servant passed the discouraged painter, who moved
in the other direction, wheeling his easel from the presence room.

Ducking his head respectfully, Thomas took a step forward and
delivered his scroll into the sovereign's hand. Then he stood obediently,
his feathered cap in his hand, as James anxiously perused it. The king's
eyes dulled as he read. At length he rolled up the document, briskly.
"Well, this is a new kind of soothsaying. No mention of—by Cock, your
hair's wild, Thomas Percy! Put on your hat, man, cover, cover. I give you

good leave. We'll give you a comb before you go. Cock! Comb!" Again the high, short laugh.

Thomas replaced his hat, feeling awkward.

"Your master writes most movingly of the plight of you English Catholics," the king said. "I have long heard of it, and sorrowed for you." He looked unconcerned. "Do you also bring news of your gracious queen?" He added a quick, smooth compliment. "I wish her long life."

"The queen hath lately suffered an abatement of vigor." Thomas stopped. The king was looking at him warningly.

"Leave us," James said, to no one in particular. "And one bring this man a chair." The servants who were standing by the doors left the room hastily. The man who had ushered Thomas in returned almost immediately with a velvet-covered stool, then withdrew once more, this time closing both doors to the chamber behind him. The stool looked delicate, and Thomas sat down on it as gently as he could.

"Continue, Master Percy," the king said in a lowered voice, after the thud of the doors' closing. "But be warned, there are spies peering through there" — he gestured vaguely at the room's east corner — "and there." He pointed at the closed doors. "They're all hunched there with their ears to the crack."

"Ah," Thomas said, then stopped again, baffled. "The queen is in good health, and sends you ..." What to say? "Sends you ...."

"You bring me no word from the queen or of the queen, not even by indirect messenger," James said shrewdly. "This you should straightaway confess. The sum of your message is that the queen's minister harries Catholics, that masses are restricted —"

"Forbidden outright, Majesty," said Thomas, then felt abashed at himself for interrupting.

But James didn't reprimand him, or seem to mind. "Yes, forbidden," he said. "And good priests tortured or killed. Those of the old faith suffer. I am not myself a Catholic, as was that poor lady my mother, whose misfortunes I regret."

"She was a holy martyr!" Thomas blurted, his face suffused with sudden passion.

The king looked at him quizzically. "A martyr? Some say aye. I applaud your reverence, Master Percy. I think you have a pious heart." He leaned forward as though to share a confidence. "Do you know, I languish in grief for the Catholic families of England. Yet what can I do?"

He spread his hands helplessly. "I can but remonstrate with your gracious sovereign for mercy towards them, for tolerance of their peaceful practice of their faith. She, who is my kind cousin, is also the prince of her realm."

Thomas saw the canny glint of James's eye, and seized a chance. "She will not always be prince of her realm." There. He had said what it was treason to say in England. The spies who ran like rats in James's palace had surely heard it. But those were Scottish spies, not English ones. And why should it be treason to state such a bald fact of nature?

Now he chose his words as carefully as it was in him to do. "Would Your Highness find himself empowered to . . . improve the condition of the faithful in our realm, our gratitude would be immense. And were we to have such assurances, be certain that the Earl of Northumberland . . . ." What should come next? "That the earl —"

"Is not without influence." Raised at court, James was far more skilled in wordcraft than newcomer Thomas. He knew the art of the prompt. He followed his words with a nod. "This I know." He thought for a moment, scratching his bare big toe and still nodding. "You have my promise," he said at length. "I will do what I can to make your land safe for the practice of your pieties. Proselytizing, of course, I cannot countenance. But by my own faith, I abhor the bloody violence and the sneaking! Let all have liberty of conscience."

"And the priests?"

"*All* should have liberty of conscience," the king repeated, with emphasis. "I give you leave to tell the earl so. And you to go. But wait!" He rose and walked over to a heavy desk that stood under a high window. Producing a key from somewhere in his clothing, he unlocked a drawer, then returned to the now standing Thomas with a slim book. "Och, the floor is cold! Here. Give this to the earl. It may serve as a wholesome warning. There is much witchery in the island of Britain of late. Let him not in his dark experiments say an evil word and summon up one of these several devils. For they are hard to dismiss once they are raised, and may do harm. I tell you, the Earl of Gowrie was led by such fell spirits to stock me briefly among his linens, until my loyal guards freed me. And not all of those linens clean, neither. I shall never forget that day. To make things worse, Gowrie sent a fiend in to plague me while I was packed in with his fouled shirts. An invisible fiend, but aye, I felt his pinches, and had marks on my body afterwards. Why do you stare at me, man? You may open that book."

Thomas fumblingly turned to the book's frontispiece, and started. His eye was met with ink images of devils and witches soaring through castled landscapes. He felt a chill. The book's title page read *Daemonologie. Made by James VI, in Scotland.*

"I have spent much time reckoning up the names of several demons both Scottish and English," James said proudly. "Let the earl read it and beware. Depart, then, Thomas Percy. I give you good leave."

Thomas bowed, tucking the book inside his doublet something fearfully. He decided that once outside the castle he would stuff the king's book in his saddlebag, keeping it as far from his body as possible. He moved to replace his hat, then remembered he had already done so at the king's behest. Not certain how to leave the royal presence, he walked backwards from the room, and bumped into the doorframe. James, reseated and again perusing the earl's letter, looked up in fright, then relaxed. "Begone, good sir," he said, waving a ringed hand. Thomas bowed, turned, and walked frontwise through the door.

Pausing to put on his gloves outside the presence room, flanked by the two nearly motionless guards, he heard the patter of receding feet down dark passageways. *Rats.*

"Your face speaks of a suit granted," said a dry London voice. He looked up and saw, to his right, a soberly clad, flat-capped pastor seated on a bench next to the wall. The man was holding something large and rectangular on his lap.

"You . . . bring him news of the queen?" Thomas asked.

The man laughed. "I have no news of the queen. The queen lives, for the present. I bring a plea of my own, on behalf of the godly of East Anglia." He tapped the thing on his lap. Peering closer, Thomas saw it was no box of documents, but a thick Geneva Bible. "I bring him a good word, and a warning against fat bishops," the man said. Under his gospel hat, his face glowed like a saint's.

Thomas burst through the doorway at Huddington Court, pushing past the servant who had answered his knock, then galumphing up the stairs. His entry was brash, but what matter? He was known here in York, at the ancestral home of the Catholic Wintours, and behold, he brought tidings of great joy.

On his return from Scotland he'd gone first to Alnwick Castle, but had been disappointed there. Deep in a book in his study, the earl had seemed indifferent to the message from James, and had nettled Thomas by asking if he'd been given something in writing.

His reception at Huddington Court proved more satisfactory. Fifteen grim, frightened faces stared at him as he stood in the doorway of the second-floor room. He saw before him not only Gawain and Bors Wintour and their wives but Eliza Vaux, Eliza's grown son Edward, Francis Tresham, William Monteagle, four servants, and three wide-eyed children who had not reached age ten.

"What *is't*, Thomas?" hissed Anne Vaux. "Pursuivants?"

"Nay! A good message from our future king!"

"From King *Arthur?*" the smallest Wintour boy asked wonderingly. His mother hushed him.

"Blessed be the name of Arthur. But again, nay. I speak of James of Scotland! He promises tolerance to all English Catholics!"

Amid the babble of happy exclamations came one cry that sent Thomas to his knees in terror. "*Gloria Patri, et Filio, et Spiritui Sancto!*" The ghostly voice seemed to emanate from the ceiling or somewhere above it.

Thomas ripped off his hat, threw it to the floor, and crossed himself. "God hath blessed us!" he said, quaking. "He speaks, here in our midst!"

Laughter was rippling through the assembly. Eliza Vaux tugged at a young girl's sleeve. "Upstairs, niece, quick," she said. "Tell Father Garnet to come out of hiding."

Chapter 12

March 25, 1603. Feast of the Annunciation of Mary (Lady Day).

"Nothing, then." The small lord gazed intently at the man in the travel-stained cloak who knelt, uncapped, before him. Idly, the lord touched the heavy gold chain that circled his neck, its medallion at rest on his velvet breast. "Nothing at all. No townsmen massing on the precincts of Alnwick Castle. No visitors of note."

"I saw nothing out of the usual way, my lord. And the earl was indeed in residence. He rode out once, unaccompanied. I tried to follow, but lost him in a wood near the castle. He returned in three hours time."

"With?"

"Naught but a basket of herbs. Muttering to himself in Latin, if I can read lips."

Cecil laughed. "Yes. This was Henry Percy." He tapped the arm of his chair. "And the sheriffs, in York and elsewhere?"

"They have your message, and are indisputably loyal. They keep close watch. Your brother in Northumbria also finds things quiet. You have his letter. That was five days past, of a surety. I rode hard."

"I know you did." Lord Cecil snapped his fingers. A servant approached with a flagon of wine. "No, not that." The spy's face fell, but regained its cheerfulness when Cecil said to the servant, "I want you to see this man paid. And take him through the postern gate."

Once alone, Cecil sat nearly motionless, his chin sunk in reverie in his hand, his elbow propped on the chair-arm. He seemed to sleep, but his mind was busy, weighing the possibility of a northern rising against the chance of Catholic patience. Which was heavier, papist anger or papist hope?

He'd labored to build the hope. He himself had been one of the many southern petitioners who'd lately sent to the court of Scottish James. And his letters, he knew, had been those to which James, employing his own scales of deliberation, had given greatest weight. By all signs and reports James behaved like an outland clown among his courtiers and before his foreign visitors, but he was no fool. No fool at all. His letters to Cecil confirmed that James knew whose voice mattered most in the matter of the English succession.

A linnet chirped in the gilded cage Cecil kept on a low shelf. Aroused from his thoughts, Cecil rose, walked to the bird's pretty prison, and tapped the wire. The linnet hopped from his perch and pecked at the man's fingertip, drawing blood. Cecil grimaced as he quickly stepped back from the cage. Pulling a silk handkerchief from his breast pocket, he wiped the finger as he strolled to the window and looked out. The sun was setting.

Impossible not to smile, however sadly, at the irony of nature.

He put his head out the casement, scanned the greening fields and the houses, and was once more taken by the stillness of all of it. Strange how quickly rumor ran, bringing messages *gratis,* for no fee. For somehow, everyone knew. No proclamations had been posted, and yet the hush that had lately fallen on Richmond Palace had spread to its precincts, to the town and the great city of London beyond. No bells or bugles sounded.

So it had been for three days.

There is a tide in the affairs of men which, taken at the flood, leads on to fortune, yet, not taken, brings all to pox and hell-fire, or something of this type which is not happy and must at all costs be avoided. No, that did not scan as well as the lines in the play he'd heard quoted *ad nauseam* in and out of councils every day of these past three years, when each moment was thought by every ambitious lord and minor court-climber to herald that particular tide which must be sailed on, or all beached forever. But this, this very now, *was* the moment. Cecil felt it.

More, he was in a position to know it.

A knock sounded on the door. He turned quickly. "Yes. *Ingredere.*"

A servant opened the door. "My lord, she is the same."

"I'll to her." Quick on his short legs, he entered the torchlit hallway.

Long practice had taught him to ignore the sort of whispers that followed him as he passed the small knots of noblemen, lesser gentry, ladies, and servants huddled in corners of the palace. *Derry,* he heard twice, and once, *Tom Thumb.* Only once, years before, on a day of particular vexation following an audience with the queen concerning her commissioning of Essex in Ireland, Cecil had stopped to confront one of the mockers, a young, foppish courtier who'd gigglingly chirped, "Beagle!" as he'd passed. Cecil had paused and slowly turned. "And *you* are a parrot," he'd rebuked the man, who'd already turned pale as his cohorts scrambled to desert him, running back to their palace holes like mice in the face of candleflame. Cecil's voice had risen with his fury. "Yes, a parrot you are. A mindless bird who repeats whate'er he hears. A — " On the verge of ordering a flogging for the youth, he'd stopped himself. It had not been that he thought it well to tolerate loose speech. The opposite was the case. But he knew the dignity of his position was compromised by his slightest acknowledgment of these brainless insults, these air-bullets fired against his person. He hated the nicknames, but after all, they did nothing to lessen his sway at court. Recalling all this, mastering his anger, he'd turned on his boot-heel and left the man cowering. Even that short, self-indulgent interchange he'd regretted later; had, in truth, regretted it ever since, because "Parrot!" was now added to the litany of comic names that followed him down stone palace passageways. Even *she* had used it once, he winced to recall.

In the anteroom of the queen's chamber, three others of the Privy Council were gathered. All were standing. They looked at Cecil as he entered bearing letters in his hand. He held the documents high. "The north is quiet," he announced. He scrutinized the men's guarded faces. "I shall interpret those sideways movements of your eyes as expressions of glad relief." He tucked the letters in the inner pocket of his velvet cloak, choosing to say nothing of the one that was signed, in the code he'd invented, by "*Number 10, Decimus.*" That letter, dated March 20th, read, "*I await with all patience the bestowal of the honorable and glorious burden God may deliver me through his earthly ministers.*" How long, he wondered, had James toyed with that troublesome word "may"? No need to speak of that letter now, at any rate. The Scotsman's hopes were well known, by all from the merest London draper's apprentice to Sir George Carey, guzzling wine by the window there.

"So the north is sure. And the midlands?" asked Francis Bacon.

"A guard has been issued to Lady Arbella Stuart," Cecil said smoothly. "As we agreed in this room, the queen's most Catholic cousin will be brought south from Derbyshire. This will protect her from papists kidnapping her and duping simpletons into rioting in her favor."

"Aye, those zealots besotted by the religion of their grandams. Their banners emblazoned with all the counterfeit signs of holiness, the five pentangular wounds of Christ and a painted communion cake. A true Satan's garrison." Bacon's voice was dry as powder. "And you'd wish to *protect* their idol? Let us give Arbella Stuart the same protection we gave her kinswoman Mary."

A dead silence greeted this sally — if it *were* a sally, and not a serious suggestion that the mild gentlewoman Arbella Stuart should be beheaded simply because she was Romish. Cecil loosened the tension by smiling tiredly. "Let us pray, for all our sakes, it does not come to that. The lady is no Queen of Scots but a loyal subject."

"Loyal now, yes," said Bacon. "But in the coming days, loyal to whom?"

Now Cecil's eyes snapped. "To the peace of our Protestant realm."

He felt their eyes on his back as he entered the queen's chamber.

The heavy curtains over the windows were drawn. Her old face was dimly lit by a single candle, itself a compromise. Two days before, when she'd still been capable of speech, she'd asked for absolute darkness. Cecil had cautioned the women in attendance to think that request mere poetry. Elizabeth would have darkness soon enough, he'd thought grimly. At this time, to keep England from total night, it was necessary to read her sounds, her face, her very gestures, for word of the succession.

Word of the succession! Through her whole life, in her obstinacy, she'd not only refused to speak of it, but forbidden others to discuss it as well. Ten years before, for even broaching the subject openly in the House of Commons, a respected Puritan pastor had been sent to the Tower, where he'd sickened and died. Lords took note, and whispered in private, or in code. In her superstition, Elizabeth thought that to admit the need of a next monarch was to allude to her own passing, and that to speak of that coming end of life was to bring it on. In this her seventieth year, she'd often seemed really to believe the fanciful compliments her younger self had cannily fostered so that she might hold sway over ambitious male courtiers. She was Astraea, Gloriana, a new Holy Virgin, half a goddess! *In my time, have I not defeated the Spanish and the smallpox?* she'd once jested in the presence of a nervous council. *Indeed, I may live forever!* They'd cheered her vociferously, of course, Cecil among them. *Yes, milady, you may! God make it so!*

Cecil's father had been the queen's closest advisor before him, and Cecil had been raised to inherit his father's part. He knew the queen better than anyone living—better, he was convinced, than had his own sire—and had perfected ways of urging her toward the choice they all knew must be made. He knew how close to the cliff he might dance in his speech, what urgent requests for intelligence would pass for compliment, what words presented ugly truths sufficiently veiled. For Elizabeth, there was no impending death. Instead, there loomed "that sad event that I hope mine eyes shall never see." There need be no present naming of the monarch to come. Rather, Elizabeth might "quiet the fears of her loving people by indicating which of her loyal British countrymen she deemed most regal." The words "British countrymen" Cecil had chosen with particular care. They gestured vaguely northward rather than southward. For God forbid that, after so many decades of brave resistance to the pope's minions, the daughter of Henry the Eighth should incline toward the king of Spain! And that Spanish king's sister, the Catholic Duchess of Flanders, would be no better choice, for all there was some English in her blood. No. "Heaven preserve thy realm from the wars that might break forth between true English Christians and the slaves of Pope Clement, should a Spaniard see cause to put a toe in Southampton!" Cecil had warned the queen. "Yet, your Majesty might forfend such an unlooked-for invasion with a single word." She knew exactly what he meant, of course. But this artful eloquence saved him—usually—from the hottest flames of her anger.

Yet even his skilled attentions had yielded no final fruit. She had never named an heir, nor forbidden one. And now, her heart and breath failing, she could say nothing at all. All, all his statecraft for nothing.

But the beagle still had a trick.

He knelt by the bed and gazed at her face. The skin was pock-marked, sallow, and hanging. The linen cloths with which she'd lately plumped her cheeks when greeting her ministers had been laid by. In her age she seemed sexless, like the phoenix she'd played for nearly five decades of her life. He pitied her, and sorrowed for her. The great queen was his friend.

And like a friend he would save her by saving her one beloved. England would not be torn by Catholic rebellion in the north. Quieted by

James's pledges, by the promises Cecil had urged the Scot to make, the recusants and church papists would wait patiently to see what good things their new monarch would bring. They would continue to pay their fines: no small benefit to the state's coffers, at two hundred pounds a year per Catholic gentleman. Cecil's lip curled at the memory of his old enemy Essex. A dreamer, who'd hoped to be named heir, and would have banned all such fines in the name of tolerance! A fool with no knowledge of what it cost to manage a country. Even Elizabeth, so fond of Essex, had seen in the end that he was an idiot.

Elizabeth's eyelids fluttered, then flew open. Her left hand lay curled on the pillow next to her nearly hairless head. She looked childishly, questioningly, at Cecil, who bowed his head. "My gracious sovereign." With his left hand he signaled to the woman who guarded the door. She turned to admit them: George Carey, Walter Raleigh, Francis Bacon, other men of the council. Word of Cecil's coming had traveled, and the crowd in the room outside had grown over the last few minutes. As expected. As planned.

The men filed in and stared at Elizabeth, aghast at her appearance. "The sacra ....," Carey said, then stopped at Cecil's dry look of warning. Was Carey mad? Whatever the queen privately believed (for who knew?), and however her father had died a Catholic, would she, to say nothing of they, defeat the Protestant life she'd lived by such a travesty? Freeing a Peter-priest from prison to administer the last rites, with his damned Roman gestures and mumbling? No. Cecil himself would perform the only ritual necessary.

Cecil bent his upper body forward and once more met the queen's bewildered gaze. In a clear, loud voice, he said, "Your Highness, it is not meet that you should speak. Only touch your head with your hand upon hearing the name that you favor." He cleared his throat. He was self-schooled against all emotional display, but his heart was now racing. *There is a tide in the affairs of men which, taken at the flood ....* With the peers as witnesses, the thing must be most carefully timed.

"Isabella, Archduchess of Flanders," he said. He heard a faint intake of breath from Lord Carey, which he took note of.

Elizabeth gave no sign.

"The Duke of Parma."

The queen's eyes flickered as at an old memory, but her hand lay still.

"Henry of France, late of Navarre."

"Madness." He knew the scornful hiss came from Walter Raleigh, who was bolder than the others, bolder even than Bacon, who hated Raleigh for his daring. Cecil did not bother responding to the whispered insult. Ambitious Raleigh was too big for England, which was why he spent so much time sailing the Atlantic. Sooner or later he'd fall afoul of whatever new monarch took the throne, with too strong an expression of a point of view. It would not be the first time. Cecil didn't waste spies on Raleigh, who would dig his own grave.

He drew in his breath. Now he said clearly and slowly, "James Stuart, King of Scotland."

For a moment the old woman did nothing. Then, slowly, her still-curled hand moved toward her forehead, touched it, and rested there.

Hardly breathing, the lords moved forward and leaned over the bed. Cecil looked up at them and nodded.

George Carey withdrew hastily from the room. Cecil smiled at that. Carey was a church papist, he suspected, but not enough of a fool to foment a Spanish invasion now that Elizabeth's choice was clearly made and likely to be popular. No, he was gone to spur his horse onto the old Roman road north, ready to kill himself with haste to reach Scotland before anyone else, to beg from James an excellent appointment at the king's new court. Fresh horses already posted along the way, no doubt. Carey would not waste a moment after the queen drew her last breath. The other lords would be rousing themselves to like busy errands of self-advancement, sweating over letters and dispatching them by swift riders from Richmond Castle, waiting for the end. All of them were swirling cloaks, turning to go. None expected further signs of consciousness from the queen. Her lady saw them out.

Briefly alone in the room, Cecil withdrew his hand from beneath the queen's mattress, where he'd placed it before the men had entered. He was not physically strong, and his fingers felt cramped from the slow pressure they'd exerted, lifting the heavily upholstered mass until the queen's hand had finally slipped down to her forehead. He flexed the fingers, one of which still bled from the peck of the caged linnet. Then he stood and reseated himself on a low cushion by the wall. He fixed his eyes on Elizabeth.

Her lady returned. The air was stifling, and at Cecil's request the woman drew a curtain and opened a casement window slightly to admit a breath of the night air. Then she sat down by the bed of her royal mistress. Cecil said nothing more to her. With the woman, he watched, as the last Tudor's breath grew shallow and then, in the grey dawn, utterly ceased.

Chapter 13

A town in mourning, the dyers busy as witches on All Hallow's Eve, blacking white garments in bubbling vats and profiting, profiting, profiting. Never had so much black been seen in the London streets. On the day of the burial fourteen hundred persons walked in funeral procession, wearing cloth to match their quality. Representatives from each English sphere of life were brought forth by the College of Arms, to march. Here, to the slow beat of drums, came prelates, earls and knight-marshals, clerks, musicians, judges, law officers, apothecaries, servants from the royal laundry and scullery, seamstresses and ruff starchers, and three hundred seventy-six men and women of the poor, paid pennies for their trouble.

"A heretic, and an excommunicate, she was," said Thomas, when word of the funeral's dark splendor reached Northumbria. "No counterfeit and most secular rite can save her from Hell's hot fire."

"Nay, it cannot." Martha and their daughter nodded. Both the woman and the girl had seen armed Crown agents break into private homes, beat good husbands with the flats of their swords, and hold terrified children at knife-point to force their parents to reveal priests' hiding places. They'd seen walls broken through with axes and holy men drawn off in carts. On Queen Elizabeth's due punishment they could all agree.

The North did not rise. Lent ended, Easter came and went, and no soldiers galloped south to kidnap the dead queen's Catholic cousin Arbella Stuart and force her to rule them. Unlike his most notable ancestors, Henry Percy, ninth Earl of Northumberland, did not summon armed men and ride forth to demand a reckoning of the lords in the haughty south. Instead, hardly aware of the time, he stayed in his high tower, reading, muttering, and adding sheep's urine, boiled for three days, to pinches of powdered gold and sweetgum to make a paste for eternal adhesion. In the midland and northern towns there was no massing.

There were, however, masses. These were conducted by priests come from hiding, one of whom blessed the elements of the sacrament in the open garden of Baddesley Clinton. In London there was mourning, in York, thanksgiving. The faithful prayed and offered blessings for their delivery from forty-five years of fear and torment. They waited, suspended in hope, for the advent of James, friend to Catholics.

Thomas collected his rents, waiting with the rest. These hopeful days he did his best to limit sword-waving in the exercise of his duties. He reminded himself that a Percy quarreled only with gentlemen, not with farmers and tradesmen. At times, seeing the sweaty sheen of a blacksmith's or a cooper's skin at a residence where he'd come to collect moneys, or the hard bare hands of a shepherd counting coin into his own gloved palm, he felt the melancholy descend on him. He was nagged by the fear that he was more like these men than he pretended, or at least, that he might have been. He could never entirely free himself from the memory of his father milking a cow during a year when harvests had been bad and farmers weren't paying their taxes. The Percys had had to discharge their servants, for a time. His father hadn't seemed fully to understand the shame of it, though little Thomas, practicing his reading on penny ballads, saw it well. Percy hands, which should have grasped the hilt of a sword, raising it high in defense of a Catholic king — such hands, on the udder of a barnyard beast! Now grown, Thomas thought admiringly of golden-haired Robin Catesby, who, whatever the decline in his fortunes, still engaged in activities befitting a gentleman. Catesby fenced, hunted, and spoke with wineglass in hand of heavy matters of state. Always Robin Catesby showed fine manners and honorable gallantry among his peers. *And I am Robert Catesby's peer, or better,* Thomas thought fiercely, urging the roan to a pointless gallop along the dusty northern road as he made his rounds. *I am a Percy of Northumberland!*

Coming to his own gate, he saw the bird he loved most, the broadwinged golden eagle, soaring above the slate roof of his manor. A good omen! The sight inspired him. He reined in and watched for several minutes as the bird swooped and dove. Then he dismounted, gave his horse to a servant, and hurried inside the house, calling exuberantly for Martha. "Wife, you must ready your spirit! The great families of this high country will be honored in England's new day!"

Martha looked at him with eyes wide, less surprised at his suggestion than at his broaching of such topics with her. A rare occurrence, indeed. Busy with household cares, she'd just summoned the cook to complain about the poor quality of the leeks he had bought at market. Now, when the servant entered the room, she instantly dismissed him to listen further to Thomas. "How honored?" she asked. "What have you heard?"

" 'Tis rumored through the land. Catholic gentlemen need no longer skulk and stay far from London. All say it. The king will give places at court and in council to men of the north."

She knew that this was, in truth, the rumor that raced through the hamlets and towns of the north and the midlands. Many hopes had been shared in a talk lately overheard by Martha after a mass, among Thomas, Robin Catesby, and her brothers, Kit and Jack Wright. She knew those four companions had long resisted turning church papists like William Monteagle and Gawain Wintour, both of whom had earned places at Elizabeth's court by swearing the oath of allegiance to her. Robin Catesby in especial had thrown all possibility of advancement away, not only in falling in with Essex, but in stubbornly and (the familiar thought pained her) *obviously* maintaining his recusancy after Essex's failure. But perhaps they all might safely persist in their faith now. With James coming, there was every hope that the court might be open to Catholic gentlemen, and Catesby rewarded for his unswerving honor.

Now Thomas voiced his true hidden hope to his wife. Once restored to public favor, Catesby could open the way for Thomas Percy, kinsman to the earl. Thomas might, after all, be knighted.

Thomas did not share with Mary all on which he now brooded: his deep, tangled welter of memories and dreams. He dimly understood his religious fervor to be rooted in a personal history he could not fully speak of, or change even if he would. He was just practical enough to understand that mere conversion to Protestantism, real or feigned, would never have elevated him to a place among the noble. He'd been a private soldier, a paltry adventurer, when he'd met soul-changing Mary, whose image still fired his soul. Few chances of worldly advancement had been lost when, moved by Mary's piety, he'd turned true Catholic. And once he'd lost her, wandering homeward bereft to Northumbria, it was Catholics who'd redeemed him. First Robin Catesby, met at a mass, had afterward approached and befriended him. Catesby had urged him to supplicate the earl for employment on the strength of their shared lineage. Thank God and all the saints for Catesby! Next, the Wrights, who'd also come back north, and Francis Tresham, another highborn Catholic — all liegemen to Northumberland — had welcomed Thomas into their circle, even urging him to remarry within it. Only among these faithful had Thomas been granted the honor due his name.

So he loved them.

"Knighted? A place at the king's London court?" Hope warred with the natural skepticism in Martha's face. She placed her fists on her hips. "Do my brothers say so?"

"Jack thinks it more than possible. Great things are afoot, wife."

At this Martha permitted her eyes to shine, and gave a little birdlike hop. Though content in Yorkshire, she had long dreamed of seeing London once more, on higher terms. She started to hum. Indeed, she found Thomas highly tolerable of late.

Again she summoned the cook, and dealt more cheerfully with him. So taken up was she in the cares of her kitchen that she did not notice her husband fall silent again, or his eyes cloud over.

Despite all newer hope, the melancholy was afflicting Thomas. He had meant, truly meant, freely to share his hopefulness with Martha, to bind them both in a joy best expressed in loving embraces, and whatever might follow those. For indeed, he loved her best when her bustling energies set her racing cheerfully about the rooms as she did now, the lines of her long, strong legs visible beneath her straight-falling gown (for Martha scoffed at petticoats, so hooped and stiff). He would like to have caught her, raised the hem of her garment, and stroked those lean legs with his large hands. But some nameless gloom stayed him. And now, as she disappeared into the rear of the house with a last swish of skirts, he felt a disabling grief rise as it did so often when London was spoken of, when he recalled his last happy residence there.

And the way it had ended.

Suddenly he smote the tabletop with his hand, hard. He stood, walked to the window and glowered at the crocuses in the courtyard. Why had God waited to strike down this red-headed queen? It almost appeared He had blessed her with long life. Why had the faithful been punished by her evil counselors and nearly endless rule? Had Elizabeth died on a more predictable date, say twelve years before, on the anniversary of her murder of the good Catholic queen of Scots, all might have been well. Then the queen's obstinate chastisement of the faithful, revealed as black sin, would have ended. Then heretic English bishops might have been banned, and Roman priests might have blossomed in churches, appearing as needed to shepherd the faithful on dutiful pilgrimages undergone without fear. No obstacle then would have impeded his and his Mary's fulfillment of their pledge to Saint Winifred.

Yes, he loved Martha and Claire. They were blessings. And yet, to have kept in his arms his first wife, the wife of one year, the wife of his passion? She who had lovingly teased him for his clumsiness and ill-spokenness, not impatiently upbraided him nine times out of ten?

He now gazed sullenly through the window at Martha, who had gone out to the courtyard to survey her garden. There she was, squatting and muscular, vigorously digging out weeds with a stick. A servant would have done it, but she couldn't wait. Yes, lively Martha, the young girl in the Wrights' London house whom Mary had been tutoring on the day he and Mary had first joined eyes and blushed pinkly at one another. Thomas had barely noticed Martha then, but now — as he thought of it — he dimly recalled that she'd looked to be penciling figures in the margin of her catechism book that afternoon, as though toting up the numbers in her private budget for expenditures, instead of attending to her instructress's lesson about why God made the world. Ah, worldly Martha! Martha was not the woman God had meant for him. Surely, had he and Mary kept true to their holy promise to Winifred, it would have been Mary standing in the yard where Martha now squatted. And Mary would not be strenuously weeding, dirtying her hands. She would be gazing at the pale pewter sky, smiling softly, mysteriously. And then she would turn and walk toward him with her hands outstretched, and in her eyes he would see acknowledged his most secret self. Loved. Known.

He closed his eyes in bittersweet memory. With Winifred's blessing Mary would have borne him many sons, healthy and whole sons, instead of harboring a cold child who never saw daylight.

Angrily, Thomas shook his head, scattering tears like a wet Shetland dog. "*Aaarrrgh!*" he cried, stamping about the stone hearth room. "God forgive me my *wroth!*" He missed his dead child fiercely, though he'd never seen or known him. They had planned to name him Henry. Henry Percy. Namesake of the present and ninth earl, and of the first one.

Forty minutes later Thomas was back at the window, still brooding, though he had dragged over a heavy chair to contain himself and his clotted musings. For some minutes he had been urging his stubborn brain in a more hopeful direction, reminding himself that Martha was not old, and that despite past disappointments in the area of childbirth, he might yet have a son. Not only namesake of Northumberland, but — Thomas dared to think — perhaps heir. The present earl had no son or brother, and did claim, or at least had claimed, on one well-remembered occasion, to regard Thomas as close kin.

The momentous words had been spoken on a day of great noise and tumult in Flanders, two and a half years before, during his sojourn there with the earl. Certain images from that day were permanently engraved in his memory, forever a haunting. And the words and sounds still echoed.

There were the explosions, of course, coming mostly from the English gunships assaulting Ostend down the coast, doing battle with what remained of the Spanish Armada. Thomas had been following the yelling earl, one of ten soldiers pushing and lugging the guns into place over sand-dunes, turning their muzzles toward the walls of fortified Nieuport. In the dead of the prior night the English engineers had laboriously dug a tunnel in the damp, shifting ground under the east wall of the fortified town, stocked it with powder, and laid and lit a fuse, but it had come to nothing. The moisture of the air and a sandfall had snuffed out the wick. Now the earl's men were bringing cannon to raze the wall, but the guns kept bogging down. They ended by abandoning three of them in the grainy muck, and used their concentrated might to emplace the largest brass gun, the long-barreled one with the ten-inch bore, which they knew could do the most damage. Sweating, Thomas had readied the charge, and awaited the signal. He watched the earl approach in his blowing cloak. The earl knelt, then stood again, measuring the gun with a metal quadrant, chanting arcane computations of ball-density and range, a Euclidian geometry of death. The signal came, and Thomas fired. The ball fell fifty feet short of the wall. Twice more, cursing, he fixed the charges and fired. Each time, the ball fell short.

The earl was beside himself. "They should go *straight*, but they arc *downwards*. It is almost as though some *force* is pressing them to earth!"

Thomas knew, in retrospect, what the force had been. It was the hand of God, standing for the Flemish and Spanish. But in the moment of battle the English were disinclined toward this unhopeful interpretation of their misfortunes. Shaking their heads at the mystery of the sinking balls, they increased the powder in the breach and managed to push the gun farther forward until it stood only one hundred and forty paces from the fort, though this placed them well in range of defensive arrows. "Ready!" the earl had called for a fourth time. "Aim! *FIRE!*"

The force of the explosion threw them to the ground. All sound ceased. By uncanny, devilish luck, the fourth ball, though it too missed the wall, had hit and sparked the fuse of the massive charge the English had abandoned beneath the fort the night before. Lying entangled on the earth, all that he and the earl could now see through the smoke was the horror. A rain of rocks mingled with severed Spanish and Flemish arms, legs, and armored heads flying through the pitchy air before them, pieces of soldiers, not to be rejoined until the Day of Judgment. Thomas would never forget the unearthly sight of a bleeding man, on fire, who'd risen into the sky with the speed of a comet and then plummeted, crashing, til he lay black, dead, and broken on the burning ground right before the two deaf, dismayed Englishmen. Truly this, the smoke, the flames, the soundless screams and unjointed bodies, was a vision of hell.

As though dreaming, or else suddenly awake, he and the earl cowered, fearing God's swift punishment for the part they'd just played in the destruction of England's enemies, who were their own Catholic brethren, who should be their friends. Their ears rang like bells. Huddling on the sand, their hearing slowly returning, they waited in fear for their deaths, longing for a priest to hear them confess and to bless them. Amid the din and smoke, sure that their lives would soon be over, the earl pulled Thomas close and cried out, "Brother Percy!"

They had not, however, died, and by the evening the ninth earl had composed himself. The secrets of the earl's soul were his own, but, once the English were ensconced in the captured fort, Thomas suspected that Henry Percy had postponed his search for a priest for confession — though English Catholic priests weren't hard to find in Flanders — to return to his study of powder and gun placements.

The day after their shared vision of hell, seeking a more honorable confrontation than powder could afford, was the day Thomas had sallied forth with his sword to the fields near Ostend, and forthwith been captured. Brooding in a Spanish cell, he had recited, over and over, two prayers, the *Gloria Patri* and one more particular to himself: "*Brother Percy. Brother Percy.*"

Yes. So the earl had called him, and the name bespoke his destiny. This present earl might scant the ancient honor of the Percys, but Thomas would redeem it. He could only believe that he would indeed have a son, and would name him Henry, now not for the ninth earl, nor for the first, but for another Henry Percy, he of ancient days who would have been the second earl, had he not so gloriously, youthfully, sword-in-handedly died. Thomas would name his son for Hotspur.

Back to the now of things. He began to fret, looking once more through the window at the dream-displacing figure of Martha, with her stubbornly flat belly. There she stood, dusting hands from the weeding she'd been at for over an hour, straight and narrow in her red wool gown bought with money from the coffers of the earl. She was a tall woman, only half a head shorter than Thomas. And she was more hale than little Mary had ever been, but she had women's troubles of her own. Since Claire's birth, Martha, like his first wife, had proved unable to bring new pregnancies to term. The vexing result was that after almost ten years of marriage, son and heir Percy had still not arrived. The thought of his old aborted pilgrimage to Saint Winifred's well plagued him anew when he thought of Martha's several miscarriages. Surely he was punished therein! Unfairly, Martha too was being made to suffer for Thomas's quailing faith. What had he done but grumble idly in taverns and fret about Mary, during those months set aside for pilgrimage, while Father Quindle sat manacled in a London prison? He winced, thinking of the priest's scarred hands as they'd lately rested on Anne Vaux's fine linen tablecloth at Baddesley Clinton. Quindle had absolved him at Baddesley Clinton, but still, Thomas's soul was black and heavy and freighted with failure.

Thomas wished he could go on a pilgrimage. Despite frequent confessions, he was haunted by his own uncleanness. He had not done well as a father, as a husband, as a Catholic. He longed impossibly for some purgation by water and fire. Above all, his heart yearned for Winifred's shrine.

Now he pulled out his Winifred medal and held it in his hand. He stared at the simple engraving. To his eyes the saint looked like Mary, mother of his never-born son.

Thomas had never made pilgrimage to any holy place. In England, after all, where was there to go? In Canterbury and Durham, the shrines of the blessed saints had long ago been dismantled, their stones pulled apart by rude, irreverent king's men in the days of Henry the Eighth. Only in wild, far-off Wales did anything like the old shrines still stand. Yet gone were the days when Englishmen and Englishwomen traveled to

Wales and elsewhere as they would, roaming the blessed earth freely. Now, holy travelers had to reckon with laws against vagabondage. And when pilgrims prayed to those who blessed their walkings, they spoke to saints now banished. Did the saints even hear their English faithful anymore? Ursula, guider of vessels. Ninian, who cured blindness. Columba, protectress of virgins. Cuthbert of Durham, the incorruptible, bringer of luck and guarder of city walls. Those holy ones had been chased away. England had gone grey with the breath of Protestant pastors, those cool, black-clad men of reason who proclaimed that the age of miracles was past, and that God lived in a homely way in the English Bible. Those men were wrong. God was never so easy to find.

But how go in quest of Him? Now not only thieves and pursuivants but sheriffs and town guards troubled the holy wanderer, requiring proof of a sanctioned errand, forbidding "vagrancy," stocking palmers, jailing men and women they deemed masterless however much they served God and the saints. Martha was even less inclined than gentle Mary had been to brave such modern dangers. His new wife balked at any suggestion that she leave her home for perilous travel, yea, even for Winifred's blessing. She was not overfond of Saint Winifred, for reasons Thomas did not well understand.

Still. Hope. In a kingdom restored to holiness, even Martha might flex and soften. Might become someone more like Mary.

Come, James, he prayed. *Make thy realm safe for pilgrims!*

Chapter 14

That James would come was sure. The sovereign had been publicly declared Elizabeth's heir, king now of England and Scotland.

True, he dawdled in his progress toward London, fearing the plague that had erupted in that city shortly after Elizabeth's death. Yet even this sad delay figured in Thomas's prophecy. "The black plague punishes the irreverent!" he declared triumphantly to Martha, when word reached the north that the fearful disease raged in the capital. He glowered at his wife when she snapped back that this was not probable, that anyone with a sliver of brain could see that pestilence slew faithful Catholics right alongside Protestant heretics.

It was true that the plague struck less frequently in the more rural north and midlands. In these parts, no high-piled death carts clattered down lanes. Still, the disease was on everyone's lips that spring. Huddled in Baddesley Clinton with Father Garnet, Anne Vaux mourned for the poorer faithful, scores of them in London, who would now succumb to the grim pest, their bodies discolored by buboes, as disgusting to themselves as to others, lacking the benefit of priests to perform their last rites. And the unholy burials, the saintly and the sinners tumbled into common graves!

"God sees it, and will act," Father Garnet told her. Today he had dressed, as he often did, in his gardener's garb, and was actually trimming a hawthorn hedge, as Anne followed him fretfully. These grounds were not his, but he'd come to feel a proprietary interest in their care. He adjusted the straw hat that shaded his eyes, and snipped a twig. "Think, Anne, how our own patience has been rewarded with a promise of tolerance from James."

She laughed a little. "Then thou'lt not long for thine old cramped berth, standing in water two feet below the floorboards?"

Henry laughed. "I will visit there, now and again."

Garnet was weary, having spent weeks traveling the midlands and the north, performing masses for fifty families. He was glad to be at Baddesley Clinton, though he knew the place was frequently watched, and though over the years he'd spent nearly as much time in its dank priest-holes as in its garden or spacious welcoming hall. Despite those discomforts, this house was the one place on earth that was something like a home to him. It was Anne, of course, who made it so. He turned and smiled at her worried face. He wished to pat her hand gently in gratitude, but refrained.

South, south James finally came in summer, to rule England, to ride the horse of St. George. His whole way from York to London's Whitehall Palace was lined with cheering English faces. With him he brought his three princely cubs and his Catholic queen, whose adult conversion to the Romish faith he thought foolish, but tolerated with affection.

As they passed through York, Thomas Percy watched the royal pair's velvet-gloved hands waving from the windows of their carriage. He stood three men back in the thick crowd, but was, as usual in such gatherings, large and high enough to see and block the view of others. He took off his hat, not for James, but as a concession to a grumbling towns-man behind him. He felt satisfied, thinking, *This queen may make our king Catholic in time.*

Thomas knew the power of pious wives.

After King James, the ninth Earl of Northumberland traveled south, having finally agreed to Thomas's nagging plea that he deliver a petition from loyal English Catholics to the king at Hampton Court. From thence the earl rode to Syon House, again to host his science-minded friends, Walter Raleigh and Francis Bacon and the mathematician Thomas Har-riott. Together these men conversed about the shape of the earth and the speed of the moon. At times they were joined by George Carey, who loved experiments; Carey, the lord who'd bolted from the room of his dying queen and ridden north far and fast to be the first to tell James of his royal fortune. That hard journey had ruined Carey's health, and, to his greater sorrow, had not gained him any special court appointment. Now he visited the earl, hoping for favor that way, now that the earl Henry Percy had been named Captain of the Gentlemen's Pensioners, the king's royal bodyguard. The duties of that position were light. The earl knew well that the king had honored him thus so as to keep him in the south, and a close eye on him there. Since the first Earl of Northumberland revolted in 1403, his northern banners flying and his son Hotspur raising his spear against the royal House of Lancaster, no English king had ever fully trusted a Percy.

"This is the fruit of my letter sent in all innocence to help you and your friends," the ninth earl said angrily to Thomas, who had followed him south alone, leaving a vexed Martha behind him. "This! I must now be resident here at Syon or over at Petworth eight months of the year, and all my best materials behind me in Northumbria!"

"I will fetch them forth, lord."

"You? You'll confuse ammonium with mercury. And some of the elements are not transportable. This is your mischief, Thomas. Or, better said, Robin Catesby's."

Thomas's eyes flashed sudden fire, and he stood. "God has called thee! Thou art champion of the faithful at the king's court!"

"Calm yourself, Thomas. Remember your station." The earl's voice contained no real rebuke. He'd been distracted by the sight of the king's book, *Daemonologie*, which lay on a heavy oak table at his elbow. He raised the book and shook it in the direction of Thomas, who covertly crossed himself. "But what a king is this! To send me a catalogue of demons and their variant powers! For whom does he take me, an *auld* Welsh sorcerer? 'The foul fiends Flibbertigibbet and Hoppededance'? Men of science are not frighted by old wives' tales. This, now." Replacing *Daemonologie*, the earl lifted from the table a thicker book with a featureless cover page. "A more scholarly inquiry into the secrets of nature, by Pico della Mirandola. In Italian, bought me by a servant in Paul's Yard. I'd sent him to seek Aristotle's *Physics*, and the man was so bold as to purchase this too, which delighted me. I gave the man a purse of silver, I was so glad. Do you know, this work can only be lawfully printed in Protestant lands? The Roman church has placed it on the Index — "

"The *Roman* church? Do you not mean *the* holy Church?" Thomas cried.

"Yes, yes. Soft you now, Thomas." The earl had seated himself on the velvet settle, and was caressing the volume of Pico. "You and the rest must have patience. You have seen blessings already. The fines — "

"Aye, the fines may be repealed, but what of the priests in the unholy prisons?"

"Look you, Thomas, the king has not arrived in England to straight-way welcome priests and make Rome-leaning pronouncements regarding the Church. He's not a fool. There are bishops and ordinary Londoners to contend with, and folk of a hundred towns that are not much like York. And there are Puritans, whose pastors draw crowds on street-corners here."

"Mad crowds," Thomas said sulkily.

"And the Puritans think papists are duped by the devil! Think. The king has now met with the English bishops and seen they are glad to owe no loyalty to an Italian pope. These are not the early days of old Harry the Eighth, when the country was tossed back and forth like a tennis ball between the pope and Martin Luther. When it *could* be tossed."

Still smoldering, Thomas glared at the earl. "What meanest thou, lord? That England cannot now be moved?"

"Gently led, I think, Thomas. Gently led. Ah, out the window, there. Look. A servant has watered your horse, and there he stands, impatiently pawing. Fine beast! Anxious to be on the road."

Thomas rode into London, fuming, lost among the carts of menials, the horsed gentry, and the throngs of loud pedestrians. Thinking to find a short way through the cloth fair, he found himself blocked front and behind by two wagons filled with woolen goods, and had to wait as the commodities were unloaded and stocked in booths. The men seemed to have noted his fine-clad impatience and to be slowing their pace deliberately. The good roan was quiet, but Thomas seethed and swore, thinking, *Patience! saith the earl. By God, has there not been enough of it?* By the time the knot of carts cleared and he reached Aldersgate Street, he was enraged nearly to the point of apoplexy, brooding on the rudeness of London tradesmen and the dashed hopes of most of the northern lords who had hoped to be appointed to James's London court. Yes, James had appointed nobles from the north. The *far* north. Stinking Scots! Lousy *lairds* with outlandish accents, accents even Northumbrians could barely understand! And the Scottish lords were not Catholic, but Presbyterian, every one, save a few Catholic ladies specially chosen for the queen's household.

And so, if the ninth earl ceased to argue for the Catholics' cause, what would come of King James's promise?

Thomas was in too unholy a humor to stop in Crutched Friars Lane today and dream of his lost Mary. He stalled his horse in a mews and himself in the Irish Boy, where the sharp-eyed host, who remembered him, brought him a tankard of Left Leg. The ale did not calm him, but the spirits that rose to his brain confirmed his direction. By mid-afternoon he was in Southwark, watching another history play.

"A triplicity of evil, royal sir," Cecil said. "I would not trust Raleigh, Carey, *or* the Earl of Northumberland. Mad wizards all three, babbling of science there at Syon House. Though they pull in different directions, not one of them pulls toward loyalty. Each has a private desire. Raleigh wants to build his own empire in Guyana. Carey wants only his own promotion, however he can come by it. And Henry Percy, as you have seen, speaks for the Catholics."

"If the earl's Catholic alliances are a danger to me, I wonder that you so strongly urged me to place him at the head of my very bodyguard," grumped James. He was seated in his new council room at Whitehall, sweating in the unaccustomed heat of a London summer. The fur robe he had worn to address the English Parliament that morning lay loose on the floor, and he sat in his linen shirt. Hearing a door close some rooms away, he started, then steadied himself.

Cecil regarded him with veiled amusement. He thought the king's skittishness understandable in one so often kidnapped or threatened since his youth, by this or that castled lord seeking to use him as a pawn or do away with him altogether. Yet the same could have been said of Elizabeth, and she had never, never shown fear.

"Well?" asked the king. "Speak!"

Cecil had anticipated the question about the Gentlemen Pensioners, and answered thoughtfully. "You will control the guards' appointments, majesty. If one dislikes you, he will be dismissed without question. Have them all Scottish knights, if you wish."

"I've had to bring them to England or risk their revolt, but I'd not trust *them* close." James's voice was peevish.

"Then whom you will, lord. As for the earl's captaincy, some position needed to be found for him. The earl poses far less danger with you here than he does out of sight in the north. Let him not serve as a beacon

to unhappy hinterland papists who think themselves wronged." Cecil
smiled. "Let him be a happy Londoner, and make new friends."

"As *I* must." James sounded irked by the prospect. The glamour of
new kingship was already fading. He had sat for three hours that morning listening to audacious Englishmen, men of the commons who seemed
to think their voices as worthy a hearing as his. Every pronouncement
he'd made had provoked a *response*, and furthermore he'd been handed
a pile of petitions, which now lay stacked on the table before him, awaiting his perusal.

"Oh, sit, will you?" he said testily to the patient counselor. "By Gog's
wounds, little man, I'd thought you *were* sitting!"

Cecil laughed pleasantly and took a seat. In the weeks since James
had arrived at court, Cecil had become armored to his crude and often
unseemly jests, so distinct from the dry, witty sallies of his old friend,
the late queen. Scottish James was a different breed of royal animal. Of
course, unlike some others of James's council — a council newly consti-
tuted, but retaining, at Cecil's advice, a good portion of its old membership — Cecil did not underrate the king's intelligence. James had perfectly played his hand with the formidable English Catholic families thus
far, and with the puritan zealots, to whom he had also lent his ear. The
result had been a more peaceful succession than Cecil had dared hope
for.

The thing was to preserve that peace.

Cecil cleared his throat. "Your decision to suspend the fines for
recusancy — "

"Only for those who will sue for remission of the fines. Those willing
to make themselves famous as Catholics, if they are not already."

Cecil bowed his head in a nod. "There is that caveat. Yet the fines
have long netted the royal exchequer upward of five thousand pounds
a year. The Crown would be hard pressed to make up this payment
elsewhere."

James brooded. "Hmmm." He glanced sidelong at Cecil. "Would the
hotter sort of Protestants pay fines?"

Cecil was taken aback. "For what, Majesty?"

"For abstaining from church services, as the Catholics do. They do
not like the services. I first knew of this from an English priest — though
he refused to be called such, pastor was his word — who came to me at
Edinburgh toting a big thick Bible on a day when my very *feet* were sore

taxed, with chilblains. What I heard from his brethren in Parliament today confirms what he said. It appears that thumbing noses at the pope is not enough for these precisians. They want no bowing at Christ's name or to the Eucharist, no ceremonies of confirmation, no bishops who may excommunicate, no high altars or puffed priestly caps, and worse, now they wish me to lend my name to a new translation of the Bible!" James sighed with vexation, then brightened, recalling his original thought. "And so, perhaps they would pay fines, to stay home from churches and hobnob with the Holy Spirit, in small groups. I think they like to do this."

"Puritans will not stay home," Cecil said firmly. "They will not give you their money, or England the Church. They think the work of reform is half-done and not to be relinquished. In the meantime, when one pastor likes them not, they seek another, with a name like Praisegod Scripture-man, who cuts his hair short and wears a flat cap. If they like not short-haired Praisegod Scriptureman, they send their own sons to Cambridge to take orders. They –"

"They wish not to defy but to control all English churches." James nodded bleakly.

"Not only the churches, but what is done in the streets outside of churches, whatever the weekday. They dislike women's frippery. Men's frippery they like worse. They abhor Maypoles. They hate plays. Lately they preach against bear-baiting. The sport depraves the souls of the watchers, they say, who were better saving their groats for pocket Testaments. And they bark that the sport is cruel to the blameless bear."

"I have seen this in Scotland," James said broodingly. "The presbyters preaching about *hair*, and railing that the lukewarm middle-grounded Church of England is neither flesh nor fowl, and that God will spew it out of his mouth. And I heard enough of the bold blattings of their English counterparts in Westminster this morning. No, you are right, wee man. There would be no profit in fining a Puritan. So zealous and precise a Protestant would throw all his money to a beggar before he'd pay one penny to a king."

Cecil thought it the wrong moment to remind the king that such a practice was recommended in the gospel. Prudence, before all. "It is so," he said merely. "And, to be blunt with you, it is Catholics, not Puritans, who have the money. The fees they have long been willing to pay will prove crucial to the expenditures you propose for the coming year. Our childless queen had no separate royal households to maintain, as do you, blessed, as we are, in your offspring." He bowed slightly. "And because of the many masques and other entertainments favored by our beauteous new queen — "

"Catholics must remain recusants, and the fines must be reinstituted in time." James nodded. "Yet let us be gradual, Cecil. And –" He reached forward and pulled from the pile of petitions a large scroll tied with a blue ribbon. "This, from the Catholic families of the north, humbly presented to me by my new Captain of Gentlemen Pensioners, the wizardly Earl of Northumberland. Along with a new horoscope. I have not read either, but I predict the letter proposes clemency for priests."

Cecil stiffened slightly. "Clemency for Peter-priests? 'Tis treason to be English and to be one."

"May they be banished rather than drawn, quartered, and hanged?" James, Cecil knew, was not asking Cecil's leave to do one rather than the other. The king was looking at the ceiling and addressing his own royal self. "I have heard of the English punishments of these priests."

"Your Highness has long approved the hanging of witches in Scotland," Cecil said, his tone carefully mild.

James raised a warning finger. "We hang witches, not priests."

"There are some in the south of England who see small difference between a witch and a Roman priest."

"But the Jesuit Campion, who tried only to catch Queen Elizabeth in St. Peter's net? He wished to try his luck at converting her, and then — torn bloodily limb from limb, to your own father's approval!"

Looking evenly at the king, Cecil debated with himself whether to recite, in defense of the famous Jesuit Campion's execution, the tired and usual words about Jesuit treason, Jesuit loyalty to foreign masters, Jesuit sowing of devilish dissension. Execution was a delicate subject. Cecil sensed behind the king's affable gaze a glint of malice at the English, who had killed his mother.

Yes, James would require as much careful treatment as Elizabeth, in his way. He was no brainless pawn. But to please his silly papist wife he'd witnessed many plays and pageants and shows, and might therefore understand a new way of putting this case.

"You are right, sire. Edmund Campion tried to convert our queen." Cecil kept his tone somber. "Though not until he was captured. Before then, he tried to fracture the kingdom; to incur disloyalty to her sovereignty in all four corners of the realm. He did so in obedience to the pope who had said God would bless any Englishman who contrived her murder. And Campion kept the pope's wish no secret. All this was a defamation not merely of our sovereign but a dismembering of the four-limbed cross of our loving Christ. That others might not fall into Campion's error or be swayed by such as him, it were necessary that he be visibly punished in a way that matched his crime. And, before spectators, he was."

James nodded slowly. "And this was proclaimed?"

"The meaning of his quartering was proclaimed, yes, and posted, and preached by royal command in every church. Except by four or five Puritan pastors who saucily refused to read the proclamation."

"Puritans!"

Cecil shook his head. "There is no understanding it, except to say that they dislike *all* signs and ceremonies, including bloody ones. But papists we know. Papists are like sheep. Fear them not! Fear only their shepherds, who come from France in their masks of piety, handing forth rosaries and other trinkets for the children to play with." Cecil relaxed his grimness and half-smiled. "Remember, *the very beadsmen learn to bend their bows against your state.*"

"Who says this?" James looked alarmed.

"The principal playwright of your own company, sire. The King's Men. In a play of old England."

"Ah, that man. He has a . . . ."

"*Lean and hungry look?*"

"Is that more of him? He's lean enough. Do you train your eye on him, wee man?" James reached out to pat Cecil on the head.

Cecil supposed he would need to get used to this. "My eye is on all things, my lord," he said courteously. "I wake to preserve the health of your royal person, and to enact the just purposes of your rule."

That compliment he thought at least half true. Now two months crowned, this outlandish Scotsman must be thought to incarnate England. It was not just the body politic, but Cecil himself who must think it so.

Chapter 15

At summer's end the order was proclaimed. For the remainder of 1604, King James would allow Catholics to avoid English Church services *gratis*.

That fall Thomas Percy, Robin Catesby, and their recusant friends had coin for new household stuff. As for Eliza Vaux, she had plenty to keep Father Quindle in fresh doublets of the latest French cut, feathered caps from Flanders, and tight hose of peacock blue and vermilion. Quindle thanked her, telling her that a fop's wear, however constricting, was still a hiding place greatly to be preferred to a priest-hole. But he warned her that, to his observation, the close-fitting hose worn by every gallant during Elizabeth's reign was now seen less and less among Protestant gentry. And men's hair was cut shorter, too.

"Not in men of our rank," Eliza assured him. "Believe it, you carry this disguise more convincingly than you'd manage the look of a Puritan."

"I, uh . . . thank you," said Quindle.

The surplus of money they all enjoyed was owed, indirectly, to Quindle himself, as well as to Henry Garnet and Anne Vaux. One day, following the performance of a secret mass in Warwickshire, Father Quindle had heard some troubling talk between two unknown Catholic gentlemen — church papists, one of whom, by his words, was a guard at the king's palace at Whitehall. The gentlemen's dialogue had touched on a serious plan to bind and kidnap the king and store him in the Tower until he'd sworn to grant full tolerance to any stripe of Christian. Ever distressed, as was Garnet, by threats of violence, and shrewd enough to know that the enactment of such a plan by Catholics would mean the end of Catholic hopes in England, Father Quindle had written to Father Garnet, his elder, for counsel.

On a late spring day in the garden at Baddesley Clinton, the pair of priests had worried the matter bare. What to do? If they said nothing and the plot went forward, surely all the promises James had made to Catholics, and those he would further be forced to make, would be broken the very moment he was freed. Yet if they themselves came out of hiding to make the mad scheme known to the king's council, they would be imprisoned as peter-priests, and quite possibly executed, despite their good work.

The two men debated for hours. Evening found them inclining toward the view that in spite of all, one of them should convey a warning to Whitehall, and at a stalemate over which should take the risk. Garnet thought it would be madness for Quindle to do so. Quindle was a warned priest who had been explicitly banned from re-entering the country years before. Quindle disagreed with this judgment. He felt confident of certain covertly Catholic friends in Parliament to whom he could write, men who would be glad to curry favor with James by discovering the plot to the king.

"But if you *were* caught, you would surely be sentenced," Garnet said. "As for me, if I were questioned as to my priesthood, I could answer honestly and still escape detection."

"How honestly?"

"Through equivocation, as we were taught in France. Instance, if asked directly if I were a priest, I could say no, because I am no priest of the English Church."

"And if asked whether you were a *Catholic* priest?"

"I could give the same reply, since the English Church calls itself holy and catholic, however falsely it does so. The question, in other words, might still be construed to pertain to the English Church."

Quindle laughed shortly. "The thickets of logic grow denser. How if asked whether you were a Roman priest?"

"No again, for I am English. I've ne'er *been* to Rome, man."

"A peter-priest?"

"Even less, for that is a Protestant saying, and we never use it."

"Good sirs, though I never cease to delight in your debates, I must call you to supper." The men looked up. Anne Vaux, mistress of the house, was standing in the yard, frowning a little. "The cook has prepared mutton with chives. Yet, no! Sit still." She moved toward them brusquely. "You'll not taste a bite of the meal before the deep substance of your talk is made known to me. You have sat here a whole afternoon."

Quindle and Garnet looked at each other and sighed. Reluctantly, Henry told her the story.

But in the end they were glad. By supper's end Anne herself had resolved the matter in her own thoughtful way. The priests sopped up mince jelly with bread and sipped claret as she explained. She herself would speedily write to the new king, in a letter to be delivered by means of a cousin who served at court. Why not? She had little to lose. She was a known Catholic already, and could easily have overheard the things Quindle reported.

"Brave Anne!" Garnet began, but she stopped him. "This needs no special courage, my Hen —" He stiffened, and she amended her word to "friend." In the company of other priests, he grew abashed at Anne's familiarities. He shot her a warning look, which her eyes registered. "We can afford the loss of neither of you," she briskly continued. "As for me — what will I seem but a garrulous spinster, eager to see her neighbors arrested?" She smiled quickly, to allay the slight bitterness that had crept into her tone.

Henry was now looking at her gravely, but Quindle's mind had run elsewhere. "And that is a thing that grieves me," he said. "If faithful neighbors *are* arrested because of this charge — a charge against fellow Catholics who happen to be lunatics —"

"Or lunatics who happen to be Catholics," Henry said.

"Either way, it will not go prettily for the neighbors."

Anne thought for a moment with furrowed brow. Then she brightened. "But I have no neighbors' names to report. Surely I can write a missive sufficiently vague to set the king on mere alert. And in it I'll speak for the loyalty of English Catholics. And if the crazed attempt is made, well, then, a Catholic warned of it!"

Reluctantly, the priests nodded. There was no toppling the sense of this argument.

"I may do us great good," Anne said, now hopefully, as she rang for a servant to clear the plates. Logic always cheered her. "So dense is the forest of spies in Whitehall, belike the great Cecil knows of the plot already, and awaits the attempt, only to step forward and tell the king how misplaced was his trust in all of us. My letter will frustrate Cecil's argument before he can make it." She smiled at the priests over the rim of her wineglass.

Henry still looked at her worriedly, but Father Quindle laughed. "Anne, you would have made a queen to rival Eliza."

In fact, Lord Cecil *had* known of the plot against James, by means of a hidden speaking tube that snaked through a palace wall into a room where three gentlemen he disliked habitually played cards. He had been particularly gratified that one of the gamesmen who'd spoken mid-hand, approving the absurd plan and revealing some of its finer points, was a notable church papist whom he'd long mistrusted, and that another was Walter Raleigh, who was chafing at the king's flat refusal to back another of his New World expeditions. Cecil knew the date in August that the plotters proposed and the groom of the king's chamber whom they planned to corrupt so they could seize and truss James in the night. His plan had been to catch all of them in the act, in a spectacular display of statesmanlike prescience and consular capability.

Thus he could hardly contain his dismay at the letter an irate James pushed into his face shortly after the treacherous card game, on a warm July day near the royal stables, as Cecil greeted the king after his daily hunt in the royal park. James was still panting from the exertions of the deer-chase. He caught his breath as he dismounted, pulled a paper from his cloak, tossed his horse's reins to a nervous, scurrying groom, and shrilled, "What's this?" He waved the wrinkled parchment back and forth before Cecil's nose. "What's *this?*"

Cecil stilled the letter. In a glance he took in its contents, noting the writing's fine feminine hand. He looked at the signature. *Anne Vaux, a Catholic lady and a loyal servant of the king.* He knew of this gentlewoman, a moneyed spinster of the midlands, rumored to be a hostess to priests and other Romish vermin. He took quick note of the fact that she'd somehow made herself privy to the details of a pernicious plot against the sovereign, one he himself had only lately heard of. Cecil was struck far more by this suspicious circumstance than by the charity she'd shown in exposing the plan.

But James thought differently. Once he'd calmed himself with a few paces of walking, he said, "This Catholic lady shall deserve a place among the angels for this warning!"

"And so she shall," Cecil equivocated, thinking, *Would she might assume that place without delay!* "Highness, I will sound this matter to the bottom."

"See it *done!*" James strode quickly into the palace, clutching his riding cloak close. He was trailed by several members of his bodyguard, whom he seemed to be trying to elude.

Cecil ordered arrests, then imprisonments. He tried not to fret at the mishap, and told himself the thing might have turned out worse. Thinking it best, now, to conceal his prior knowledge of the conspiracy, he reaped praise from James for his uncannily swift unmasking of the identities of those plotting against the royal person, a most admirable feat, since the letter had not named names. In the end, Cecil's own standing at court rose higher even than before.

But Cecil worried for the future. England's future. The message from meddling Anne Vaux had done its bad work, convincing James indeed to free some Catholics from prison instead of jailing more. It had persuaded the king that there was, after all, a difference between loyal English Catholics and power-hungry assassins who *might* be Catholic, or might simply be Walter Raleigh.

Cecil did not believe in that difference. In this matter, the king was unschooled.

Throughout summer and fall, Cecil paid unusually scrupulous attention to the reports of the royal exchequer. These showed King James was spending almost double what his predecessor had in the last years of her reign, with less takings-in. Shrewd Elizabeth had made her richest nobles pay her household expenses for much of the year, undertaking progresses through the country, stopping at the fine estate of this or that earl who was then expected to feed her and her train, down to the last horse and dog. Once she had stayed a month at Penshurst, the rural seat of the great Sidneys, where the lady of the house had whispered to Cecil in confidence that the queen would surely beggar them if he could not persuade her to leave soon.

James liked his lavish comforts no less than Elizabeth had, but had not yet perfected the art of the progress, or perhaps merely liked to settle into a place and call it home. He had a family, after all, as Elizabeth had not. At James's order the park of St. James had been well stocked with deer for his hunting pleasure, and the several nearby palaces of his wife and children vied to offer tables laden with the freshest and most savory stuffed fowl, sweetmeats, roasted venison and even boar, and spiced wines, to say nothing of the lavish masques and plays performed after dinner. What was more, the new king had added dozens of Scottish courtiers to the rolls of the royal employ. The English nobles disdained these men for clownish, crude upstarts. James himself was certain each Scot was only awaiting the right moment to stab him, but felt the need to safeguard his continuing rule of the north by offering southern opportunities to Scottish nobles and gentry. Cecil was only dismayed by the money they cost.

Yet in this pile-up of royal debts he saw an opportunity.

"Majesty." Several weeks after the receipt of Anne Vaux's letter, he placed the record of royal intakes and costs before the sovereign, who sat comfortably soaking his feet. James had spent the evening watching a performance of *Julius Caesar* enacted for him at his palace, and had listened to Brutus's speeches with a kind of horrified fascination. "These expenses" — Cecil gestured at the paper — "must needs issue in higher taxation."

"Then that is what we shall have," James said blithely. He drew a silver toothpick from a pocket case and inserted it into his mouth.

"Lord, in this way you give the Puritans in Parliament cause to grouse against the high-handedness of kings."

James replaced the toothpick in its case and frowned at Cecil. "'High-handedness'? What *should* my hand be, if not high?"

"It will be *their* word, sire, and they will not use it with reverence."

James stared at the fire, still frowning. He tapped his breast as though checking the strength of his armor, which in fact he was. He'd commissioned the royal seamstress to fashion him stiletto-proof double-quilted doublets — quadruplets, in fact — and now wore them routinely, still starting at the odd scrabbling of a rat or a mouse in the walls. The king thought back on the bloody action of the play he'd just seen. "Might these Puritans plot, think you?"

"Plot?" Cecil thought carefully. "Majesty, I think that were those who call themselves the godly ever one day sufficiently angry and strong, they would not plot, but openly rebel on a battlefield, shouting out words from the book of Isaiah concerning the holiness of the Israelites or some such misapplied rant. Their way is not . . . secret. Nor subtle. Nor very quiet."

"In truth, they are most horribly loud." James pondered. "So were their Scottish brethren."

"Yet others besides Puritans might plot."

"Whom do you mean, wee man?" James squinted at Cecil. "What is your drift? I've stuck Raleigh in the Tower. Who should join him, for a merry game of cards there?"

"I speak of no man—"

"Of a woman?"

"No, though clearly women may plot as well as—" He stopped himself. That had been a blunder. James was bristling. Since he'd come to England, the king was always on guard against any insinuation against the memory of his mother, whom Cecil's own father had finally persuaded Elizabeth to behead for the danger she caused.

"Take care what you say," James said warningly. "My mother was more a victim of plots than a plotter. And she was brave as well as bonny. Indeed, she stood firm when one treacherous laird raised his pistol, aye, pointed it at *me* when I was a wee babe in the womb!" James had convinced himself he remembered this incident. He looked grave. "Know that I pray for the soul of that poor Queen of Scots every day."

This was no time to remind James that prayers for the dead were both banned and useless; banned, in fact, *because* useless. The dead went straight to heaven or hell, and that was the end of the story. Naught could be done for them by King James. The king had been schooled by Scotch presbyters, of course, and knew this. But he would have his superstition.

Cecil inclined his head slightly in deference. "I meant no such imputation, Majesty, and beg pardon for the offence. I should have said thus: I speak of no man—nor no woman—in particular, but of those who can never be trusted, as their loyalty will ever lie elsewhere, to a foreign power. I speak of the English—"

"Papists. Ah. Yes." James sighed. "In truth, I would that my Nan had never embraced that faith. Her mumbling prayers and her continual self-crossing begin to wear on me. She presses me to proclaim Romish priests forever legal inhabitants of England, which—"

"*That*—" Cecil controlled himself, and spoke in a milder tone. "My lord, for all the queen's well-meaning, that would be a most dangerous course."

James looked shrewdly at him. "In that, I agree. But these Catholic gentry! They claim I have made all manner of unfulfilled promises. They are like children running after their sire and whining that they were meant to get some sugar sops. I spoke of liberty of conscience, not of enfranchised priests! Not of open masses! Let them *believe* what they like, as the queen allowed, and there an end." He tapped the document on the table before him. "We wander from your purpose."

Cecil picked up the paper. "Yet here indeed is the point. Your Majesty might make it, again, more costly to be a Catholic than not to be one. And certainly this might appease the Puritans."

"It may please them," said James. "It may mitigate their anger at my standing fast for my Protestant bishops in the face of all their wicked complaints about good church ceremonies and laws and tithes. I must stand fast for my bishops, for if the godly do away with those, they will next do away with me! By God, I will say so at the next Parliament."

Cecil was a little alarmed. Though he agreed with the king in principle, he feared James did not fully understand the independent English temper. He thought quickly. "Sovereign, your mind is keen. Verily, this — this 'standing fast' for bishops — would go down more easily were you to give the lords and commons reason to know that in defying those leveling Puritans, you are not embracing the Romish faith of your queen."

"Ah," said James. "Yes. I had thought of this first, you know. Before you."

"Of a surety. *Videlicet,* might the time not have returned to show sufficient disdain not only for Puritans, but for papists as well? As Queen Elizabeth so wisely did? Is there not a way?" Cecil placed the sheet scrawled with figures before James's nose and gave it a shake.

James looked down at the document, and light dawned. Smiling, he said, "I bethink me of one."

Chapter 16

April 23, 1604. St. George's Day.

"**H**e is a churl and a faith-breaker!"

Thomas's voice shook the walls of the Irish Boy. Catesby raised playful eyebrows at his friend's tone and volume, but the Wrights, Francis Tresham, and the Wintours looked dismayed. The men had engaged the Pomegranate, a private room, but even so, Tresham shushed Percy. "Patience, Thomas."

"Call it not patience, man, it is despair!" Thomas howled. "That which in mean men we entitle patience is pale, cold cowardice in noble breasts!"

"Whence got you this vaunting speech?" asked Kit Wright in alarm. "'Tis higher than thy usual vein. Pray, speak lower!"

Thomas dropped his voice, but would not be swayed from his subject. "The king promised us *tolerance*," he hissed. "And now! To openly renew, nay, to *increase* our fines, should we miss the unholy church gatherings where we hear naught but a man like ourselves, a counterfeit priest, blatting at us from a crude English Bible! I tire of this fat English Bible."

There was general assent at the table.

"For further insult, we must hear this profane priest who is no priest *mock* our ceremonies rather than perform them. We receive *no sacrament*, no true one, but an unblessed mouthful from an ordinary oven, as though men's faiths were wafer cakes. And God's real priests still banished from our shores!" Thomas hit the table with a fist, making tankards jump.

The host of the tavern appeared at Catesby's elbow. "Gentlemen, my ale likes you not? Your distress is audible. I'll not offer you small beer, but I have in the room farther back some brown beer — "

"The drink is well." Kit Wright gave the host a coin and the man left them with a careful backward glance. "Thomas Percy, you'll have us hanged," Kit whispered fiercely.

"Thomas's behavior is mad, but he is right." Robin Catesby's eyes glowed with eerie fire. "This subtle king means to drain our wealth. He made us gracious offers, and then graciously rescinded them. Now all comes to naught."

"What a candy deal of courtesy that king of smiles showed me in Edinburgh! He plotted to please all, only for the English throne." Thomas tapped his hilt. "Would I could make him taste the blade of this sword."

Tresham opened his mouth again to object, but Catesby spoke first, his voice low and intense. "If thou wilt be a traitor, Thomas, thou shalt be, to some great advantage. So may we all."

"What mean you?" Thomas stared at him. His fingers sat frozen on his sword.

Robin waved his hand gracefully, gesturing southward. "Is there not Spain?"

Thomas frowned. "You propose we should remove to Spain?"

"No. I propose that Spain should come to us."

"There is still hope of that, though less than before." Gawain Wintour spoke in a half- whisper. "There is talk of a meeting between King Philip's emissary and James. Even now the Spanish agents are in Flanders, preparing to cross the Channel."

"When they are here, it might be a time to make ourselves known," Catesby said. "Known, I mean, to them."

Francis Tresham shook his head. "Most perilous."

"The exploits of honor are perilous!" Catesby sprang to his feet with the grace of a cat. "We shall speak of this further. But now, since we return north to our homes tomorrow, and since naught is to be done with Spanish Philip's man still in Flanders, let us betake ourselves to a play. With Percy I heard some most stirring speeches at the Globe in Southwark yesterday, of double-dealing kings who never come to good."

"The man who wrote them surely takes our part, in secret," Thomas said fiercely. "Some of his plays are printed, and I have bought them. I know it."

Catesby laughed and adjusted his feathered cap. "I'faith, you may speak true. Would you could find him! Ply him with red ale, then put the question."

At Baddesley Clinton, where she tended Anne, who was ill, Eliza Vaux was on her knees. This was not a posture of penitence, but of abject grief and rage. Alone in her chamber, she spat on the notice of recusant fines that lay crumpled on the floor before her. The figure it requested surpassed the sum it took to maintain her priest for a year. She wiped her lips, touched the rosary under her bodice, then raised both hands to her face. "Oh, I could eat this king's heart in the marketplace!" she sobbed, too angry to pray.

The Spanish ambassador arrived at James's court, clad in cloth of gold and a huge ruffed collar, haughtily forgiving England for ravaging his country's Armada fifteen years before. He paid a visit to Oxford. Much shouting from Thomas and smooth pleading from Catesby had persuaded Gawain Wintour to accost the Spaniard on his way back to London, after the conclusion of the Oxford entertainments (three student-authored plays in Latin dramatizing debates among Temperance, Virtue, and the Genius of History, through which the ambassador yawned). Gawain Wintour was chosen by Catesby for good reasons. He spoke Castilian, and had met the Spanish king. On such a skill and such a history, he could build a case for an audience. Gawain cautiously agreed to bring the ambassador word that three thousand armed Catholics would rise for King Philip should Spain choose, just once more, to attempt an invasion. He felt compelled to bring the message when Thomas Percy—who, in the Wintours' private view, mismanaged even his native English when he wasn't quoting plays—threatened otherwise to do it himself.

Thus came a strange encounter on a muddy road ten miles south of the Oxford city gates. As the Spanish procession passed near a copse of ash trees, the ambassador was startled by the sudden emergence of a silk-clad horseman wearing Cordovan leather gloves. His servants fumbled for their swords, anticipating the sort of highway robbery they'd been told to expect in this cursed rainy country full of shrubbery. But the horseman only removed his velvet cap, dismounted, bowed gracefully and sweepingly, and said, *"Un servidor humilde de Dios y amigo del buen rey Felipe pide una audiencia, señor."* The interview was made.

A day later, Wintour reported back sadly to hopeful Catholics of northern and midlands circles. It seemed that Privy Counselor Cecil had foreseen a Spainward approach on the part of distressed recusants. Before his ride north, Cecil had told the ambassador of the fair treatment King James had accorded to those of the Romish faith in England. Cecil had even shown the ambassador a letter from a Catholic woman that betrayed a plot against James, a letter which professed the loyalty of Catholics to the king. As a result, the Castilian was not convinced by Wintour's promises of a rising.

When, a week later, the ambassador sailed back to his sunny country, King James proclaimed that a peace would be drawn up between England and its new friend, Catholic Spain, including the prospect of an Anglo-Spanish marriage alliance between royal offspring. A politic solution to a long and tedious war.

In Northumbria, Thomas was vexed by Martha's glee. "This is not the good tidings it appears, wife," he said sullenly. "For the other England, the counterfeit nation, it is cause for joy. But not for us! What if the king has agreed not to send warships to slay Spaniards? You are wrong to think this betides his grace toward *English* Catholics. You know of his new proclamation. The fines are renewed, and priests must decidedly leave our shores, or be violently sent, as he thinks, hellward. Indeed, another holy priest has lately been drawn and quartered, for all the king's gracious promises of tolerance. The cankered royal ingrate! Let him look to his crown."

"Thomas!" Martha covered the small ears of Claire, whose hair she was combing.

"What say you, woman! Have you a heart to do more than fold linen? We are still to hide and sneak, still to pay, still to wait! You, smiling foolishly because Spain is now friend to England! To *what* England, I say? Had Spain rejected the ignoble peace, and joined with *us*, we might have had a Catholic sovereign, and a coronation mass at St. Paul's."

"Well." Martha shrugged as she smoothed their daughter's wind-tangled locks. "Have patience, husband. James remitted our fines once, and may again. May not full tolerance follow? All of us heard how warmly the king embraced the priest in the train of the Spanish ambassador. A *Catholic* priest."

"For he knew the man would take his leave in two weeks' time, and not stay in England to convert Protestants."

"You are melancholy. Be cheered, husband! May not the earl call you presently, to serve him in his new post in London?"

Claire coughed, and Martha knit her brow, still combing. "Poppet, you must dress more warmly in this damp. Cold can be caught in summer as well as in winter-time."

Thomas stalked into the courtyard, there to exercise with his sword. *Yah!* The *stocatta!* The *imbrocata!* The *punta riversa! Yah!* and *Yah!* He practiced feints and passes for twenty minutes. Then he calmed himself by walking, panting, in a circle. *Patience!* he thought with scorn, as he sunlessly orbited. *A woman's virtue.*

In Thomas's mind there were two Marthas. One of these Marthas pleasurably exhausted his energies. On breath-frosting winter nights he would often find her naked beneath their bed's thick counterpane, her hair loose, smirking and waiting. At such times she would grab his big hands and put them where she willed, would laugh when he lifted and rolled her on top of him. Or tensing beneath him, her long legs gripping his frame with uncommon strength, she would bite his shoulder, grip him tightly, and in the end cry out in her passion. He could find no fault with this midnight Martha. But the daytime Martha dissatisfied, with her apron and her pinned head and her scoffing. At worst she enraged him, at best left him vaguely uneasy. At times she seemed unfaithful to religion. In her pettiness, she cared more for the state of their house's shutters and the quality of her chickens than about things that mattered: courage, valor, the *punta reversa*, the clear and open exercise of faith.

Or honor!

"I tire of that word you will not cease muttering," she'd once told Thomas, as though honor were *only* a word; as though the things of real importance were their own carnal revels and the warmth of a home and the health of children.

And despite all his hopeful journeys southward, the earl had *not* called him to service in London. The great Henry Percy had left Thomas to shiver in Northumbria, collecting his paltry debts.

Thomas stormed through Martha's house for weeks, til she so tired of his surly tramping that she ceased speaking to him altogether. He brought his unrest outdoors as well, and glowered as he rode through the greening countryside. Nature's beauties were a mockery to those who must hide their worshiping, who must pay out of their substance or else risk their souls. Here was the dilemma. To be a Percy *was* to be a Catholic. His parents had practiced the rites of the faithful. *And shall I seem crestfallen in my father's sight?* Let the old earl live a life of shoddy compromise. Thomas Percy would hearken to his true ancestors, the noble ones. *Esperance!* Muttering, he spurred the roan to a gallop, riding from holding to holding, angrily gathering rents.

One day in May he returned home to find a message closed with Catesby's seal, delivered by the hand of a mild-mannered man whose face he did not recognize. Avidly, incautiously, he tore open the letter in front of the unknown messenger. *Reply to inform us of the date of thy next London visit,* Catesby had written. *We will meet there to speak of events to come.*

"What events? *What* events?" Thomas said in vexed excitement.

The messenger laughed. "The letter is not precise enough for thy liking."

Thomas glared at the fellow, who had not even shown the breeding to doff his cap. "What's that to thee?"

The man shrugged affably. He was nearly as tall as Thomas, but much sparer. His beard was as thick, but where Thomas's was black with white patches, the hair and beard of this one, who seemed some years younger, was reddish-brown. His cheeks were fair, though scarred by smallpox. He wore an oddly cut shirt of a type Thomas thought he had seen before, with wide sleeves and a rounded collar.

"Flanders," the man said, noting the direction of Thomas's gaze. "I served in a company there."

"What company?" Thomas laid his hand on his sword, suspecting for the first time that this man was a spy; that Catesby's message was counterfeit. Someone, some agent to the pursuivants, might have stolen Catesby's seal.

The man laughed. "I do not merit thy distrust, and I do not fear thy sword. 'Tis big enough, but I saw how badly you wielded it in the Lowlands. Marry, it was not hard to disarm thee there."

"*Thou!*" Thomas frowned deeply. "I was taken prisoner by Spaniards in the Lowlands. I abhor thy fleering insults. I have not seen thy face before." He quickly crumpled Catesby's letter and stuffed it in his doublet. "How came you by this letter you brought?"

"I was given it by Robin Catesby, who counts me a friend. As do Gawain and Bors Wintour, who were boys with me, together in York, at St. Peter's School, five years after you. And you *have* seen my face, however smoke and mud did mask it on the field. 'Twas I who brought you to the Spanish captain who jailed you in Flanders, and you owe me thanks. Had I not garnered thee mercy by telling him of the Percys' proud history, thou mightst well have deserved worse than a prison. Couldst have gone on with thy bluster, calling thyself a descendant of Hotspur, but my captain of Valencia knew nothing of the Ballad of Chevy Chase, and had little time to pause and write to thy fine earl for ransom. 'Twas I who persuaded him the gold would be worth his spent quarter-hour."

Thomas stared at him, baffled and abashed. "Why did you so?"

The messenger's mild face lit up with a smile. "Art not thou my countryman? I was born in York. Like you I know the torment of living a stone's throw from that scabrously Presbyterian realm of Scotland. I am from the north of England, though I dwelt long in Spain, and learned the trade of a soldier there."

"Who art thou, man? What's thy name?"

Now the man removed his hat. It was high-crowned, made of rough leather, and dusty from its wearer's traveling. "'Tis Fawkes," he said pleasantly. "Guido Fawkes."

Chapter 17

"Yet it *is* lawful." Gawain Wintour, accoster of Catholic diplomats, held the floor. He shook his finger at his auditors. His humiliation at his failure with the Spanish emissary had transformed his caution to zeal. "It is not only lawful but a necessary Christian *duty* to remove tyrants."

"So say many, among them Pope Clement." Jack Wright sipped his canary, then swirled the pale liquid in his goblet. He sat opposite Gawain at a large round table. The Duck and Drake in old St. Clement's Parish, London, boasted only one such article of furniture, and Robin Catesby had specifically requested its use for the men's meeting this day. An added benefit he'd craved was the room in which the table stood. This was a den near the rear of the tavern, with an entrance not easily visible from the house's crowded common area. Here the men sat in relative quiet and comfort, in upholstered chairs.

Jack Wright continued to gaze into his pale yellow wine as though it held the answer to his conundrum. "Many say Christians must dispense with tyrants. But when the tyrant is an anointed king?"

"A vice of kings!" Thomas Percy loured from behind the remains of a roasted capon black with Indies pepper. "A king of shreds and patches! A counterfeit king! We have all seen the play —"

"Ah." Catesby tugged gently at his bright beard. The corners of his lips twitched. "Plays again."

Thomas was wounded. "Yes, plays! You may make me your table-sport, but you, Robin Catesby, have not disdained plays on your visits to London. You too have seen them. Plays which summon the noble houses of old to the good fight. Plays in which honorable fathers speak from Purgatory, urging the faithful to scourge rotten kingdoms! I say that the man, the *Warwickshire* man it is said, who writes these calls to arms is of our true party, whether or not he doth know it!"

"Well, it may be so." Catesby made a gracious gesture of concession, shifting his posture. His shirt was partly open, and a shaft of May sunlight caught his gold crucifix, making the metal flash and the men blink.

"Damnation is what you fear." All turned to look at the auburn-bearded man, newest to their company, who sat quietly in a corner, slightly back from their table. Guido Fawkes's stated purpose for this self-removal was his desire to enjoy a long-stemmed pipe of tobacco, which stank and whose smoke hindered the breathing of his new friends. From the corner he could wave the smoke toward a partly-opened window. But his corner position gave Thomas Percy the sense that he observed them, and possibly judged them. Guido Fawkes had treated him with friendliness, even with honor (after his initial irksome delay in removing his hat in Northumbria). And Fawkes, a man of the minor Yorkshire gentry, had a self-effacing manner that the others found most congenial. Still, Thomas felt even more awkward in his presence than he sometimes did among the higher-born gentlemen. The shame he harbored at having been captured by Fawkes in Flanders — at having been bested so easily in sword combat — stiffened his manner with this rugged man, to whom the others deferred, since they admired his long service to the Holy Catholic Spanish monarch.

Catesby answered Fawkes boldly. "Well, Guido, for all thy skill in southern languages and time spent abroad, thou knowst how to make a blunt English sentence. And thou art in the right. We fear damnation daily. And why should we not? In our benighted country, we may die by accident, with no blessed fathers by to hear our confession and give us last rites. We may go off in a graceless state. Our very sons may go unbaptized."

Thomas winced.

Catesby went on. "We endure weeks, sometimes months, without tasting the holy Eucharist. And we stand by idly while true priests, on whom our souls' health depends, are most brutally hunted down and then horribly slain. Shall we bequeath this life to our children? To our children's children?"

"*Nay!*" said Thomas in a voice like thunder. He jumped to his feet, and was roughly pulled down by Jack Wright, who wearily cautioned him, once more, to speak lower.

Catesby went on. "And fellow gentles, even now —"

"We go on no pilgrimages!" blurted Thomas. It was no good. He could not contain himself. This morning he had stood for an hour in Crutched Friars, staring at his old casement window, remembering his Mary and the lost child, and weeping inside. He would always feel their blood on his hands. Now he fingered the medal of Saint Winifred that hung from his neck. He thought of his unbaptized baby, floating Godlessly in Limbo for eternity. There the souls of unchristened infants lay lost, with no hope of Heaven. Poor little ones! Nary a rag ball to play with, there. Could any saint intervene for his son?

He looked with plaintive eyes at Guido Fawkes, this man of the strange Italian first name. Fawkes had been twelve years across the salty sea, residing in more blessed places than benighted England. "Hast been on pilgrimage?" he asked Guido suddenly, plaintively.

Wintour, Wright, and Catesby hid smiles behind their hands. But Fawkes answered graciously. "I have traveled to Santiago de Compostela in Galicia. And to San Pietro in Rome, and to Jerusalem." His accents were sure. Catesby was right. Like Gawain Wintour, this Guido Fawkes knew the angel tongues of Catholic lands.

"The shrines of the saints were heavenly," Fawkes added. "They give much comfort to the people, and the saints work true miracles."

"Here our erring rulers have done their best to destroy the saints' shrines," Thomas Percy said bitterly. "Certain it is that we must destroy *them*."

"Marry, 'tis so. And *this* action is not damnable when the enemy has broken a contract," Catesby said quickly, seeing Jack Wright look at Thomas uneasily. Robin spoke calmly, reasonably, not pressing Jack. "James made a firm promise to Catholics that he would tolerate our presence in his kingdom and permit us to worship as we would. Such was his message to the Earl of Northumberland, through Thomas Percy."

"It was." Thomas could not remember exactly what James had said to him in Edinburgh Castle the year before. Perhaps, so hungry to be King of England and for all to wish him so, James had equivocated. But Thomas knew what the king had wanted him to believe, and was that not as good as a promise?

"In return for this promise, the earl pledged our loyalty." Catesby's tone grew warmer. "And loyal subjects we would have been, had James served us as he said he would do. Instead, he is cowed by his advisors. Unholy men, men of craft, who care nothing for their souls and everything for their royal exchequer! Men like Cecil. Soulless lords whose mischief is to tax our holiness. Ever and again in Parliament they have levied grave fines for simple recusancy. In that den of serpents called Westminster they have imposed harsh penalties on our priests. And now they have treated with Spain, and ended our hopes of a just invasion. "

"Gentlemen!" Thomas popped up again like a firecracker, his hand on the hilt of his sword. Startled anew at his motion, the others looked toward the door, but saw no one there. "Gentlemen!" Thomas roared again, not heeding the finger Catesby was holding to his lips, the whispered shushings, or the hands tugging at his garments. What honor lay in caution when the heart must be eased? "Words, words, *words!*" he trumpeted, beetling his brows over his proud hooked nose. "Shall we always talk and do nothing?"

"Nay, we shall not, my good jack-of-the-clock!" Robin said. "Drunk with choler! I'faith, thou *art* pursy, Percy! Ever full of gas and prone to blow. We shall *not* always talk and do nothing. We shall have talk, but we shall also have deeds. Now speak *lower,* lest you mar all. But no, stay standing." Catesby rose to join him. "We will take a vow."

Gawain Wintour, Guido Fawkes, and Jack Wright rose as well, and Guido came forward, so that they all surrounded the table. Catesby unsheathed his sword and held it pommel-up above the table's midpoint, clutching it below the hand-guard, so its gold handle and the bar formed a cross. "No more words before this swearing. Let us vow to consecrate our lives to the freeing of Catholic England by what means are necessary. So swear, by Christ and his saints!"

The five men placed their right hands on the shining sword-hilt with Catesby's. Five hands touched one another and the weapon. "By Christ and His saints, we so swear!" they said in unison, their voices hushed.

"Good!" Catesby dropped back to his seat and sheathed his sword. "And now, boys!" He looked sidewise at Guido. "Tis the hour to propound."

But even the two bottles of canary that followed did little to allay the men's shock at the plan Catesby revealed, and appeared to think they had sworn to.

After an hour of fierce argument, they agreed to take the sacrament and pray. In some turmoil of soul, the five of them trooped up to a second-story room where lodged a man Catesby knew to be a priest. Robin had visited him earlier in the day, and the priest had been expecting the men since. With the father they kept mum about their burgeoning scheme, and none of them requested confession. Secrecy one from the other would have been hard to keep in the priest's small room, and a knot of them in the hall outside the door, waiting, would have looked suspicious to any servant passing by. So the man granted them the sacrament without shriving them. After he said a brief mass, Fawkes, Jack Wright, Catesby, Thomas, and Gawain Wintour returned downstairs to the round-table room to sup and talk some more, in calmer voices. Guido Fawkes reseated himself in the corner with another pipe.

The room was now grown so dark that the men's expressions were hidden from each other. When the host entered to light two candles, they shifted into idle talk. Fawkes and Jack Wright moved to play at a chessboard set on a smaller table by the wall. The companions' worry of being overheard was not so great in the Duck and Drake. Catesby had frequented the tavern with Essex in years gone by, and was sure of the host, who cared to hear and see nothing out of the usual way as long as he was paid good coin for ale and food. This was a safety not always guaranteed at the Irish Boy, with its long-eared proprietor. Still, even in safe surroundings, so momentous was the plan now starting to grow that the men spoke of no more than recent plays, the strength of the wine Jack Wright had brought, and the quality of Catesby's riding boots, until the host's clomping footfalls had faded well down the hallway.

Then Guido and Jack stopped their half-played game. Jack reseated himself at the round table, and Fawkes in the room's corner. "Here is how I shall persuade you," Catesby said, leaning forward, his eyes strange in the candle flame. He tapped the glinting hilt of the sword on which they'd all sworn. "Think of it thus. Our old honor was swords. Our new honor shall be fire."

"Yet guns are cowardly," said Jack Wright. "Any man might fire with one, and from far range. Men without skill, grace, valor, nor breeding."

There was a murmur of assent at the table. Gawain Wintour said, "I've heard that in far Japan they have outlawed the arquebus that an Englishman brought to their shores sixty years ago. The guns are dismantled, and 'tis death to own one. Why? Their knights have for centuries lived by honorable swording. They do not consent to be felled by any odd peasant crouching behind a wall. Who uses muskets? Men who are hiding from valorous combat. This troubles me, Robin."

"I speak not of guns, but of a vast and holy conflagration." Catesby tapped the table for emphasis. "I speak of powder. Do we not honor our battlefield engineers, who wreak blazing judgment on insolent towns? Our work is as theirs. *Only* with powder can we sweep England clean of its yoke-masters. Think widely, sir! We have not one enemy, but many. For years upon years they have hunted us down like rabbits. And like rabbits, we scurry for our warrens. Can this be honor?"

"No," said all the men, frowning.

"Our brethren forswear themselves, falsely speaking the Oath of the King's supremacy for a place at court or in government, while in secret they profess themselves true servants of the pope. Indeed, some of you have done the same. Can *this* be honor?"

The Wintours gazed at the tabletop. "Nay," Gawain said in a low voice. "Nay, it cannot."

"Yet time serves wherein you may redeem your banished honors. Not in the old way. Our northern nobles are denied their ancient privilege of summoning armies of liegemen. And Spain will not help us. How, then, can we fight? Marry, this is how. With powder. The valor of this act lies in the skill of its execution, and in the coolness with which we will daily face fear of discovery."

"That is just the — "

"Yet we will master that fear." Catesby held up his hand to stop all protests. "Why will we do so? It is required. *God* requires it. Whose task is it if not ours, not only to punish our guilty lords, but to make a show of their conviction and redress? The Parliament has long been the site of all their mischief and deviltry, the crucible of their unholy statutes and laws. *No more.*" Catesby banged the table. "We will end it."

Thomas was staring at Catesby, transfixed by the ardor in his face. For all his bluff anger, he, too, had at first been horrified by Robin's suggestion. Now, something shifted inside him. In Flanders, long ago, he had attacked the wrong stone fortress. The enemy was here, at home.

The men were all slowly nodding. Gawain Wintour sat slightly back from the table with his arms folded. Fawkes puffed silently in the corner. Jack Wright looked uneasily at Catesby and Thomas Percy, and asked, "But if we fail?"

"We, fail?" Catesby looked incredulous. "But screw your courage to the sticking point, and we'll not fail. Can you for a moment doubt that

God appoints this? Or for a minute believe England will not rise to follow us when it sees the good work done?"

"Yet none rallied to Essex when — "

"Speak not to me of London sluggards, who fear to leave their shops for an hour's loss of trade." Catesby would not slow. "*We* will ride to the midlands, and thence to the north. There thousands of the faithful will rally. There is no choice in this, and we have sworn. Wouldst turn cold now?"

"Nay." Wright shook his head. "Honor pricks me on. I wish only that our plans be well laid. Heed. When we mean to build, we first survey the plot, *then* draw the model."

Gawain Wintour rapped the table. "Good, Jack. 'Tis so."

"He has that conceit from a play," said Catesby. "He's as bad as Percy." The men smiled, their tension loosened. But Robin raised a hand, turning them serious once more. "Look ye now, all." He leaned forward with intensity, holding their circle of faces rapt in his golden gaze. "We are *sworn*. And have we not God on our side? Does he not appoint us saviors of our fallen realm? I'faith, it is meet that Spain not help us. It is meant. I will say again, it is *our* work. English work."

"It *must* be thus." Thomas was enthralled. He thought of his years of clumsy swording, the shame he'd long felt among Catesby and Kit Wright, men so deft with the all-honored blade. Suddenly, all this mattered not. Catesby, wondrous Catesby, had revealed Thomas's destiny. He would fight with a new weapon, though not a paltry musket, no, nothing so dishonorable as that. *Gunpowder* Percy. Might he not rise, like a dark and thunderous storm, over the low houses of London? A cataract, a hurricano, a tempest of fire! Fire, which was not one element, but many virtuous elements combining together. Who had said that? Fire was the *doing* of a thing.

Thomas remembered the exploding castle in Flanders, the Spanish and Flemish heads, arms, and legs severed and hurtling through air. That bloody spectacle would now be avenged, and his guilt for such English horrors atoned for. Now it was Protestants who would pay. They would tremble as he and the earl had trembled, unwilling slaves of a Protestant queen, huddled on the wet Lowland earth. Powder . . . . mystic powder, lying inert, then fast alive, speaking with the voice of God, leaping up suddenly to dazzle its beholders, like Lazarus, or the risen body of the Christ. To stun! To astound!

"England's sickness demands so sharp a remedy," Catesby said quietly, stoking the slow-burning furnace of his listeners' zeal. Their rage was deep, awaiting its mining. Catesby's tongue was quicksilver. "It is necessary that our governors be visibly punished in a way that matches their crimes. And they will be. 'Twill be the edifying spectacle of God's wrath. They have fractured the Church in the place of unity, and the place of unity will thus visibly be fractured. They have rent the body of the Church, and so will their bodies be rent. Ripe justice will rain hot vengeance on the offenders' heads."

"Offenders' heads, yes," said Jack. "These would be men like Cecil. And Francis Bacon."

"We'll cook Bacon," Fawkes muttered in the corner.

"And the king's family," Jack went on. "The loss of the crown prince is to be regretted, but he has been raised a Protestant, and is too old to be saved."

"The . . . ." Thomas felt suddenly cold. But the other men were nodding. He knew they were thinking of Harry the Eighth's young son Edward, sixth of that name, long dead, who had been taught by Protestant bishops. As an adolescent king, sixty years before, Edward had approved an English Book of Prayer and the English bishops' official proclamation that saints' miracles were superstitions. He'd done much damage in his six-year reign. Nine when he was crowned, and already too old to be saved.

But. . . .

Jack Wright was nodding with the rest, but a slight frown creased his brow. "For this king and his kind, henceforth we will not have to do with pity. Blows and revenge for us. No mercy toward offenders, and none towards the baby snakes, hard though this be. But the Catholics in Parliament? Monteagle? Thomas Howard? How can you make their deaths good, Robin?" Jack spoke pleadingly, wanting to be convinced. "Without them, there would be none to speak for us. How have they offended?"

Catesby's eyes flashed. "They offend by *not* speaking for us, for one. They have joined a rogue church and done nothing since. They have treacherously taken the Oath of Supremacy, acknowledging the king as their spiritual leader. Outwardly they reject the pope and his bishops. Then they sneak to mass in private and say paltry penances for this selling of their souls."

"Aye, but .... Some have been most grievously pressed to do so. After Essex's martyrdom, Monteagle was threatened with — "

"*I* was so pressed," said Catesby firmly. "I have lost everything. But I did not turn church papist." Seeing the worry on Wright's face and the hurt on Gawain's, he softened. "Perhaps, though, Monteagle might be warned."

Racked by conflicting emotions, Thomas sat, furiously rolling a small ball of candlewax between his thumb and forefinger. Staring at the shortening taper that half-lit their faces, he forced his mind from the thought of King James's young sons. He spoke. "What of the Earl of Northumberland?" This was something he needed to ask, despite his mixed feelings toward his lord. He had been growing steadily angrier at Henry Percy since the ninth earl's removal to London. Lord Henry Percy seemed content to leave Thomas forever in the lowly position of rent-collector, and not even to employ him on his southern estates, closer to the seat of power and rule. Still, he owed the earl some loyalty. It was because of the great Percy's regard, he knew, that these men thought him a member of a noble house at all.

"The Earl of Northumberland!" Catesby laughed. "Fear not for him, Thomas. Indeed, he will be most amply warned. For he is the centerpiece of our plan."

"How so?"

"To begin, he will furnish us with knowledge of the powder, of emplacements and earthworks, and of sources for supply."

"You think the earl would do this?" Thomas was incredulous. "*My* earl?"

"We know thy dear ninth earl likes to share his wisdom. He need know nothing of the purpose. Not as yet."

"But how will you gather intelligence from him?"

The men looked expectantly from Catesby to Thomas. Catesby smiled and said nothing. Thomas knitted his brow. "Do you mean . . . ."

Catesby nodded. "We will supply you with a list of questions. Fear not. These will be simple interrogatives, easy to remember, concerning ingredients, compounds, the laying of mines, and so forth. Our haste is not tremendous. Parliament will adjourn in summer and not meet again until February. You will visit the earl once more this month before leaving London, I guess. You are his familiar servant, are you not?"

Thomas cringed at "servant." He said, "As his *kinsman*, I am often in his company."

"Of a surety," Catesby said smoothly. "And your service with him in Flanders will prove good ground on which to build any conversation you like. You may learn much."

"I may." Thomas was doubtful. He knew little of mixing powder. In the Lowlands he had lifted, breach-loaded, and fired, and that was all. He knew, of course, that the earl could be tempted into long discourses on the properties and types of explosives and their variant uses. Had he not sweated and inwardly groused under the weight of the man's rambling speeches? But would he remember later what the earl had said? Did the grave act they'd sworn to perform hinge on this chance?

"Guido knows much of munitions, and will guide us," said Jack Wright.

Thomas felt relieved.

"Do not tell the earl of our plan," Jack cautioned Thomas. "Leave him in ignorance, and fetch him out later. For the nonce, let him busy himself with his books and his sizzle-games for children. His time will come after, when all is done."

"His time?" Thomas was perplexed. "What can the earl do then?"

The voice of Guido Fawkes spoke from the shadows. "He shall be our Catholic king."

Chapter 18

"Saltpeter, dug out of the bowels of the earth. This is a staple ingredient, you recall, though sal ammoniac has been used." The earl made a clucking sound with his tongue. "But that too can poison."

"Indeed, yes." Thomas nodded, thinking *Not sal ammoniac. Never sal ammoniac.*

"You recall also that a good flame flares red and white. Not blue. The quality of the flame can be predicted beforehand. The powder tastes sharp. No salt in the compound, nor animal fat from the packing. And the powder must look fair." The earl rapped on his table in vexation. "This is not so sturdy, no, nothing so satisfactory as my worktable at Alnwick. Months it has taken for the transport of my materials southward, to say nothing of my books. Indeed, I have you to thank for much of the labor. There was some danger in it."

Thomas bowed. "'Tis my appointed service, lord."

"And yet, I am forever finding that this or that box or bottle has been left behind or lost on the way."

"Not lost, I trust, lord."

"Left on a shelf at Alnwick, more like, as what you have brought does tally with the list I gave you. 'Tis not your error, but my forgetful brain."

Thomas had long wondered whether the ninth earl's distraction was natural to him or a byproduct of his frequent contact with odd materials. Likely both factors combined to produce an occasional chaos in his thought. Today it was difficult to keep him on a dialogue's single track. The earl kept starting off like a fox after new subjects, of great interest to him, if not to his hearer.

"Do you know," Henry Percy said now, "were it not for the far greater amplitude of books to be had in London, I could hardly bear to remain here."

Thomas seized this opportunity. "Is it through books you acquired your knowledge of Greek fire?"

"In the beginning, yes. That knowledge I have long possessed. Do you know, the Greek fire spoken of by the ancients is thought by many to have been gunpowder, yet it was not, Thomas. In the seventh century Greek fire was used in Byzantium for warfare, just as we use our black powder. Yet, though Greek fire burned fiercely and long, it was not known to leap upward to destroy high battlements with a great storm of sound, as gunpowder does. Thus we must needs conclude that, while saltpeter may have formed part of its mixture, either sulfur or charcoal were missed." The earl knit his brow. "Perhaps both were missed."

"Indeed!" Thomas masked his impatience with a face of enthusiasm and a thoughtful nod. "And — "

"No, Thomas, we must look to the Chinese as the true authors of powder. 'Twas they who first practiced the art of explosions. And such explosions! Beauteous flowers in the air! 'Chinese snow,' said the Arabs who wrote of them in the thirteenth century. This was those infidels' term for the saltpeter the men of Cathay used for their sky-works. And the Saracens studied the Chinese art and used it against Spain, ha ha!"

Thomas looked pained, but Henry Percy didn't notice. "Marco Polo was also much taken with Chinese tricks," he went on. "But Chinese powder was not merely for spectacles. The Chinese warred with their fire, too. Fire-lances, they called their weapons. Sticks which aimed exploding pellets of tar and willow-charcoal and — you'll not credit it — charred grasshoppers, to make the balls jump! *Fire lances.*" He laughed. "Guns, we would say, though we omit the grasshoppers. Europe was many years in refining this art, which was centuries old when we came to it. There was, again, Roger Bacon, and his flawed formula. Saltpeter, sulfur, and *Luru Vopo Vir Can Utriet.*" He drummed his fingers on his worktable. "The code, you remember. Whatever it meant."

"Yes." Thomas nodded sagely. "I recall our discussion."

"And I have told you, I think, of Berthold the Black, who heated sulfur and saltpeter in a pot until it exploded. Yet this did not kill him. He tried this mixture once more in a closed vessel, and that blew his house apart. Him, too."

"Ah. And this made him Berthold the Black?"

"Nay, nay. He was Berthold the Black when he began. *Schwartz*, as they say in the German. Though it is thought he might have been a Greek." The earl pondered. "Or was he a Dane?"

Thomas stifled a yawn. All this was useless, but he did not know how to guide the earl's discourse to the subject of most moment, this being the readiest means to the acquisition of powder in England. Sulfur, charcoal, and saltpeter, yes. All knew these to be powder's basic elements. But there were more questions to which Catesby craved an answer. Would it be easier and wiser for their band to collect sulfur, charcoal, and saltpeter separately? Or should they seek to purchase the mix already made, on some open market? What was the cost? And how long could powder sit before it decayed?

He must try again. "Saltpeter is dug from earth, you say," he ventured cautiously. "Yet it has other sources —"

"Most assuredly. It comes from dead men. Did you not know that?"

Thomas was momentarily speechless.

"Aye, friend Thomas. It can be culled from rotted corpses. Fire springing from death."

Thomas recalled Hotspur's lively death on the London stage. *Gunpowder Percy. Might he not rise?* He gave his head a dog-shake. "Yet this is not the . . . usual way saltpeter is found?"

"No. Only in times of great and prolonged warfare. The more ordinary way is by culling through the common rot that turns into soil. For my experiments I have often harvested saltpeter from decayed matter and filth in the barns and dovecotes of my tenants. Yet there are powder mills —"

"Oh, aye?"

The earl raised his eyebrows at Thomas's eager tone. Off-handedly, Thomas added, "I have, indeed, heard of such mills in England. They were much talked of a few years past, when another Spanish invasion was hoped f — was feared."

"Ah. Well, our governors watch over the making of powder as well as they can, but they cannot keep eyes on everything. Since peace with Spain has been declared, and the wars in the Lowlands abate, there is much surplus material, and tradesmen eager to sell."

Thomas straightened. This was what he wished to know.

"Yes." The earl sat down in a chair, placed his hands behind his head, and gazed up at the high ceiling of his Syon House room. His hair, like

Thomas's, was disheveled, and his doublet loose. "Yes, yes, yes. This, the surplus, was also found ten years ago, in the years just after we trounced the Armada, and this, the superfluity, was helpful to me, for then I needed powder for my investigations into the combustibility of granite. Large boulders, you recall, were my subject. Yet 'combustibility' is not the word. In truth, I wondered what charge might be required to reduce them to stones useful for building. I had in mind a wall on the grounds of Alnwick. The landslide that crushed two goat-sheds was an unfortunate outcome of my endeavors. Another was the slight deafness that I have borne in my left ear since that day." He pulled his earlobe distractedly. "Yet there was profit. Knowledge was acquired. No experiment is truly wasted." He fell silent, nodding and tugging his ear.

Exasperated, Thomas sought the right words. "And the . . . the store of powder then. You acquired it whence?"

"Was it in Godstone?" The earl pondered, again looking up at the ceiling. "Or Faversham? Faversham, I think. Though it decayed during transport north, and I was constrained to remix it. I would have done better to start with mine own stock."

"Thy talents are evident, and much admired."

"Ah?" The earl looked pleased.

Perhaps this was the tack. "Yes. Thine experiments are often spoken of among the gentry with whom I consort."

"With whom *you* consort?"

Miffed by the earl's tone, Thomas struggled to stay calm. It would not be to the purpose to quarrel with the earl, especially now, when they had most need of his good will. "Yes. My friends," he said shortly. "Men of the faithful."

"Ah, the Catesby and such."

Thomas nodded. "These take particular interest in your knowledge — "

"Of powder?" The earl frowned. "Now, that is strange."

"Not so. They think only that your skill might teach them how best to defend England on our own soil, should Spain make such a shift necessary."

The earl looked at him suspiciously. "Your Catholic friends fear invasion from Spain? Despite the new peace?"

"No, not Spain, to be sure. Spain is now a friend. I meant to say . . . uh . . . Wales. Or Ireland."

"Or the Land of the One-Legged Monopods?"

Sweating now, Thomas spoke quickly. "Of a surety, foreign threats to our shores have recently abated. But this our dear England is always at risk. And the faithful are most ardent to demonstrate their loyalty to the crown in any . . . in any future engagement, in hopes of kinder treatment from King James. They look to you because of your friendship and your gallantry in Flanders."

"Gallantry in Flanders." The earl's tone was half-amused, half-bitter. "*Gallantry.*" Abruptly he rose and returned to his worktable. "Well, tell Robin Catesby that this shift is now a distant necessity. No need to stock powder to drive out the bravos of the South, who were the only ones we had to fear. I for one am pleased that we now smile on Spain. I was stuffed to the gills and made sick with war three years ago. James is less bellicose than was our queen. He wants peace with the world. I will not be called again into perilous service."

So you believe.

Thomas, Catesby, and others of the sworn band had met once more before Catesby had dispatched Thomas to Syon House. In an ale-house in Eastcheap, they had spoken in detail of the part the earl would, in the end, be asked to play for them — aye, for England. Thomas had proposed that when the time came, though the earl might balk at a royal title, he would agree to act as regent for one of James's children, whom the men could kidnap and keep safe. The nine-year-old daughter, perhaps. And surely the two-year-old son, Charles, might be let to survive. Still troubled on the point of the princes, Thomas had argued fiercely for Charles's preservation. Such a baby could, after all, be brought up to the true faith even more easily than a nine-year-old maiden. Catesby had answered that while this was so, the king was likely to bring both his sons to the opening of Parliament, to display his royal virility and the reassuring fact that he had heirs, and if this happened, even the child must fall prey to the clean sweep.

Unhappily, Thomas had put the question of the children aside, and agreed that whichever of the king's progeny inherited, the men would have need of the Earl of Northumberland. As the highest Catholic noble — for he'd have no reason to hide his true religion in the restored England — the earl would see there was no other course but to take up the reigns of government. The ninth earl would guide the horse of St. George.

Not, of course, that the earl would lack the counsel and assistance of the faithful. Other Catholic nobility would do much in the redeemed realm, and among those nobles the primary redeemers hoped to be counted. For new nobles would be needed to replace the fallen. Aided by these, the earl would find much time still to engage in his studies, if governance were not to his liking. Catesby had argued persuasively that Thomas himself could hope for no less than an earldom, once the justice of their cause was made obvious by its success. To whom else should the Percy title fall, when the earl blew himself up in some new mad experiment, like Berthold the Black?

"Was there aught else, Thomas?" The earl was looking longingly at a book. "I thank you again for transporting my northern rents, along with these bottles and volumes. Your dedication to my house is estimable."

My house. Thomas gritted his teeth.

He was on the verge of a dishonorable retort when the earl spoke again. "Indeed, I have made a petition on your behalf. You shall be made a Gentleman Pensioner."

Thomas's sour look vanished into thin air. He vaulted from his chair, knocking it sideways, and stood with his mouth agape.

The earl smiled. "I have stolen your tongue, have I not? Yes. Long service should be rewarded. I have earned the king's trust this year, it seems. I keep from his path, he says, and cause no trouble, unlike some of his other English earls, who are too much underfoot. Owing to his regard, all subjects with the Percy name have been removed from the recusant rolls. This benefit may be withdrawn in time, when English church absences again become conspicuous to pesky Protestant sheriffs. But for now, the king looks graciously on the Percys. I might better say, he looks graciously away from them! There is, then, no bar to your advancement. And because some of his upstart knights have incurred his anger, brawling on palace grounds, they've been stripped from the Pensioners' list, which leaves several vacancies. I am charged with filling those." He sighed. "I find this a difficult task. My studies have made me so ... insular ...." Percy gestured widely about his room, which, though large, was fast growing as dense with books, instruments, and vials as his cell at Alnwick. "To conclude, I spoke on your behalf."

"I ...." Thomas felt tears welling in his eyes. To be made, at last, a knight! "I know not how I should thank you, my lord."

"Tut, tut. Good service is thanks enough. For your service to me *will* continue. You'll have a berth in London, but I will expect your continued ferrying of rents from the north. Though I think these might be collected at less frequent intervals. The king's hand has been generous with me, far more than was the hand of.... Well."

"Thank you, my lord." Should he fall to his knees? He knew little of the protocol, not having been born to the manner, for all his pretenses to the contrary. Thomas settled for removing his cap, making a leg, and bowing deeply.

"Your wife will perhaps regret your more frequent absence, but then...." The earl winked. He had put himself in an affable mood. "There will be a royal stipend to quell your Martha's complaints."

Thomas thought this would not be a time to propose bringing Martha to London. The earl did not seem to foresee his setting up a smoky household here, and indeed, this was well. A solitary berth in the city would suit Thomas best, for now. He felt a stab of worry, thinking that, on hearing of his impending rise in rank, Martha herself might argue for an occasional-house in the capital, like the one her parents had owned, before, weary of taxes and the off-handed treatment given them by London's Protestant gentry, they had finally sold it and gone back home to York. Now Martha might see her own position improved enough for a new foothold in the south.

But though he could never tell her so, Thomas himself did not want Martha in London. London had been Mary's place. And other things were afoot now, that wives should be kept well out of. He would simply bear with Martha's storms.

In any case, her anger would be much allayed by the knowledge that she might now be called Lady Percy, like the earl's own wife (who had removed to Alnwick Castle as soon as her husband had re-ensconced himself at Syon House).

"You are to be installed this Friday next," the earl said, rising briskly. "I shall supply garments; fear not. I had meant to tell you sooner. The oath will be administered, and then .... well, what is it? You cannot have a more pressing engagement."

"Nay, lord," Thomas said. His face had fallen. "Nay. It is ... something else."

"What, then, man?"

Thomas mustered all his scant self-control and took a deep, ragged breath. Then, holding himself proudly erect, he said stiffly, "The oath. I cannot, my lord, swear the Oath of Supremacy. I cannot declare King James the Head of the Church." With the heels of both hands, he wiped his eyes.

"Ah." The earl regarded him gravely, then looked away. "No, Thomas. Of course you cannot."

The two men stood for a moment, separately gazing at the rush-strewn floor. Then the earl said gently, "I . . . will see what can be done. James has a Catholic wife, by God. Can she have taken the oath? Or perhaps I will simply . . . . 'Tis I who administer the ceremony, Thomas. I'll put the case to the king. He's no Henry the Eighth, thank God; he'll see the way of it. The thing might be omitted."

Thomas felt tears spring to his eyes again at the earl's unexpected kindness. Did Henry Percy think him true family after all? He walked forward and bent to kiss the earl's hand, which tasted of a chemical.

"Wipe your lips, Thomas. This was mercury," said the earl, clearly embarrassed. "Now, off to thy plays and thy haunts. Go to the Globe. Don't wander into the powder mill at Rotherhithe Street and light a pipe. 'Tis hard by, and one so dizzy with new-granted glory as you might easily make the mistake." He laughed. "The players should learn not to fire live cannon in their history plays. Not with the mill so close. Just now I hear there are many pounds of surplus powder sitting dormant, awaiting a single spark. Though three weeks brings decay, and remixing is necessary. Still, they must be anxious to sell before the price drops below twenty-five pounds per barrel. There is always the danger of an accident. So have a care where you walk, Sir Thomas!"

Thomas's white teeth flashed in a rare grin. Once more he bowed deeply. "My lord."

Outside Syon House, he mounted his roan and took off at a gallop toward Catesby's borrowed dwelling in Lambeth, near London. His chest expanded, and he gave a savage whoop, like an Irish warrior. He could feel his destiny unfolding. A knighthood, to be claimed with honor, with no forswearing of his faith! God's hand in this design was clear. He, Thomas Percy, had been blessed for his boldness, for the holy venture he had now undertaken with his band of Catholic brothers.

He was on fire to tell Robin Catesby the news.

Rotherhithe Street, he thought excitedly as he rode. *Sal ammonium! Something about decaying, and twenty pounds per barrel! Or was it twenty-five? Taste of the powder sharp. But fair? What can this mean? Powder is black, not fair. Fair meaning lovely? No matter. Rotherhithe Street!*

Back at Syon House the earl paced the floorboards of his workroom, tapping his brow. "*Luru Vopo Vir Can Utriet,*" he said. "*Luru Vopo . . .* 'Man Can'? Marry, what *can* old Friar Bacon have meant?"

Chapter 19

Wide scarlet sleeves, a furred cape, leather boots, and black silk galligaskins. A fur-lined cap pinned with the badge of the Gentleman Pensioners. A shorter and more ornamental sword than the long blade that had clattered by his side for years. With some relief, Thomas had unbelted that sword the day after the recent meeting with Catesby and the others at the Duck and Drake, when powder had been revealed as his destiny.

Martha combed Thomas's hair and trimmed his beard, unhappy with the ragged job a servant had made of it. She had ridden for a week to reach London for Thomas's installment as a royal Pensioner, then busied herself at clothiers' and jewelers' shops. With money from Thomas's new gold she'd bought a blue satin gown, a stomacher of French lace, heeled shoes, earrings, and a dyed ruff. After all this preparation, she was nonplussed and then annoyed by the shortness of the ceremony — the dubbing, then a brief kneeling and swearing of loyalty to the ruler, made fleeter in this case by the earl's studied omission of the Oath of Supremacy, by which Thomas would have placed the king above the pope. Henry Percy had decided, in the end, not to consult the king on so trivial a matter as one knight's oath, but simply to leave out the troubling words on his own initiative. King James, ever busy with the hunt during morning hours, would not even be there to notice.

Thomas Percy was glad of the king's absence. With him in attendance, it would have been hard to swear even simple loyalty, since he was plotting the man's death. Not that the mere loyalty oath was a lie. He *did* swear that one, since Catesby had assured him that, unlike the Oath of Supremacy, the loyalty oath held no dishonor. After all, the king in his person represented England, so fealty to the king meant fealty to England, which in the powder brethren's case would mean killing the king. James's body would be sacrificed for the England he stood for, and hence the conspirators' action *was* loyal, in an ultimate sense. Thomas accepted this logic, but was glad, all the same, not to see James there in the face.

Martha was irked, however. Unlike Thomas, she did not hate the king. Indeed, she shared nothing of her husband's temperament, which was choleric and melancholy by dizzying turns. His savage humors drank and fed on dreams in which doom figured frequently. In those she was too practical to partake. With stubborn hopefulness, she assumed Thomas's new honor signaled James's actual acceptance of Catholic families, lying hidden under the words of intolerance he set forth for his Protestant counselors. So the king's absence from Thomas's investment vexed her for workaday reasons. She'd seen the monarch just once, from a distance, during his passage through York before his coronation the year before. Thomas's knighting today might have given her a chance to view James more closely, and, more importantly, for him to view her. Not that she was a child, like Claire on the high street in York that day, hopping up and down in hopes of a glimpse of a crown and a wave from ermine-clad majesty. No vain or trivial woman, Martha had chosen her garments for this London occasion with care, hoping she'd look an honorable Catholic woman as she knelt before the new sovereign. She'd even hoped she might see and be approved by Queen Anna, a Catholic lady like herself—also, regrettably, absent today, like her royal husband. Might not such a scene have led to a quicker official softening of the monarch's views regarding the faithful?

Her disappointment made her peevish. Thomas knew not what to do with her in the London afternoon but to take her to a playhouse, where they sat in a lord's box, their rich garments attracting the gazes of the idle. The play at the Fortune was a comedy of Friar Bacon and Friar Bungay, featuring a priestly magician. Thomas thought it not as great a thing as a history play at the Globe, and yet a like confirmation, however deeply encoded, of the wisdom of Catholic clergy, and the justness of his own looming cause.

Martha thought it a stupid play.

Thomas's knightly duties would be light. The earl, who remained his master and captain, dispatched him to Northumbria the day after the investment ceremony, that he might there continue his money-gathering as before. Of course, Thomas needed the London berth of which the earl had spoken earlier, so he took care, before starting, to lease a small dwelling in Gray's Inn Road, and, at Robin Catesby's direction, another near Westminster.

"With my frequent absences, a caretaker will be necessary," he told the earl late that morning in Syon House. "The pay need only be modest."

"Ah." The earl was squinting through a glass at a trapped ladybug. "You may speak to the steward here. We have many idle servants who –"

"Begging pardon of your lordship, I have already hired a man I think trustworthy."

"Good!" The earl straightened and looked hard at him. "Then nothing hinders your departure."

"No, lord." Thomas bowed and retreated.

"May I know your caretaker's name?" the earl called just as Thomas reached the door.

Thomas paused. He had not anticipated the question. "It is . . . John Johnson, sir."

"Hmm. John Johnson. Well enough, Thomas. Goodbye."

Thomas rode quickly back to Westminster, where he confirmed with the new caretaker the earl's approval of his appointment. Then he met Martha at the London home of the Wintours in the Strand, where the pair of them had lodged, and together they rode north.

In the yard outside Sir Thomas Percy's rooms, the caretaker took stock of his surroundings. He was a quiet man, lanky, tall, and observant, with a bushy, red-brown beard and slightly pocked cheeks. The street he surveyed was home to two bakers and a cooper's shop. Some yards past these establishments stood the entrance to a large courtyard which was shadowed by the House of Lords.

Save Guido Fawkes, the plotters all left London. They met sporadically that summer at their own estates in the north and midlands and at those of their friends. At Huddington Court, at Harrowden Hall, at Twigmoor, at White Webbs, the men debated their plans.

Thomas had told them what he'd learned from the earl concerning powder. He and Catesby had charged Fawkes to form acquaintanceships with workers at the Rotherhithe powder mill, and to find other close sources for the acquisition of the mighty weapon. From his long soldiering, Fawkes knew a great deal about the setting of charges, and from Flanders Thomas remembered enough. For the placements, they would later depend on Fawkes's judgment. For now, Thomas reckoned thirty barrels would supply them. The purchase of these should be made — of course — gradually.

Late August found the conspirators at Harrowden, the midlands home of Eliza Vaux. By now their group had widened to include Jack Wright's brother Kit, Gawain Wintour's brother Bors, and Catesby's brother-in-law Francis Tresham. "These friends will rouse our gentry in the country," Catesby said. The men were gathered at a table in Eliza's garden. Nodding assent, the Wintours proposed also bringing in a Warwickshire Catholic named John Grant, brother-in-law to one of them. Grant was a shielder of priests, known to all the plotters from many years of shared secret masses.

Thomas had no complaint about Grant, or Kit Wright, or Bors Wintour. And though he felt contempt for Francis Tresham — such a cautious church papist! — still, Francis was cousin to Catesby, and Thomas was willing to believe his nobler blood was stirred by the news of the impending exploit. Tresham might prove true Catholic yet. Yet the general spreading of the net worried Thomas. Now, hard on the heels of the Wintours' suggestion, Catesby was proposing to share their plans with the caretaker of Catesby's own rented house in Lambeth, across Thames, where the powder might be stored.

Thomas shook his head. "Nine men might pass. Three is the Trinity, and this will be three times three. But ten makes too unwieldy a number," he said grumpily.

"Thirty barrels also make an unwieldy number, for all it is ten times the number of the Trinity. Thirty barrels of powder! And it may come to more barrels before we act. Who will guard it all?" Catesby looked tauntingly at him. "You, Sir Thomas, great Gentleman Pensioner?"

"You know I cannot do it! I have my duties to perform for the earl."

"Ah, wizard earl. We might use him for both guard and storage. There is ample room at Syon House and Petworth — "

"By the Rood, no!"

The men looked at Thomas in surprise. He lightened his tone. "No. Not well thought upon. The earl would put the powder to his own use, blowing up a stable to observe the effects of ash on winter hay."

Robin laughed. "Good! Good, Thomas."

"But —"

"A moment, friends." Kit pointed. A large dog had found its way into the garden and was bounding toward them, pursued by a youth calling, "Back, Whip! An' ye spoil gentry's roses, ye'll be hanged!"

"Ah. The four-legged scamp of the shire. He hopes Garnet is with us, to give him another sweetmeat." Robin rose to intercept the dog and prevent his young master's further progress. "Rabbits abound in yon forest for this valiant hunter." He pointed beyond the wall, smiling at the young man's apologies while he led boy and dog toward the gate. The latch closed behind them, and Catesby returned to the table. "Now. Thomas, and all of ye, let worry on this matter abate. I warrant my man Keyes at Lambeth can be trusted. In converse with Fawkes — "

"Then you've told him already," said Jack Wright, who had been gathering his energies during the interlude with the dog.

"Ha?"

Wright looked hard at Catesby. "I say you have told your servant Keyes of our plan, and this seeking of our counsel is a kind of show."

Catesby kept his eyes steady. "Aye, I have told him. He's a good man, and there was need for haste. Guido has already begun to purchase powder, and had need of an ally. Had I not made the thing sure in London, this arrangement must needs have been done by letter. Our plans put in writing. Do any of us wish such a risk?"

No one said anything for a moment. Then Jack grunted, "No."

Catesby spread his hands. "Doth any man here doubt my loyalty, or my powers of reason?"

"No." A chorus of firmer voices responded.

"Good. " Catesby nodded. "We may speak later, then, of the probable need for tunneling. Much discourse must be postponed until several of us return to London and meet again with Fawkes. Here, today, we need only prepare for confession and mass when Father Quindle arrives from Staffordshire."

There was an awkward silence. Kit Wright finally broke it. "I had . . . not thought to make confession this day."

"Nor had I," said Jack Wright.

"Nor I." Bors Wintour looked at his hands.

"Nor I," said Thomas. "Instead, I had wished to speak to Father Quindle of a journey I would perform. A journey of the faithful, to be shepherded by him, if he would do it. To Wales."

"Gentlemen!" Catesby studied their faces keenly. "Mass is no good without confession. Pilgrimages to Wales instead of confession? What is the hindrance in this matter? The priests are not often with us. We must take every opportunity to embrace *all* sacraments." He leaned close to Thomas. "Sir Thomas, why do you long to go on pilgrimage? Can I believe that you think our present enterprise a sin?"

"'Tis no sin!" Thomas spoke gruffly, disentangling his legs from the struts under the benched table.

Robin widened his eyes in mock fear. "Let me see thee pop up and declare it, in thy usual jack-of-the-clock fashion."

Thomas needed no prompting. He was already pushing himself to his feet. "'Tis no sin, I say!"

"Hush thee, Percy!" Kit Wright tugged at Thomas's sleeve. "We must bring no further trouble to this good house. Do you not think the women can hear us above?"

Looking up, Thomas saw both Eliza and her maidservant at the manor's high window, staring down at him in perplexity. The maidservant's hands bore a blue priestly cope, which Thomas recognized, having bought it himself for the Vauxs from a company of players, the only sort of folk who could legally own such a garment now. New copes had been common on the costume market some forty years past, but this one was now threadbare.

Eliza vanished from the window, but the servant remained. She'd been unfolding the cope, and now stood stock still, holding it before her like an offering, as she looked with considerable interest at the men.

"What are you thinking? It is worse when you stare up," Wright hissed. "Be seated!"

Thomas waved weakly at the woman just as Eliza's voice called her from the window. Then he sat.

Robin Catesby smiled at all of them, but his eyes were grave. "We must resolve this question of confession. Why do you hesitate? Surely we embark on no sin, but on a just and zealous work to which God has committed us. And when there is no sin, no sin need be confessed. This is apparent, good sirs, and not open to argument."

Most of the men nodded slowly. Still, no one spoke. Catesby sipped his wine and looked at the sky. They sat thus, until a servant rounded the house to tell them Father Quindle had arrived.

They were gathered upstairs, conversing after their mass, when the pursuivants came.

At first they thought the knock signaled the arrival of Martha and Claire Percy. Thomas's wife and daughter had been expected for today's ceremony, but, as Thomas would later know, Martha had deemed the road too rough and the risks of travel too great for a midlands mass that season. Yet "There is Martha Percy," Eliza whispered, and turned, just as her maidservant bustled into the room hissing that they must straightway hide Father Quindle.

Familiar with the rough door-pounding of searchers, Quindle was already stripping off his chausable and cassock. "You are taken," Eliza whispered to him frantically. "The closest hiding place is beneath the steps, and they are on the steps already!"

Some of the guests were already running down the hall to a servant's stair that led to the house's rear entrance. Others were busy distributing themselves among the various second-floor rooms of the manor, striving to look merry and convivial, as though they'd all randomly gathered to play games, drink canary, and admire oil portraits in the afternoon. Amid the hurly-burly Kit Wright vaulted through a window, landed in a hedge, rose, righted and dusted himself, and began strolling the grounds, whistling. The three pursuers were not fooled by any of this, but none of them chased the men and women who were rapidly leaving the house. Instead, they rushed upstairs and into the very room where mass had just ended.

There they found Eliza, Robin Catesby, and a bread-munching, silk-capped gentleman clad in tight orange-tawny hose. The three gentles gazed at the intruders in apparent surprise from their chairs by their blue-covered table, their hands clutching cards in a suspended game of primero.

Catesby rose, frowning. "Whom do you seek? Rudesbys, you'll find nothing here but our game."

"We know it." The man with the royal badge spoke harshly. "We come to *halt* your game."

"Must you do so? I was winning." The silk-capped man spoke in a lazy whine. He raised and drained an over-full wineglass, then fussed with a dangling earring.

"High stakes, indeed," said Catesby. "But I will win my stake back, fear me not, if these intruders will give us leave to play."

One of the pursuivants sniffed the air. "Candlewax. Why have you lit tapers in the bright midday?"

"I was trying to fire a smoke, though I failed. See here." Catesby withdrew his long pipe from a pocket of his doublet. "Methinks there's a flaw in the draw."

"You should put some tobacco in it," the agent said scornfully, glancing briefly at the pipe.

"Marry, well bethought!" Catesby returned the pipe to his doublet. "I will do so."

"Why are you gathered here? What is the occasion?"

"'My birthday," said Eliza. "Can you guess which one? Think, sir, I pray! None has guessed rightly yet." She tittered foolishly.

"Whatever your age, madam, whether you truly were born on this date can be easily ascertained."

"Go, then, to the hall of records in the town to inquire," trilled Eliza, and gave another brainless giggle. "I shall stay for your return."

Shaking his head impatiently, the leader of the searchers gestured to one of his followers. "Tap the floorboards, there. If need be, get the crow and rip them up."

Catesby gave his hostess a pained look. "Mistress Eliza, I fear we must now shift our contest to another venue. Now will come loud searching, rough questioning of your gentle guests, and a blunt end to all the day's merriment. You may send for us at the Swan in Stratford, if by some service we may repay your hospitality."

"O, la, be off, gentlemen." With a pout, Eliza rose. "These men have troubled each inch of my loyal house before, and I must watch them closely with my linens."

"And that is where we'll begin, lady." The searcher frowned at the group, having been given this new idea. "In your ample closets! You." He gestured to the pursuivant who was now on his knees, ear to the floorboards, knocking the wood with a practiced hand. "Up, fellow. Leave that for now. We will start down the hall, with the linen closets."

The silk-bonneted man at the table rolled his eyes in disgust. With an elegant sniff, he minced from the room and trailed Catesby down the stairs. His jeweled earring swung as he tossed his head peevishly. The pursuivants followed them out of the room, then turned down a corridor.

Eliza quickly snatched off her single remaining ruby earring and dropped it inside her bodice. Then she followed the agents of the Crown, complaining heartily of the stain of their muddy boots on her new-strewn rushes.

Outside, Thomas Percy waited behind the barn with his roan, patting its nose to keep it quiet. In a minute Father Quindle and Catesby rounded the corner, walking more quickly than they had on the stairs. Catesby was smirking. "Ha!" he laughed when they came close to Thomas. "Sport royal!"

Quindle tore off the silk bonnet and scratched his head furiously. "I'd not wear *this* longer even to avoid the rack. How do women abide such gear?"

"Ah, the uses to which cloth may be put! Father, thy cope did well as a table-cover. I only wish we'd had time to hide the Eucharist before you were compelled to swallow it."

"Yes, Robin, I regret that." Father Quindle was swinging himself onto Thomas's horse. "God forgive us! Ah, this." He pulled Eliza's other ruby earring from his lobe and handed it to Catesby. "*You* might wear this, Robin. As for the next mass, let it be known I'll return in a week."

"But not *here*." Thomas spoke with alarm.

"Nay. Baddesley Clinton. I'm for John Grant's house now, where you may later claim your horse. Tomorrow . . . well, I will see. Farther north." Quindle kicked the horse into a trot, and rode hatlessly off.

Catesby turned to Thomas with a grin. "Let us, then, to the Swan, after all. We'll play chess there. Here, there'll be naught but a house turned topsy-turvy."

"How for horses? The priest has mine."

"Shall we steal one from the pursuivants? Nay. Eliza's mare is recovering from the bots, but we'll borrow and saddle it for you nonetheless. Come with me, Thomas. You may tell me more of our future regent, the wizard earl, and his thoughts on Greek fire." Catesby clapped Thomas's broad back. "My horse is in the stable as well."

"Marry, *you* ride the mare," said Thomas, but he followed.

Chapter 20

By October Thomas and Robin were back in London, staying alternately in Gray's Inn Road and at Robin's house upriver in Lambeth. Thomas was little found at his second berth, his Westminster rooms. Guido Fawkes made sure of this. The day after Thomas's arrival in the south, after he first visited the earl, he went to Westminster to speak to Guido and to watch with him the comers and goers at Parliament Place. After half an hour Fawkes was pleading with him to remove himself, so conspicuous was Percy with his startled staring, his obscure muttering, and his silk and fur garments of the Gentlemen Pensioners.

"Let thy 'John Johnson' calculate the traffic," Fawkes said, with a wintry smile. "I have spent many weeks doing little more than this. As foolish an alias as thou hast given me, I can better play a gentleman of small note than thou canst. I will meet thee with Catesby and his man Keyes, at Lambeth."

"When?"

"Tonight, at five of the clock. Tell Robin I'll bring a town-bred goose for supper."

Thomas left him and crossed to Southwark by way of London Bridge. Passing between two rows of tight-packed shops and houses on the bridge, he was dripped on, not by rain, but by new-washed sheets stretched on ropes between upper windows. Thus dampened, he met in a tavern on Tooley Street with Robin Catesby. Jack Wright and Gawain Wintour were there also. At Catesby's behest the two had ridden south the day before, and now sat sharing ale, bread, and mutton pottage baked into a thick pastry coffin.

"Why did Francis Tresham not come with you?" Thomas asked the two of them, as he shook the water from his hat.

Wright grunted as he swallowed a mouthful. "As always, Catesby's cousin Francis is distressed by talk of the powder's operations. He says he has business in Northumbria. I think he finds comfort in distance." He patted his chin with a linen handkerchief.

Thomas scowled. "Will Francis Tresham prove true?"

"He swears he will prove a valiant soldier at the rising, once the deed is done."

"Let him do that then," said Catesby. "At the rising. Each to his sphere. What more said Fawkes today, Thomas?"

"That he will meet us at supper in Lambeth."

"With my steward Keyes we will be six, and I have nothing for supper."

"Thy *steward!*" said Jack Wright. "La."

"I have a skeleton staff, which he commands."

"A potboy."

Catesby shrugged and puffed his pipe. Fawkes had introduced him to tobacco. Now he smoked whenever his friends would let him.

"Fawkes says he will bring a goose," Thomas said.

"Ah. Did he mean you?"

The four men went to a play.

———

"Here." Sucking marrow from a goose-bone, Fawkes swept to the side a litter of goblets, plates, and breadcrumbs. On Catesby's long table he unrolled a wide sheet of paper. Six heads bent to stare at the neat, blocked outline of Parliament square he'd sketched on the backs of two playbills stuck together. "Just here," Guido said. "What was't you said in the spring, Jack Wright? *When we mean to build, we first survey the plot, then draw the model.* So I have done."

"And well have you done." Catesby chuckled. "Only we do not mean to build, but to raze."

"Aye." With the hollow bone Fawkes tapped a rectangular box marked "X." "The lords meet here. And at the opening session, that pestiferous Scotsman James and his family will most certainly be in attendance." The bone tapped another spot. "Here is their place."

"Is't still expected that both sons will attend?" asked Thomas anxiously.

"The brat Henry will, of a surety. As for the younger brat Charles, if he is brought, he will perish with the rest."

The men sat silent. Catesby surveyed them all coolly, saying nothing. This, the matter of the children, was always a point of discomfort. At last Jack Wright nodded reluctantly. "One fell swoop — "

"Fell?" Catesby shook his head vigorously. "Never fell. Blessed! The arm of God shall strike with us."

"A boy for a boy," said Thomas, sunk in himself. "A lad for a lad."

The others looked at him strangely. "Not for one lad. For all our children," said Gawain Wintour.

"Aye." Thomas nodded. "Aye."

Fawkes touched the paper again. His eyes were calm in his scarred face. "Let us not argue the merits and justice of our action. This was all done before. Let us now look to the doing of what was vowed. There is, you see here, a vault beneath the room where the lords meet, but no privy access to that vault. The other buildings in the place are all ramshackle and whatnot. The lords ply their evil and politic trade near a bakery and a tavern. The yard is busy with lords and servants and panniers and vintners and coal carriers in the day, and guards watch the houses at night."

Catesby looked at Thomas, who was still wearing his Pensioner's silks, though they seemed less fine than in the morning, stained as they were from beer he'd spilt on himself at the playhouse. "We may work to influence the choice of guard, may we not, Sir Thomas?"

Thomas shook his head. "There is little chance that a Gentleman Pensioner would be sent to stand guard in Parliament Square. Our duties — "

"Are in the main ceremonial."

Thomas bristled. "Like those of most knights in our fallen day."

"Aye." Robin conceded the point ruefully. "This cannot be denied."

Thomas smiled a little. "At any rate, our duties chiefly concern standing in palaces with right hands behind our backs, clutching pikes with the other."

"'Tis so." Jack Wright nodded. "I have seen those great sworded lugs louring at me in chambers. Indeed, I thought, when Percy was given this duty, he might use it to our purpose in Whitehall, yerking the king hard between the ribs — "

"I thought of it. But 'tis said the king wears a thrice-stuffed doublet."

Catesby held up a hand. "Why all this chat? Killing the king would not do enough. It would leave Cecil. It would leave Prince Henry. It would leave many odious Protestant bishops and lords. We know this. We have concluded this. Let us listen to Fawkes."

Obediently, the men returned their eyes to Guido, who stood patiently waiting with his finger on the sketch of the House of Lords. "I thank you, Robin. Now. Without question, we must tunnel. There is only the question of where to begin." Fawkes slid his finger along the paper to a smaller box adjacent to the X-ed rectangle. "This house belongs to the Keeper of the Wardrobe. Robin, I have spoken of him to you."

"Yes. I know him to be Catholic."

"We cannot be so reckless as to share our plans with any and all who have *this* mere commendation," said Jack Wright in alarm.

"'Tis no *mere* commendation, Jack. Yet I think as you do. We shall not include the Keeper of the Wardrobe among us, at our core. Still, we will persuade him to rent his house."

"Can this be done?" Thomas asked eagerly.

Fawkes nodded. "The present tenant's lease expires on St. Nicholas's Day, and he has already pulled up stakes and moved elsewhere. I am confident that we can strike a bargain with the landlord in a trice." From a shelf by the wall Fawkes picked up a wooden rule he'd brought in a sack with the goose. He placed one end of the rule on the center of the small drawn box on the paper and the other on the spot that marked the king's seat in the House of Lords. He then took a stick of charcoal from his pocket, drew a line between the two points, and scratched a number above the line. "D'ye see?"

"I do." Thomas's eyes shone. "We can traverse that distance underground. We shall work with shovels, and creep into the belly of the enemy, like Ulysses in his Trojan Horse."

"Something like," said Catesby.

"Then this question is settled," said Gawain Wintour.

"Yet there is another question." The speaker was Robert Keyes, Catesby's caretaker at Lambeth. He was a large, red-bearded man and, like Fawkes, a grave and quiet listener.

Catesby nodded. "Aye, Francis. I can guess your thought. Where will we get money for all the powder?"

They had put off discussing this matter. Now the men gazed at one another perplexed. More than one of them put a furtive hand to his purse, and none could think of a word to say.

Six weeks later, after still more journeyings back and forth between London and their estates at home, the men had not yet resolved the issue of money. The problem was now pressing. Their own resources were sorely taxed by the price of powder, which Fawkes and Keyes had begun buying in small lots from several mills between Rotherhithe Street and Faversham and covertly transporting to Lambeth. The weapon was costly. Decayed stock might be remixed, but there was no saving the two barrels that fell one night from their boat to the bottom of the Thames. And since the English had withdrawn their artillers from the Lowlands and Ireland, the mills, to avoid glut, had been manufacturing less. Much of the English powder that existed had been bought by foreign agents, and supply was growing scarce. Consequently the price of a barrel had risen by late fall to more than twenty-eight pounds.

"We *must* have more wealth in our enterprise," Catesby told Thomas, Fawkes, and the Wintours one cold afternoon at Lambeth. It was St. Andrew's Day, almost December, and though it was only half-past four the sky was dark. Catesby lit another candle. "More wealth. We must have Rookwood."

"What wood?" Thomas was mystified.

"Ambrose Rookwood is a gentleman of Bury St. Edmund's, a good friend of mine, and a lover of our cause."

Thomas pushed his chair back from Robin's table and stood. The Wintours looked back and forth between Catesby and Thomas, not sure which of these two friends alarmed them more. "A lover of our cause, is he?" Thomas growled. "Doth he *know* of our cause?"

"Nay, nay." Catesby's voice was smooth and calming. "I mean only that he is Catholic, and longs, as we do, for release from our miseries. He has agreed to give money that will garner us fifteen more barrels, and to store these fifteen — "

"To what use doth he think this powder shall be put?" Thomas yelled, banging the table so the salt cellar toppled and spilled white grains on the cloth.

Catesby laughed. "Thomas, for one who desires to creep into the belly of a Trojan Horse, thou dost make a poor Ulysses. *He* thought before he spoke. Do you doubt that I do the same, and have answers to your challenges? I have devised a counterfeit assault to mask our real one. Ambrose Rookwood thinks we buy powder to send to the English regiment at Flanders."

Fawkes smiled. "My old regiment! The soldiers who fight for the Duke of Parma and for King Philip. A good feint, Robin. It is not unlawful to collect weapons for this purpose. Since our peace with Spain, any Englishman may fight in that country's service against the Protestant Dutch."

Thomas sat down, absorbing all this. Robin and the Wintours smiled, but Thomas's frown remained. "Why, what a . . . ." Words failed him.

Understanding, Catesby came to his aid. "Aye, Thomas. What a farce it has been, for our rulers to have spent fifteen years aiding those Dutch Protestant rebels, aiming our own cannonballs not only at the Spanish but at the English among them who stood firm for the true Church, only to turn and make it lawful to join those true English, and kill the Dutch Protestants! It dishonors thine and the earl's service for the queen."

"This king hath no soul." Thomas's voice was hushed. "Wrong though she was, Elizabeth believed in her Protestant cause. But this king believes in nothing."

"And soon he will be nothing, made all naught, by a cleansing fire," Catesby said with satisfaction.

"It is so." Thomas's voice grew louder, exalted. "The best and holiest flame is a red and white mingled, like the red and white roses of England. The powder that makes the flame rise shall be sharp to the taste, and fair . . . ." He paused. He was still puzzled by the earl's instruction to this effect, since good powder was so clearly dark in color. Could dark be fair? No matter. "The earl once told me that the secret of the first exploding fire, Greek fire, was revealed by an angel to Constantine the Great, and that holy Joan of Arc praised black powder as an instrument of God's justice."

"Truly?" Amusement struggled with wonder in the men's faces.

Thomas rose again, more slowly than before. "Gentlemen, for the success of our great purpose, and that God may find us worthy of our high charge, let us pray."

As one, the other men rose, and all crossed themselves. Thomas knelt to lower his heavy body to the floor, but as the others bent their knees Fawkes suddenly said, "What was that?"

The group froze. From beneath the window came the crunch of footsteps retreating on frosty ground.

Bors Wintour and Robin Catesby ran to the casement and looked out. Fire logs lay scattered on the snow-coated grass under the window.

The back of a brown-capped man carrying some thin sticks of wood could be seen rounding the barn.

"'Tis my servant," said Catesby. "He tends the horses and the fires."

The men stared at one another, their prayer forgotten. Even Catesby, usually resolute, looked flummoxed.

"The window is shut," he said after a moment. "I know not what he can have heard today. He's a simple fellow, at any rate."

"I think we must send for him," said Bors Wintour. "He climbed on the woodpile to listen. He only picked up sticks to cover his action after it toppled, I am certain. If he fears he is discovered, he may run. Then there'll be no stopping his mouth."

Catesby left the room.

"What will we tell him?" Thomas asked nervously, thinking, *A wood-carrier is no gentleman.* Even Robert Keyes was a gentleman, though a minor one, and though he now posed as a servant well beneath his station. The same with Fawkes. But this one?

Jack Wintour shrugged. "We will sound him. Then we will know."

Catesby returned with a frightened-looking young man clad in a cloth cap and coat and rough woolen breeches. Robin sat the youth down. "Bates, you are in someone's pay," he said affably.

Young Bates shook his head violently. "Nay. Only yours, sir."

"Then why did you spy on us?"

The youth's face lay open. "Forgive me. I were only struck curious by all the comings and goings."

Thomas thought, *He hides nothing, or everything. He is either very stupid or very wise.*

Catesby looked shrewdly at Bates for a moment, then nodded. "I will believe thee. Tell me, why do you think we gather here?"

"I heard little. Only something about powder. And the name of King James."

"Speak true, man, and say all."

"Sirs, I heard talk of Westminster at the start."

"And what have you seen in the barn?"

"Black powder."

"What do you think it is for?"

The youth swallowed. "I . . . "

"Ba-aates? Tell the truth."

Swallowing, Bates said, "Sir, I think you may mean some harm at Westminster."

"And what do you think of that?"

The young man looked at the floor. "Marry, I think nothing. These are gentlemen's matters. I take no part in them. I wish no part."

"Do you value your employ?" Catesby's voice was thoughtful.

Bates had looked nervous. Now he looked terrified. "Yes, Sir Robert! And I hope I do good work."

"And so do we. We hope we do good work, and we *do* do good work. As for you, you may believe that what we do is in the service of God and His Church. We must trust your silence, sirrah. Can we do so?"

Bates crossed himself. "Aye, sir."

"Then go, and listen no more."

Bates left the room. The Wintours looked satisfied with the dialogue, but Thomas was frowning. "Are you sure of him, Robin?"

"He's a farmer's son from Wiltshire. He knows no one. And he values his place with me. There is naught to fear."

Reluctantly, Thomas nodded. As always, Catesby's shining eyes warmed his trust and fired his zeal. "Then we go on."

In the kitchen, servant Bates was kneeling, not to pray, but to stoke the cooking fire. He hoped he had done the sign of the cross well enough, never having been precisely taught it. He'd meant only to please his master, who sometimes brought a Roman priest to say masses in the house. He thought the men's conspiracy deep and dangerous and something Catholic.

It occurred to him that he might be a made man, did he report what he'd heard to someone great. But that thought was fleeting. For how could he know who was for or against these gentlemen? Bates had heard there were many in England who seemed good Protestant and were not so, who held secret masses in hidden rooms, like Catesby. The rumor ran that some of these could even be found in Parliament. Depending on what lord he spoke to, Bates might be rewarded, or might, on the other hand, find himself in some danger. Most likely in his ill speaking he'd be laughed at, and lose his place at Lambeth to boot, whatever his listener's religion. Protestant, Catholic, those words meant little to Bates. He was sure that in the end, all the gentlemen would hang together.

Chapter 21

G od was watching and blessing them.

Thomas was the best with the shovel. Catesby was good for only two hours a day before his body turned sore, numb, and all but useless. Jack Wright was in like case. Neither Catesby nor Wright was an indolent man. But the muscles exercised by horseback riding and quick bouts of swordplay, however frequently used, were not those required for this dull, steady pack-and-heave, pack-and-heave. Thomas too rode, often enough, but his back and arms were thick, and he showed an uncommon aptitude for the repetitive work.

Beneath the heart of London they labored, below the house of the absent Keeper of the Wardrobe in Westminster. They would come above stairs singly, an hour before dawn, each with a face smirched with the umber of the earth, looking — had torches been lit, and any been there to see them — like a demon arisen from hell, or an actor playing a devil or a Moor.

They worked deep in the city's fundament, which was well, because their work was fundamental. Catesby had pronounced this truth as they'd lit their lanterns on the first night. Here, down below, they would lay the groundwork of England redeemed. This could only be done by destroying the base of the counterfeit England, blasting the foundations of the false house. Strict husbandmen, they would delve to the evil's bad root and hack it away; burn it until it crumbled into ash and nothingness, like Northumberland's mercury snakes.

The labor was cold, wet, and tedious. Guido Fawkes would squint in the light of a lantern, scrabble with a pick, and dislodge the biggest stones. Then Thomas or Catesby or Jack Wright would shovel, and if a third man was present he would come behind the shoveler, sweep the loose earth into buckets, then toss the dirt up the angled passageway they'd made to the cellar floor. With every yard gained in the tunnel, one would scratch a tinderbox and hold up its light to Fawkes's leveling tool, to keep their track on the true. With every three yards gained, the men would stop to place the six-foot oak support beams and roofing pieces that "John Johnson" brought to the place piecemeal on a cart below bags of foodstuffs, all of it covered with a rough blanket. Fawkes made these deliveries during the busy morning in Parliament Place, when carters and suppliers with their barrels and wares were everywhere, their tracks crossing as they brought goods to this building or that. In the predawn the men swept, pushed, and tumbled the loose and piled dirt from the cellarage floor into barrels. They rolled these out to Guido's cart as quietly as they could, since the barrels were too heavy to lift. Then Guido drove to various woodsy spots on the Thames bank, where he dumped the dirt into the muddy river. Catesby or Wright would sneak back to Lambeth by an indirect route, and Thomas would stagger like a drunken man to his nearby rooms, brush and splash himself clean, and gain a few hours of sleep before reporting to the palace in his scarlet sleeves and silk galligaskins. At times, during the day, he dozed standing, his pike against a wall, his head propped against a doorframe.

The men worked wrapped in woolens, clad in thick leather gloves and boots to warm their feet against the creeping damp of the earth. Their hands grew blistered despite the gloves, and their toes turned numb so they had to stop and stamp, ever worried that in so doing they would shake the tunnel-roof loose. The first six feet of burrowing had broken the hardest ground, earth near frozen in December, and cost them a full week of nights stolen from sleep. Three feet down, the shoveling had gotten easier, but as they'd deepened the vertical shaft, moisture had started to creep in and wet their feet as they stood in the hole. The earth grew softer as the shaft grew deeper, but the damp was bone-harrowing, and the shovel-heave to the lip of the ditch got more difficult. Often the dirt would cascade back down onto the digger's head and need to be scooped up again in dim light. Once the shaft had taken a turn into the horizontal vault, they could dispense with the loose dirt more reliably by tossing it behind-hand for the sweeper, but tall Thomas's and Catesby's need to stoop while digging caused them excruciating discomfort. To make things worse, until Fawkes could place and secure the covering roof-slats, dirt continued to fall from above onto their heads, sliding down their collars to tickle and trouble their necks. These annoyances became less frequent once it occurred to them to scratch three crosses and the words *In Excelsis Deo* at each corner of every roof-piece. But still the occasional dirt-clod tumbled.

"We should have begun last summer," Thomas grumbled to Fawkes more than once, though the house had not been available for lease at that time, their plans were then ill-formed, and the thing would have been impossible. Besides, summer digging, too, would have brought its trials. The earth would have been softer, yes, but yielding earth was quicker to tumble and fill in tunneled spaces, which would then need to be shoveled out again. Now, they met several dazed earthworms and crawling beetles, struck out of dormancy by Fawkes's pick, but these would have been everywhere in July, crawling on their flesh. Fawkes reminded them of this, and of the fact that the traffic in the yard was thicker at night in summer than in winter, and their chance of discovery greater.

Even now, that chance was fearful enough. Though three, four, or even five of them worked at a time, Kit Wright joining when he could, still, so great was their fear of being heard overhead that little banter passed among them to relieve the monotony, and few jests. Now and then to relieve the tedium Fawkes would come forth with a whispered gibe against the Scotsmen he so hated. *How may the king disband a mob of Scottish rebels? Send a beggar among them to ask for alms.* But their laughter was nervous, stifled, and easily killed. Every close footfall, every rattling turn of a cartwheel in the yard outside the rented house made them freeze and stare upward, shovels in hand, as in a charcoal sketch Thomas had once seen, of colliers struck dumb by a vision of angels. As they moved farther into the vault the digger and the sweeper could no longer hear the world outside or anything but their own scraping and brushing. But sometimes the whistle would come from the man left wielding his bucket in the hole, and all of them would stop, suspending their work for five, ten, fifteen minutes or longer, until danger seemed to have passed. Over time they'd grown used to the carter who rolled loudly past the house each morning at three. One night Fawkes had stood above-ground, in the shadows of the entrance to Parliament Square, to observe this driver, and had come back to report that he was a pannier, delivering dressed fowl to an eating-house at the far side of the yard, across from the Palace of Westminster. He would not trouble them.

What would the men say if found? They knew no story of theirs — a need to expand the house's storage space? — would convince any curious guard come to call. Certainly not when it was known, as it shortly would be from their accents, that it was gentlemen who were soiling their hands and muddying their faces in an earth-dug hole. Their hope lay in their secrecy, and in their conviction that God knew and approved their purposes.

Catesby reminded Thomas of the proofs they had of God's blessing. Had He not allowed them easy access to powder? Had God not opened Ambrose Rookwood's heart to Catesby, leading Rookwood to make a generous gift of twice the amount of gold for which Catesby had asked, so zealous he'd been to aid English Catholics fighting for Spain in Flanders? No help came to those true English from the king, Rookwood had said, with such heat that Catesby felt sure his friend from Bury St. Edmunds would approve even more gladly the use to which his money had truly been put, once the great thing was accomplished.

This would be at the start of February. In February Parliament would meet. The king would reopen the august body of lawmakers, his royal family by his side wrapped in ermine and all wearing heavy crowns. It was now St. Lucy's Day, in mid-December. The powder brethren must be busy, devilishly busy. Angelically busy. They had little more than six weeks to dig through the twenty yards of earth that Fawkes figured yet lay between them and the bottom of the House of Lords. The men had already encountered one enormous stone, which had blocked their passage and required four feet of sideways turn in the tunnel. They must pray no new obstacle prevented them.

Indeed, Thomas prayed constantly as he worked, thinking of tiny Nicholas Owen, with his life spent crawling on his back or his stomach, carving holy spaces in safe houses for priests. *I am like Owen now*, he thought. He prayed for secrecy, and that Parliament might be postponed and allow them time to complete their work, some time to emerge from the night darkness, to sleep full hours, to journey homeward, even to go, perhaps, on pilgrimage, to plead with a saint for success. He prayed that little Prince Charles might be spared, kept home in his separate London residence on the Day of Judgment, so that Thomas, admissible in his Pensioner's silks, might enter the royal house, pick up the sleeping child, and gallop away with him, far to the north.

But mostly he prayed not to be buried alive.

"A big man walked in one night with a bundle of shovels wrapped in a sheet. I could see the shovel blades sticking out at the top. And John

Johnson comes and goes every day, driving barrels on a cart. One night I saw him peering at me from the shadows of the gate."

Cecil nodded. He sat with his elbows resting on the arms of his chair. He made a triangle with his thumbs and forefingers, and tapped his lips with its point. "And? Did he see you note him, master pannier?"

"Marry, that I know not. His face was in darkness, but I knew from his cap and his height it was he."

More lip-tapping. "Is there more?"

The pannier shifted his weight, pondering. "Nay. Naught out of the way."

"The big man you saw, with the shovels. What was his face like?"

"I know not. I saw his back only. He was muffled in wool from head to toe. I thought it were an odd thing, and since it concerned that house which you had spoken of—"

"Yes." Cecil rose and paced. "Thank you. There's pay for you, over there." He nodded at a small purse that lay on a silver plate by the closed door.

The man bowed, picked up the money, and walked to the door.

"Yet one more question."

The pannier turned and bowed again. "Yes, lord?"

"Have you found the name of the man who rents the house?"

"Aye, sir. I spoke to a baker who delivers bread to the place. Leaves it on the stoop, where he finds his coin. He says he understands the house to be leased to an Andrew Andrews."

Cecil made a small sound of disgust. "Andrew Andrews. Indeed! Go, then. I thank you."

When the door had closed behind the pannier, Cecil sat thoughtfully for a while. Then he opened his desk, pulled out a stiff sheet of parchment, and began to write a letter to his younger brother, a man officially titled Lord President of the North, whom he'd installed in Northumbria. "To Beloved Septimus," he began the missive. "I earnestly entreat you not to abate thy close watch on the castles of Nonus. In all obedience, at my request, Nonus has chosen his northern agent, one of his relations, for the assumption of knighthood and the office of Gentleman Pensioner. The selection enables close watch of this damnable family in the south, yet the watch yields reason to fear the stirring up of disloyal men in Northumbria, and perhaps elsewhere. Nonus has petitioned to spend three weeks at X Castle, and stays there now, as you know. Straightway report to me any communication arriving to Nonus there by southern post. Your loving brother, Primus."

He sealed the letter with candlewax, then sat and drummed his fingers on the table. Briefly, he brooded. He was not a prayerful man, but in the quiet of his study he now gave short thanks to God for the time he'd been given to solve this riddle, to play out line to those fish who he strongly suspected were guilty of something more than a petty, profit-bound scheme, some illegal stockpiling of goods, or local theft. No. These men were plotting some ill-doing against one or more of the lords of Parliament. Harm, perhaps, even to Cecil himself.

Now there was time. By king's messenger he'd received word this very night, two days before Christmas, that Parliament would again be postponed months past February for fear of lingering London plague, that disease so easily transmitted when many souls were close-packed together. The earl might stay busily happy in Alnwick Castle, the king frolic in his hunting grounds, until well into the new year. And the realm's lords would stay a far distance from Westminster Palace until summer's end, at least.

God was watching and blessing them all.

Chapter 22

"**O**ur prayers are answered! I have said it before and will say it again. Faith shines like gold in a furnace, and is rewarded." Catesby punctuated his praise with a slam of the door. "Up, Percy!"

Thomas, abed in his room in Gray's Inn Road, opened a groggy eye. Catesby was dancing, his face radiating light like a saint's in a Flemish painting.

"Has the king turned Catholic?" Both eyes open now, Thomas stared at Catesby as he capered.

"Ha! When hell freezes and Tottenham turns *French*, he will. No. But the opening of Parliament has been postponed until autumn. King and lords will not meet in full assembly until then. The king has bought himself close to a year. Corpsed he shall be still, but not before October, at the earliest. We've time to complete the vault!"

Thomas sat bolt upright. "Thanks be to an all-seeing God, who rewards our service!" With a callused hand he tossed off the counterpane. He rose and lumbered to the side of the room, where he cracked the casement window and urinated into the alley below.

"Clothe thee, Thomas! The room is chill!"

"Wilt light the fire?" Turning, Thomas fumbled for his strossers, then for his knights' livery, which lay piled in an untidy heap on the floor. His duty was to stand guard at Whitehall this Christmas Day.

"The merry king will stay with us only through Twelfth Night. And then he'll go north, a-hunting!" Catesby said with satisfaction. He sat on the bed. "Where is thy servant?"

"I keep none." Thomas pulled on his leggings.

"Most evident." Catesby wrinkled his nose, surveying the clutter on the floor. "*Foh!* The place smells of decay."

"Surely that is the remains of the fish Guido and I supped on here last Friday." Thomas adjusted his strossers.

"Dost not know to cast out thy scraps?"

"I go about blear-eyed, thinking only of dirt and shovels. I see nothing but the bed when I come here."

Catesby smiled, and bent to light a fire in the grate with a spark from his tinderbox. Then he lit his pipe. "Come, then, Thomas, tonight we'll not delve. 'Tis Christmas Day. My pipe-smoke will sweeten the air —"

"Ack."

"— and when this bowlful is mere smoke and ash, we'll to your post at Whitehall and watch the revels. The King's Men will play for our wretched Scottish sovereign today, and we are welcome at court."

Thomas snorted, tying on his sleeves. "*You* are not. You fell four years ago along with Essex's star. Methinks you are reckless e'en to show thy face at a public *play*house, to say nothing of —"

"Ah, but like any anonymous gentleman in the company of a Gentleman Pensioner, I may visit the palace for Christmas Revels. Do I not walk with a Percy?"

Thomas beamed. He knelt, broke the ice in a porcelain bowl that sat by the bed — the room lacked a table — and splashed his face with the frigid water. Then he wiped his teeth with a soaped rag, and spat, and combed his hair and beard until Catesby approved the sight of him. The pair went below stairs and out the door and set off on foot for the palace.

Revels were in full course at Whitehall. So festive was the mood in the great hall that even the guards on duty were sipping wassail and wine and sampling foods from the long tables that lined the walls. The choices seemed infinite. To the left, rabbit stuffed with hazelnut dressing, a five-foot sturgeon topped with jellied pike, and ranks and rows of prawns sauced with wine, cinnamon, pepper; cloves too, by the scent of it. Near these delicacies were stretched large herons and egrets, roasted with their skins whole, and propped, wings spread, to look alive. Then came partridges and curlews and an even larger though unidentifiable baked bird. On the right side of the room a second table groaned under sweatmeats: baked custard coffins, cakes drenched with honey, pies filled with dried fruits and almond sugar, marchpane, and, last, an enormous pastry swan. Thomas was stunned by the richness of the Christmas offerings. Suddenly ravenous, he moved to take a morsel of the largest fowl. It tasted of woodsmoke.

"What is't?" he asked a gentleman who was also sampling meat from the wing.

"Golden eagle, from the Scottish border. This king's master cook can bake any bird. Ah, you have spit on my sleeve, sir!"

"Pardon." Thomas wiped his mouth and moved back from the table, assuming a post by the door. Nauseated, feeling like a cannibal, he took a deep breath to steady his stomach.

Robin was already deep in the crowd of revelers. He had been straightway recognized by many, most quickly by Cecil, who stood in the shadow of the throne, following Catesby with his eyes. Here and there the Catesby went, back and forth, darting gracefully.

Lord Cecil noted with interest the frequent exchanges between Catesby and the Pensioner Thomas Percy, who stood guard by the largest entryway. Were they particular friends? Dark and light, stolid and graceful, the looks and manners of Percy and Catesby could hardly have differed more. Both men were of a height, but Percy was dark, with a wide face and a salt-and-peppery beard. He stood stiff, paw on his pike like a trained bear, constantly eyeing the company as though they dazzled him. Like those of many others, his eyes seemed especially drawn to King James, who sat laughing in shining white ermine on the central dais, flanked by his sons, the handsome Prince Henry and the frail little Charles. Though three, Charles was only beginning to toddle about. He fell frequently, and was raised up by spare gentlemen of the household who tried to wrap him in furs and keep him still. But always he struggled free. Thomas solemnly watched the royal group, and Cecil continued to watch Thomas, the big guard, so resplendent in formal livery which, for all it fit him snugly, did not hang quite right.

Unlike dark Thomas, light-haired Robert Catesby was paying little mind to the king. He glided about the room artfully, mercurially, in his silks, lace collar, and peaked fur hat. His blue eyes gleamed and his ringed hands flew as he exchanged words with this lord, or that lady. Remarkable, Cecil thought, how the men were opposites and yet a pair; twinned or, rather, complementary in their movements. Thomas bulked and towered like the foot of a compass, standing still by the door and only leaning, occasionally and slightly, to see, it appeared, where little Charles was running, or where Catesby had gone. Catesby moved like the other foot, ranging far afield, circling, turning, then returning to Percy, his starting point. Closing the arms of the compass.

Though Catesby came back always to Percy, Cecil's eyes returned always to Catesby. The man made his ears prick up for danger. Cecil knew well the history of this old friend of Essex. So he continued to watch closely as the golden young man danced the second coranto with Lady Percy, the Earl of Northumberland's wife, who was merrily resident in London though — or because — her husband currently lay in the north.

Thus Cecil missed the small, innocent gesture Thomas Percy made to little Prince Charles as the baby toddled close to the doorframe where the big man stood guard. Percy suddenly knelt with a smile, reached into his silks, and handed something to the wide-eyed little boy.

It was the rosary given Thomas by Father Quindle over a year before at Baddesley Clinton. The boy laughed and clutched at the pretty beads, which Thomas helped him tuck into a breech pocket. Then a satin-clad nursemaid emerged from the throng in nervous pursuit of her charge. Thomas smilingly raised him and handed him over.

The centerpiece of these Christmas revels was a comedy performed by the King's Men, watched by all but Cecil, who was busy watching its watchers. Thomas Percy proved eager, at the play's conclusion, briefly to abandon his post and waylay one of the players as, after their bow and dance, they all moved toward makeshift tiring rooms off the grand hall. "Is thy poet present?" Thomas asked him.

The actor looked puzzled. "My po — ah, our playwright? Nay, sir." The powder-faced fellow looked warily at Thomas. "Our playwright had the king's leave to journey north to the midlands this Christmas."

"Ah." Thomas's face fell. "To where?"

"Stratford-upon-Avon, sir, and...." The player bowed deeply — mockingly? — and concluded, "A blessed holiday to you, sir."

Percy was vexed at the poet's absence. Back in Gray's Inn Road that evening, he lay on his bed, thinking what a rare opportunity a chance Christmas meeting would have given him to sound that man's leanings. Yet, no matter. He would find him, on another occasion. And then! To begin with some words of flattery touching this day's play, which treated so broadly of a subject close to Percy's heart, that of pilgrimage. The play had featured a young woman — a boy actor, of course, in woman's clothes, but convincing, compelling — disguised as a palmer undertaking a holy journey to the most sacred site in Europe, the cathedral of St. James, Santiago de Compostela, St. Jaques le Grand!

The writer should know his meaning had not been lost on the faithful among his hearers. How would their dialogue go? Thomas pondered, hands behind head, staring at the darkening ceiling.

First he, approaching, would reveal himself as a Percy, giving a meaningful intonation to the name. Then, "Thou hast written most touchingly of holy pilgrimage," he would say. These — the self-revelation and the deft remark about holy Catholic journeyings — could uncover much, jewels perhaps to be dug out of the playwright at a supper in Lambeth, to which the man should be invited. What wonders were hidden in him? Like Thomas Percy, the poet posed as a king's man, was a man patronized by the monarch, a man who wore king's livery on ceremonial occasions and had access to the palace when the king was in residence. Where might this lead? Better than Thomas, the man had the ear of Londoners who paid to hear his golden words. Had not Thomas, Catesby, the Wrights, the Wintours — yes, now, even the caretaker Robert Keyes and rich young Ambrose Rookwood and the soldier-come-home-again Guido Fawkes — had not all of them been to the Globe again and again, and been transported by this man's high verse? Had they not been inspired to the audacious feat they now undertook? The man was their muse, and what remained was only that he should know that he was.

In the slow-burning forge of Thomas's thought, known facts, observations, and dreams softened and fused like molten metal. All things adhered. He felt happy. Desire, purpose, and reason were one, and nothing could balk the full prospect of his hopes.

He drifted into a half-dream. Drowsily, he recalled a jest made by Catesby today as, giddy with wine, the golden-haired lord had departed the palace with him, squeezing his arm before walking riverward alone for a boat to Lambeth. "What are the three parts of powder?" Robin had said, mixing blasphemy with reverence. "Anger. Nostalgia. Love. And the greatest of these is love." And was it not so, for all Robin's smiling? The path to England's redemption would be bloody horror, but the end, Thomas knew, would be love.

And the poet?

He sat up suddenly. The deep thought surfaced. A poet, practicing his craft, could *help* the English understand them, the powder brethren; and history's hard necessity. If, indeed, after the stunning event, help were needed. And as Thomas's drunk settled into sobriety, he conceded that it probably would be. For all to end well.

Chapter 23

March 25, 1605. Lady Day.

Plump, rose-cheeked Eliza Vaux sat staring balefully at the letter. She had read it three times, and was still only starting to grasp its import for her son. *If your family seeks this match in earnest, Edward might reflect on his prospects at court, and how they might best be advantaged. It is our duty to guide our daughter Elizabeth's choice, and with things as they are we must needs incline toward her betrothal with Lord Knollys.* The letter was signed by Catherine, the wife of the earl of Suffolk, one of the more prominent members of the great Howard family. Like her husband, Catherine Howard was rumored to be a secret papist, but when in London she could be found every Sunday in a fine pew in St. Paul's, listening dutifully to Bishop Jewel's homilies concerning the depravity of the Roman church.

So Eliza had heard.

She folded the paper carefully and stowed it in her bodice. Lord Knollys was fifty-seven. The news of this match, she knew, would break the heart of her son, who was so much in love with seventeen-year-old Bess Howard that he'd thrice ridden fourteen miles to one of her family's manors to sing madrigals under her window. So he'd confessed, when Eliza had found him at dawn one day, muddied, exalted, and climbing the trellis to his own chamber on the second floor of Harrowden. Young Edward, Fourth Baron Vaux of Harrowden, was a passionate youth, devout and single-minded in all his affections. His heart would not easily turn to another young lady. But neither would it cast off a long-held faith to curry favor with an ingrate king and sit in a pew in St. Paul's — no, not even to sit with his true love and, one day, their children beside him. Yes, he loved a Howard. But it was not in him to be as trifling as a Howard. This, Eliza knew.

On the stairs, Eliza steadied herself and rubbed her eyes with the heels of her hands. This would not be easy.

An hour later, she softly closed the door outside her son's chamber and stood a moment in the rush-strewn hallway. She'd left him with the letter crumpled in his hand, sitting listlessly at the window, exhausted and embarrassed by his own tears. "I am too spent to pray," he'd said, when his mother suggested they kneel.

Eliza was not spent, though she found that she, too, was not inclined to kneel at this moment. She fairly glowed with the rush of angry blood to her limbs, and moved down the passage with vigor. Her face was dry. She would not loose a tear for this king's severing of families and breaking of hearts, any more than she'd weep for the last priest lately disemboweled in Paul's Yard to the cheers of a thousand raucous, bloodthirsty spectators. Any one of those holy victims might have been Father Garnet or Father Quindle. But tears did no good. And as for prayers . . . . Perhaps, at this moment, God required some more active service from his faithful flock than prayers.

Early the next morning Eliza ordered her horse saddled. She rode the long day's journey through a biting March wind to Rushton Hall, the estate of her and Robin Catesby's cousin, Francis Tresham. This opulent manor had often been mocked by the very family to which she'd wished to join her Edward, namely the Howards, who called the place a "triangular folly" because of its shape. The devoutly Catholic and recently deceased Tresham patriarch had made sure that in his home triangles were everywhere visible, and in keeping with his whim the doors, windows, and gables had each been fashioned in some wise to signify the Holy Trinity. Privately Eliza thought the Howards' laughter at the triangles of Rushton Hall quite justified, but today, no matter. This was not a time to jest about Tresham mysticism. She was coming instead to argue her bond with the Treshams. She was coming to see Francis.

Though Francis had hidden his religion since his punishment for the Essex affair four years before, Eliza knew he had stayed closely tied to their mutual and confederate cousin, Robert Catesby. All northern recusants were stubborn. Francis was not like his sister's husband, William Lord Monteagle. Yes, Monteagle had ridden in the street waving a sword on Essex's day, and not for the glory of the queen. But everyone knew that afterward, when taken, he had literally kissed old Queen Elizabeth's foot, all the while repudiating his Catholic sympathies in a most igno-minious access of self-abasement and spiritual treachery. Monotonous persistence in this line had gained him the right to sit in the House of Lords, while his worthier brother-in-law Francis mouldered in the north.

Or didn't moulder, quite. Of late Francis Tresham, shaking off his country dust, had begun to make frequent visits to London, for purposes Eliza could only guess at. She would now discover whether these visits meant what she thought they meant.

She had something to barter for the knowledge.

Two hours after her surprising arrival at Rushton Hall, Eliza sat closeted with her cousin. Francis sat stiffly, regarding her with suspicion and some fear.

"Yes, I had heard of the Howards' decision to reject Edward's suit, Eliza," he said cautiously. He spread his hands. "I am sorry. But believe me, I can do nothing in this matter. The Howards have had naught to do with me since James took the throne and restored them to high favor." A look of scorn crossed his face. "'*I love the whole house of them!*' the king said." He laughed shortly. "And they have all been quick to repeat that saying widely. Well, the king has no love for *my* house. We have been far too Catholic for far too long. Too Catholic for the Howards themselves, now."

"Yes. I know it." Eliza's tone was bitter.

"I *am* sorry, cousin. Your Tresham tie is a bane to your son. I can do naught, and there's no profit in speaking of it. But . . . ." Francis leaned for-ward. "Eliza, if it's Father Quindle's whereabouts you seek to know, I can tell you that he is presently in —"

"I know where Father Quindle is, better than thou dost. He has removed to a safe-house in Sussex, and I helped him get away. What are the effects of ash on winter hay?"

Francis blinked. He stared at Eliza's smoldering eyes. A candle on the three-sided table behind them cast a halo around her bright, coiffed hair. "What can you mean?" he asked nervously. "Winter *hay*? How should I know this?"

"A remark concerning the effects of ash on winter hay was made by Thomas Percy, in a scornful voice, to many rapt men at table in my garden at Harrowden last summer, the day the pursuivants came and

Father Quindle minced off like a fop with my pendant swinging from his ear."

"Ah, this!" Tresham laughed a little uneasily. "*That* was nearly a day of reckoning, that was — "

"Perchance you will tell me the meaning of Thomas Percy's words. They were said loudly enough to be heard in the house upstairs. It was hot. The window was open. Percy made his scoffing jest about ash and hay, and then he said most firmly to our cousin Catesby, 'It is no sin.' What is no sin, Francis?" Eliza leaned her stout body forward and hooked her cousin's eye with hers. "*What* is no sin?"

Francis shifted in his velvet-covered chair. He looked at the lush Turkey carpet that hung on the wall. Though an infidel's handiwork, the rug was yet patterned with mystical interlocking triangles. So God's mysteries were made manifest even in the works of the pagans.

"Do *not* go into a trance, Francis. I have asked you a question."

Francis cleared his throat. "Eliza, I cannot recall the . . . . We were meeting for a mass, as I think, and speaking of the troubles of the faithful in — "

"What is afoot in London?" Eliza shook her head impatiently. "Where do you go every month, stopping at my house on the way? Your story of wool market business is a foolish one."

Francis's mouth worked like a fish's, but no sound came out.

With a cry of disgust, Eliza rose. She began to pace the room, wringing her hands with agitation. The low heels of her slippers made little clicks on the floorboards, and two gold pins in her hair, catching the light of the wall-mounted candles, seemed to shoot angry sparks. "With my sister Anne Vaux, I make places for priests," she said in a tight voice. "There are days when Anne is so troubled with her ailments she can barely rise from bed to direct her servants, to show how the men must be fed and clothed, and where hidden. We harbor those priests, as well as you who come to be blessed by their hands. We offer our manors for masses. We employ carpenters to make houses safe. Do you wish this to continue? Do you wish to use our houses for your meetings and masses?"

"*Our* masses, cousin."

She turned to face him, her hands clasped before her breast. "If they are ours, then share with me — "

"Hark." Francis rose as abruptly as Eliza had, and approached her. He was a burly and compact man, an inch shorter than she, so she found herself looking down into his eyes as he covered her knotted hands with his own — thick-fingered, the Tresham signet adorning the left — and gripped them tightly. "Out of my regard for thee, I will tell thee this much. We plan a thing which the faithful will applaud. We work in London to put an end to tyranny. Even now there are . . . *inroads* being made — "

"*What* inroads? By the name of the mother of God, I conjure you, *how* is this work proceeding?"

"I cannot — "

"Ah, but I say, good cousin, that you *can.*"

As Father Quindle's longtime patron, Eliza was well practiced in wheedling to obtain gifts from the Catholic gentry of England. Money for carpentry, since fresh hiding places were always needed; provisions, clothing, and silver for priestly travel; safe havens for Father Quindle and his brethren. Over the years she had polished her persuasiveness to a sparkling art. And in the end, Francis told her what she wanted to know.

"I yet hope things may not come to this pass," Francis concluded softly, with something like shame. "Before then, James may — "

Eliza made a wordless sound of contempt, this time for the king. Francis fell silent.

They had reseated themselves. For a minute the cousins looked without speaking at one another, quiet and still in the richly appointed room. The chamber was ghostly in the long light of the low-burning candles in the three tripartite candelabras.

Daunted by Eliza's lengthening silence, Francis Tresham began to sweat. What he had revealed was not a tale of persuasion, or of long-suffering patience, or of prayer. He could not guess how a gentlewoman would be taking it.

At length Eliza spoke, softly, as though to herself. "The holy martyr Father Campion's entrails were drawn out before his eyes."

Francis drew in his breath. "They were. And our king has renewed the persecutions."

She shook her head. "James is not my king. My king is in heaven."

"Then God knows that they . . . ." He coughed. "That we shed blood to end bloodshed."

Eliza nodded. "All's well that ends well. God steel your hearts to the purpose." She rose to leave the room. But she turned at the door. "Thank you, Francis. Now I may sleep."

But she did not sleep, right away. Above, settled in a shadowy bed-chamber, Eliza sat on a three-legged chair whose carved triangular back ended in a sharp point behind her head. She put pen to paper, construct-ing a letter to a Catholic friend in London who had lately asked how sped the match between Eliza's son and Elizabeth Howard.

"Our plans may yet bring fruit," Eliza wrote. "Fast and pray. Those of the faithful who wait may soon see such a miracle that—" She paused, tapping her quill to her lips, seeking a conceit that was sufficiently vague, but that a Catholic might well understand. "We shall see Totten-ham turned French," she wrote, and sealed the letter.

Below her, in his private room, Francis Tresham rested his short legs on a fabric-covered settle and brooded over his cousin's last words. *God steel your hearts.*

At Tresham's last meeting with the powder brethren in London, Catesby had spoken unflinchingly of the necessary damage the tunnel-ers would wreak not only on the king, not only on the treacherous lords in Parliament, but on the king's wife and her eleven-year-old son, Prince Henry. Francis was not a father yet, but had lately come into his estate, and was newly married. He had a wife he loved. He wished there was a way this terrible plan might spare the king's woman—that she could be warned to keep her distance from Parliament—but such a warning was unthinkable. Other Catholics, even peers of the realm, might be cau-tioned, those known for their Catholic loyalty and zeal. But the spouse of the targeted king, the mother of the doomed heir, could not keep their secret unless she were kidnapped, and that would be a complicated undertaking indeed. On this the men had agreed, and reluctantly Fran-cis had conceded that, if she were present on the day of judgment, Queen Anna must also be sacrificed.

The coming catastrophe hardly bore thinking of. Francis had never seen the effects of a large-scale powder detonation, but Guido Fawkes had, and had coldly described these to the whole group of them, while Thomas Percy had sat nodding, cold-faced and mute. When the holy fire rained down on London, Tresham knew he would be far from the ground of impact, rallying Catholic countrymen in the north. But now, and per-haps then as well, his mind would not easily shed the images Fawkes's words had raised, of splintering roofs and stones tumbling on horses and men, of teeth and bones and body parts flying in air. There were rich pas-sages in the Old Testament which Francis might have cited to justify shedding the blood of the innocent to redeem the holy. Every Protestant knew them. But Tresham wasn't a Protestant, and knew little of his Latin Bible beyond the Paternoster. The priests knew more, of course, but neither Father Quindle nor Father Garnet was now resident at Rushton Hall to share his knowledge of scripture. God knew, in any case, what those gentle men would think of the intended massacre, of which they'd not yet been forewarned. Catesby had wanted to seek Garnet's spiritual counsel, but had thus far been overruled by the other men, who held that the knowledge of the coming vengeance must be kept closed in the breasts of men steeled to the purpose.

And the breast, now, of one woman.

"God steal our hearts," Tresham whispered, as the candle flickered. Without noticing, in his mind he had changed the spelling of the verb.

Chapter 24

"Have a care," Guido Fawkes whispered urgently. "There is water seeping here."

"I cannot stop the water," Thomas snapped. "There is no other place to dig but where I am digging."

He was alone with Fawkes in the vault, and in worsening temper. Early in this Lenten season, he'd returned to the north, and been frustrated both going and coming, in his passage through the midlands. He'd made a shift to seek the poet, the powder-brethren's muse, at the man's fine Stratford home, but was told both times by a maidservant that despite the season and the closing of the theaters for the holy days, the fellow was again in London. Having returned to London, Thomas had sought him in his residence on Silver Street, only to be told he had gone back to Stratford for Eastertide. The whole thing seemed a jest at Thomas's expense. He was beginning to wonder whether the man existed at all.

To make things worse, just when the tunnelers had burrowed nearly sixty feet in a horizontal track under the Westminster earth, and seemed in reach of their goal, they'd encountered a second wall, thicker than the first. And this wall had proved impenetrable. It was the remains of an old foundation. Fawkes thought it part of the cellar of an old mews. They'd had to guess in which direction it ended quickest, and strike out that way, hoping the wall would not present an absolute obstacle to the base of Westminster Palace. Eight feet to the left the wall had petered out, and with relief they'd angled their tunnel back toward its original path. But the new earth was wet. Fawkes was worried.

"We must move to the *right*." Fawkes swung the lantern in that direction.

"I *am* moving to the right."

"Dig at a sharper angle. This soil is moist from underground streams that feed the Thames."

"I *cannot* dig at a sharper angle. There's a piece of the foundation still." Ankle-deep in brown water, Percy dug his shovel forcefully into the earth-wall at his left, saying, "I must delve *here* — "

A gush cascaded over his shoulders, instantly turning the earth before him into mud. Within seconds the water in the tunnel was midway to the men's knees and visibly rising. Guido and Thomas dropped lantern and shovel. Splashing water, they turned and ran.

"So it is destroyed."

Thomas sat at Robin Catesby's table in Lambeth with his head in his hands. He could not speak. Cool Guido sat in his customary corner, smoking a pipe. "So it doth seem," he said. "No more tunneling there without drowning in mud."

"Well." Catesby gazed at the wan faces of his companions. The usual litter of plates and glasses and crumbs and bones lay on the cloth before him, but there was more flesh on the bones than usual. The men lacked appetite this evening.

Nine were present. The Wintour and Wright brothers and the Lambeth caretaker Robert Keyes sat on the long benches that ran down either side of the table. At the end of one bench sat John Grant, the wealthy Warwickshire farmer who was brother-in-law to the Wintours. Grant had come south with his relatives as the newest member of the group. He was the only one of the band who was cheerfully eating.

"Well," said Catesby again.

"Well, indeed," said Fawkes wryly from the corner. "That's what it is, now."

Catesby laughed. Kit Wright and Bors Wintour managed humorless grunts.

Robin propped his elbows on the cloth and scrutinized the careful drawings of Parliament Square that Fawkes had once more patiently set forth. The young servant Bates silently circled the table. He was one of them now. Catesby had raised Bates from the low status of kitchen bottle-scourer and stable hand, and he was now pouring wine.

"We have, at worst, four months." Catesby tapped the broadsheet with a silver spoon. "Forget the other hole. We might start again, over here."

A muffled groan came from Thomas. The men shifted position. All looked dispirited, save three: Fawkes, who was now calmly blowing smoke-rings into the spring air beyond the open casement; the newcomer John Grant, whose brow furrowed with interest as he leaned forward, a sweetmeat in hand, to stare at Fawkes's drawings; and Catesby, whose blue eyes scanned the room with their usual fire.

"Shall we abandon our high design?" Catesby challenged them all. "Does God not put trials forth to test the faithful?"

Bors Wintour cleared his throat. "Our faith does not flag, nor our purpose. Yet think. A tunnel made under *that* section of the yard must be dug in broad daylight."

"Or by night, costumed as —"

"Madness, Robin Catesby! To dig in the unroofed square, with guards on the watch?"

Robin's eyes gleamed. "May not God blind the eyes of the unholy?"

Even Thomas lifted his head to stare incredulously at Catesby.

The silence in the room held for some seconds. Then John Grant said in a practical tone, "What lies directly under the meeting room of the House of Lords?" He tapped the place on the map.

"A cellar." Fawkes's voice came again from the corner. "A storage vault."

Grant leaned back on his bench and looked inquiringly at Catesby. "Why do you not rent that place?"

"Rent . . . ."

"The lowest floor of the building. The storage vault. Property is always leasable, for a price. You've money enow with what Ambrose Rookwood has given you, and then, no more digging required. The cellar exists. Roll powder into the place in barrels — flour barrels, or what you will — cover them up with something, and leave them til we're ready to use them. We will bring our fire that much closer to the king."

All the men were standing now and peering at the map. "*This* would be daring," said Catesby excitedly.

Grant shrugged, taking another bite of sweet. "No more daring than sloshing through a subterranean tunnel," he said through his mouthful. "Our John Johnson" — he gestured at Fawkes — "may be caretaker of the powder. No doubt the denizens of the yard are well accustomed to his beauteous face and flowing red hair."

Fawkes laughed. "Catesby, you are a prophet whom we all honor. Ah, but John Grant! John Grant is a midlands farmer."

Grant shrugged, still munching.

"Indeed." Catesby grinned widely, and raised his wineglass in a toast to Grant. "Would you had longer been party to our plans!"

Grant shook his head in self-deprecation. "Well —"

"*No* more wells," Fawkes laughed. "All's not well that ends as a well."

"*Well* said," jested Catesby.

Good humored groans came from all sides, amid smiles and raised glasses, but Percy was silent and still among the men. He knew Grant had redeemed their plan, and was grateful. But he felt lingering shame that he, Thomas Percy, had caused the day's disaster, and his feet were still damp.

Chapter 25

Each night Father Garnet quailed at the sound of footfalls on Thames Street. The London lane was too narrow for cart traffic, but people frequently passed through it at a walk, stepping below his window on their ways to the river. He steeled himself not to glance out. Once, his will failing, he had done so, and had shuddered at the sight of the gray bulk of the Tower. The prison stood off in the distance, but was a little too close all the same. He loathed the look of it. So he would wait, only half-involved in his prayers, not breathing easily until this or that set of footsteps had rounded a corner and faded from hearing.

The house was owned by an absent friend, and he'd been directed to it by the person he trusted most on earth, Anne Vaux. He'd come to London to minister to a small body of Catholics in the Strand. And he would celebrate mass for a larger group on Corpus Christi Day, the sixteenth of June. He was here as he was everywhere, to good purpose, in the service of God. But he hated the city, was weary of travel, and missed the greenery of Baddesley Clinton. He'd not sojourned there for several months now.

And the house on Thames Street held no hiding places.

That truth sent him into a near panic on his third night there, two days before Corpus Christi, when the footfalls did not fade around the corner but stopped below his window, and were followed by a rap on the front door. He heard the door's latch drawn and the top of it opened, and an interchange between the woman who kept the house and two men standing outside in the lane, though he could not hear what the men said. As quietly as he could, he walked to the bed, lifted the mattress, and flattened himself against the bedframe. He pulled the mattress over him. Sounds from outside the room were barely audible to him as he lay near-smothered, but he could still just hear. *No, no . . . .* The woman should have sent them away, but she hadn't! Or else they'd pushed past her, because now two sets of feet were coming up the stairway. The wall next to his shoulder vibrated. And now, very now, the feet were in his room, treading the floorboards. *Fool!* he chided himself, his heart beating loud in his ears. He'd forgotten to blow out the candle.

"Father Garnet!" The voice was a hushed whisper, but he knew it instantly, and his heart slowed with relief. Robin Catesby. "I am here with Father Quindle," Catesby said. "We can plainly see you, you know."

Sheepishly, Garnet helped them lift the mattress from his body. "I had no word of your coming."

"We thought it best not to send." Delicately, Catesby brushed from Garnet's shoulder some straw that had escaped from his bedding. "A foul bed, this."

"I much prefer the feathers of Rushton Hall and Baddesley Clinton." Garnet's voice was light with relief. He wiped sweat from his brow with the back of his hand. "But for this servant, straw will serve. Is there danger?"

"Always there is danger, sir!" Robin seemed to shimmer with light, *energia* made visible. He sat down at Garnet's table and pushed aside the Catholic Bible, printed in France and smuggled from Antwerp, which Garnet had been reading. In its place he set a bottle of Rhenish, which he swiftly uncorked. "I spoke to thy woman. She will bring us goblets."

Garnet glanced sideways at Father Quindle and said in dismay, "She is a married Catholic servant!" The suggestion that he might be disloyal to his Christ! An adulterer! But Quindle only raised his eyebrows humorously.

"Laugh, then, brother," Henry muttered.

"And I will." Quindle patted his fellow priest's shoulder. With God's help, Quindle had long ago mastered his own erotic inclinations, fasting and praying during his years of imprisonment in the Tower (which he, too, thought too close to this house). In his half-cape and bonnet Quindle looked the most trivial of court butterflies, but his soul was charged with iron. "What a Puritan you are, priest!" he jested now, pinching Garnet's arm until Garnet half-smiled.

"Of course I know she's not your mistress." Catesby, who'd sprung up to draw a curtain, sounded impatient. "And she knew me. She'd seen me at a mass."

Garnet bent his head in sudden, private prayer—a habit of his—while Quindle looked at Robin's gold-bearded face in thoughtful puzzlement. Catesby had been a man of family. He was father to a son who was now the ward of a prominent recusant and his wife, good friends to Robin. Wifeless for years now, Catesby was unshackled by priestly vows, but had by all accounts lived like a monk since the Essex uprising. More than a few of his many followers, his fervent admirers, were women whose motives seemed, to Quindle, a mixture of the pious and the carnal. Though his purse was light, Robin could have remarried, or, despite the sin (for the flesh was the flesh), he could have taken a mistress. He hadn't. "Families? Suffering compounded," he'd said cryptically, when Quindle had once questioned him on the matter. "And a woman *will* know your secrets. A man possessed of a vision does better alone."

Possessed of, or possessed by? Quindle had almost replied. What prophet's zeal owned Robin Catesby, body and soul? Both priests feared Catesby's visions, though at times, in Father Garnet, they provoked the sin of envy.

The servant entered with an armful, three goblets and two stools. Mutely she set down her freight, then departed, closing the door softly behind her. Garnet crossed to the table and poured cheer for his guests. "Is there particular danger, Robin? Why have you sought me here?"

"For spiritual counsel."

The two priests seated themselves. "Do you wish the sacrament of confession?" Garnet asked Catesby.

"Confession? Not now. I seek not penance for wrongdoing, but direction for right doing. You know that war persists in Flanders, and that English Catholics now fight openly there on the side of the Spanish."

Garnet nodded.

"The Lowlands are an amphibious place of betwixt and between. All things are mixed there. The land is like water, the English mingle with Spaniards, and—" Catesby paused and leaned forward in his enthusiasm — "swordfighting accompanies powder explosions which by their nature slay the innocent along with the guilty. It is not unknown for women and children to perish when forts and city walls are destroyed. Yet these forts are blasted in the service of a just war against the rebellion of Protestant rogues. How, Father Garnet, does God make this conundrum good?"

"Ah." Garnet nodded. "I have heard of thy plan to send munitions to soldiers in Flanders."

"You *have?*" Catesby frowned.

Garnet bit his lip. He had lately served as confessor to the gentleman Ambrose Rookwood, who had spoken of his suppliance of powder to Catesby for this purpose. Though such schemes were not unusual among Catholic gentry, only Rookwood had specifically tied Catesby to such an enterprise. But the seal of confession must not be broken. Garnet equivocated. "I . . . hear some talk among gentry of assisting the English there. And I know some who have gone there to fight, or give gold. I thought your involvement likely." This was all true, Rookwood or no Rookwood.

"Well, and why should English Catholics not go to Flanders? Why should they not assist brother Catholics?" Catesby's handsome face was defiant. "Father Quindle is of the opinion that the war is just."

"What is your question, Robin?"

"I wish to know what you think of the justice of powder."

"Of powder?"

"It was my word."

Garnet wrinkled his nose. "In and of itself it is an inert substance, incapable of good or evil."

"What think you, then, of powder put to the use I have described?"

Garnet thought for a moment. "Often," he said, measuring his words, "the innocent are punished in war. This is an evil that shows the corruption of the world in general, yet one which cannot be laid at the door of the perpetrators — "

"Meaning the evil cannot be blamed on the artillers and engineers."

"Yes. It cannot, if two conditions apply. First, the assault must in itself be indisputably just. It must be no heedless butchery, but a necessary action to punish evil and redeem good."

"Ah." Catesby's eyes were shining unnaturally. Father Quindle regarded him with dismay. Garnet too felt uncomfortable. Despite his hidden passion for Christ, he was a reasoning priest, and excess of visible zeal disturbed him.

He cleared his throat and continued methodically. "Second, the deaths of the innocent must not be intended, but a simple byproduct of the deaths of the guilty."

Catesby frowned slightly, pondering. After a moment he said, "This may work. This may do well. I shall think on it."

"*What* may work? What are you thinking on?" Merriment had fled. Quindle's voice was quiet and tight.

Catesby looked from Quindle to Garnet and back again, and said nothing. Then he spoke. "If you are caught in this room, Father Garnet, you will be taken there." He gestured with his head. Then he rose, went to the window, and pointed in the direction of the Tower. "There. Father Quindle has been there."

"Yes." Quindle looked soberly at him. "I would not stay long there if caught a second time. They would swiftly execute me."

"Drawing. Quartering. Entrails extracted. Perhaps you could look at your beating Catholic heart before you died."

Father Garnet rose abruptly and angrily. "We know all this. Why be cruel? Do you think to frighten us with images?"

"No." Catesby came swiftly to Garnet's side and knelt, his face suddenly suffused with love and gratitude. He took Henry's hand. "I want only to say that this . . . ." With his left hand he made a sweeping gesture that encompassed the small, bare room, the dislodged mattress hanging half off its bedframe, and the Tower beyond. "All this cannot much longer be borne."

Garnet took his hand away. "It is for God to say how long suffering must be borne."

"But how does God speak?" Robin rose. "He may speak through soldiers, may he not?"

Garnet didn't answer. He reseated himself beside Quindle.

Quindle now spoke in an even voice. "God doth speak through soldiers, even now, in Flanders. But you seem to hint at something other than a Spanish victory there."

With a wave of his hand Catesby dismissed all the talk of Flanders, though he himself had introduced it. "A Spanish victory there will do little to help English Catholics now. King Philip values his English peace. There's talk of his wedding his daughter to Prince Henry."

"Let us pray for it!" Garnet said forcefully. "She may convert the prince."

Catesby paced by the table, too vexed now to sit. "She may, and the queen may, and marry, may she! In the interim, *we* will sneak and sweat, and go to the Tower for harboring *you.*"

Both Quindle and Garnet looked stung. "I ask no one to protect me who is not willing, full willing, to shoulder the risk of the pursuivants," said Garnet stiffly. "Nor does Father Quindle."

Catesby turned on him the full force of his blue glare. "Ah, but we *must* protect you. We must have shepherds. We must celebrate mass, and we must confess, or our souls are forfeit. Do you know, yesterday as I walked through Paul's Yard, I passed a wild-eyed Puritan who stood on a box with his Bible and yelled that all priests held sinners in shackles of superstition. And for an instant I believed him!"

The priests stared, not knowing what to reply. At last Quindle said gently, "If you will turn heretic, Robin, we will pray for your soul. We have given ours to God, and can do no other than what we do." Quindle knew, as he spoke, that in one way this was not true. Either he or Father Garnet could have left England any day on a boat, could have served God freely, openly, in a Catholic country to the south. But they were English pastors. Theirs was an English flock.

Catesby reseated himself at the table and placed his head in his hands. "Forgive me, fathers," he said in a muffled voice. "Forgive me my wrath. It is not for you. But I will say to you that the patience of English Catholics wears thin."

Quindle gently touched Catesby's shining hair. "Peace," he said, more like a father to a wayward son than a priest to a supplicant. "Peace."

The three men spoke of other, lighter subjects for the remainder of the evening. But the next afternoon Father Quindle came to see Garnet alone, his face pale and taut.

"What is it, friend?" Garnet gripped Quindle's shoulder. "Has something befallen Robin?"

"I must tell you, but . . . ." Quindle swallowed. As always, he looked almost comically fashionable, like a fop on the stage. Today he was splendid in peacock-blue trunk hose, an embroidered satin doublet, and a velvet feathered cap. "I must tell you in confession."

Such was Quindle's agitation that Garnet invited him to walk in the garden behind the house and speak to him there. "A walking confession," he called it. So the pair of them strolled from stone bench to apple tree, from apple tree to rosebush, then back to the bench and around again. Their talk was long, and when it was done Garnet's face had turned as ashy as Quindle's. He gave his friend a penance, but could see that the sacrament brought Quindle little comfort. The giving and taking of it left both men still in confusion.

After Quindle departed, Garnet sat on the bench, listening to the cries of river birds and staring at the top of the Tower down Thames to the east. At length he rose, went to his room upstairs, and began to write a letter in Latin to the new pope, Paul the Sixth.

For hours he labored on the missive. He must word it specifically enough that the Holy Father would know to what rash designs the faithful in England were now driven. On the other hand, he must keep it vague enough to hide Quindle's particular confessed sin, a sin of harboring the terrible secret Catesby had finally shared with Quindle earlier that very day, seeking at least one priestly blessing, and that Quindle had now shared with Garnet. How say it? *I fear the faithful among us may be driven by their despair to attempt some abominable rebellion* — no, "rebellion" was too precise, and too dangerous. Garnet scratched out the word and replaced it with "action." He worked, sweating, and ended the letter finally with a fervent plea to Pope Paul strongly to direct the English to the virtuous path of patience, patience, patience.

On the day of the Feast of Corpus Christi, Father Garnet celebrated mass for twenty-eight Catholics in a large, fine upriver dwelling. He had meant to bestow his letter to the pope on Gawain Wintour, who would go on court business to Italy in August, but at the last moment he thought better, and gave it to another trusted messenger at the gathering. The mass was performed with a solemn procession about the high-walled courtyard garden of the house, a parade which was muted, but joyful. Only the chief celebrant was not radiant, though he knew he should be as he held the blessed wafer aloft. "*Ecce signum!*" Henry announced. He wished it was easier to believe what he did believe, which was that the bread was more than a sign, it was God, and that through the English bodies of the faithful God would accomplish his dark purposes.

Swallowing the bread, he looked around the crowded yard. He saw both Wintour brothers, and reminded himself that it was unusual for Bors Wintour to be in London alongside his diplomat brother, Gawain. There was Thomas Percy, yes, who had taken Garnet aside before the mass and pleaded with him earnestly to come with some of the faithful on a pilgrimage to St. Winifred's shrine. This was not a new subject from Thomas, but, indeed, the idea appealed to weary Garnet now more than it ever had. There was such need for succor! A body of the faithful from the midlands and the north wished to go, it seemed, including many women, though not Thomas's Martha. Percy stayed almost always apart from his wife now, as much a hermit as Catesby or as Garnet himself. By God, this faith turned all of them to monks and wanderers! And here were the Wrights, whom Garnet had also never before seen in London; and the childhood friend of the Wrights, the tall soldier from Parma with the flat, redundant name. Tom Thompson, it was, or John Johnson. And Catesby?

Robin Catesby was not there.

Chapter 26

By July the men had purchased thirty-six barrels of powder and stock-piled them in Ambrose Rookwood's and Robin Catesby's barns. They began the next stage of transport with twenty barrels, first tamping the powder down to fit as much as possible into each hollow, then covering the powder's surface with a hand's-breadth of flour. By night Percy and Catesby and the servant Bates assembled the lot on a barge, which they poled across the river from Lambeth to a secluded spot on the Thames' far side. There on the bank, Fawkes met them with his provisioner's cart, and then coolly drove the barrels to the rambling house that was Westminster Palace. Percy went with him. Once there, the men carried the barrels into their newly leased warehouse, which formed most of the cellar of the House of Lords. Percy sweated the while, but Fawkes stayed cool as a fish.

The next night the men repeated the process, until all thirty-six of the barrels stood stocked in a dark corner of the Parliament storage vault. Old bits of masonry and pieces of trash already lay scattered over the floor when the men took possession, which they did more easily than they could have hoped. They left the trash where it lay, and to it Fawkes added stacks of firewood and barrels of real grain, which they placed in front of the powder barrels.

Then, as the days passed, Fawkes watched. He occupied himself with meaningless tasks that looked industrious. He drove the cart in and out of the yard, stocked wood under a sheet and carried it out, stuffed the sheet under a blanket and drove the wood back in again. Westminster Place was crowded with tradesmen and customers, and John Johnson was by now so familiar as to be practically invisible.

What all of them knew but none of them said was that Guido's task was the most perilous of all of theirs. If apprehended in Northumbria or Warwickshire or even in Lambeth or Gray's Inn Road, any of the other conspirators could deny knowledge of the powder. The questioned one could claim slander, profess loyalty, speak angrily of the slurs that were always hurled against Catholics. None of them thought he would do so, but all of them knew that they could. Yet Fawkes woke and slept with the powder. He could not feign innocence if a city guard happened to search the increasingly crowded vault. For this minor Yorkshire gentleman, childhood friend of the nobler born Wrights and private soldier of Parma, there was no route of escape but success. Add to this that he alone stood the danger of being blown apart. For wordlessly, without discussion, all had arrived at the general agreement that it should be Guido Fawkes who lit the fuse.

Having first disdained Fawkes' lack of breeding, Thomas had come to admire him beyond what words could tell. True, all of them had sacrificed, mortgaging estates, selling much of what they owned to buy powder and to purchase the rights to the building that now held their dark treasure. But Fawkes was daily sacrificing the most, living closest to the flame. It unsettled Thomas to think that the most valorous of their group was the man of lowest estate, saving the servant Bates. Fawkes was not highborn, but he was honorable. All in all, it was a paradox.

Thomas resolved his confusion on the matter through prayer. He prayed fervently for hours each day in his room at Gray's Inn Road. When he was not performing his duties in king's livery at the palace, he was hunched on his knees holding his new rosary, one he'd taken from Martha's jewelry chest after he'd handed his own to little Prince Charles at the Christmas Revels. The rosary was not missed by Martha, who'd fallen out of the habit of using it, and cared little for jewelry or "trinkets" in any case. Thomas used the rosary, and other aids to devotion. A psaltery lay by his bedside, next to a sliver of St. Dunstan's clavicle and the quarto texts of three plays he had bought in Paul's Yard. Next to these relics he knelt, his lips moving silently. When he journeyed between north and south on rent-duties for the earl, he prayed a-horseback. In London, when free of palace duties, often he stayed in and told the beads of his rosary.

He did this, and he went to the plays.

All Catholics prayed in the same way, but each man also prayed in his own way. Little Nicholas Owen, creeping through midlands manors digging holes for priests, was praying. Guido Fawkes, pulling canvas-covered barrels of powder back from damp Westminster walls, was praying. And Thomas Percy, sitting straight and tall on a hard sixpenny bench in the Globe, was praying, too.

Today Thomas adjusted himself on a purgatorial wooden plank, midway between the hellishly crowded yard and the paradise of the private lord's boxes. He was flanked on one side by a trio of richly clad Dutch merchants whose outland speech he could ignore because he did not understand it. He attended, instead, to the play.

On this day on the stage, wicked Prince John, the brother of Richard Lionheart, had sent a servant to kill his royal rival Arthur, the boy prince and his nephew. A horrid crime against innocence! Yet here the loyal servant came, riven by the war between his duty and his tenderness. He carried cords and with them bound the lad, who quaked and cried piteously for charity, charity, and the staying of the murderer's hand. The man bade him cease his wailing. He threatened the boy with irons heated by the coals. *Mercy!* pleaded the piteous child. And in the end the servant relented, and the boy was spared from the fire.

Thomas saw all this, rapt on the bench in Southwark. Afterwards he brooded over an ale called Left Leg in a tavern called Mermaid on a street called Bread in Shoreditch. He thought long on what the play meant about present-day England, as though it were not a history play but an allegory. God had revealed some of its meaning to his thought. Not all of it, yet.

The truth was that Thomas was sorely in need of spiritual blessing. It was one thing for Francis Tresham and the other powder brethren in the north to contemplate the destruction of distant Westminster. But Thomas lived in Gray's Inn Road, and walked frequently near Parliament. Daily he was forced to note that it was not only treacherous Protestant lords who frequented the area, but tradesmen and their families. Even children, playing with balls or at barley-break, or doing their chores. Children! What great work could compensate for the burning of these? How could St. Winifred bless it?

This sin, as yet uncommitted, was not one he could confess to Father Quindle.

He touched the medal of Winifred that hung from his neck. Undeserved, the medal was, since he had not yet managed to visit his saint's shrine. For the thousandth time the feel of its metal pricked his conscience, telling him he must truly earn this badge before he was through.

He must go west. There, in Wales, in the holy place of Winifred, he would pray.

Though now he worried. Would the saint accept the prayers of a man who was bound to kill children?

Then it came to him fully, between the tenth and eleventh swigs of Left Leg, amid the din of song and the clack of falling dice in the Mermaid. He suddenly knew precisely why he must go a-pilgrimage. He must travel to Holywell, fearful and trembling, not despite but *because* of the love of Winifred for children. Only she could answer his troubled prayer.

Chapter 27

These families did not lack horses. Even some of their servants rode. Father Garnet too was supplied by Anne Vaux with a stallion, though he, spry for his fifty-three years, often chose to walk. He would stride ten paces ahead of his fortyfold flock with the aid of a palmer's staff, climbing grassy hillocks in the late August heat, scanning the green fields for footpaths through farms, and once leading the group through a tangled and magical wood, singing *Derry derry down-a!* all the while. When the sideways were absent or treacherous, Garnet kept them to the open and well-traveled highway, though that road was often busy and dangerous. On it their large group caught curious gazes, which made all fear for the safety of the priests. When other riders or walkers approached, Garnet would melt back into the group, where Father Quindle and two priests of private chapels already rode inconspicuously, wearing garb lent them by the various households who habitually supplied them. The four priests looked like any English gentlemen. They chatted of blades and horses, and had false names at the ready should a sheriff challenge them. Thus pseudonymous, they braved the risks of the main thoroughfare, because that road was easier for the weaker ones among them.

Yet most in the group were quite strong. Here was the sturdy gentleman farmer of Warwickshire, John Grant. The Wintour and Wright families were well represented by Bors and Kit and their wives. Robin Catesby had hung back in Lambeth, wishing to stay close to the seat of all his plans — and perhaps, Father Garnet suspected, to avoid the company of at least one priest who knew of his design, and did not well approve of it. Yes, Catesby had stayed behind, but here Thomas Percy rode, stalwart and tall in his saddle, looking straight ahead, his face radiant with prayer and with purpose.

Trotting next to Thomas was Ambrose Rookwood, supplier of powder for — as Rookwood thought — the English regiment in Flanders.

Rookwood had declared himself anxious to pray for the triumph of the Holy Church over all its unruly factions. In the middle of the group rode Eliza Vaux, with scarlet hose as fine as the Wife of Bath's. Her eyes sparkled above her sun-reddened cheeks as she pressed the others to ride longer, faster, another five miles today! only stinting her exhortations out of charity when she saw the weariness of her sister-in-law Anne.

By Eliza's side rode her son Edward, his face a study in sad hope, wondering as he wandered whether some saint might after all grant him his sweet, beloved Elizabeth Howard. *Saint Cupid, be my speed!* Thinking of the wife he'd so wanted, young Edward gazed longingly at the clasped hands of a couple only a few years older than himself. These were a lady named Mary Digby and her husband, Everard, a Buckinghamshire gentleman. Digby was a fine horseman and swordsman who'd been converted to a zealous Catholicism by the joint prayers and persuasions of his wife, the priest whom her family had granted them as a kind of dowry, and his much-admired friend Robin Catesby. At the moment, he knew no better way to express his zeal than to ride on pilgrimage.

Unlike Edward Vaux, who regarded them wistfully, Thomas Percy looked away from Everard and Mary Digby, keeping his eyes on the far reaches of road before him. The laughter and easy speech between the young married pair reminded him too painfully of himself and his own lost Mary. To make the sting worse, Mary Digby was visibly pregnant, as his Mary had been when they'd both hoped to make this very journey, to travel this same road. He must not think of her now, he knew, but.... On one of their haltings, at a safe-house in Hereford, Thomas had heard the amorous sighs and passionate groans of young Digby and his Mary coming from the far side of the wall that divided his room from theirs. As Thomas's bed was too heavy to be pushed away from the wall, even by him, he'd risen to escape the noise, and had slept like a monk on the floor. For hours he'd tried to banish the sweet images that the sounds of marital joy had made rise in his mind. No midnight Martha, his own Mary had been shy in lovemaking, but her sweetness had been beyond compare. Yet what good could it do him now to recall the only times on this earth he'd felt happy and whole and beloved and known, the nights like these, in a bed like the Digbys', spent naked in her arms?

Ah, to journey toward Mary — to pass through Wales and keep on across the Irish Sea, to that wild green country wherein, some said, a

dark entrance to Purgatory lay! There he might lay down his earthly bur-
dens, walk into the otherworld, and see . . . .

No. None of it. He'd a new purpose now, and wives must be — nay,
were — distant things. Instance Martha, who'd refused to come on this
pilgrimage, despite her lack of any sons to show for her eleven married
years, and the obvious possibility that a prayer to Winifred would result
in a Percy heir. She had not felt well these several weeks, she said, and
could not stomach the two weeks of riding. She had enraged Thomas by
saying that if God was pleased, then she too was well satisfied with one
daughter, nay, a host of daughters should God choose to send her more
of them, and that it were a waste of good time to limp and stumble over
rocks and through fields toward a Welsh well that was, when all was
said and done, no more or less holy than the well lately dug in their garden with her oversight and direction, and dug without (mark you) the
help of Thomas Percy, who was always away in London. A Northumbrian
well which gave sweet water but was in need of some mending of the
superstructure which she herself would quickly see to, did the all-honored Gentleman Pensioner grant her the silver for the work. Exactly two
pound six for the materials and labor of a stonemason in York, whose fee
was higher than that asked by Peter Giles who was closer at hand, but
then, Giles's work on the wall by the barley field last summer had been
something shoddy; half the capstones had tumbled in the last storm. But
Giles would repair that wall, *gratis*. He would indeed. She would see to
that.

Martha sounded more like a Protestant every day.

Thomas had not tried overhard to persuade her to come with him.
Before he'd even spoken of the journey, now planned, now agreed to, now
imminent, he had sensed that she would not make one of the pilgrims'
party. Her refusal would not alter his plan or his destiny. Though he still
only dimly apprehended God's intentions for him, he knew that the part
he must play in the powder plan did not depend on a woman, or even on
an heir of his own body. Something else, something grander and larger
and more glorious, awaited him. He need only be faithful.

And faithfully, he rode. When the train of travelers moved slowly,
he mastered his desire to canter ahead, to reach his destination, to say
at Holywell the prayer that had burned in his breast for years. Along
with Bors Wintour and Kit Wright (though not the imperturbable John
Grant), Thomas fretted about the time they were taking. A meeting had

been set by Catesby for Michaelmas, September twenty-ninth, in Lambeth. There the powder brethren would make final plans for all the roles they would discharge on that great coming day. This could not, then, be too lingering a pilgrimage. But Thomas compelled himself not to race forward, but to go at the pace of the group, in the faith that God would see to his presence in London at the appointed time. These were a community of the faithful, and he was one of them.

Once only did he ride apart. This was after an old farmer, asked by Kit Wright what town lay in the distance before them, followed Wright's gesture with his eyes and said briefly, "Shrewsbury."

Thomas sucked in his breath.

Though the place was not on their way, he made vague apologies to the group, and galloped a league toward it. By a flock of sheep, he stopped on a hill overlooking the fields near the town, surveying the sweep of wood that gave onto the wide, famous plain. Now that plain was filled with swaying wheat. But within the wheat he could see warriors.

There, on the far flank, crowded the blue-capped soldiers of the mighty Scot Douglas, a friend to Hotspur. Nearby, the army of the devout and priestly Archbishop of York, come to bolster the Percys' rebellion. Across, the massed men of the treacherous English king Henry the Fourth.

And there, now, down the sweep of the middle hill like a tearing thunderbolt on his warhorse, came charging the greatest of all possible Percys, the Hotspur! Leading his hosts, trumpeting his war cry. *Esperance!* The hills echoed his shout. Now the armies bore down on one another, noble Scots and both loyal and treacherous English in all their colors, swinging maces and flails and deadly broadswords, braced against their glittering shields, and high among them, on a horse hung with the banners of the Percy crest, shone the noblest spur of them all. Two hundred years of the heavy time since were gone like a dream, and Thomas saw Hotspur raise his blade in anger against a lying, deceitful king, and fail, and die nobly, plucking bright honor from the pale-faced moon.

He had fallen, had Hotspur.

But might he not rise?

Alone on the hill, Thomas lifted his sword high. "*Percy!*" he yelled. He called down the spirit of Catholic England, from a time when his island country had not hung apart, frayed and lone, like a ragged remnant of torn altar cloth, but stood knit tightly to Christendom and the Mother Church. One fabric. Whole.

"*Esperance*," he whispered, like a prayer.

Then he sheathed his sword, spurred his horse to the gallop, and sped back to his tribe.

The sheep stared after him for a moment, then returned to their placid grazing.

They rode for two weeks, sleeping in safe houses or, sometimes, in fields. All were careful of the frail or halt among them. In need of frequent rest was Nicholas Owen the carpenter, who had worn out his body carving priest-holes, and was often afflicted by bone-ache. Also Anne Vaux, whose cramping abdominal pains had returned in force on the journey. The task of lifting sore, cheerful Nicholas on and off his horse fell to Thomas, who hoisted him with ease, as though the dwarf were a bag of flour. Father Garnet himself saw to Anne. On some days she rode crouched over the neck of her horse, half-supported by Henry, who would then walk by her side, a steadying arm on her back. There had been no question of Owen's staying home, or of Anne's. They had heard of Winifred's Well all their lives. Now the well shone in Anne's mind like a beacon of health, hope, and blessing. *St. Winifred*, she prayed as she rode, leaning forward from her saddle, through Bewley and Bridgenorth and Wenlock. *I am suffering. Make me well.*

Her inward prayer silently echoed, enlarged, among those Catholics who walked and rode with her. *St. Winifred, we are suffering. Make us well.*

By St. Bartholomew's Day they had reached the large English town of Chester, near the border of Wales. Two of the horses had the bots, and one had been lamed crossing a field of boulders. So while the bulk of the party rested by the River Dee, in the green fields outside the walled Roman town, Thomas Percy and Everard Digby ventured in to find a horse trader and buy provisions for the last part of the journey. Thomas at first felt stiff discomfort alone with twenty-four-year-old Everard, who was so well-born and polished that his manners prompted Percy's old fears that he himself walked and spoke like anything but a knight. Yet Digby's sunny graciousness soon melted these worries. The two were speaking in a lively way of the events of the journey by the time they came under the great gate of Chester and joined the flow of holiday traffic. They rode among festive folk and carts bearing hay, wool, and foodstuffs to the fair of Bartholomew. They did their business quickly, and on the return road stopped before a tavern whose swinging sign proclaimed it "The Trader's Hazard," under a picture of a ship and three silver coins. Beneath this, in smaller letters, was painted, "Joseph Buckmaster, prop."

They entered, and found the host genial enough to share a tankard with them. They were guarded when he asked them their destination, but Buckmaster quickly guessed it was Winifred's Well, since many of Winifred's pilgrims came through Chester. He disappeared into the garden behind his establishment, of which — of both garden and house — he seemed proud. He returned with leeks, carrots, and five large onions, for which he added a very precise number of pence to the scot. Percy and Digby paid him their coins, one of which the man bit to prove to himself and the world that it was not counterfeit. Finding the payment good, the host bade them add his vegetables to the bags of saltfish and cheese and bread they'd bought on the high street in town, and the pork they'd purchased on the fair-field outside it.

Then he amiably told them their travel was wasted.

"And why should that be?" So appealing were young Everard Digby's fresh skin and lively hazel eyes, his new beard and pearl-white teeth, that his loose jaw, now hanging in amazement, did not make him look stupid. He looked, instead, like a younger version of Catesby, open and disingenuous, astonished that any man could find his faith laughable.

The host polished a glass with a towel. "There are chapels and wells enough in London, where I take it you come from."

"Near enough." Digby took a sip of his ale.

"If your business is there, can you not say your prayers locally, without spending weeks away and buying new horses?"

Eyes flashing, Thomas informed the man of a fact that should have been obvious: none of those local London wells and chapels was the shrine of St. Winifred. After that, he was stumped for words. Vague impressions troubled his mind. Had he been articulate — had he been Robin Catesby — he would have spoken of the charity engendered in the very act of pilgrimage, of the daily discipline the holy walk provided in kindness to the weak, patience with the slow, good humor in the face of vexing chatter. He would have told of the deepening of human affections that might flower from conversations sprung between man and man, woman and woman, woman and man, on a long road — this, though he himself had stayed mostly quiet on this journey. But Thomas, who knew all these things in his heart, lacked a tongue to say them in defense of pilgrimage, that shrine-bound journey that had been banned and mocked in England since the latter time of old Henry the Eighth. So he said instead, "Winifred is a healer."

"I know not that." The man gave a mild snort. "Some things heal by themselves, in Wales or anywhere. Any Englishman knows it, or should. Thirty years ago the ice nearly broke on the Dee from the barefoot women hobbling across to see Winifred on her holiest day. November the third. I'll not forget hauling my own aunt out with her frostbitten foot. Then off she limped to Winifred to pray for healing of the foot! They came to the chapel in crowds then. Mark you, there are fewer now. Less every year."

Thomas was getting angry. He banged his tankard on the table. "This is because our devil-led governors have tried to stop our devotions! They think they can turn us all from one faith to another in the wink of an eye." He ignored Digby's warning look. His heart had caught sudden fire. "Against our shrines they light a fuse that runs quicker than thought, fires a cannon, and out comes a ball that destroys a wall or a fort. So have the Reformers done to England's piety, with their new religion! But mark, what is so quickly done can as quickly be undone, and a false-built house destroyed quicker than a true one."

"Hoo-hoo! New religion!" The host was smiling. Hot disputes over ale were the stock of his trade. "Big man, there is no alteration so quick as you describe. You see surfaces only. England has long been changing, in its heart, in its soil underneath. The seed of a plant takes root in the earth over a long winter, and then in the spring comes a sprout. This sprout of Protestantism was long in the growing. We may sing the old ballads, and why not? They go down well with a tankard or two. But we are not the people we sing of. And this religion you call new . . . Have you not heard of old Luther?"

"A devil!"

"Of John Oldcastle? Of John Wyclif, now two centuries dead, who gave us a Bible in English? Or so he tried to do."

Thomas frowned, thinking. One of these last two men he'd heard spoken of in a play, and the other by a master at Cambridge. But he could not remember which was which, or the importance of either.

The man grinned, a fine wide stretch of the lips, showing a row of strong teeth with only two gaps. "I'faith, there were cracks in our cathedrals as far back as old Hotspur's time."

Now Thomas was truly stung. He drew himself up in proud affrontedness. "Thou art speaking to a Percy."

"And you, too, are speaking to a person," said the pert old man, who was deaf in the right ear. "I speak no more than what I know."

Everard Digby was staring in surprise at the tavern host. "Here, now, man. Thou art no scholar. How canst thou know any of these things?"

"I can read," the host said proudly. "I am lent books by our pastor, here in Chester. More, he says these things I have said in his homilies, and other things as well, and says them in plain English, mark you, not the garbled Latin of the priest of my youth. When I was eight I was told by that poor country priest that if I bowed three times, popped bread in my mouth every seven days, and once a year dipped a foot in Winifred's well I would live forever. Christ, I never knew of."

Wounded, Thomas barked, "You may jest at the sacrament, but the Eucharist is a knowing of Christ that transcends all reason —"

"Hear and understand me, man. I speak not of arguments concerning the meaning of the sacrament, whether 'tis *sign* or *substance*, wine or blood. That matters little to me. When I say I never knew of Christ, I mean I'd never heard of the fellow. Not of his birth or his death on the Cross. Nor of the Holy Spirit, nor of Adam or Eve or any one of the Ten Commandments. I thought the Virgin Mary was a magical lady in the sky."

Is she not? thought Thomas, puzzled.

"And as for the Our Father . . . ." The innkeeper laughed sadly. "Poor country herb-gathering priest. His life was spent 'healing' parish matrons on odd afternoons, and, twice a-Sundays, stammering through some Latin text he understood naught of. May he rest in peace with his ignorance, and be forgiven for ours."

Thomas was silent, thinking of the learnedness of Father Quindle and Father Garnet, of Garnet's noble celibacy. Of both those priests' knowledge of Church and scripture. Of high discussions of theology among Quindle, Garnet, and the Wintours and the Wrights and Catesby, feasts of argument that more often than not sent Thomas to sleep. "You were ill served," he said finally.

The man shrugged. "I was as well served as any man or woman in this parish. But I am near sixty and a widower, and Queen Mary's time was long ago. Things shift and change in our English soil, mark you, though they do so underneath. The *new* priest has been at Cambridge. As I say, he preaches in English, and taught me to read, and to do accounts — "

"A priest taught you reckoning!"

"He taught every man in the parish who did not already know."

"Much pleased he must be to see how you used the knowledge," laughed Digby, tapping his tankard, then gesturing toward the full pocket of the man's leather apron.

"*For the laborer is worthy of his wages,* says the gospel of Luke. I read this in a Bible I bought at a bookstall. And I also read in one of Christ's parables, that a man should be crafty and sell all he has to buy a field if he knows a treasure is buried in it. That is why I sold my farm and bought this inn quicker than thought, when it came on the market. I saw it was very well placed on the high road."

"That cannot be in the Bible," said Thomas loftily. He thought of the powdery treasure for which he and his fellows had sold many properties and leased the cellar of the House of Lords. He squinted at the crass host. "I tell you, Catholics do not speak so much as you about the getting of money."

"Only because they already have it. They have profited from the labors of the people. Psalms one hundred and five, verse forty-four."

"Marry, thou *art* a book-reading man." Digby winked at Thomas.

The man was so pleased to have deftly quoted scripture to these young gentlemen that he failed to notice the wink, or else didn't mind it. "My father could not read, but I can," he said proudly. "And three of my grandsons now learn Latin at the grammar school!"

"Thou art a wondrous fellow." Digby doffed his cap and gave it a flourish.

As Digby and Percy rose to go, the man rose as well, and said directly to Thomas, "But you, sir. One thing more. Mark you, my pilgrim fellow — "

Fellow? Thomas was ready to protest, before he recalled that this antic had called even Christ his fellow.

" — believe me when I say that the powder you speak of, that burns and destroys, is a surface thing as well. Cannonfire does not change a country, down below. To topple a fort is no more than to topple a fort."

This brought Thomas short on his way to the door, and he stopped and stared back at the man. Did he know something of him and his business? But no. The host was now bowing and smiling amiably, clearing the clutter of tankards and his glass, looking to his till and some new customers, a group of carters who had noisily entered and were calling for stew. He had only meant to display his wit by questioning Thomas's earlier conceit of the cannon.

Thomas was not given to forming conceits, or good at defending them. But as they left the house he thought the man had been full of nonsense, after all. For how could powder be a surface thing when it needed deep tunneling under earth to do its work? Under earth, or in a basement vault, when tunnels proved faulty. From thence powder would push upward, would raise its dark flower. This was the earth and change Thomas understood. And this English inn-keeper, and everyone like him, would be made to understand it as well.

"This was a mad old man, was he not, friend Thomas? What think you?"

Thomas glanced over at Digby, who was laughing as he mounted his horse. "He is a coin-counter, an ale-server, a man of pocket pence and carrots," Thomas said gruffly. "His faith is his till. He knows naught of true religion." Privately, Thomas thought this fine tavern host would have proved a fit old husband for his Martha.

And so they came to Holywell.

The humble stone chapel was almost a part of the hillside from which it rose. The group had been singing all morning as they rode toward the shrine, but when they saw the church they grew hushed. As they approached it nearly and dismounted, they fell entirely silent. In small groups of four and five, then, they climbed the crooked stone stairs and greeted the priestly keeper of the place, an old man in a plain grey robe who bowed and collected their offerings in a wooden box. Then they walked down again into an open space where a clear spring of water flowed before a statue of St. Winifred.

Seeing it, Thomas fell to his knees and sobbed. He wanted to say "Winifred," but the name that burst from his lips was another's. "Mary," he prayed thickly. "Mary!"

Anne Vaux put a hand to his back. She too had tears in her eyes. She, like Eliza, knew something of Percy's history and of his first, thwarted desire to make this pilgrimage. She herself ached, with true bodily pain, to step into the water, but she waited, helping Thomas Percy to pray. He was murmuring the name of Winifred now, whispering prayers, crossing himself.

At length the big man's whispers ceased. He sat with his head bowed for another minute. "Yes," he said softly. An expression of peace softened his features. "Yes," he said again.

Then he rose and dipped his hands in the holy water and touched them to his forehead, making the sign of the cross. He knelt again and bowed his head, and stayed there motionless for a long time.

Anne moved away from him. Closing her eyes, she stepped into the water.

Later, outside the chapel, Thomas patted his horse and gazed at the sky. His face was serene. It was as he had hoped and prayed. The fullness of his purpose had been revealed to him.

He had prayed to Winifred for the souls of Mary and their child, for the children of Westminster, and for the salvation of baby Prince Charles. And when he had done so, Winifred had blessed him with a certainty.

The innocents who would die on the day of holy destruction would not suffer, but be sealed under her protection and taken straightways to Heaven, where Thomas's lost Mary and baby would soon reside. For his own dead infant, though never baptized, would be saved by his father's great work, and allowed to leave Limbo for eternal bliss with God. All this Winifred had promised. As for Thomas, he was not to despair of paternity. For Winifred had at last shown him the truth. Thomas was to be earthly father to a son after all! When the evil royal father was destroyed, Thomas Percy would become the good father. His task was to save the child Charles.

Now that knowledge lay in his heart, just as Hotspur had lain on a stage, in place of the infinite possibilities he had ousted. There was one place for Hotspur, and one road for Thomas, now. Bright shone his destiny. The ninth earl of Northumberland would stand as regent and figurehead of England redeemed. But Thomas alone would be little Prince Charles's guide, charged by God and all the English saints to love and nurture the Catholic faith of the tender babe, of the boy who would be king.

Chapter 28

G od was still watching. His hand was plain.
Because of God's care, Parliament's opening had been stayed a third time. Now it would not meet until November the fifth, which gave the brethren nearly five more weeks to stockpile powder in Catesby's barn, for surplus, in case any of the barrels in Westminster turned irretrievably counterfeit.

Catesby rejoiced. In London, he and Fawkes were the first of the powder brothers to learn of the new parliamentary prorogation commanded by James. But the news went swiftly forth throughout the realm, and soon all were aware that the lords and commons would not gather in London on October third as last proposed. The reason was the same as before: plague. James feared some dregs of the late contagion still festered in the pest-threatened city. Warm weather brought forth the sickness, and until the air once more turned chill the king thought it safest for his royal person to hang back from all gatherings of men.

So, following Queen Elizabeth's precedent at last, King James now made his own festive pilgrimage through the rural parts of his domain, dining at the houses and expense of the gentry. He even spent a night at Eliza Vaux's Harrowden, because he felt friendly toward all things Vaux, forever. How could he not, after Anne Vaux's letter, warning him against Walter Raleigh's mad plan to imprison him until Raleigh were given a costly ship and licensed to sail off in search of El Dorado? (This, at least, had been one of the several charges thrillingly made against Raleigh in Anne's letter, though Raleigh — from the Tower — called the accusation absurd.)

At Harrowden Hall the king was graciously received by Eliza Vaux's servants. These expressed regret that their mistress and the young lord her son were away with friends in the north. The Vaux retainers kept mum about the particulars of Eliza's real whereabouts, and the king, merry with his retinue after a fine day of riding, proved not overly curious. Six of the clock on August twenty-ninth (the feast day of the beheading of St. John the Baptist) found King James seated at Harrowden's great table, lifting to his lips a forkful of roast from a swan that had been sacrificed in his honor.

At that same moment Eliza, the mistress of Harrowden Hall, was rising from her knees on the stone chapel floor in Holywell, having finished her devotions to Winifred. She had come to pray that Elizabeth Howard might one day bear the child of her lovelorn son Edward, despite all impediments. But in uncanny correspondence with events at Harrowden, her prayer had also mentioned the festive king James, and asked blessing for a coming sad but necessary sacrificial roast.

They had said their prayers. They had left notes and flowers at the base of Winifred's statue and more pieces of gold in the chapel box, and cleansed themselves at the holy well. Now the pilgrimage party dispersed. Thomas Percy rode back to Northumbria to collect rents for the earl, who was back at Syon House in London. The greater part of the group returned to Warwickshire, where, after ten days' riding, Anne Vaux dismounted with the flush of health in her cheeks. At the shrine, Henry Garnet had bathed her from the spring as her friends prayed fervently on their knees on the stones beside the water. That afternoon and the following day her pains had been sharper than ever, delaying their departure from Holywell, and she had despaired, thinking her hard weeks of pilgrimage had come to naught, since Winifred had refused her devotions. But on the third day she had risen with a curious lack of sensation in the womb that had troubled her for weeks. The pain was gone, and it did not return on any day of the journey homeward. She rode joyfully. By her side Garnet smiled, sharing her gratitude, though some lingering worry — about what? — still hung on his brow.

Now free of pain, Anne was able to look about her and observe such details as the shadow in Garnet's grey eyes. She questioned him sharply about his concerns. He parried, answering only that he was anxious for the fate of English Catholics in days to come.

And this was true. "Days to come" was sufficiently general. Henry thought it essential that Anne not know he was in a stark terror about one specific day to come. The day on which the explosion was planned was one day and not "days," but "days" was not dishonest, because certainly Garnet fretted also about the days between now and that day, wondering whether a message from Pope Paul to English Catholics, enjoining their continued patience and restraint, could possibly arrive from Rome in so short a time. Had the pope even received his request for this message? Garnet had been to Rome once before, and knew how a letter might get lost, might be secreted in a functionary's pocket and then magically produced in exchange for gold; how purloined missives were used to enhance position at the papal court. His letter might have been seen, stolen, and suppressed by some lay person or even a cleric who wished a Catholic rebellion in England, and wanted to prevent any papal caution against one.

Anne persisted. "Has this . . . anxiety of yours to do with my cousin Catesby?"

Garnet looked at her warily. "What mean you? Why say you this?"

"Robin has been much absent from our masses of late. And I wonder why he did not join our pilgrimage. I sometimes fear he has fallen in with another like . . . like Essex. Do you know aught of this, Henry? Does Father Quindle?"

"Would that Robin had come with us! He endangers his soul when he strays from our company. He hath no other priest that I know."

Anne continued to pester Henry, and Henry continued to evade her questions. He longed with all his soul to share what he knew with her. The burden of it was so heavy! But he knew of Robin's plot only from Quindle's confession, and as long as Quindle said nothing, he himself must say nothing. And there was more. Whatever Anne came to know, she would be obliged to reveal to any officer who arrested her, if it came to that — if it came to the worst, to the general arrest and detention of Catholics throughout the realm. Garnet could not put his dear friend in the danger of his new intelligence. What guilt he bore, he must bear alone.

Or almost alone. He glanced over at Quindle, who returned his worried look. Covertly, Quindle crossed himself. Henry smiled wanly. He knew Quindle, too, was tense with fear about the papal letter.

But courage! God was watching and blessing them. Time was short, and yet, from westering travelers on the road, they heard that Parliament had been prorogued. Surely in these five additional weeks the pope's letter would arrive! And when it did, what could Robin Catesby do? What *was* there to do, with a direct command from the head of the Church to desist, but simply obey it?

Martha frowned at Thomas. "And why is this?"

He spoke brusquely. "There are things in hand."

She felt an urge to pout. Mastering it, she came closer to her husband, took his hand, and placed it on her waist, not far from her left breast. "There *might* be things in hand," she said slyly. "There might, had you not turned monkish on your pilgrimage. You are home two days, and gone again? We have not shared a bed these five weeks." This circumstance was bothering Martha more than it ordinarily would have. She was, after all, used to her husband's long absences, and they'd been married eleven years. After such a passage of time (as she knew from frequent chats on this subject with her sisters-in-law), it was ordinary for ardent embraces to grow sparser, and less hot. Martha accepted this fact as she accepted all truths of nature. But to see, in his brief visits home, Thomas retire to another chamber — this was a new trial. The night of his return from Holywell, she'd come to seek him, wrapped only in a woolen blanket to provoke his interest, and had found him on his knees in a corner of their house, praying before an image of the Virgin! The next evening he'd spoken gruffly, almost apologetically, of the Knights Templar in Jerusalem and how the strength of their arms was increased by their chastity. Her jesting response (a carnal speculation about the real reason for the strength of their arms) had angered him, and he'd left the house fuming to ride his horse through the neighborhoods, pointlessly, since he'd collected all the earl's rents earlier that day, and since the affairs of their own lands were well ordered, thanks to Martha's industry.

To make Thomas's grim celibacy more unsettling, these days she found her body undergoing a mysterious springlike awakening. Longings were stirring in her loins. Also, since Thomas's installment as a Gentleman Pensioner, his absences from Northumbria had been so numerous and extended that she'd grown lonely.

Holding his hand near her breast now, she regarded him evenly. Now a knight in occasional call to palace service, he'd grown used to grooming himself more carefully, and to cutting his beard in the military style like the ace of spades. His hair, too, was shorter and less outlandish. He looked handsome, standing tall in their courtyard before her, his face ruddy with health and zeal, preparing to mount his roan horse for yet another ride southward. Indeed, he *was* a man of parts. She kept her fingers on his, seeking his eye, inviting intimacy. He'd spoken so little to her this year! There were things she would like to tell him.

But he took his hand from her waist in order to adjust his saddle.

Hurt made her peevish. "What carries you away?"

"My horse."

"I cannot laugh at that. Can you not stay an hour? And why cannot Claire and I travel with you?" Against her will, her voice was sharpening to a point. The nagging wife! Well, 'twas his fault.

Still busy with his saddle, he did not even look at her. He spoke loftily. "This is no world to play with mammets and to tilt with lips!"

"What say you?" Her voice was a needle, jabbing. "*Tilt?* You are no knight of King Arthur's court, Thomas, but a Gentleman Pensioner who helps make up the retinue." She stepped three paces back from him and put her hands on her hips, watching, narrow-eyed, as he mounted his horse. She felt his vexation at her growing, radiating toward her, but could not stop, needing to ask all questions now, in this small space of time before he rode away. For who knew when she would see him again? She raised her voice, as though shrillness could penetrate the shell of his indifference. "Why can we not set up household in London, as the earl does? This is time of peace."

This sparked the explosion she'd half feared, half desired. "*Peace?*" he roared, dropping the reins. She hated the loudness, wanted to block out the animal sound, but at least he was looking at her now. The roan, used to its master's outbursts, only flicked its ears slightly. "*Peace?*" He raged on. "What know we of peace, woman? The faithful are threatened daily. Our priests are bedeviled, tortured, and hanged. Only last month a gentleman in Snitterfield, Warwickshire, was imprisoned for giving home and food to one of our holy shepherds. And –" At last noticing the pain on Martha's face, he softened his tone a little. "And I have no fit lodgings for you and Claire there, Martha. I have told you this. My pension is not yet so great as to allow for two separate houses."

"I know why it is not great enough," she said sourly.

Thomas knew she didn't know. In fact, Thomas could have afforded two households, had he not expended the bulk of his year's earnings on powder and the leases of rooms in Westminster as well as in Gray's Inn Road. But he'd told her nothing of this, and now he played out the game. "Why is it not great enough, wife?"

"You are stinted by the king because you have not taken the loyalty oath. Thomas, I think you must swear it."

He stared at her. "Now I think thou art truly mad. I am to sell my soul to the devil for a ten-pound increase in salary and a house in the Strand? This, when the earl was so gracious as to omit the oath from the ceremony for my good?"

Martha met his hard gaze and did not drop her eyes. She was thinking of Gawain Wintour's wife, with her London house and her pair-drawn carriage. Her husband had taken the loyalty oath for Elizabeth, and had taken it again for King James. Both sovereigns had employed Gawain Wintour as an emissary to Spain and rewarded him handsomely, whatever dark double dealings he had done down there.

"Thomas, I think you must swear it," she repeated. "Confess the sin after, if you will, and do penance. You need only swear the oath once."

Thomas continued to stare at her, until she felt beads of nervous sweat pop out on her back. What was wrong with him? Her suggestion was reasonable. She would press her case to the limit. "If you love me, you will swear the oath. What have you to say?"

He raised his hand and brusquely crossed himself. "Avaunt thee, miscreant! I say thou art no wife of mine." He mounted the roan, snapped its reins, and cantered through the iron gate, his cape billowing behind him.

She looked after him forlornly until he disappeared around a curve in the road. Then she shook her head and turned back to the house. *Well. It's clear he no longer loves me. Better so, perhaps.* Her busy mind sought a way to make his abrupt leave-taking good, and found one. Had she told him now of her pregnancy, he would only have railed at her further for not having gone with him to Holywell, where prayers to Winifred might have snared the child a safe passage into the world. He would not have accepted Martha's reasoning, which was peculiar, perhaps even faithless, though she stubbornly clung to it. She'd believed — *mea culpa*, she prayed as she thought it — that the growing babe would be safer at home. Safer than it would have been in the womb of a mother who bumped over rocky Welsh hillsides, got coughed on by a mob of pox-ridden, ague-suffering, contagious travelers at Winifred's chapel, then turned around to bump down more rocky hillsides in return.

She placed a protective hand on her abdomen as she went in her front door.

Chapter 29

Thomas's meeting with the earl at Syon House proved short. Henry Percy was preoccupied with a book on medicines and a messy experiment involving a purgative he'd administered to one of his bloodhounds. He received the rent payments with ill grace, then dispatched Thomas to the Tower with a book for Walter Raleigh.

Raleigh held a kind of court in his prison apartments, which included a library, several plush settles, a chamber for his wife, and a schoolroom for his young son Wat. Lush, but still, an inescapable river dankness hung in the air of the place. The stink of tobacco was everywhere, and it was cold. Thomas shivered as he sat on a bench in the domicile's entryway alongside a brace of courtiers who also bore things for Raleigh — letters, in fact, that were now being opened and scanned by a Tower guard. After these writings passed muster, the guard appropriated them for delivery, then beckoned Thomas and leafed quickly through Thomas's book, which the earl had purchased from a man on Lime Street, and which concerned botany. The guard poked its covers and binding with a knitting needle, tearing the book apart in the process. He began to place the dismantled pages in a box with the letters, then suddenly took note, for the first time, of Thomas's livery and Gentleman Pensioner's badge. His manner became deferential. He handed the pieces of book back to Thomas. "You may wait, sir, if you wish to speak with Sir Walter."

Thomas did not wish to speak with Sir Walter, having no idea what he should say to him. But at the invitation he sat mechanically back on the bench.

There were voices coming from behind the wall, and he found that if he listened carefully he could catch some fragments of dialogue. It made little sense to him. One voice barked, "*All* saw your hand move under that pillow. Did you think us utter fools?" The other, milder voice replied at length, in a hum too low to follow. In time this hum began to put Thomas to sleep. He drowsed, his arms folded across his broad chest and his head dropping to his shoulder, until the slam of a door startled him upright.

Lord Robert Cecil stood before him, looking at him with raised eyebrows. "Sir Thomas Percy, is't not?" Cecil glanced briefly at the guard at the main door, then back to Thomas. "What business hast thou with Sir Walter Raleigh?"

Percy scrambled to his feet and awkwardly bowed. "None, lord. Only a book, sent by my lord the earl."

"It was carefully perused, my lord," the guard said officiously.

"Let's have it anyway." Cecil held out his hand. Obediently, Thomas delivered the book, which was now in three parts, like the Trinity, or Caesar's Gaul. "It seems not much of a book," Cecil said. "But I shall make sure. Will you walk with me?"

Thomas could do naught but assent. He followed the high counselor into the main passageway outside Raleigh's innermost apartments. The guard locked the door behind them.

"*Faith shines like gold in the furnace*," Cecil said. "What does this mean, Sir Thomas?"

"I beg your pardon, lord?" Thomas looked down at the man, bemused. He towered above Cecil, and found himself hoping, as he often did when among the highborn, that his height might prompt a touch of respect.

But this little lord seemed unbothered, unreduced by his need to look upward at Percy as they walked. He was always the smallest, and used to it. At court, short men generally wore high heels, and thus made themselves look more absurd by art than they already did by nature. Cecil could never see the benefit of such vanity. He differed from most gentlemen of the age, who thought power an attribute of physical bearing and badges and chains of office. Long before, when he was a boy pushed by bigger boys, Cecil had learned to derive a sense of authority from less visible sources.

"*Faith shines like gold in the furnace*," he repeated now, not varying his pleasant tone. "These were Robert Catesby's words to you, as the two of you spoke at our last Christmas Revels at Whitehall. What did he mean?"

"Ah . . . . my lord, 'tis hard to remember. This was many months past."

"Did he mean that the faith of English Catholics is burnished by their sufferings?"

Thomas could think of nothing to do but cough.

"Marry, Sir Thomas, all know Catesby of the flashing crucifix is a recusant. He's on the rolls, and doesn't hide it. You're not protecting him by keeping your mouth shut."

"Then I think this must have been what he meant, lord," Thomas said lamely. "What you said. Though I cannot well remember."

"I shall applaud Catesby's patience while I pray for his conversion." Cecil's voice was dry. "For gold can also *melt* in a furnace, Thomas, and be put to new uses." This last was too deep for Thomas to sound, but fortunately Cecil prevented any need for a reply by saying, "Ah, here's my turning. You may assure the Earl of Northumberland that his book will reach his friend in short order, and with a mended binding."

"Thank you, my lord." Thomas bowed once more, then took his own path into London, his heart beating quickly.

In fact, Thomas remembered very well Catesby's remark about the furnace, which had signified the fiery hell the powder brethren planned to make of Westminster. Now he tried to master his fear at the realization that they'd been spied on that day at Whitehall, by Cecil or one of his servants, and that other things must have been overheard as well. He and Catesby had done their best to speak obliquely, and he doubted Lord Cecil had collected anything truly incriminating. But the very fact that he and Catesby had been watched disturbed him.

It must simply be that he'd been with Catesby, he decided. Though Catesby had been pardoned after the Essex rising, he'd done nothing to redeem himself since, not with crown or with parliament. Unlike some others, like Lord Monteagle, he hadn't slavishly abased himself in apology to the queen, hadn't begun attending services at a Protestant church. Never Catesby! In his mind Thomas rehearsed the familiar litany of Catesby's accomplishments in stubbornness, reigniting his admiration for the man as he did so. He strode faster, his inspiration growing. Robin was honorable, and true to the faith. He must always be watched, then, by such as Cecil.

By the time Percy reached Gray's Inn Road, he'd convinced himself that Cecil had no particular suspicion of Catesby, much less of Thomas himself, and only a general distrust of Robin and his associates.

He was wrong. Cecil had taken the opportunity of his short walk with Thomas to compare the big knight's form and face, feature by feature, with a description he had received of Andrew Andrews, lessor of two small properties in Westminster. That description had been provided him by a baker in the vicinity, and he found it matched this Percy uncommonly well.

Alone in his palace rooms, tired from his walk, Cecil sank into a comfortable chair and flipped the pages of the disassembled book he'd taken from Thomas. "*A Dictionarie of Plants That May Induce Lethargie,*" he read aloud. "Now, *this* shall be enthralling." He held a candleflame to the text's margins, watching hopefully for the telltale appearance of any cipher written in orange juice.

Thomas came late to the next day's meeting in Lambeth. He'd been imprisoned in chat by the earl, to whom he'd thought it his duty to report the waylaying of the gift for Raleigh. The news had unsettled Henry Percy, who'd meant only to continue with one of his science-minded friends a discussion about the curative properties of certain leaves and stems. Distracted, the earl had brushed off Thomas's opaque inquiries about proper fuse lengths and qualities. He wanted to talk about Cecil and the botany book. He stalled Thomas for an hour, parsing his servant's words, trying to extract from them some specific reason King James's chief privy councilman should suspect an honest English earl's plain present to a fellow man of science. "Perhaps Lord Cecil is interested in plants," Thomas said at one point, angering the earl, who called him an idiot. At last Henry Percy dismissed Thomas. In the Syon House courtyard Thomas spurred his horse to the gallop, racing off in a cloud of autumn dust. But he still failed to reach Catesby's house until a half-hour after the appointed time.

Thomas knocked on the door, gave sign and heard countersign, and was admitted. He handed his cloak to Bates in the hallway. Then he strode quickly into the dining room, where a murmur of voices and a scraping of chairs told him the men were assembled. He touched his various tokens as he walked: his newest rosary, the St. Winifred medal, the onion he'd stitched, with clumsy fingers, into his doublet as a protection against the plague.

At the room's entranceway he stopped short.

"But sit, Thomas," Catesby said, though he himself was standing tall, with his right fist clenched before him. "*Ecce signum!*" Loosening his fist, Robin let a thin stream of black powder trickle from his hand down to the table, where it accumulated in a small pile on the white cloth. He performed the whole operation dangerously close to a lit candle.

Scowling, Thomas, with some others, wagged his head, disliking Catesby's sacrilege more than his physical recklessness. But in a moment his eye was caught by someone else. He stared, barely hearing as Francis Tresham spoke worriedly from his place near the curtained window. "Will you blow all of us up, Robin?"

"No. This is *my* body" — Catesby jerked a thumb at his chest — "and I like it whole, not dashed into pieces to be shared among you."

The whole room went silent at this blasphemy.

Catesby did not apologize, but smiled. "There is no danger, cousin. Guido has tested a pinch of this stuff from each barrel. It is counterfeit. All irretrievably decayed, despite a second remixing. The stock must be replenished. But fear not. God has given us time to do this. We may thank Him, now, for this second prorogation." Lowering himself onto the bench, Catesby gestured at the table. "Sit, Sir Thomas." He wrinkled his nose. "I'faith, you should change your onion. Sir."

But Thomas would not sit. Hardly cheered by this news about the powder, he was still trying to absorb the first shock, which dwarfed Catesby's reckless irreverence. He said, still staring, "The table's full."

It was. The youthful face at the far end of the bench. The friendly smile, showing pearl-white teeth. There, in Thomas's usual place, sat his companion from Chester on the way to Holywell. Sir Everard Digby.

As Bates brought another chair, Digby rose and bowed to Thomas. "Welcome, fellow pilgrim! You see I have joined this band of brothers."

Thomas nodded slowly. He could not begin to say what he felt. How had this come about? Had Kit Wright or Bors Wintour enlisted young Digby somewhere along the road to Winifred's shrine, or on the return journey? Would they do so without speaking to him of their plan? And Digby himself, with his cherished, adoring wife .... did he know what he was risking now?

Bates had gone out, and now came in again with yet another chair in hand. He cleared his throat. "Gentlemen, here is —"

"They know me." And here, five steps behind Bates, came another young man, elegant in a webbed lace collar, a fine woolen doublet and pair of trunks, and a tooled leather cap studded with a brooch. It was Ambrose Rookwood, their supplier of monies and Catesby's fellow harborer of powder, whom Thomas had also met on the pilgrimage. Rookwood had stabled his horse at the rear of the house and entered through the side. "Friends," he said, nodding.

Thomas sank into a chair.

"Thomas, th'art flap-jawed and goggle-eyed." Catesby's grin stretched wider. "Did thy horse throw thee? Didst thou land on thy head?" Robin came around the table to clap him on the shoulder. "I myself have persuaded these two to join our enterprise, though not much argument was needed. Sir Ambrose came last week to question me closely about the uses of his powder. Fawkes was here at that time, and together we brought him into full knowledge. He has pledged to gather a hundred war horses to deliver to John Grant's keeping for the rising in the midlands."

"I embrace the work." Ambrose looked reverently at Catesby.

"As do I." Digby spoke with zeal. "I'faith, I guessed at thy high design on the road to Holywell, Thomas. Your talk in the tavern in Chester, of destroying a false house — It put me in mind of what might be plotted."

"But I only meant . . . ." Thomas stopped, recalling the conversation with the wry tavern host. For what else *had* he meant, if not . . . what Digby had guessed?

Some of the men frowned at Thomas, but Catesby only smiled, first at him, and then at Digby. "We say 'planned,' not 'plotted'," he gently corrected the younger man.

"Forgive me." A gracious duck of the head. "Thomas, you said Robin Catesby stayed presently in Lambeth, and I resolved to seek him out here. And did, and have been transported. Transported. For God, priests, and country, I put myself at his service!" Digby's face was inflamed with passion. "Thomas, why look you so white?"

"It is only . . . ." Thomas's gaze slowly scanned the group about the table. Robin Catesby, Guido Fawkes, Bors and Gawain Wintour. His brothers-in-law Kit and Jack Wright. The aptly named Keyes, gate-keeper at Lambeth. Bates, the servant, who now stood in a corner, his face a mask of servility. John Grant, their midlands gentleman farmer. Rookwood and Digby, their new members. Francis Tresham, cousin of Catesby and of Eliza Vaux.

And himself.

"We are thirteen," he said bleakly.

A pall fell on the table as each man surveyed his fellows, silently counting. Catesby broke the quiet with a short laugh. "That Thomas should find this! And he is right."

"Then it is settled. We *must* include my brother Monteagle." Francis Tresham spoke with sudden force. Monteagle, seemingly, had been a subject of discussion prior to Thomas's entrance. Francis slapped his hand on the cloth, making the powder-pile jump and the black grains scatter. "Monteagle will make fourteen, which is twice seven. A good number."

"Nay, Francis." Thomas shook his head. With heavy tread he walked to the chair Bates had placed at the end of the benched table. "We cannot—"

"We cannot what, man?" asked Tresham brusquely. "You have met my Catholic brother-in-law at a mass or two. Would you consign him to the flames?"

"He is not a true—"

"Stop." Tresham held up a warning hand. "No more sour talk of church papists and false Catholics. I hear you yourself have somehow vanished from the recusant rolls, Thomas, by a stroke of wizardly luck. Not all have a mighty magical earl to protect them."

Thomas sat, silent and glowering.

"I do not challenge thy valor and honor," Tresham went on in a softer voice. "I mean only that had we no church-papist friends, no hidden Catholics, like the Keeper of the Wardrobe, who has rented *you* the Westminster properties, we could gain no foothold in the den of the enemy. I think, at the least, William Lord Monteagle must be *warned.*"

"Warned? That, we may further speak on," said Catesby. "Yet I share Thomas's view that thy kinsman is too comfortable in the devil's den to be trusted with the whole of our plan."

Bors Wintour nodded. "Monteagle sits in Parliament, yet it is said that he spoke nothing against the renewed statute banishing priests. He stayed home on the day of discussion, and sent a proxy, who cast no vote."

Francis Tresham twisted his lip, looking pained. Finally he spoke. "Well, then. We'll not tell Monteagle of . . . of all. But let him obliquely be signaled."

"I shall speak to him," said Catesby smoothly. He knit his brow. "Yet without his full membership, we still have the difficulty of the thirteen."

A difficulty owed to thee. Thomas was suddenly angry at Catesby's high-handedness. Inviting members without consulting the group! Without consulting, at the least, *him!* He began to speak, but let his voice die. Francis Tresham was speaking again, after emitting a nervous laugh. "Nay, Robin, there is no cause for concern. It ... uh ... comes to me now. We are not thirteen, but fourteen."

"What say you?" Catesby barked. Thomas was also alarmed — yet *another* made privy to their secrets? — but a little glad to see Robin Catesby's smile leak from his face. Their golden-haired leader pushed back the bench and stood. With rare ferocity, he snarled, "Have you told all to Monteagle, after all? Is this a game?"

"Nay, nay!" Tresham held up his hands. "I've told my brother-in-law naught. But .... Aye, I must tell you. There is a fourteenth, and it is ...."

"What, man?"

Tresham cleared his throat. "Thy cousin."

"My cousin? *Thou* art my cousin. What other cousin?"

"*My* cousin. Not thou. Mine other cousin. And thine."

"What's thy babble?"

Tresham dropped his hands. "Eliza Vaux."

The group sat, stunned again, as though the small black pile on the table had actually exploded. After a few seconds Catesby spoke in a voice of controlled anger, fierce and low. "How could you have done this? To tell our secrets to a *woman*?"

Francis Tresham again held his hands up in defense. "I could not choose, Robin! Eliza all but guessed. Do you recall, three years ago at Baddesley Clinton, how precisely she divined our plan to petition Thomas's earl to approach James? This was the same. She deduced the plot —"

"The *plan*."

"The *plan*, from close observation. She rode to my house and threatened to withhold sanctuary from our priests if I did not speak."

"She would not have done that!"

"I know! I know this was her bluff, but Eliza is a .... Robin, had I failed to confirm her guesses she would have gone forth asking questions of others, and rumor would have spread that way. I had to prevent it!" Spreading his hands, Francis looked helplessly around the frozen group. "At all events, she urged her service to us and the priests, and her sister Anne's —"

"*Anne* Vaux knows also?"

"Nay." Tresham shook his head vigorously. "I am sure she does not. I swore Eliza to silence on the body of our Lord. Robin, if you are set on this bloody course —"

"'If *you* are set'?" Half the group stood now with Robin, hands on sword-hilts, but the shouting came from Thomas. Knocked back with the force of his rising, the bench hit the wall. "Should your *you* not be *we,* Francis Tresham? You, too, have sworn! He who has a sword, a hand, a heart —"

"Of a surety!" Francis held up a hand. "I have sworn. Calm thyself, Thomas. Sit, all! Let me speak! If *we* are so set, says our cousin, she approves our plan. She has sworn to be of help —"

"But a *woman!*" Thomas and Catesby cried together. The other men stayed silent, gone wooden, hands still on their swords. Only their eyes moved, darting warily between Tresham and the other two, Thomas and Catesby, at the table's other end.

After a moment Catesby let out a long breath, and the men relaxed slightly. "Francis, it was not well done." Robin shook his head. "You should have come to me."

But Francis was tired of defending himself. "You, Robin Catesby, have invited men to join our band before obtaining *our* good leave. I speak not against Rookwood and Digby. They are welcome. Ambrose was indeed half a member beforehand. But what was I to think when you told me you had shared your secrets with Father *Quindle*? Which will make us, as I think on it, *fifteen!* Why did you so?"

Catesby sat back down and folded his arms, but the men still stayed rooted, hands clutching scabbards, absorbing this new surprise.

"I sought Father Quindle's blessing," Robin said quietly.

"And did you get it?"

Robin said nothing for a moment. Then he declared, "A priest is not a woman."

Francis snorted. "Father Quindle is something like it."

"But not in the way of chattering."

"Our cousin Eliza does not chatter. Sound her yourself if you do not trust her faith."

"No! It is done." Jack Wright had been silent since Thomas's entrance, but now he spoke. "Sit down, all. There will be no sounding. Women and priests shall be our partners. So be it."

"One woman," said Francis, as the men slowly lowered themselves back onto the benches.

Robin smiled sardonically. "*Perhaps* one woman. "

"And perhaps one priest!" Francis snapped.

"The priests will not betray us," said Thomas.

"Nor will my cousin Eliza."

Kit Wright spoke. "My brother Jack says true. It is done." Kit spread his hands, encompassing the group. "Does any man here wish to forsake our endeavor because Father Quindle and Eliza Vaux are privy to the plot?"

"The *plan*."

"Aye, the plan, Robin. What say you, men? Doth any man falter?"

All shook their heads vigorously. *No.*

There were reasons for the other men's silence in this debate. Some of them, indeed, had let slip word of their doings to their wives. Save Thomas Percy and the wifeless Catesby and Fawkes, each man had a woman he thought eminently trustworthy. None of them had spoken of his small indiscretions to the others when those had occurred, and each was even less inclined to reveal them now.

"No man falters." Kit nodded. "Then make peace, my good friends, before supper."

Francis leaned across the table to clasp Robin's hand. Then he reached for Thomas's paw. "Peace." Robin Catesby and Thomas Percy echoed his word.

Catesby now straightened and smiled. Having suddenly convinced himself that Francis Tresham's breach was pardonable, he dispensed his golden confidence to the rest. The sun rose again in his face, and answering smiles broke forth around the table.

"I'faith, this is just." Catesby filled his glass with yellow canary. "The realm is true powder, awaiting the touch of the spark. All the faithful pant for their liberation. Women as well as men, and priests to boot." Catesby did not tell the men of Father Quindle's wan look when, halfway through Catesby's disclosures to him the prior July, that priest had laid a hand on Robin's very lips and begged him to stop speaking. That didn't matter. Whatever Father Quindle's delicacy, Catesby knew that in the aftermath of the miracle, once released from their cramped priest-holes and dank attics, Quindle, Garnet, and all the other shepherds would rejoice in the free air. Catesby would save the priests so the priests could save him. He raised his glass. "We walk now in danger. But out of this nettle, danger, we pluck this flower, safety. Safety for all!"

They toasted with him. "Safety for all!"

Their group was expanding, widening like ripples in a pool, and in that growth lay danger. They all knew it, but at this moment were less alarmed by the pool's spread than comforted by the proof that they were not, after all, thirteen.

Chapter 30

The sky was a deep blue, the sun dazzlingly bright. In a large gravel pit behind Ambrose Rookwood's manor in Suffolk, Thomas Percy and Guido Fawkes were testing fuses. Bates and Robert Keyes circulated in the woods near the pit, aimlessly firing blunderbusses. There were partridges in the wood, but the men were not trying to bag birds. They shot only to shield the sound of the blasting of small amounts of powder in the pit.

Thomas watched from the edge of the hollow as Fawkes knelt, lit the far end of a length of oil-soaked twine with a spark from his tinderbox, then rose and backed quickly away from the burning fuse. As Fawkes came nearer to him, Thomas looked down at the face of the watch Keyes had given them this morning to time the fuse-lengths. Behind Guido the hissing spark snaked down the length of the twine, faster than thought. When Fawkes was still three paces from Thomas the powder exploded. From the trees crows scattered, cawing.

"The pox!" Fawkes swore. "A whoreson fuse!"

Thomas showed him the watch. "This burned in only a little less than a minute."

"*Less* than one minute is worse than *more* than one minute. I must leave the vault at a walk, else I bring suspicion. I might stay in the vault, but then I blow up. Hoist on my own petard." Fawkes looked down at the spool of twine at Thomas's feet. "If the fuse is too long it may sputter out before it gets to the powder. But I must lengthen it." He knelt. With hands marked by powder-burns, he unspooled the twine, spliced the cord with his knife, then spread oil along the new length with a greasy cloth. "We will try again."

That night found Thomas in the Irish Boy, where he'd come to tell Catesby of the progress of the testing. He'd thought to meet Robin alone, and was surprised, when he entered the Pomegranate room, to find a large supper party in progress. It included not only Catesby and Kit Wright but several men whom Thomas had not seen before, as well as a high-browed fellow who looked faintly familiar. Thomas doffed his cloak and pulled a stool close to Robin.

Catesby greeted him with a clap on the shoulder. He was busy singing a catch with a large, festive fellow who held half a boiled egg in his hand and waved it in time to the music. The room was too raucous for introductions, though the noise had its merits. As the men sang their chorus for a third time, Thomas seized the opportunity to ask Robin in his ear what all the mayhem meant, and why these strangers were here.

"They provide some color for our enterprise," Catesby told him gaily, through hands cupped over Thomas's ear. "Too many meetings of the same knot of men will turn eyes toward us. But see us now! Your random flock of drunkards."

"Aye, well." The host of the Irish Boy brought Thomas a pewter cup for wine, then moved to the left of him and Catesby, gathering plates and wiping crumbs. On this table, for a rarity, the host had placed a cloth.

"You promised Francis you would speak to William Lord Monteagle," Thomas said. "Did you so?"

Catesby snorted. "Yes, by St. Geronimy! I spoke of the weather. We have had clear skies, saving the late eclipse. Such was our discourse. Then we parted."

Thomas laughed. "A fine equivocation."

"And did thy trials go well?"

"Aye, at the last. We have arrived at an oiled fuse that burns two full min —"

"Enough." Catesby nudged him in warning. "Speak no more of it. Two minutes is good. It will bring our man well out of the yard."

"Aye, so we found it. And tomorrow, before the cock crows, Fawkes will go to Faversham to fetch more —"

"Yes. *Pauca verba.*"

Thomas paused and looked about him. In a lower voice, he said, "I had thought Jack Wright and John Grant would be here."

"Nay." Catesby took a bite of apple tart from a baked dough coffin, then pointed at his plate. "Excellent pastry! Have a bite. Nay, Thomas, the two of them have posted to their homes and will remain there. Grant is gathering horses in Warwickshire, you know, and Jack performs a like duty in the north. God *grant* they acquire enough mounts! Grant! Ha! And hey, hey! The devil rides on a fiddlestick!" Robin Catesby was antic. "Drink, Thomas! You and I have naught to do now but watch and pray."

"And take the sacrament."

"Aye. To do that, we may repair to Buckinghamshire, where Digby keeps a priest."

"Good." The singing had stopped, and was now replaced by a clatter of dishes and a buzz of merry conversation. Thomas lowered his voice further. "And my part is well approved? Concerning the young Duke of York?"

"Speak more guardedly, Thomas. Yes. You will nab Charles. Small children will be happy at Syon House. They like wizards and magic tricks. Grant is in Warwickshire, near where the little boy's sister's household is kept. He will obtain her without trouble after our work is done, and she will be brought south to join her tiny brother."

"Then the earl —"

"Between you, you will keep the two children." Catesby had perfected a way of talking by which his lips barely moved, though the words came forth plainly to a close listener. "Be not offended, Thomas, when I tell you that the lords of the faithful who find themselves still on this earth on November the sixth will be more likely to honor the earl's title than yours, and to name him Lord Protector. This will be so whatever service you have performed in his shadow. So you must ensure that our fine sorcerer, our Merlin, our Percy and Glendower in one, remains in Sussex, and does not whimsically spirit himself away, riding a rocket to the moon." Catesby was cheerful indeed. He raised his voice. "Thomas, you are not drinking!"

"I am." Thomas poured some Rhenish into his cup from a half-empty bottle. The large egg-eating man across from him was now calling for a new catch, about the trials of wedlock. "All married men must sing!" he shouted. He pointed fingers at Robin and Thomas. "You two."

"Robin Catesby and I are widowers, and cannot," said Thomas.

Catesby looked at Thomas curiously. "'Tis well that Kit has gone to pluck a rose in the alley, and cannot hear you. A brother of Martha Wright would grow warm at your saying."

Thomas shook his head impatiently. "Let us sing a different song!" he said, and swigged his Rhenish as though it were ale. He banged his empty cup on the table just as the door swung open and Kit re-entered the room, fastening his breeches. "Let us have the Ballad of Chevy Chase!"

"Ya-hah!" Kit Wright raised a fist.

"'Afore God, an excellent song!" said the high-browed man, and started them off.

With fifteen hundred bowmen bold,
All chosen men of might,
These knew full well in time of need
To aim their shafts aright!

An hour later the crowd in the room had grown, and places at table had shifted, owing to the movements of Catesby, the egg man (who was also egg-shaped), and the smiling high-browed fellow, who had all risen at some moment to dance a jig. Now Thomas found himself sitting next to the high-browed man, who, when he caught Thomas's eye, graciously half-rose and bowed to him, and said he had seen him once in the yard of St. Paul's, glancing at books, near Michaelmas some three years before.

"I lack such a memory as you have," Thomas said, trying not to burp.

"You are from Northumbria."

"I am," said Thomas proudly. "And from your speech, you are of Warwickshire."

"A native."

"What do you here in London, sir?"

"Counterfeit."

"Ah?" Thomas felt confused.

The man laughed. "I counterfeit. I feign. A player and a poet am I. I write plays, as does my fat friend, there."

"Ah!" Thomas grew interested. "Then you know of a play of Hotspur and the Battle of Shrewsbury?"

"I do, having written it."

Thomas gaped. "Say you true?"

Smiling, the fellow gestured widely at the tableful of singers. "Ask any man here."

Thomas was dumbfounded. This, this slight smiling fellow, was the muse he had so long sought! And the hour was just. Surely God had brought him to this tavern, at this moment, that he might inquire of

the man, to sound his faith! Nothing like a full partnership in the powder brethren was thought of, of course, not after the hard passions of
the brethren's last supper. But if this man was who he claimed to be, he
could be made useful. He owned the largest house in Stratford-upon-
Avon. Thomas himself had seen it. Such a fine midlands manor could
well serve as a base for the gathering armies of the faithful, once all in
England knew that the miracle had been performed; when the news of it
was published in every hamlet and city street. And after the event, here
in London — a London redeemed — what might this thin man not do? He
remembered the idea that had struck him after King James's Christmas
Revels. What wonder might this poet not dream into being, presenting
the glory of the powder brethren in a play?

"What do you write now?" he said stammeringly.

"Now? I incline toward tragedy. Black deeds, to be performed on a
sunny stage. A paradox. Dark things done in fair light."

There was an odd, knowing glint in the man's eyes. His words
prompted Thomas, against reason, to question him regarding the earl's
strange words about the color of good powder. *Useful* powder, Henry
Percy had said, was not grayish, but the blackest black. But he had also
said good powder was fair. "Think you, sir," said Thomas, "that a black
thing can also be fair?"

The poet gave a short laugh. "I *know* that black can be fair. To my
pain, I know it."

He knew it! Thomas's heart now sorely tempted him to give the man
some hint of what was plotted. Was planned. But soft. He could not trust
so far, especially after his recent explosion at tongue-loose Catesby. He
sought other words with which to continue the dialogue, to sound this
poet's inclinations. *Ah. St. Winifred.*

"Do you know," he said cautiously, "I set out from your country of
Warwickshire some weeks ago, with a passel of pilgrims. We journeyed
to Holywell."

"To Winifred's shrine, as I take it."

"Dost know her story?" Thomas spoke with excitement. "She is a virgin saint. Centuries ago, when Winifred spurned the unchaste advances
of a churlish suitor named Caradoc, the knave struck her head from her
body. But lo! When Winifred's head came to ground, a spring of water
jumped up in that place. And then Winifred's blessed uncle joined her

head back to her body. And now the water of her well heals all who touch it. Cures them of all manner of fleshly ills."

The man's eyebrows had arched up so they stood nearly as high as his hairline. "Rejoining heads to bodies?"

"Even this might Winifred's water do."

"Wondrous! And to think some folk charge the pilgrims with superstition! With belief in fantastic tales!"

"Scoffers and rudesbys know naught of true religion," Thomas looked at the poet meaningfully. "Yet you, sir, know something of the faith of Catholics."

"Something I know, indeed. 'Tis a rich man's religion, is't not?" Assuming a mock-haughty look, the man gazed heavenward. "'A-hawking I will go, followed by a light repast of wine and pheasant pie, a change of shirt, and then, to fetch out my priest for a mass. Ah, but so many houses have I, how can I recall where I have stowed him?'" He looked back at Thomas with a smirk and a cackle. "Yes, I know my English Catholics."

Thomas's brow darkened. "Are not *you* a rich man?"

"It might be said that I am, sir, though I was not always. And I did not earn my silver to spend it on fines for recusancy."

Thomas's disappointment was violent. He kicked back his stool from the table and rose so abruptly that ale sloshed and spilled. Hands reached to grab and cover cups, and several men, including Catesby and the poet to whom Thomas had been speaking, looked at him in surprise.

"Sit down, friend!" said the poet, mopping spilled ale with a handkerchief drawn from his doublet. "I meant no offense. Believe as you like, and eat a hazelnut."

But Thomas could not stay. He said an abrupt goodbye to the company at large. As he left the table he heard the thin poet musing, "It might make a play, were Caradoc to repent and him marry Winifred at the end. But how to make the water spring onstage? To say naught of the beheading."

"Pox on all that!" came the fat egg-eater's reply. "Leave magic tricks for . . . ." The voices faded.

Thomas strode the streets near the river in a fury, clenching and unclenching his fists. Talking to this all-admired poet had been no better than speech with the wizard earl. The cares of both poet and earl were petty. This poet, he now knew, was a thoughtless mouthpiece for the God who spoke through him. He was the barrel of a gun, but not the gun's fire.

Hotspur was fire. Catesby was fire. And Thomas was fire. "I am the powder," he said, not realizing he was speaking aloud. "*I* am the *powder.*"

Within half an hour Thomas had reached London Bridge. For no conscious reason he strode across it, muttering and fuming, as late-evening walkers eyed him askance. He passed under Traitors' Gate, not pausing to look up at Essex's head, which stood moldering on a spike like a black apple. He turned to the west, still walking briskly. He slowed when he reached the looming, thatch-roofed bulk of the Globe theater. The playhouse loomed, topless, like an upended pistol.

He walked softly toward it. Passersby were few here at this hour, and there was no one in sight. The wattle walls of the building glowed eerily, as though the place were lit from within. Though he knew the light was only moonshine on whitewash, those walls frightened him. This church where he had long worshipped seemed of a sudden to house a malevolent spirit.

There must be a hired guard, he knew. But either the man was asleep or now rounding the far side of the structure. Or he was scanting his duty, guzzling grog at one of the alehouses nearby.

Thomas came up to a wall and touched it. For some reason he'd thought to find it warm, but of course the wall was cold in the October air.

He looked down at the ground, where some loose thatch from the half-roof had fallen. Kneeling, he took from his bag one of the tinderboxes he and Fawkes had used that morning to sample the fuses. He lit the straw, which flared up quickly. He peered at the fire intently, as if he might fan it with his gaze. Yet there was no need. In a moment flames began to lick at one of the wooden posts that held up the wattle-and-daub superstructure of the house.

He watched the fire for a moment or two, transfixed. Then he shook his head as though to wake himself from slumber. Quickly he unclasped his cape and smothered the flames with the garment. He stamped on the ground until all sparks were extinguished. He left the half-burned cloak on the ground then, and walked down the path to the road, shivering in the wind from the river, feeling in his doublet for Keyes' watch, before he remembered that Fawkes had kept the timepiece.

He struck out for the river-stairs. His reeling head held only a dim notion of the hour, but he knew it was late. Traitors' Gate was likely locked, and the bridge closed. He'd need to hire a wherry to cross the water. He glanced back twice at the playhouse, but kept walking riverward.

That was not my duty.

He'd another house to destroy. As for the whited sepulcher at his back, God himself would strike it down when it had no more usefulness.

Chapter 31

October 26, 1605. St. Bean's Day.

The man plucked nervously at the cloth cap in his hands. He wore a leather jacket with crystal buttons and good woolen netherstocks. Naught in his dress could bring shame; he was far from a beggar. But this was Whitehall Palace. To dress like the lord who sat before him, in a cloak lined with cloth-of-gold and a jeweled cap, would have violated three provisions of sumptuary law, though he could have bought the wear had he wished. The Irish Boy was a lucrative establishment. He was a tavern host, dressed, rightly, as a tavern host. But as the only tavern host in view on the long stony walk to Lord Cecil's apartments, and one led by a guard dressed much more finely than he, he'd begun to feel a small bit abashed.

Even though he had been invited.

"You say they intentionally met."

The tavern host nodded. "Aye, my lord. The two poets, some loud players, and those three."

"Christopher Wright, Thomas Percy, and Robert Catesby."

"Aye, lord."

Cecil had assumed his customary listening pose in his armchair, his forefingers slanted and touching at the tips, two thumbs forming the base of a triangle whose point grazed his lips. "What was discussed?"

The man half-smiled. "The limpness of September lettuce. The treachery of absent wives. The vile pentameters of a certain London poetaster, and —"

"What spice of treachery was mixed with this word-salad?"

"I heard nothing but babble from most, but there was something said between Master Percy and Master Catesby. Something of interest, perhaps, to you, my lord. Percy asked after men he had thought would join them in the tavern this night."

"Did you hear those men's names?"

"Yes, and I have done my best to remember them, though the place was crowded, everyone calling for Huffcap since we'd run short of Dragon's Breath, and never enough mugs–" The man glanced at Cecil, who was beginning to tap his foot. "Well. I mean to say, it was some time before I could write anything down. But I am sure that one of the men Thomas Percy'd expected was another Wright, and then John Grant. And he spoke of one named Dickby, or Digby. Aye, and one more. When Percy first entered Catesby said something of Lord Monteagle."

Cecil turned to his desk. He inked his quill and wrote quickly. "What did he say of him?" he asked as his pen scratched.

The tavern host shifted his feet, considering. "Of Monteagle?"

"Yes."

"Let me see. I think ... some nothingness. That he had sworn to speak to him but had only spoken to him about the fineness of the weather."

Cecil smiled faintly. "Good. Yes. Continue."

"And then it was that I heard the name of the Duke of York, and of a Zion House as I think, and something of a Thresham, or Tresham, in Warwickshire, who had horses. The din was great, and I caught only pieces," he said apologetically. "They spoke something, too, of an oiled fuse."

"An oiled fuse?" Cecil looked up from his busy writing, frowning. "You did not mention this before. Are you sure those were the words?"

The host nodded vigorously. "Aye. I had meant to come to it. The big man, Percy, spoke to Catesby of a success he'd had lately had with an oiled fuse. In connection with this, he spoke of someone called Fox, as I think, who was bound for Faversham on the morrow, in the small hours, to get something. Catesby stopped him from saying what it was."

"The morrow? Meaning today?"

"Aye, it would have been. And Thomas Percy smelled . . . ." The man wrinkled his nose. "Like —"

"Smoke."

The man's eyes widened in admiration. "Yes, lord. This was it."

After the tavern host had departed, his coin purse the heavier, Cecil sat nearly motionless for ten minutes. He gazed at the fire. Once he leaned forward and pushed at the smolder with an iron. Blue and yellow flames leapt upward, and a charred log snapped. He squinted at the flames, imagining explosions, earth-thunder, the stones of a building falling, and a fire such as this at the heart of it.

His bird chirped and hopped in its cage on the shelf, frightened by the sudden noise of the logs. Cecil paid the linnet no mind. He sat and thought.

After a few more minutes he rose, slowly, but with a purpose. He cloaked himself warmly, muffling his face, and let himself out of his rooms. On foot, he left the palace. He had resolved to walk. It was not too far, and a horse might bring unwanted attention.

Within an hour he was at Westminster. Parliament Place stood dark and mostly quiet. The baker's and pannier's shops were closed. At the far end of the square, a few hired caretakers lounged dicing in front of an alehouse as its host locked its doors. A cat yowled somewhere. Cecil quenched his lantern and held close to the shadows, hoping that if the dicers caught sight of him he might, despite his low stature, be taken for a guard like them.

The caretaker of the place to which he sought access was absent, he trusted. This would be "Fox," if he had guessed rightly that "Fox" was the real name of the "John Johnson" who watched the property below the House of Lords. According to the host of the Irish Boy's report, that man was on his way to Faversham now, which left Cecil free to delve into the mystery of this building. In his pocket he fingered the key he'd acquired from the Keeper of the Wardrobe, the man who had leased the vault. In all good faith, he'd told the Keeper he wished to ensure that all was ready for the Parliament that was to open in only ten days; that needful commodities — wood and coal, for example — were well stocked. He'd held this key for a week, awaiting his opportunity for night-work. The tavern-host's report had come in good time.

Cecil turned the key in a side door, opened it, and walked into blackness. He closed the door behind him and knelt. He lit the lantern with his tinderbox. Then he stood and held the light high.

The lantern cast its beams over a capacious space. He saw arched enclaves for storage, and a high ceiling crossed with wooden support beams. Wood, old stone, and barrels of– coal? powder? — were in large supply. Black shadows hovered at the edges of the vault. He lifted the lantern higher. "Is there any man here?"

His voice echoed in the hollow chamber.

Careful. Careful, he told himself, and began.

For an hour, holding the lantern or placing it with extreme care, he searched through the motley assemblage of boxes and caskets and barrels scattered through the cellarage. Nothing. Nothing. Nothing. Most of the containers were empty. Others held dust and moldy traces of oats or bran or millet.

After an hour and a quarter, Cecil began to wonder whether he had been wrong.

He stood at one end of the floor, biting his lip and pondering. Then his eye was caught by a mountain of firewood that lay five yards from his elbow.

He walked toward the pile. This was more firewood than would be burned in the braziers of this house in six months. Moving closer, he peered at the stack. Certainly, there was something behind it. Back and forth he paced, swinging his lamp close — but not too close — to the wood. The third time he stopped, noting some carved marks on a log that rested atop the mid-section of the pile. He bent and gently lifted the log.

His heart flooded with dark joy. There, underneath the wood, lay the lid of a barrel.

Carefully, carefully, he moved enough of the firewood aside to free the barrel's lid, so he could lift it. He leaned closer, taking care to raise the lantern very high.

Millet. His face drooped in disappointment.

He began to replace the lid. Then he paused. It was not, after all, his way to stop at the surfaces of things. *Why should millet be hidden?* He plunged his right hand into the barrel, as deep as he could get it, then pulled it back, clutching a handful of grain.

It was millet all the way to the bottom.

Still. Why should millet be hidden?

He replaced the barrel-top. Behind the millet he could see the brown staves of another barrel. Gently shifting more wood, he pushed the lid of the second barrel to the side. He was leaning over the first barrel now, his feet dangling above the ground, his left arm still holding the lantern aloft. *Careful, careful!* He saw a glimmer of something white in the second barrel, and dipped his right hand into it. *Flour.* He pushed his hand through the silky substance, two inches, four inches.

Five inches into the barrel his fingertips met something grainy. His grim smile returned. *This. Praise God, this!*

He withdrew his hand and looked at what he held. Black powder. He tasted a fleck of it. *Sharp.* He grimaced and wiped his tongue on his sleeve. No spitting. The mark on the floor might be seen by Fox, or whatever the man's true name was.

Peering into the hole he'd made in the woodpile, Cecil saw more barrels behind. But he could not count them without dismantling all their covering. This was more than he could do alone, and, more than he could do without leaving signs that he'd been there. He replaced the lid of the second barrel and the wood over it, noting the particular marks on the split logs. Then, stepping carefully so as not to leave tracks in the dust of the floor, he walked back to the side entrance of the house. He blew out the lantern flame, came out into the cold, clear night, and locked the door.

He stood for a moment, envisioning the unsuspecting boy who would have brought wood for the braziers of the king and lords above on Parliament's opening day; the baker and pannier and their wives, who would ply their wares close to the great house, the customers buying, the children playing pennyprick in the dust the very moment the sky fell on their heads. For a moment, he allowed himself to think of such plain English folk. Then he returned his thoughts back to the welfare of the man who was England, the sum of their parts. Cecil himself would have been in attendance; would have died, too, in the blaze. But to this sure fact he gave small attention. He thought of the king.

By the time he'd again reached the palace his feet and back hurt, and his arm was full sore from holding the lantern so high for so many minutes. Still, he brushed away the servant who offered to bring him soup and wine, asking only that the fire be replenished. Once the wood had been piled high and relit and was crackling merrily, he sat gazing at the flames once more. This time, however, he did not conjure burning buildings in the yellows and oranges and blues. His mind was busy counterplotting.

The presence of poets at the Irish Boy introduced a new puzzle. What had those rhymers to do with this horror? Cecil doubted any benefit would come from questioning them directly. The Essex event had taught him well enough what to think of London stage-poets. They were workmen who did anything for money. Some were masters of verse and spectacle, but all were fools in the realm of the politic. Only one of them had ever shown a gift for both spycraft and playwriting, and that one had been dead twelve years, and could no longer be blamed for anything. The plays themselves bore close watch, of course. England bred mad lords like Essex who were now and again inspired to flights of dangerous self-glorification which some stage-verse or other had taught them to confuse with honor. But the poets and players themselves wished only to compete in extracting coin from those lords, who had enough. Indeed, why not tempt such hare-brained gentry into the theaters by prancing on scaffolds, portraying the feats of their ancestors, and embellishing those feats greatly in the act? No, it would be a waste of time to sound the poets, as it had been four years before. They said many words which, boiled down, came to nothing at all. This was true even of the fat one, a man oft seen at court, much praised for his masques, and almost as often thrown in jail for his stage-mockeries of the Scottish knights who now swarmed through Whitehall. Very humorous mockeries they were, in Cecil's private opinion. And their author was a known recusant. But in the main, he, too, was a man of mere talk. He and the other poet had doubtless been brought to the Irish Boy last night only to mask Catesby's sedition with some trivial noise and color.

But the others who had been seen or mentioned at the gathering were a different matter. Cecil looked at the list that lay before him on his writing desk. He knew every man on it, save the one called Fox, alias John Johnson. *Christopher Wright. John Wright. John Grant. Francis Tresham. Everard Digby.* One of these five professed Protestantism, but all were members of well-known Catholic families in the midlands or the north, as were Robin Catesby and Thomas Percy. It was not difficult to link any of their names with conspiracy. And *this.* Cecil tapped his quill on the parchment. *Zion House.* His lip curled. That could be no other place than Syon House, the earl's London palace, to which Thomas Percy reported. The wellspring of this poison.

Yet he should not say so. Syon was not *quite* the wellspring. Surely these men had met there, had conspired with the wizardly Earl of Northumberland, who stood to reap great gains from their fiendish antics, no question. But who, at the start, had prompted the men to form their cabal? Who kept them so wrapped in chains of fear, fear for their souls, fear of damnation, that they would do anything to breathe easily? Would kill a king for the right to confess the sin to a shadowy ghost behind a screen, and receive some petty absolution? Who, indeed, but the Jesuits?

It was the peter-priests, always the peter-priests, who for fifty busy years had been poisoning English wells.

But there was time now to purge the wells. Thank God Cecil had stirred the king's fears of plague, to achieve this last Parliamentary prorogation! James had disliked Cecil's suggestion of postponement, until his royal mind had been shaken by his counselor's lurid descriptions of the rotten, discolored bodies of London dead during the worst times of plague, of how the buboes swelled in the skin and every orifice bled red fire. At this, James had thought he would, after all, betake himself again to the country where deer were plentiful, until the autumn was well advanced.

Now that he had done so, leaving Cecil time to fish for his enemies, Cecil had not only found this plot, but could take days to prevent its horrible unfolding, and to stop it in no blunt, crude way. The king would not return until the eve of All Hallow's Day. For the rest of this month, then, Cecil would let the powder lie, until out of this nest of traitors he had coaxed a savior.

But who should this savior be?

Cecil had not slept for eighteen hours, but still he sat, working the complex machinery of his thought. At last he chose. Inking his quill again, he wrote a letter. The missive was not long, but it took him an hour and many cross-hatchings and new starts before he was satisfied with it. Then he folded it, scrawled a name on its outside, and locked it in his drawer.

Dawn was breaking as he swiftly penned two additional, short letters. One was to his household steward, saying his return to his house would be delayed some days further, on a pressing matter of state. The other was to Lord Monteagle. He sealed the last two letters with wax, and rang for a page to see to the swift delivery of both. Then, exhausted, he half-walked, half-hobbled to his bed.

"My lord, I assure you I knew nothing of this." It was not his face of shock and dismay but the woundedness of his tone that convinced Cecil that William Parker, Lord Monteagle, was telling the truth. "Nothing," Monteagle repeated. "I was not warned."

You were not included, Cecil thought, studying his eyes. *So good a church papist are you that your Catholic friends did not trust you. They would consign you to death rather than risk you dropping hints of their plot about London, leaking it like water from a broken bucket.* He said none of this, but only "Hum."

"I swear I was not sounded, lord." Monteagle drew himself up tall, evidently resolving to make what advantage he could for himself out of the painful slight. "I think all in England know I could not be tempted into any device that brought danger to the realm, most particularly to our king." He spoke with dignity. "I know the men you speak of, but have not seen them in a group since a ma — since a gathering at Huddington Court more than two years ago."

Cecil erupted, banging his hand on a table. "You *know* these men? You *know* them? In 1601 you and three of them rode with Essex, brandishing swords before the gates of this very palace. Riding back and forth through the Strand like madmen, shouting threats to our queen! I would agree, you *know* these men."

"Foolishness of youth, lord, and now I — "

The little man's voice rose to a roar. "*Further,* your wife is sister to Francis *Tresham!*"

Monteagle went down on one knee and bent his head. "Lord, I concede the relation, but . . . ." He had begun to shake, and Cecil felt a twinge of pity for him. He suppressed it. "I was not . . . *warned!* " Monteagle was pleading, his voice now a half-muffled moan. "I know nothing."

Cecil resumed his normal, even tone. He touched Monteagle on the shoulder. "Get up, man. I believe you, as it falls out. You shall see why I believe you. Now you know how wise has been your choice, in swearing fealty to the sovereign and to our Church."

Monteagle got to his feet in relief.

"I do not care what you think about masses and sacraments, Monteagle, though I would not be pleased to find a peter-priest hidden in your larder. If you would commit no treason — "

"I swear it."

"Then I know how speedily you would have come to me with this letter had I not intercepted it before it reached you." Cecil opened a drawer and brought forth the letter he had worked on hours before, while night was fading from the sky. "Sit. You will see you *were* warned, or would have been."

Monteagle sat. Ill-disguised pleasure flooded his face as he bent to look at the document Cecil placed before him. He was to have been told after all! He read aloud. "*My lord, out of the love I bear to some of your friends, I have a care of your preservation. Therefore I would advise you, as you tender your life, to devise some excuse to shift of your attendance at this Parliament, for God and man have concurred to punish the wickedness of this time.* Whence came this?" He looked wonderingly at Cecil. "It is unsigned, and I know not the hand. Certainly it is not Tresham's."

Cecil was piqued at Monteagle's last observation. His fingers still ached from the unnatural position they'd held as he'd scribbled the letter, discarding the refinements of the secretary style, attempting to shape words like some northern Catholic gentleman might, or like anyone might who was not Cecil. "Whence and from whom it came need not precisely concern you," he said brusquely. "Suffice it to say — and suffice *you* to say — that it came to you, and that you brought it to me. As you would have."

Monteagle nodded uncertainly. "Yes. You must see that the letter itself shows I knew — "

"Nothing. I know. If you cannot tie the letter to any . . . specific source, merely leave it with me. I will bring it to the king's attention when he returns to London."

Cecil folded and stowed the letter. Monteagle followed it with his eyes. "That is sound reason, lord. Please tell his majesty I was aware of — "

"Nothing. I will. But as you know, I have every reason to think the warning ensues from those gentlemen I named to you, of whose villainous enterprise I have clear proof. You must keep clear of them."

"I will stay clear. And I will share with no one what you have uncovered."

"Say to me what it is I have uncovered, sir."

"A plan for some treason at this Parliament, which you know . . . some . . . to be on the threshold of achieving." Monteagle swallowed, and his voice became strained. He disliked even thinking the words he meant to say next. But he had a wife with whom he shared everything, and children, for whom he would have died. He would not have died for his brother-in-law Francis Tresham, or for the right to a Catholic mass in an English church. Nor to confess to a Catholic priest, at least just yet. He had come to think confession a deathbed thing. Lord Cecil had taken his measure correctly. Indeed, this Monteagle was not the sword-waving rebel of four years before. Then, Essex had intoxicated him, had nearly cost him his fortune and his life. Afterward, he had resolved never again to follow a dangerous man.

Drawing a deep breath, Monteagle said, "You may proceed in all trust with their arrests." He hurried on. "I will not speak to my brother Tresham, or to any of the rest. Keep me under close watch if you doubt my word. If any more letters come to me, I will—"

"You shall be trusted." Cecil rose. "I bid you once more, keep mum."

Of course he had Monteagle followed. Yet he felt sure the lord would not compromise the glorious reputation that would come to the Parker name out of this contrived event. By the bogus letter, Monteagle would be made the gentleman who had saved England.

Cecil did not think Monteagle had thought far enough ahead to realize what other excellent things the letter would conjure forth. He himself, of course, had. The news would be published that peers with Catholic ties were warned to avoid Parliament on the day it was to explode. Perhaps, indeed, the conspirators intended to warn those peers. Perhaps they did not. But whether or no, the warning letter to Monteagle, a suspected papist, would argue that only Protestants were to perish. And then, how villainous, how un-English, would all Catholics seem! How blacker than the black they already were! And blackest of all would be their shepherds, the peter-priests, when they were found (as they would be), brought out (as they would be) to disclose the hand they had played in the plotting! For there would be priests in it. There would most assuredly be priests in it, at the plot's very heart and festering core.

Yes, young Monteagle would shine forth a hero. Verses would be written and so forth, perchance by one of those poets who'd drunk with Robin Catesby at the Irish Boy two nights before. Buying freedom from suspicion the only way poets knew.

But this, the glorification of Monteagle, was peripheral to Cecil's main aims. In truth, Cecil cared more to make still another man a hero, a shining star of royal wisdom whom all subjects might adore.

No simple task, when the man in question shook at each slam of a door, and spoke so repeatedly of pinching devils named Hobbididance and Flibbertigibbet.

Chapter 32

November2, 1605. All Souls Day, The Feast of the Dead.

They were gathered for a mass at White Webbs, Anne Vaux's house in Middlesex, when the word came. Reclining on a settle in the parlor, merry Catesby was voicing regret that he'd not joined the king's hunting party at Royston, since so rare a king-hunter was Robin Catesby, aye, your only gentleman for king-hunting! The men were all laughing, but Anne Vaux was looking askance at Robin, her face tight with dread. She had just decided to seek Father Garnet, who was donning his massing clothes above, when three hard knocks came on the door. This was the signal, the slow knock of three they had used since Father Quindle's near-capture at Harrowden the year before. Even so, the men quieted while Anne peeked through a curtain. On the stoop she saw Young Everard Digby, his twin six-year-old sons, and his wife Mary, all of them flushed from their brisk ride. Across the courtyard a groom was leading their horses to the stable.

Anne opened the door. "In, all!" She pushed the boys into the arms of a trusted housemaid and gestured their parents toward the dining room table. "Mary, you must rest and eat something for that babe in the womb. Hard riding!" She clucked her tongue.

"I am well." Smiling, Mary Digby removed her cloak. "Do not vex yourself. I must not in any case take food before mass."

"'Tis the babe who would take food. Some wine, at the least. And Everard?"

But Digby was already going. With a quick bow to Anne, he vanished into the parlor, from whence, a moment later, they heard him consulting in low tones with the men. Anne's dread returned. She frowned as she gazed searchingly at Mary Digby. "What is afoot?"

Mary shook her head so vigorously that one of her auburn ringlets escaped its ribbon binding. She pushed it impatiently behind her ear. "I know not," she whispered angrily. "Something to do with the coming Parliament. But Everard will say no more than that. No more to *me.*"

The two women clasped hands and gazed at each other helplessly. The brow of each reflected the fear of the other, and made that fear grow. A servant wordlessly brought wine and glasses, placed them on the table, and as quietly departed.

Suddenly impatient, Anne pulled her hand free. "Rest, Mary." She poured wine for her guest and bade her sit. "Fretting will harm the one in your womb, so avoid it. I will speak to Hen — to the father."

She climbed the stairs and knocked softly on a door. "'Tis I, Henry." "Yes. Come in."

She entered to find Henry Garnet in full massing clothes, just rising from the prie dieux, where he'd been kneeling before a painted image of the Virgin. "Forgive me, Father," she said gently. As always, they spoke formally to one another when he was in vestments, shifting parts awkwardly from close friends to priest and penitent. Now that Henry was standing, Anne knelt before him. "Forgive my intrusion. But I plead with you to tell what you know of this *plot!*"

"What plot do you mean?" Garnet asked with alarm. "What have you heard?"

Anne put a hand to her abdomen and kneaded her belly, her angular face contorted with woe. Her pains had returned of late, and now they combined with her worries about the group in the parlor to leave her discouraged and frightened. "I have heard nothing but hushed voices and murmurs of men, talk that stops when I come in a room, as though naught Robin Catesby does should concern me, though he dines in my house. And now Everard Digby has come, with some vexing news of the coming Parliament, by the sound of it. He has closed the door to the parlor! What can I think, but that something is plotted? And Robin, no doubt, at the head of it."

Henry felt uncomfortable looking down on her, so he knelt by her side. "Anne, Robin has spoken to me as little as he can for months. He avoids confession. Or avoids confessing to me." He could not tell her what Quindle had revealed to him. Still, he was not lying.

But though she'd begged his help, Anne was barely listening. "What is worse, my sister Eliza knows something, and only tells me not to speak of coming days. She has not come today, even on All Souls' Day, so as not to be sounded by me, I think. She says God will let fall his judgment, and there an end. But how can she know this if you do not?"

"Rise, Anne." Garnet made shift to do so himself.

Anne stayed stubbornly on her knees. "And this letter you always ask for. What letter do you expect? At White Webbs, at Baddesley Clinton, you look for a letter. From whom?"

"I have written the pope for direction for English Catholics. I have done this before —"

"Do not think me a fool!" Discarding patience, piety, and form, Anne got to her feet. "What is the present urgency?"

Henry mopped his brow, then noticed he was using the sleeve of his chasuble. He dropped his arm to his side. "Anne, I have seen what you have seen. I fear what you fear. I can say no more."

"Cannot, or will not?"

"*Can* not." Pleadingly, Garnet met her eyes. "But Catesby —"

"Since he is at last here, will you speak to him, at any rate? Today, after mass?"

"I will do so, Anne. And dear Anne —"

"Yes?" Defeated, she had turned to go, but when he grabbed her hand she turned to look again at his worried eyes. She suddenly had to summon all her will to keep from embracing him, not in the way forbidden, like a lover, but like a mother comforting a child.

His eyes still pleaded. "You will see if any letter for me has come?"

Her vexation matched her fear. "As though I would keep it from thee!"

In the parlor below, Francis Tresham sat white-faced. "'Twas *thou*," Catesby said with contempt, hurling the words at Francis. "Thou! In fear and cold heart thou hast run to thy kin and laid open all our proceedings. A dish of skim milk for thy honor!"

Digby had come with the news that a Catholic peer had approached him in the Strand and urged him to stay home from Parliament on the opening day. When Digby had asked him why, the man had said that he himself had been warned by his wife, a dear friend of the wife of Lord Monteagle, that arrests of Catholics might be made on that date, there in Westminster.

Tresham spread his hands helplessly. "You must believe me. I myself have received no warning, not even from my sister — "

"Because *you* warned *her*, and *she* warned her husband Monteagle! You have betrayed us!"

"But Robin, *you* were to have warned my brother Monteagle! So you said in Lambeth! After that, I felt no need to do it!"

"I . . . ." Robin was taken aback. In his anger and fear he'd forgotten his equivocal promise to Francis, made weeks before at the counterfeit-powder supper. He looked sidelong at Thomas, who was staring around the group, his face blotchy with rage. "I had not done so yet," Robin said. "I had meant to approach your brother-in-law on the eve of the act before I rode westward, to prevent loose talk floating about London. There would not then have been time for wives to gabble."

"But if they *have* gabbled, there is time to give up the plan." Francis said this with a mixture of urgency and relief. "Our scheme is now too dangerous. And as I have said, though I have horses, I have some doubt that the men of York you call on will rise this year. We eat the air and promise of supply, we use men's *names* instead of men. None but we are truly committed. Can we not wait? We may lie low this season, and should praise God for this delivering news, as, from what Digby says, nothing is known of the powder. We can remove it, just as we placed it there."

A low rumbling had been coming from Thomas's throat. At Francis's last words, the volcano blew. "*WE?*" he thundered, as seven men bade him hush. "*WE*, infidel? As *WE* placed it there? Marry, didst *thou* fill and roll the barrels with us? Or didst thou stay safe in thy stone triangle?" Thomas shook off Catesby's restraining hand. Kit Wright made a move, then sank back on the long settle next to his brother and the Wintours. Why bother to rise? Thomas's rage must burn itself out.

Thomas turned violently to Catesby. "We have labored for this caitiff, for this churl, who has undone us!"

"I am persuaded he has not," Catesby whispered fiercely. "Speak lower, Thomas!"

Thomas dropped his voice to an angry hiss. "Then *you* have undone us! In the Irish Boy you said you spoke to Monteagle, you — "

"I said naught." Catesby held up a warning finger as Tresham looked at the pair curiously. "Nothing."

"Too much, you have said! Always, too much!"

"And you, Thomas Percy jack-of-the-clock, a man of pure choler, would accuse me thus? I hurl thy taunts back in thine angry face."

Thomas felt desperately for his sword, then remembered he'd unbuckled and left it in the hall, at Anne Vaux's insistence. He clenched his fist. "Thou hast menaced a Percy. Thou . . . . Thou . . . ."

Catesby sat down lightly in a chair and crossed his legs. He raised his eyebrows at Thomas, who stood mute, gruff, and wild-haired before him. So far for so long from Martha's scissors, his mad beard had begun to grow out again. Robin smiled at his friend with some affection. "Come, Thomas. Forgive my harsh words, and fear me not. I will say again, I have said nothing of substance to Monteagle. Nor has anyone, i'truth. As you say, Francis, Digby's news proves only that someone thinks he knows something, but no one knows of the powder. This augurs no mishap for us."

"That is not all I said, Robin." Francis spoke with some heat. "I spoke of our lack of friends — "

"An excellent plot, very good friends." Catesby cocked an eyebrow higher. "But I forget myself. I should say, 'tis an excellent *plan*, for, as I have said before, only players and villains plot, and we are none. As for men, Francis, see how Rookwood and Digby have sought *us*, without our stir! "

The three-part knock sounded again on the door. Robin sprang to look out the window. "To speak of the devil — or saint! — Ambrose Rookwood is here now, to tell us of a hundred horses stalled at Bury St. Edmund's. Courage! No quailing now." He opened the parlor door. "Four days, and we will be free of the yoke."

"Aye," said Kit Wright. "Aye!" The other men nodded assent. Even Francis did so, though his face showed pain.

Thomas stood in the middle of the room, confused and deflated. With a flash of fading anger he looked at Catesby, who was now bounding to greet Rookwood in the main hallway, moving as gracefully as a greyhound.

And Thomas suddenly knew who Catesby was.

By his light did all the chivalry of England move to do brave acts. He was the mark and glass, copy and book, that fashioned others. Remembered lines of verse tolled like bells in his head. *O wondrous him! O miracle of men!* O Catesby! It was Catesby who wore Hotspur's mantle. Golden

Robin, not lumbering Thomas Percy. Robin, not Thomas, would leap like a spark, to pluck bright honor from the pale-faced moon.

The anger drained from Thomas's breast. He felt suddenly humbled by the hand of providence. Still he would follow Catesby. Indeed, he must, even more so, now that he saw things clearly. The pair of them were linked like chain-shot. He had, after all, his own destiny to fulfill, and it was tied to Robin's. He thought of little Charles, ensconced in the London house, on a street that Thomas now strolled more frequently than he went to Crutched Friars where he'd lived with his Mary. A Gentleman Pensioner could pass through Charles's gate without arousing suspicion, and Thomas knew every entranceway from the courtyard to the palace beyond, knew the moment each morning when a servant carried slops to a pit in the back and left a rear door open. He had seen little Charles high at a window in his white nightgown. The tiny prince had waved to Thomas. Poor, lonely Duke of York, away from his parents like his siblings were too, in separate royal residences. Yet he was the smallest. Thomas had waved back to the boy with infinite love.

Charles was waiting for him.

Tomorrow was November the third, Winifred's sacred day. In the morning he would pray for the showing of that saint's long-awaited favor toward himself, Thomas Percy, soon to be the new father to royal Charles. Thomas would be blessed.

Father Garnet and Anne Vaux huddled together on a stair outside the parlor, around a bend in the hallway. Both were shaking. "Can I give the sacrament to these men?" Garnet asked her. If only Father Quindle were here to advise him! "Anne, what must we do?"

"Could you hear them? I tried —"

"Only Thomas Percy's shouts, about placing something somewhere. And a mass of voices." Of course he knew more. He prayed silently that the men had given up what they planned to do, though he had been tantalized by one other phrase, by four words he'd heard just before Catesby had pulled open the door to greet Rookwood. *Free of the yoke*, Catesby had said. How Garnet longed to be free of the yoke!

"I know you can say naught of what's heard in confession," Anne boldly hinted.

"You say right. I could not. But none of these men has confessed a plot to me." *Yes. True. The plot was revealed to Quindle. It was Quindle who confessed his knowledge to me.* "This means they feel no need to confess a thing that is not yet done, *or* that they have confessed to another priest." Garnet quickly leapt from this suggestion to one farther from home. "Or that they have no consciousness that what they plan is sin."

"And perhaps it is not sin, though I fear it is," Anne said miserably. "Still, to betray them could be to consign them to death. And I know not what I would say if I wrote to Lord Cecil as I did once. I could not betray . . . ." She let the sentence hang unfinished, and looked with concern at Henry. "And sure *you* must stay hidden."

Garnet rose. "Now Ambrose Rookwood has come, and they all wait for me. Let us . . . . Let us have the mass. In the parlor, today." The choice was not as rash as it might have sounded, as the parlor of White Webbs gave access to a priest-sized space of concealment behind the chimney.

"I'll send a servant to fetch Mary Digby, then. And you vow that after, you will speak — "

"To Robin, yes. Fitter then. And after today, I am for Harrowden Hall, where I will sound Eliza. Perhaps she will talk to me. Now, for this holy time, let us leave it to God to turn hearts, if hearts are gone astray."

All rose when Father Garnet entered the room with Mary Digby and Anne Vaux walking quietly behind him. And though Henry had hoped that the appearance of their priest, carrying the box that contained the host, would calm any violence in the men's breasts, it was not so. Looking at his good face and the virtuous majesty of his vestments, the brethren felt only a renewed zeal to protect him and the other brave, good shepherds who made sense of their faith. Each man there — even dubious Tresham — thought he would die for Father Garnet, as Anne Vaux had always known she would.

Father Garnet did not want anyone to die for him, save Christ, who already had. At least, he did not think he did. Now, he put aside all his fears of and for these men, as he faced the quiet group to perform the mass. He sensed only the union of hearts in the room, and was, however briefly, cheered by it. These people loved him, and loved one another. In his mind he saw the wide, gentle lap of great Catholic houses in England, arching from London to York, houses where he and his fellow priests greeted their sheep, and the lambs found each other. Ashby St. Ledgers, Bury St. Edmunds, White Webbs, Harrowden, Twigmoor, Rushton Hall, Huddington Court, Baddesley Clinton, and dozens of other manors, strung through the green land like beads on a rosary. All these high-walled places offered welcome and warmth to the afflicted faithful. Catholic marriages, Catholic baptisms, Catholic masses were celebrated like moveable feasts among them, by families so bonded their members had become as interchangeable as their homes. Behind the beauteous houses' doors lay shelter on the instant, and conviviality, and plenty, and the sense that a man or a woman was known. How much better was this fellowship, this easy hospitality, than the pinched precision of the Protestant household, with its measured charity, its wasted thrift! How petty, how poor in spirit, would England become if all this great-heartedness died!

Keep my flock strong, he silently prayed. Aloud, he praised their patience, and from memory recited the Latin gospel. A vision briefly came to him, of himself in rich new vestments, arms raised before the altar of St. Paul's Cathedral, amid holy images and statues all restored to their proper places. Incense perfumed the air, and a thousand murmuring parishioners stood at his back. He shook his head. *Vainglory!*

Here, now, before him. This small knot of trusting people. This was his parish.

He led them in prayers for those who had died and now suffered in Purgatory, souls caught betwixt this world and the next. He blessed the sacrament, and reverently changed its papery substance into Christ's living body. "*Hoc est corpus meum.*"

When Robin Catesby approached to communicate, Garnet looked hard into his shining, unfocused eyes as he placed the blessed bread on his tongue. *Give over the plot*, he prayed as Catesby bent his head and withdrew. An unquiet imp spoke within him. *And, if you will not give it over, see that you succeed.* Appalled, he shook his head again. *Out, imp!*

After the mass, Henry removed his cope and chasuble. As his head emerged from the cloth he caught sight of the vanishing left boot of Robin, who was leaving the room. Hastily he thrust the vestments into a servant's hands and followed Catesby outside. "Robin Catesby, I would speak to you!"

But Robin was mounting his horse, vaguely waving his hat. In the sun his hair looked incandescent, like torchlight, or furnace-fired gold. Garnet squinted in the brightness, shielding his eyes to dispel the illusion that a nimbus surrounded his friend's head, or that the man was on fire. Then a great gust of wind swooped into the courtyard before him, kicking up dust and dry leaves, and for a moment he was blinded. Still he stumbled forward, yelling, "I would speak to you, sir!" at Catesby's diminishing back, as Catesby galloped away.

Chapter 33

"**Y**et this is most vexing!" The king paced, nearly frantic. "The letter is dark. It is doubtful. By Jesus, I can make nothing of it!"

"Let us look again." Cecil's voice was soothing. "Surely this came to Monteagle from some Catholic zealot. The papists are like sturdy beggars, who ask favors with the right hand, but keep stones in their left to hurl if they are denied. *Stones*," he repeated meaningfully. "Like *gun*-stones. In this crude and cryptic scrawl there is, perhaps, some code that in your wisdom you may unravel — "

"*I would advise you, as you tender your life, to devise some excuse to shift of your attendance at this Parliament; for God and man hath concurred to punish the wickedness of this time.* And then, *retire yourself into the country where you may expect the event in safety.* What event, Cecil? I'faith, I should not have returned here! We must prorogue once more; I am back to Royston as quick as thought. *You* may resolve this."

"Nay, majesty, it were not good to keep peers and commons waiting for so long a year. They must meet — "

"They will do what I tell them, will they not?"

Cecil bit his lip. Though he'd ruled England for more than two years, James still failed to see that this country was not Scotland. Already some bold-spoken members of the House of Commons had widely made known their displeasure at their absent king gone a-hunting, and had raised bones they were anxious to pick concerning taxes. "Think of your subjects in Parliament as children, who crave a father's counsel and care," Cecil urged. "You are their Caesar, their — "

"Aye, aptly said! And this document argues some Brutus and Cassius, who will put knives to me if I go! I need no Calpurnia's dream. This will suffice to warn me. Meanwhile, you stay and get to the bottom of it."

"Majesty, it confounds me." Cecil tried to hide his vexation. "I believe that God will lead *you*, his surrogate in this realm, to decipher its mysteries, *and in so doing prove to the realm that you are indeed its heaven-sent sovereign.*"

The king halted his pacing. He stood and thought for a moment. "Perhaps it is so." He dropped into a chair, his dressing gown billowing, and scratched a toe, glancing down at the paper he still clutched in his hand. "*They shall receive a terrible blow this Parliament.* Well. *Who* shall?"

"This word 'blow.'" Cecil crouched by his side. "Does it not seem to augur some . . . ." He looked expectantly at James.

"Hurricano, you mean? So saucy is this traitor that he presumes to prophesy the very weather. How can he know that the day will be windy?"

"Yes, he foresees some storm," Cecil said patiently. "Or some other blow, some . . . *fiery* blow, perhaps, as some —"

"An explosion!" James leapt to his feet, as though a firecracker had indeed gone off under his chair. In fact, what had started him was an old memory of a thing recounted or seen: a Scottish palace in flames, a man hanging from a tree in its courtyard. "*Another!* By God! Could any Englishman be so bold?"

Cecil touched a hand to his head in wonder. "How can I not have noted this! Yes, a predicted explosion makes some sense of this sentence, here!" He pointed to the letter. James read, "*This counsel is not to be condemned because —*"

"Nay, here, Majesty." Cecil cursed himself for interrupting the king in his impatience.

But James was now as fascinated as he was horrified, and did not note the breach of protocol. "*For the danger is passed as soon as you have burnt the letter.*" He looked questioningly at Cecil.

"*Burnt the letter.* A reference to fire." Cecil paused. "To a firestorm, perhaps."

"Ah, yes! Someone means to burn me. To blow me up! You have hit it, wee man."

"*You* have deduced it, my sovereign. By miracle, God has given this letter over to your divining."

"Yes, so it must be." Now James chewed his lip. "And my Annie, who was to sit with me! And Prince Henry! And . . . *Charles* . . . ." He shut his eyes against the horror, then quickly reopened them. A canny and politic light was renewed in their depths. "Yet you advise me not to delay the opening? What then, think you, should I do?"

"I think we must search the palace," Cecil said firmly.

"What? All the palace? *Every* palace?"

"The Palace of Parliament, Highness. May I have your leave to summon the council? With your permission, I will ask them to approve my going to Westminster with a troop of guard. Will you give your leave, sire?"

"With all my heart." The king rose eagerly. "Yet *I* shall not go. I shall return to –"

"Nay, Majesty!" In his eagerness, Cecil interrupted him again. With folded hands he bowed to atone for the second rudeness. "I beg of you, lord, wait until I have returned to tell what I have found. Perhaps I will not be long."

James looked at him shrewdly. "Should Whitehall not be searched as well?"

"I will order it, sovereign." An idea struck Cecil. "Meantime, perhaps you could ride in the park."

"An excellent idea, wee lad."

Cecil winced perceptibly. "Lad" was new.

"I had meant to stay and peruse documents in preparation for the morrow's proceedings." The king gestured to a stack of papers piled on a heavy oaken desk. "But now all is at sixes and sevens. By God, will they always try to kill me? The dark fates have sprinkled powder at the very base of my family's tree! Can I trust only my *horse,* because hooves cannot strike a flint? And yet . . . and yet, I trust you, good Cecil."

Cecil hunched his shoulders, preparing to be the victim of another animal comparison. Was he a trusty pony? Or, more familiarly, a faithful spaniel? But James seemed too preoccupied to fashion conceits, or even to repeat the common ones. He said only, "I shall do as you bid me, friend. We shall share this ominous letter with others of the Privy Council. And then I shall ride."

Chapter 34

November 4th. The Night of St. Charles's Feast.

With seven servants, Everard Digby had ensconced himself at the Red Lion in Dunchurch, near Dunsmore Heath. He had left Mary Digby and their sons at White Webbs. He looked festive, handsome, and grand, encased in a white satin doublet cut with purple, and draped with a cloak stitched thickly with gold lace. To the host's care he'd committed a surprising number of horses. These, he had told the man, were to be used for a hunting party. Numerous companions would be joining him on the morrow. He assured the host of that.

Thomas Percy rode hard from Lambeth to Syon House. On the road outside his dwelling, Catesby had sent him westward, saying that from the earl Thomas might discover more about what was generally known and not known about the parliamentary opening. Thomas was to say he was there to ask for money. If the earl seemed in total ignorance, Thomas was not to warn him of anything.

The instruction had confused Thomas. Was not the earl to be their regent, after the blow?

"Yes. But he is not in danger. He will not go to Parliament. He will send a proxy."

"How know you this?"

"Does he not frequently do so?"

"But . . . ." Thomas had stared, aghast. "You had said he would be amply warned."

"Well, I have thought further. Look you, Thomas, we must play the hazard in this. The earl is not one of the brethren. He can be trusted after, when the dust doth settle. Then, as Jack Wright once said, we may fetch him out of his smoky den. If he foils us by going to Parliament tomorrow, well, then, there will still be high Catholic lords enough for a regent, especially as this warning seems somehow to have been floated among them. What matters most is that young Prince Charles is kept safe."

"As he will be." Thomas had sworn to that. "Yet —"

"Keep faith!" Catesby had wheeled northward and galloped toward the midlands road.

Thomas could do no more than ride south. He had presented a picture of resolve to Catesby, but in his breast there was now a new turmoil. Not to warn his master, the ninth earl?

Now he sat with his lord in Henry Percy's favorite study. The earl was distracted and out of sorts. He pushed the embers of his fire with a poker. "Why do you need money, Thomas? You have received your pay this month."

"I . . . . lost it at cards. Playing at hazard."

"And now I am to open my coffers to feed your debts. I will not do it." The earl coughed. "Indeed, you find me in an ill humor. I am only beginning to recover from an unfortunate experiment with ground poppy seed and magnesium. The inhalation was meant to clear the vapors of the mind and provoke lucid thought. Yet, whatever the great Paracelsus says of this mixture, it sickened me."

"I am sorry," Thomas said gravely.

"Yet I do not despair of poppy. My thought is that the magnesium was at fault. I am anxious to prove this, but cannot, before I am hale."

"Ah." A hopeful thought struck Thomas. "Then, feeling ill, your lordship will not go to Parliament?"

"It is my purpose to go. Tomorrow is the opening day, and the king will be displeased if I omit the duty. Parliament will meet at ten of the clock. I think I will be myself by then. I am for Essex House in the Strand tonight. There I will lie."

Thomas's heart sank. Clearly the earl knew nothing of the plan, which augured well for them, in a way. But not well for Henry Percy. How could Thomas leave him without a word?

"You must go now, Thomas. I have no money for you." The earl poked the fire again. It was dying, despite his efforts.

Thomas cleared his throat. He lacked all skill for subtle speech, but despite Catesby's warning he must try it. "My lord, I think thou wert best to keep home. There may be . . . concatenations . . . "

"There may be *what*? Thomas, your presence annoys me more and more today."

Thomas tried another tack. "You know of the many sufferings of the faithful. They have fallen most harshly on our Percy ancestors. Remember our first Percy earl, who — "

"You are most free with the name of our house, Thomas," the earl snapped, rising. He felt his gut roiling, and feared he might vomit in front of his servant. The shame of that thought made him irritable in the extreme. "That I have pleased to employ you to ferry pounds and shillings to my dwelling places does not mean I think of you as a brother and will cheerfully pay for your vices. Now, leave me!"

Stung, Thomas rose, bowed, and wheeled clumsily, knocking against some furniture as he exited. Behind him the earl collapsed once more in his chair. "Ah, God relieve me of this torment!" he wailed, then spewed the bile from his stomach into the ashes of the fire.

Outside, half in a daze, Thomas rode back to London. Night-birds shrieked at his passage. The moon peered down like a saint spying into his purposes. *Follow the man in the moon.* His brain reeled on the still road. He prayed to Winifred to quiet his spirit, but the earl's words burned within him. At the end of his years of service, insult had been his reward!

So. He must entrust the earl to God.

The church bells had tolled midnight by the time he came into the city. He meant to sleep for a few hours in Gray's Inn Road, then rise at dawn to station himself in the shadow of a wall near Charles's house. But he found himself first in Crutched Friars Lane, looking once more up at his old window. The window was black, the house silent. He touched his hand to the Winifred medal that he had deserved at last. Then he dropped his hand to squeeze the rosary inside his shirt. *Mary, save me!* He mouthed the words, not knowing whether he prayed to his lost love or to the Virgin.

Night was far along by the time Westminster's justice of the peace had been found and brought to rap on the door of the vault. The lords of James's council had agreed with Cecil's suggestion that an official of the city of London, not one of Whitehall, should conduct the search. For did this fiery plot not only threaten the king, but the citizens of London as well?

A moment passed. Then an auburn-bearded gentleman in a tall leather hat opened the door a crack, from the other side. Impassive by torchlight, he quietly confirmed that he was John Johnson, yes, the caretaker of this place. He raised a pair of reddish eyebrows. What brought him so august an assemblage of visitors?

"That is to be discovered." Cecil inwardly marveled at the man. Fox indeed, and a performance worthy of the Globe. So bland was the fellow's look that for one chilling instant Cecil thought, against reason, that he must have been wrong after all, searching alone on that night of shadows nearly two weeks before.

But he knew he was not. The powder's bitter taste could never be forgotten. "Keep this man under guard," he ordered an officer, who made the caretaker sit, and blocked the exit way. Then Cecil watched the officer's men, guiding them gently with the subtlest of directions as they sifted through corded wood and opened barrels of coal. Not here. Not here. Once he looked at "Johnson" and found the man staring back at him with impossible calm, even with something like curiosity. He looked away quickly.

Then, struck by a thought, he looked back. The man was still watching him. Cecil walked over to his side. In the hearing of the justice of the peace, he said, "Do you, sir, serve a man called Andrew Andrews?"

"Yes." As a seeming afterthought, the man added, "Lord."

"Then answer me this. Is 'Andrew Andrews,' in truth, Sir Thomas Percy?"

The man shrugged. "Not that I know."

Cecil watched him, letting the silence stretch between them. This time it was Cecil who raised his eyebrows.

"Lord," the man said, with the ghost of a smile.

"Hmm. Why did your master 'Andrews' lease this vault?"

"This I also do not know. But in the close neighborhood stand a pannier's establishment and a bakery and a tavern. I think it likely that my master has some thought to establish a business here."

"I think I know his business." Cecil turned away.

The city guards were still searching fruitlessly if meticulously, uncovering barrel lids, peering into boxes, casting contents on the floor, less tidy than Cecil had been. After twenty chilly minutes, unwilling to stand in the cellarage until Parliament day, Cecil allowed himself to move indirectly into the far alcove where he'd seen the powder. Holding his lantern high, he peered for a moment. Yes. There it still was. The scratched crosses on the firewood. Three of them, in a row.

Turning, he tried to catch the eyes of the caretaker again, but the watchful guard had turned his own lamp to allow him a better view of the searchers' work, and "Johnson"'s eyes were deep in shadow. Cecil saw the man make a slight movement, then subside once more into stillness.

Time to end it. Cecil raised his lamp as high as he could. With the thumb of his free hand he gestured, saying loudly, "Mark this! Over here!"

Dawn was greying when, after a night of phantasmagoria, Kit Wright woke fully to a disturbing noise. Through the upper casement window of his house in the Strand he heard a sharp knock below. The rapping was coming from the door of his near neighbor, who happened to be William Lord Monteagle. He turned in his bed and leaned over the sill, in time to see Monteagle's door open to a fur-gowned member of the king's Privy Council. Cocking an ear, Wright heard the king's man speak excitedly to Monteagle, directing him to call up the Earl of Northumberland from Essex House where he lodged, to raise the Lord Henry Percy *now* and to bring him to the palace, because of some happenings at Westminster.

Wright jumped out of bed. What could this be? It was barely dawn, and no explosion had sounded. He scrambled into his shirt, trunks, hose, and boots, thanking a watchful God that his wife and children lay safe at his estate near York. Bolting into the Strand, he ran to the mews and saddled his horse, then rode at full tilt to Gray's Inn Road, cloakless and with his shirt flapping.

He found Thomas Percy awake and dressed most peculiarly in an old crested armor which looked to have been brought from a playhouse. Thomas was kneeling before a brass crucifix he'd nailed to the wall, and his lips were moving silently. By his side lay his sword — not the elegant rapier he customarily hung from his Gentleman Pensioner's belt, but an old iron, long and heavy.

"Up, man, and out!" Wright cried to him. He pushed the big sword toward Thomas. "Arm, and pray as you run. We are caught!"

Chapter 35

And they are riding, riding, riding, racing the clock, the year, and the season. Wind and dust blow in their wake. Thomas Percy is booted and spurred and his armor is cumbersome, since it is not real steel with flexible hinges, but stiff painted leather. It hinders his movements. Still he wears it, straining forward over the head of his roan and fiercely whispering. "*Esperance!* Ever, *Esperance!*" By his side Kit Wright is shouting in his ear, telling him their safety lies in speed, that they will find Catesby in the midlands, that the call must go out for the rising. Past the houses of Highgate they gallop, then through green Bedfordshire. Though they do not know it, twenty miles behind them comes Robert Keyes, and behind him Ambrose Rookwood. So fine is Rookwood's horsemanship that he outstrips Keyes and Digby and overtakes Kit and Thomas on the Bedfordshire highway. In two hours Rookwood has ridden thirty miles.

Rumor spreads quickly. Rookwood has heard every detail of the capture of the powder, and he shares it with the men as he finds them. He then rides ahead in search of Catesby. An hour more and he spies Robin. Catesby flies a-horseback with Jack Wright and the servant Bates, heading pell-mell toward Warwickshire. Alerted by hoofbeats, the two rein in their mounts and turn to look at Rookwood galloping toward them. "Is't done, Ambrose?" Catesby shouts. "Are we free?"

His face goes white as Rookwood comes closer, calling out the bad news. Bates and Jack Wright exchange looks of horror.

And suddenly Catesby laughs. "Is this all? Then, to the rising!" he cries. "Die all, die merrily. *Let them come!*" He wheels and spurs his horse forward, and each man of them follows. The color rushes back into Catesby's face and he whoops savagely, like an Irish warrior, as he gallops on the northern road.

By nine of the clock on November the fifth, Gawain Wintour was the only one of the powder brethren still in London. He'd stayed purposefully, having heard the hubbub in the streets of the Strand, but wishing to find out how much, precisely, was known. Some undefined, threatening menace, with the Catholics as its source, had perhaps been guessed at. A vague story was leaking from the recusants who'd been advised to leave London on that day. To discover more, he decided to walk from his house to Westminster. Was he not a diplomat, an emissary to England's new friend Spain, a man trusted by two successive English monarchs, a member — on the face of things, anyway — of the English Church? What had he to fear? In his finest silks, he left his London house to go to Parliament.

The babble sounded louder in his ears as he rounded the corner and came into King Street. He spied knots of men and women gathered in talkative corner groups. "What is this?" Wintour asked a guard who, stopping his progress, demanded to know his business. "I am bound for Parliament. What has happened?"

"Much!" The guard's face grew lively. "There is a treason discovered in which the king and lords were to have been blown up! They have taken out thirty-six barrels of gunpowder, stocked in the Westminster cellarage by a knight named Thomas Percy, whose caretaker was to have lit — "

But Wintour was already gone, sprinting back the way he'd come, around the corner and hastening to his horse. Within a quarter of an hour he too was at Highgate, on the road, like all of his brothers.

Cecil had prevailed with London's Lord Mayor. Though not quickly enough to satisfy the privy counselor, a watch was posted to all the city gates. The ports throughout the country were closed. Withal, Parliament met, though briefly, in the afternoon. King James, repelled by his own fearfulness at last, performed the bravest act of his life. Knowing men had meant to kill him, uncertain whether the search of the cellarage had been thorough enough, or whether an assassin yet lurked near an unopened barrel of powder with a tinderbox in his fell hand, the sovereign rode openly to Parliament. There he addressed the lords assembled, and thanked God for his deliverance.

Then he went home to bed.

From the palace, Cecil sent orders dispatching an army of pursuivants to safe houses throughout the realm. White Webbs, Baddesley

Clinton, Rushton Hall, Harrowden — all would be riffled for Jesuits. Two of known name, Garnet and Quindle, were most particularly sought.

"And the man Thomas Percy?" asked Cecil's officer. "And Robin Catesby?"

"Ah. They." Cecil meditated, thinking of Catesby's wild zealotry, of the probability that the odd knight Thomas Percy shared Catesby's stubborn temper, of how unlikely it was that either one of them would betray his priest.

"What say you, lord?" The officer was a young man, eager to join in the hunt.

"Let me not see either of them alive."

The man bowed and walked quickly from the room.

What next? Cecil had spent an hour with the primary prisoner, who was being held in the palace. The calm and soldierly "John Johnson" had admitted his true name, which was not "Fox" but "Fawkes," and had made no show of denying the powder. Was he a priest? He said nay, but they all said nay, meaning they were not priests of the English Church, as though this answer were somehow not a lie. Who were his associates, and what had they intended? The man would not say. He'd shown great surprise when told that his master "Andrew Andrews" was in fact a knight of the king's ceremonial body guard. At the mention of Robert Catesby, he had merely looked blank. The powder was not Catesby's, but his own, he'd said. Yes, he'd meant to light it this day. Thirty-six barrels to blow the king back to craggy auld Scotland, and good riddance. Yes, he was a papist. But Jesuits? Fawkes had shrugged. He knew none by name.

It might be required to submit this cool gentleman to some of the gentler tortures. So great was the danger that the king had approved the measure. Yet let Fawkes sit for a while.

Cecil opened a door into another small office, where a figure rested on a settle, shivering in thin silks and looking ill. Unlike Guido Fawkes, this man was not calm. He was fretful, and clearly cold. He'd been pulled from his bed and given little time to dress. The furred gown he'd meant to wear to Parliament's opening ceremonies still hung from a hook in Essex House. The gown did not matter, of course. In the end, closed in this chill palace room, the man had missed the brief Parliament anyway.

Cecil walked to the window and gazed out over the trees. Smoke was rising from far streets, where excited Londoners were lighting bonfires, as they usually did when told God had suddenly saved them from the devil. This time God had worked hand in hand with King James, royal revelator, who in his wisdom had read the dark code of a letter of warning, or had found some gunpowder, or performed some other redemptive feat. Praise God! Praise James! Let this pernicious hour stand aye accursed in the calendar, and the smoke rise yearly to heaven! The bonfires were peril of a new kind, for wooden houses might catch fire, and flames spread. But Cecil did not think he could stop the bonfires. Better attend to the business before him.

He walked to the fireplace, lifted an iron, and stirred his own small blaze. Then he turned to regard the ashen face of the man before him, who, like London, was confused.

Five years later, safely lodged with his bottles and beakers above his friend Raleigh in the Tower, this addled man would have leisure enough to collect his thoughts. Then he would reflect and expound on philosophy, science, the magic of chemicals, the betrayals of history, and, indeed, certain events to which he might fruitfully have paid more attention back in 1605. The man would inspire one poet among his numerous Tower guests, not only handily to interpret the mystical anagram *Luru Vopo Vir Can Utriet* as "No one knows what the other ingredient is," but also to craft a play about an exiled mage, painfully regretting his past negligence, and longing for his freedom.

But here before Cecil, he cut a pitiful figure, so much so that his questioner spoke softly, though his words were hard. "And now, my good wizard Henry Percy," Cecil said. "Again we are met for a treason. What trick have you got to excuse you this time?"

Thomas and Kit Wright changed horses in Dunstable, then rode on, finding Rookwood, Catesby, the servant Bates, and Jack Wright on the way. Seeing a lone, galloping rider far behind them, they moved off the road and watched from the trees. Ten minutes. Fifteen. And then, "Francis!" Catesby rode out, an arm raised, as the others sighed in relief. The Lambeth caretaker, Keyes, had reached them.

Again they ran. The men had all tossed their cloaks in ditches for fleetness, and now went hunched over their horses' necks for warmth as well as for speed. South of Dunchurch they split apart. Keyes rode toward a safe house in Drayton. Catesby sent Bates to Harrowden bearing a scribbled, coded warning to Eliza Vaux to hide the priests. The others rode still northward. By six of the clock they had reached the edge of the fields by Catesby's home at Ashby St. Ledgers. There, by prior plan, waited Bors Wintour and a servant who bore in hand the reins of eight horses.

Catesby leapt from his saddle. "Fawkes is taken. We are discovered. To Warwick for arms!"

Bors looked as though Catesby had dropped a rock on his head. He staggered. "Undone," he moaned. "We must ride to the king. Even now, if we kneel and — "

Catesby slapped Bors hard. Thomas threw a glove to earth and roared, "Infidel and base churl!"

Dazedly, Bors regarded Thomas. "Man, what are you wearing? Is this a pageant?" He turned back to Catesby. His face showed the red mark of Robin's hand, but he was too shaken to answer either of the men's insults. "How can we hope to -"

"Our hope lies in the *rising*." The five new arrivals were already mounting the fresh horses. Gripping his reins, Catesby spoke from the saddle to the servant. "Walk those poor beasts, then follow us north if you will."

The boy nodded, whitefaced.

"Or if you won't, stay free of the house. There will be pursuivants, king's men, all manner of agents of the crown. Go!"

The boy scurried off with the tired horses, too frightened to bow or speak.

"Now for Dunchurch, to find Digby and his hunting party," said Catesby. "No fear!" His teeth flashed in his beard. "There is still time to corner a king."

"We go, then." Bors mounted a horse, though his eyes darted leftward, then rightward, like a fox seeking some path of escape.

On they went, gathering Digby and his huntsmen in Dunchurch. There Gawain Wintour caught up to them. They rode all night, calling for rising in every town, and some men answered the call. They were fifty by morning when they reached Warwick Castle and stormed it for horses. Leaving their followers barricaded there, they went on, farther north, stopping to rally what known Catholics they could on the way, for a day and a night, until they had reached a magnificent house of red stone which had once been an abbey. This was Hewell Grange, in

Worcestershire. "Here lies a lord who will help us!" said Catesby, flinging himself off his horse.

But the lord of the manor was absent.

Catesby and Thomas forced their way into the house and outbuildings, looking for arms and powder. They piled what they found on the backs of riderless horses, some of which they had freshly taken from the barn. "What next?" said Thomas excitedly. "To Tresham, or to Grant?"

"Both are to meet us at Holbeach House." Catesby named a place in Staffordshire that belonged to one of Digby's hunting companions.

Digby's lace was stained with the mud of the road, and his eyes were hooded. His wife and sons were at White Webbs, far behind them now. "Think you the townspeople of Staffordshire will rise?" he asked worriedly.

"Aye, as will these folk!" Thomas stayed his horse on the road before Hewell Grange. With a leather-gloved hand he gestured toward a crowd of villagers who stood watching the armed men with fear and amazement. A light rain was falling on them all. "Join us, for freedom!" Thomas cried.

"Join you? God's sonties, who *are* you?" said one of the bolder villagers.

"We serve God and country!" Robin declared.

The villager looked suspiciously at Catesby. Then, carefully, the townsman spat in the road-dust. "Here we are for King James as well as for God and country. And some of us have shops to open."

"*Shops!*" Thomas's voice rang with contempt. He turned back to Catesby. "Let these go. You said there was a priest here."

"Aye, I have long known of one, and have brought him here. He dodders, and has half given up his vocation. Yet he was ordained, and that in England, during Queen Mary's reign. He will answer our need of confession and sacrament."

The ceremonies were performed as hastily as could be, and after them the old priest slunk back into the grey day. The rain had become a torrent. Digby, the Wintours, the Wrights, Catesby, Ambrose Rookwood, and Thomas mounted horses outside the old abbey. They turned their heads to the northeast and set off again at a gallop.

They had measured ten miles in the punishing rain when Thomas, now in the rear of the pack, heard the dull thunder of hooves behind them. He rode forward to Catesby. "They are rising," he called to Robin. "Rising, I say!"

"They will join us in Staffordshire!" Catesby yelled back.

Catesby was right, though Percy was not. Notified by Cecil's young, eager guardsman, the scarlet-clad high sheriff of Worcestershire and his two hundred followers were trailing them, bent on their arrest. Cecil's agent rode by the sheriff's side. In their wake, speeding to join the posse, came a Scotsman named Douglas from Carlisle near the border. He had ridden south deliberately upon hearing that the Northumbrian rent-collector Thomas Percy was among the hunted. He muttered a verse from the gospel of Matthew as he rode, wincing with pain as an old thigh-wound opened, and blood stained his breeches.

John Grant was waiting at Holbeach House when they fell inside, bearing the swords and powder plundered from Hewell Grange. But there was no sign of Francis Tresham. "A dish of skim milk for his honor!" Thomas spat, repeating what Catesby had said of Francis before. "We need him not. We were followed by men — "

"Who seek to imprison you." John Grant came in with the bags of powder they'd brought on the horses. "'Tis the high sheriff of Worcestershire, no Catholic he. My servant brings word of it from the town."

Thomas sagged. Drenched to the skin, he sat in a chair, removed his hat, and wrung it. "The *pox!*"

"Where is Digby?" Catesby suddenly asked. "And Bors Wintour?"

"Were they with you?" Grant raised his eyebrows. "They came not into the courtyard."

"A dish of skim milk for *their* honors!" said Thomas.

"Fear not, brother Percy." Catesby clapped him warmly on the shoulder. "It may be they have ridden to Warwickshire to raise men there. We may come to swords with this sheriff's men, but we will cut our way through them, then meet Digby in the south, bringing such fellows as Grant has summoned from thither — "

"I brought none," Grant said flatly.

"*What?* Not a one?"

"Ten rode out with me from Warwickshire, publishing as we went that an end was come to the tyranny. But seeing the temper of the people was not disposed to riot, these ten fell off by the way. I came the rest of the way alone." Grant went into the courtyard to double-barricade the gate.

"Not disposed to *riot?*" Thomas's voice bespoke shock and disgust. "The word does not suit our high purpose or our just complaint. These Warwickshiremen were to *rise!*"

They turned their heads suddenly, drawn by a strange wheezing sound coming from the far side of the room. Catesby was laughing. He sat on a bench with his back against the wall, slapping his thigh with a glove. "Well, a dish of skim milk for the honor of Warwickshire!" he gasped. "Smile, boys!" He snorted, tried to compose himself, then dissolved into laughter again. The men watched him in fright. After a moment Gawain walked to Catesby's side and placed a hand on his shoulder. Gradually, Robin quieted. He wiped his eyes and gave them an odd smile. Then he rose, crossed the wide parlor, knelt a few feet from the hearth, and closed his eyes in prayer, signing himself as he did so.

Thomas turned his angry gaze toward the bags of wet powder he'd dumped on the stone floor. "Methinks all this may now be counterfeit." He drew his dirk, cut the sacks, and began spreading the powder on the stone floor in front of the fire to dry. As he worked he muttered a prayer. "*Ave Maria, gratia plena. Dominus tecum. Benedictaed tu in mulieribus, et benedictus fructus ventris tui, Iesus. Sancta Maria, Mater Dei, ora pro nobix peccatoribus, nunc, et in hora mortis nostrae.*"

A log popped in the fire.

"*Amen.*"

Grant came back into the room. "Thomas," he yelled, springing forward and thrusting the knight back. "What do you — "

Thomas tripped and swore. As he fell, the dirk he was holding plunged into his own thigh. He cried out in rage and pain, just as the powder exploded.

The fire engulfed Catesby and Grant. Ambrose Rookwood pulled the carpet from the wall and cast it over both burning men, pushing them to the floor. All six of them beat at the flames until they were extinguished, then carried Catesby and Grant into the kitchens.

"Blind," Grant was moaning. His face was red and black with the burns. "I am blind!"

"What say you?" All the men's ears rang from the blast. "What say you?"

Catesby's face and arms were badly blistered and his hair and head were scorched. But he had been half turned away from the powder when it blew, and unlike Grant he could still see. His blue eyes darted this way and that under his singed brows. His face was swelling.

"Water," said Thomas, cursing himself for an idiot. He himself was half-deaf and his leg was bleeding profusely, but he, at least, was unburnt. "Bring water from the well!"

A servant scurried out. He brought back a bucket of well-water and the news that two score men with muskets had surrounded the house's out-wall and were calling for the papist king-killers to surrender. As their deafness diminished, the men could hear, dimly, the cries of the besiegers.

"A dish of skim milk for surrender!" Catesby yelled, once more laughing maniacally. His shirt had blown off him, and his gold crucifix was still so hot it was burning a stigmata into his reddening flesh, but he would not touch the chain. One of his eyes was swelling shut, and his bloody burnt forearm was shaking.

Grant was brought to lie down, bandaged with cloths and cooking grease, and given a bottle of strong Scotch spirits Kit Wright had found on a ledge in the kitchen. He was moaning gutturally and only half-conscious. But Catesby, though he looked monstrous, was alert, and insisted on standing. "I mean here to die, but not abed!"

"I will take such part as you do," Thomas proclaimed, close to tears.

With a raw hand Robin cupped his ear. "Say you, what?"

"I will take such part as you do!" Thomas hollered. He pressed his hands against his wounded thigh to staunch the bleeding.

"As will we." Wintour spoke loudly and firmly. Rookwood and the Wrights nodded.

Briefly, the six men knelt in prayer, Catesby wincing in pain with the effort. Then they rose, quickly crossing themselves. Voices were sounding now from the top of the courtyard's high wall. The Warwickshire sheriff's band had raised a ladder.

Gawain Wintour and Ambrose Rookwood were the first to take action. They dashed through a side door, then squeezed through a small aperture in the wall that surrounded the yard. As they rounded a corner they slid, fell against one another, righted themselves, and ran for the stable. The rain had ceased but the ground was puddled and their heavy boots spattered mud. They meant to mount their horses and then charge into the thick of the press with swords high. But twenty feet from the barn Rookwood was ambushed by five men who had massed in the trees and were waiting there. One of them stabbed him in the stomach with a pike. Hearing Ambrose cry out, Wintour turned to run to his aid, but was felled by a musketball that shattered his shoulderblade. A man with a gun had been crouching behind the barn door. Now he and seven other gunmen hurried out of the barn to seize Wintour.

The Wrights heard the shot. They ran through the rear kitchens into the courtyard, unsheathing their swords as they ran. "*Maria!*" Kit Wright yelled. "*God for England, and Saint George!*" Muskets fired instantly from five places on the wall. One ball hit Kit full in the stomach and spun him around, whereupon he was hit again in the back, and fell dead. His brother Jack, shot in the side and legs, collapsed by Kit's side in agony, but, hidden by smoke, managed to pull himself back into the house kitchens, still gripping his sword.

Inside, Thomas had just finished wrapping his leg with cloth torn from his shirt. He and Catesby were arming. When Jack stumbled in, both men moved to his side, but Wright waved them off. "I must pray and die here," Jack panted, as Catesby cradled him in his arms and kissed his forehead with raw lips. "In a trice, 'tis only we three."

"We three!" Catesby laughed savagely. "A trinity? Or something else?" His eyes went to Thomas, who was squeezing Kit's hand in his own bearlike paw. "Percy, for these gunstones thou'lt need a better armor than that painted leather. Thou lookst a fair Richard Lionheart on a London scaffold. And I, burnt like a summer scarecrow. No matter. We have ta'en the sacrament, and God will receive us thus." Jack had fainted, and Catesby played the priest for a moment, tracing the sign of the cross on his forehead. Then he kissed Jack and rose. "Swords!"

Thomas stood and picked up his long iron. Together he and Catesby jogged to the courtyard, which was still so thick with smoke they could barely see the forms of their hunters on the walls behind their propped, ignominious guns. In the center by the well the two men stood, back to back, blades raised, just as the musket barrel of Douglas, the Scot from Carlisle, poked through the gate. For Douglas had reached the Warwickshire posse.

"Wicked husbandmen!" the Scot yelled. "You would kill the heir, and take his inheritance! Matthew twenty-one thirty eight, Geneva translation!" The man paused, taking one further moment to steady his arm and let the smoke clear.

Thomas, sword raised, was looking from left to right, seeking an enemy to honorably fight. He could not make sense of the Scotsman's hurled words, mixed as they were with the din of other shouts and exploding balls. But then came a brief quiet in which Douglas's voice rang out clearly. "*Here's for thee*, bully Percy! Th'art worm-food now!" Then the Scotsman fired.

The ball barreled into Thomas's chest. It burned through leather armor, flesh, bone, and gut, then exited through his spine, plowed through Catesby's ribs, and came to rest in Robin's heart. The men fell entangled to earth.

Catesby gurgled bright blood, then lay quiet, his hair a stiff halo, his blue eyes staring upward. Thomas still breathed. He lay leaking life, his head cushioned on his friend's still breast. With his right hand he groped for his Winifred medal, but it was gone, severed from its cord by the ball. His hand dropped weakly. With no strength to seek his rosary, he struggled to pray. "*Ave Maria* . . . ." His eyes clouded, then briefly cleared, then widened in wonder. "Mary," he said tenderly, before they closed.

Chapter 36

There was one rack in England, and it was kept at the Tower. None of the lords of the Privy Council liked to see it used, nor did James, and English common law forbade it. The choice to bypass the law in this regard was the king's prerogative. Two years before he'd spared Raleigh the rack, even though Raleigh had stubbornly refused to admit his guilt in the plot against James's life.

Yet the powder treason was different. It was different because in the earlier plot, though Raleigh had never confessed, others had, giving the justicers all the intelligence they needed to convict Raleigh and all his associates with confidence. And it was different because the scope of this newer treason was very large, and the reason for it very Catholic. Finally, it was different because Walter Raleigh was a gentleman.

What Guido Fawkes was was not entirely clear.

He had been kept awake without food or drink for two days in the palace, and still refused to accuse anyone but himself. With unquenchable audacity, he persisted in making vile jests about James's country of origin, as though he had no sense of the gravity of his situation. What could be done with the man? Cecil argued to James that so deep and wide and perilous was this conspiracy, and so stubborn and low-bred and nationally ambiguous was Fawkes, that the rack was warranted. How else could they smoke out the Catholic devils who'd enlisted his aid? How else could they find the priests? And — Cecil looked meaningfully at the king, and pronounced the words slowly — what palaces might explode if they did not?

But James's old, ready instinct for self-preservation now did battle with his newfound courage. "Aye, aye, you speak true," he said fretfully. "But we must proceed fairly. Question the Earl of Northumberland first. Go to the bottom of that strange man. That horoscope he once drew for me warned of English dangers to come. I'd come to think he meant

Raleigh, but perhaps *this* was his meaning. You must sound him. What does he know?"

"Majesty, the earl has been thoroughly sounded. He can be convicted, I think, of no more than a failure to control his Catholic friends. He claims he himself was not warned against the blow, and it appears he speaks truth. Many lords sent proxies to Parliament, but Percy had not engaged one, and his presence at Essex House argues that his intent was to attend." Cecil spoke with some disappointment.

"Then you have let him go?" asked James fearfully.

"Nay, nay, Majesty. He is in the Tower. You are right in your guess that he is not to be wholly trusted. There is some question arising from his failure to apply the Oath of Supremacy to his cousin, the gentleman who served as one of your Pensioners."

"What?"

"Yes, it is true, and most troubling. Though Northumberland's claim that he knew nothing of his kinsman's plot may be honest, surely Henry Percy was the ladder by which all these plotters descended into their pit of treason. It is not clear what should be done with the earl. But I think naught is to be got from him, save some obscure cant about the phases of the moon. We must wring the truth from Fawkes, or from no one." Earnestly, Cecil engaged the king's eye. "Such laws as we have against torture cannot stand in the face of this high degree of danger to our state. Not just your sacred person stands at risk, but the safety of the nation that you, like a father, have been chosen by God to preserve."

"You are right, little man, as always." James sighed unhappily. "I give leave to the rackmaster to use the gentler tortures on the man."

And so truth was wrung from Fawkes, by means of a severe stretching, a dislocating of ribs, and a shattering of fingers. Cecil was not present for these actions' administration, but he knew their result. After two days of torment Guido Fawkes broke at last, and, between gasps, named his brethren. By the time he had done so, Catesby, Percy, and the Wrights were already dead in the midlands, and the Wintours, Rookwood, and the scorched and blinded Grant had been taken to the Tower. With the help of the new intelligence supplied by Fawkes, Francis Tresham, Everard Digby, and Bors Wintour were swiftly seized, their families displaced, and their fine houses looted. The last-arrested men confessed their guilt without torture. They had all done what they did for love of God and Robin Catesby, whose honor they esteemed. Not one of them would name the ones Cecil knew had fired their zeal. It seemed their own honor would not permit them to betray any priests.

But there was Bates, Catesby's servant. He too had been seized on the road between Warwickshire and London, coming, he stammered, from Harrowden Hall. Though he never confessed it, Bates had had a wild fantasy of changing his name and hiding in Southwark, of becoming a tapster, or, perchance, a player. But though he kept this fancy from the king's Privy Council, he shared other things, even things that had not happened, but that the council seemed to wish to hear. He had been sealed in this conspiracy by fear, not by faith—fear that he'd be silenced did he betray the fine men in silks who sat in high discussion around linen-draped tables. As for honor, it might be skimmed milk for all the good it did a man. Bates was no scholar, but—though Catesby had thought him simple—neither was he stupid. He saw clearly that he would be racked until he said what Cecil hoped he would say, and so he said it beforehand. *Aye, aye, priests were at the heart of it, lords. I have seen them at table with the men. They spoke of ways to replenish powder gone counterfeit. Who? Two. One bore one of the names you mention. Quindle, it were. The other? He went by different names, but the one he were called most often were Garnet.*

Chapter 37

The priest sat with his chin on his knees.

He feared most the numbing of the legs, when dormancy sent the blood to sleep. But he had learned from prior confinements to stretch his legs cautiously when the feeling in them began to fade, to flex his ankles and toes (quietly, quietly) until the nerves tingled. Just enough movement to keep blood in its course, and no more. Restraint, not just to keep silence, but to conserve strength.

He could not see Quindle in the blackness of the hole, but he could hear his friend's slight, occasional movements, and knew Quindle was doing as he was.

Once he woke from a dream-infected sleep and could not feel his lower legs at all. Barely able to stifle a panicked cry, he'd turned on his side in the filth, risen to his knees, and wiggled his nether-limbs as much as he could in the limited space. Quindle had woken, too, at his movement. His fellow priest had crawled (quietly, quietly) across the few feet that separated them. Together they'd pinched and kneaded Garnet's calves until the blood returned.

That incident had terrified him, but worse was the day — or night? — when Quindle did not respond to Garnet's urgent whisperings or even his kicks. He'd feared Father Quindle was dead. He'd stretched out an arm until he grasped his friend's wrist, and found a slow pulse. Breathing a prayer of thanks, he'd lain nearly motionless, clutching the wrist as though the pulse depended on his grip, until Quindle awoke from his stupor. Garnet had feared solitude then almost as much as he'd feared capture.

They had weapons to fight the tedium. When the voices and bumps of the pursuers could be only faintly heard, they recited in whispers the Gloria Patri or the Salve Regina. They heard each other's confessions; catechized one another as though they were children, and gave the responses. *Credo in Deum Patrem omnipotentum, Creatorem caeli et terrae.* I believe in one God, the maker of heaven and earth. *Altissimi in protection Dei caeli commorabitur.* He that dwelleth in the aid of the most High shall abide under His protection. *Quoniam angelis . . . .* Dreading, they would fall silent at the sound of hard footsteps on the floorboards overhead. The steps came frequently, as there were many searchers now at Harrowden, far more than the two or three that were usually sent. Garnet had tried to calculate the number. At least twelve. Perhaps fourteen. Impossible, truly, to tell, as the footfalls were sometimes masked by the barking of local dogs impressed for the search. He knew only that the intervals when Harrowden's parlor was empty were short indeed.

For ten days they had sat below the brickwork in front of the great fireplace. Their cramped purgatory lay between the house foundations and the room above. Five days into their confinement, they'd eaten the last of the biscuits, dried fish, and quince jelly Eliza had thrust into their hands as they quickly descended. Since then their sole dinner had been thin honeyed gruel, sent by Eliza through the long tube that led from her chamber down two chimneys into their narrow vault. The men could only sit or lie in the vault, which measured a mere five feet in length and width and four in depth. But by now, they could not have stood if they'd wanted to.

The air plagued them. Quindle murmured his dread that they would choke on it. When the message had come from Catesby by way of Bates, warning them that their cause (*their* cause?) was lost and they must hide, Bates spoke of having passed a band of armed men on the road, headed, it seemed, toward Harrowden. There had not been time to gather even a close stool to bring with them into the hiding place, and now the stench of their own bodies' waste was overpowering. This, indeed, was worse than the hunger that gnawed at their bellies, and the thirst. Garnet prayed ceaselessly that his sickness at the smell would not prove greater even than his fear.

In the house above, Eliza was dealing the pursuivants the hand she commonly played when her house was searched, assuming a behavior she and Anne Vaux had long ago named "the sillies." Whenever a new hiding space was uncovered by a searcher, as had happened at least once each day since since the men had invaded, Eliza opened her eyes wide in shock.

"How did *this* come there?" she gasped, as a grim-faced pursuivant brandished before her a gold chalice and a worn blue cope he'd extracted from a cavity in the chimney.

"Do you plead ignorance of this popish trumpery? 'Tis found in your house!"

"La, 'twas my husband's house before me. That he should have been such a trickster!" She clicked her tongue.

"These were also in the chimney." The pursuivant held up the deeds of the property and Eliza's own will.

Eliza stared at the documents. "So *that* is where my husband hid the . . . the papers!" She wrinkled her nose in perplexity. "They look to be of some importance, la. I do remember signing this one, before the dear man died."

Quindle and Garnet heard some of this from their lodging below the brickwork, and even in their torment had once or twice to stifle their laughter. But they'd quickly grown somber again. It was clear that the pursuers' appetites were more whetted by their discoveries than their suspicions were allayed by Eliza's sillies. They did not depart, and in time the priests' predicament grew too dire for any jest.

On the twelfth day they could bear it no longer. These searchers were not giving over the hunt. They seemed to have set up a camp in the place. Garnet and Quindle could not stay here for weeks. They planned in whispers, stealthily exercising their limbs, raising and lowering them by inches, praying for strength. Though their legs were swollen from inaction, they might still summon the strength to crawl, perhaps to walk. When the searchers were far from the parlor, the priests could raise the panel under the brickwork and haul themselves out. Quindle reminded Garnet of the large casement window Eliza kept unlocked in the far corner of the parlor when she was hiding men here. If they could reach that window quickly and quietly, they might exit and get unobserved to the stable. They were dressed like ordinary men, and there were many such on the premises. If they got to the stable unmolested, they could take horses and ride to West Wales. From there they might leave the country.

It was a desperate plan, but to remain in the hole was impossible. They waited, listening hard to the monotonous footsteps in the house above, flexing their weak limbs constantly. Finally a moment came when the only calls, steps, and bumps came from a far wing of the house where, from the sound of it, some new cavity had been breached, and all were now rushing to see it.

"Now!" whispered Quindle, and they rose. With what strength they could muster, they pushed the panel above them, and managed to slide the counterfeit brick flooring to the side.

Light spilled in. The glare hurt their eyes. They blinked, half-blind, as they pulled themselves painfully out. *Laudamus deo!* The room was empty. Drinking deeply of the air, which gave him some strength, Quindle pulled Garnet to his feet. Stumbling, they lurched toward the window. Quindle hoisted himself with his arms and fell through it. He rose dizzily on the cold ground outside, and held out his arms to catch Henry.

But Garnet had gone back to the brickwork, having suddenly realized that were they to leave their hiding place uncovered, Eliza could no longer deny her guilt. And if Eliza Vaux were taken, then Anne Vaux might well be arrested too, and she —

A dog barked, and he heard claws scratching on floorstones. Garnet turned, and fell as he did so. In a moment the dog was there, not growling, but joyfully licking his face. In his pain and his horror Garnet recognized him as a dog he knew, a dog to whom he had spoken gently and whose ears he had scratched, a dog from the parish, named Bolt, or Whip, or some such sharp, quick thing. He tried to rise, but the hound's fierce embrace prevented him.

"What are you?"

The searcher who'd just entered the room saw his commandeered dog nosing a filthy, staring man who lay next to an open hole in the fireplace. So pale and unexpected was this man that he seemed a ghost from centuries past, from the time of enchanted woods and Robin Hood and Friar Tuck in merry England. He had the mouldering smell of the grave about him. The pursuivant felt an atavistic urge to cross himself, and began to do so.

But then the apparition sneezed, as surely no ghost would do, and the searcher dropped his hand, shaking himself back into reason. Seeing another dog in the hallway behind, Whip ran from the room, leaving Henry alone on the hearth. The glint of the bounty fee entered the searcher's eye, and his lip curled in disgust. Advancing toward Garnet, he said, "Priest, you stink."

Chapter 38

April, 1606. Maundy Thursday.

Henry Garnet was lodged in the Tower and questioned daily, in a comfortable room, by Sir Edward Coke, England's chief magistrate. Cecil watched and listened, and said little at first. Both Coke and Cecil spoke kindly to him during the first several weeks, nourished him with soups, and saw that he slept and was clothed warmly. But as the days waned and waxed, the welcome bodily comforts came less and less frequently, and the questioning grew more harsh.

The details of the plot Sir Edward Coke described squared with all Garnet had heard from Quindle, the day after Catesby told Quindle of the scheme; that terrible day last summer, when Quindle had anxiously sought Garnet in his Thames Street rooms. Then Garnet had walked with his brother priest in the garden, and Quindle had burdened him with the knowledge both would have given anything not to possess. Garnet now had only two reasons not to speak of that incident freely. The first was that doing so would mark him a fellow conspirator. The second was that Quindle had spoken to him under the seal of confession.

Yet perhaps the second reason might be used to excuse everything.

"We know Father Quindle bought powder from a mill on Rotherhithe Street," Coke said. "He has told us so."

Garnet was silent. He doubted the men themselves could believe such a ludicrous tale. But could their words mean Father Quindle had been caught and confessed . . . something? Had he been tortured?

"Did you know of the plot?"

This was the question he'd feared, the inevitable question. Garnet must shroud truth in careful speech. "To the Catholic faithful, I have counseled only patience and prayer. I — "

"Less equivocation and more truth. Did you know of the plot and fail to inform the king's Privy Council so they might stop it?"

"Rumor runs rampant in the country, of treasons and — "

"A simple yea or nay, pray." Coke spoke with exaggerated courtesy. "Answer."

"I assure you I shall, lords." Garnet tried to speak good-humoredly, though his anger was rising at this hectoring, as was his fear. Mixed in that welter of feelings was shame. For he *had* known what was plotted, and had not spoken, out of hope for the all-answering letter from Rome, out of fear for himself and his friends. In hindsight it was clear to him that any virtue in his action — his *in*action — had been shot through with spidery sin. His deeds were a mingled yarn of good and evil. *Forgive what I have done, and what I have failed to do.* He wanted badly to unburden his conscience, but not to these men, who could not absolve him. He had, indeed, asked for a Catholic priest — surely he was not the only one of those in their prison! His request had been scoffed at. The memory of their refusal sparked more anger, and he said with some heat, "I *shall* speak yea or nay when such is my answer. Then, my yea shall mean yea and my nay shall mean nay."

"Paugh, you Jesuits parse even scripture, setting the word against the word!" Coke scoffed. "Do you not?"

Did he do so? Unlike (Garnet suspected) Sir Edward Coke — if Coke considered the matter at all — Garnet believed that the tongues of men and angels, spoken of in Corinthians, were two distinct languages. Or at least, he believed that this phrase of the apostle Paul's, in Latin, Greek, or English, could be read as signifying such. The speech of angels was straight and direct, as men like Coke flattered themselves theirs was. But the speech of men was different. Men's language was fallen and fractured, with as many surfaces as moving water.

He would have liked some water.

"I ask you again," Coke said, a threat in his voice. "Did you know of the powder plot?"

Garnet wet his parched lips with his tongue. He must invoke a sacrament in which these men did not believe. "Aught I knew," he said deliberately, "was spoken to me under the seal of confession."

"Ah. Give me leave, Lord Chief Justice." Cecil rose, to the displeasure of Coke, who disliked interruptions. "*Aught I knew was spoken to me under the seal of confession*," Cecil repeated. "So you claim. But this cannot be. To a man, those traitors we have questioned perversely maintain that they thought they were acting rightly, aye, dutifully, on behalf of God, Church, and country. Though some now aver they were mistaken in this, their newfound wisdom has come after the fact."

And has been prompted, perhaps, by shrieks from the room where the rack is kept. Garnet's heart beat more quickly, thinking of that room.

"They cannot have confessed what they did not think was sin," Cecil went on confidently. "Therefore you were not bound by the seal of confession."

"Which seal, in any case, this court and this nation are not obliged to recognize," Coke put in.

Garnet blinked, thinking furiously. "Yet I have not said I was told directly of the plot." He *had* been so told, but he had not *said* he'd been so told.

"You were asked whether you knew of the plot. Your first phrase in response was, 'Aught I knew.' Aught you knew of what? Of the plot, certainly."

Cecil was right. Garnet had slipped.

"Why did you not reveal what you knew?" Cecil persisted.

Coke glanced at Cecil in vexation. He knew there was an easy answer to this. But Cecil ignored Coke's glare. *He* knew that if Garnet used the readiest excuse, he would further incriminate himself.

And Garnet fell into the trap. "The late proclamation of the king is death to priests. Were I to have come forth, into the light, with my knowledge of...." He faltered. "Of...."

"Of the powder plot," Cecil finished helpfully.

Garnet's ensuing silence did not surprise Cecil, who assumed the priest was meditating on a new alibi. He was a Jesuit, and thus by definition a liar.

Coke suddenly spoke. "Did you and Anne Vaux live together as man and wife?"

Garnet closed his eyes in pain.

Now it was Cecil who glared at Coke, before turning in disgust to the window. It was well known that the gentlewoman Anne Vaux hid priests, among them probably this Garnet, at White Webbs near London and Baddesley Clinton in Warwickshire. Out of this common wisdom Coke had derived a particular torment, having discovered that this question of his relation to Anne Vaux seemed to irritate the priestly prisoner.

His thought, he'd explained to Cecil, was to "put the peter-priest on pins and needles," that the man might more easily trip. Yet Cecil found this question not only rude but a waste of time.

"Anne Vaux is a virtuous lady," Garnet said. He wondered where Anne was. He prayed silently that somehow he might hear of her safety. "She is my sister in Christ."

"Oh *ho!*" said Coke. "Oh ho *ho!*"

Cecil sighed and turned back from the window. "To speak again of the powder plot. You need not have declared yourself a priest in informing your king of the danger. You might have sent an anonymous letter. Such was done by the woman just mentioned, Anne Vaux, in an earlier case. Why did you not send a letter?"

"I wrote to warn the pope, to ask him to admonish Catholics to be patient," Garnet said, and only then saw that he had now truly confessed to the fatal knowledge. *Why did I say 'warn'?*

"The *pope!*" Coke shouted. "Much he would care if our king were blown to bits!"

Miserably, Garnet addressed himself to Cecil, whose eyes were shining with satisfaction. Garnet would not live, and Garnet knew this. He and men like Quindle had always been these hunters' chief quarry. Now he was caught. Most likely Quindle was caught too. As for Garnet, he had been thirty-three years in God's service in England, and perchance thirty-three years was all God asked of him. It was all God had asked of a better man than he. His measure was ended.

Yet perhaps he could purchase some mercy toward whichever wretched gentlemen of the powder plot still lived. He began. "Lords, however misled these men were — "

"Aye, by you!" barked Coke.

"My brethren and I *never* counseled violence."

"But you did not try to stop it."

"My lords, I mean only to say that these men wished to redeem their country. The king did them injuries, and — "

Cecil's laugh was short and humorless. "It is the time, and not the king, that does them injuries."

"The time?" What did this mean?

Coke spoke angrily. "Fifty years ago Bloody Queen Mary burned English Bibles and Protestant clerics. What said the good Protestant bishop Hugh Latimer, before they set fire to him at the stake? *We shall this day light such a candle, by God's grace, in England, as I trust shall never be put out!* And indeed the flame of his martyrdom has *not* been put out. Has Latimer been forgotten? Or is his martyrdom not honored in Foxe's great Book of Martyrs, which all Londoners read? Is the English Bible gone?" He pointed to a Bible which lay open on a stand in the corner of the room. "Or is it not instead read by everyone in the land, from the meanest plowboy to the king?"

Garnet said nothing. Coke's questions were clearly rhetorical.

Cecil had remained standing throughout this latest exchange. Now he began to stroll the room with his hands clasped behind his back. Because of his low height, he was not at his most commanding while thus engaged, but he seemed both to know this and not to care. He hummed. He was resolved to lighten the heaviness that hung in the air. While Coke had thundered as though from a godly pulpit, Cecil, when he finally spoke, sounded detached, as though the three men were assembled for a scholarly debate in a Cambridge lecture hall. He raised a finger. "Henry Garnet, it should have been thought that Bloody Mary's failure to wrench the land backwards in time had been sufficient to warn your gentlemen, your boys playing with fire, that England is a Protestant nation now."

To this Garnet *was* tempted to reply. Queen Mary had died after only five years of rule, and her Protestant sister Elizabeth, gifted with longer life, had made short work of most of Mary's hard but necessary measures. Yet he knew it would be folly to defend Catholic Mary. This comfortable room was a mousetrap. He remembered his superiors' strict warning, delivered in France after his training and ordination, on the eve of his return to England. *If caught, let not thy questioners draw thee into any discussion of spiritual things.* To do so could only make his case worse. So it had been for Edmund Campion.

At the thought of how Father Campion had died, Garnet went cold with fear. *Jesu. Jesu.*

He must think only of his flock. He must not worsen the cases of the men he yet hoped might be pardoned.

But a deep disappointment troubled him, made him tired. The downtrodden English had not risen for Catesby. Perhaps, after all, Cecil was right. Perhaps England was so deeply benighted that it could not be redeemed. Yet could he accept a whole people's damnation? He felt ill. This argument confused him, and he must avoid it. He began again to speak for the conspirators, some of whom, he was sure, must still be alive. "Lords, I beg you to consider that the men you have arrested have children. They — "

"No more words, Garnet." Despite his reasoning manner, Cecil considered all peter-priests no equals in debate, but traitors in states of pre- or post-confession. Now that he had what he wanted from Garnet, he cut off the man's speech. It was over, and they need do no more than reveal the justice that was here achieved, through a show trial in the Guildhall, to satisfy the commons. Its outcome was sure. "These men have children, you say. Aye. So does the baker across the square from the House of Lords. And so does the king."

Back in his cell, Garnet prayed for hours, out of the depths of his despair. He then drifted into a restive sleep. Jesus's face hung before him, in its sorrowful, broken majesty, his forehead bleeding below his sharp crown. *I cannot,* Henry said. Jesus turned his back, and the priest cried out in his loneliness. Then he saw the criss-crossed stripes, and the flesh, torn and ragged. *I am your heart's desire,* said the voice of his beloved. *Follow me.*

He was awoken by the sound of a key in the cell-door's iron lock, a creak of hinges, and an arc of lamplight on the stone floor. He felt wind on his face from somewhere. Squinting, he looked up.

There, silhouetted in the doorframe, St. Winifred stood.

He rolled from his pallet to the floor, falling on hands and knees. He touched his forehead to the cold stone. Footsteps approached him, and a warm hand touched the back of his neck. The voice that spoke was tender and warm, and he knew it as well as he knew his own. It was no otherworldly voice, not Winifred's, after all, but Anne Vaux's. "Henry," she said. "Dear Henry"

Garnet had faced the weeks of hard questioning, the thirst, the sneers of prison guards and privy counselors, and the cold of his Tower cell, all without weeping. Now Anne's voice reduced him to tears. Holding his head, he rocked back and forth on the stone floor, sobbing in awkward gasps. Anne placed her lantern on the floor and held him tightly. "Ah, ah, Nan," he said. "Nan. I am so afraid!"

She gripped him close, making soothing, wordless noises. She laid her head on his back, against his shoulders, and her own wet face dampened his garment.

After a while Henry straightened. He sat with his back against the
bed, wiping his face. She gave him a handkerchief and he blew his nose.
"Ah, forgive me," he gasped. "Forgive me, my sister."

"Forgive *you!*"Anne, too, was wiping her cheeks. "It is you who must
forgive all of us. We are the cause of your trial here."

"No. No. I follow the path God has set before me." Henry grasped
her hand and looked hard at her. "I am glad you are not in prison. I know
nothing of anyone. If I asked after a friend, I would put that friend in
danger."

She raised a warning finger to her lips, and he understood instantly
that they were being spied on. He lowered his voice to a whisper. "Thy
family is well?"

She knew what he meant. "Eliza was taken."

"No!"

"They gave her a choice. Imprisonment and questioning in London,
or two hours in her parlor listening to a chastening homily from a Cal-
vinist pastor. She chose prison."

Henry gave a snort, half-laugh, half-sob. Despite herself Anne, too,
started to laugh. "Ah, bless us! After two days of listening to Eliza, the
questioner freed her. He could not send her away fast enough!"

"How did she — "

"Manage it? How do you think?" Softly, Anne feigned her sister-in-
law's trilling voice. "*La, how can you think I knew aught of gentlemen's
dealings? That a woman would be trusted not to spill secrets! My dear husband spoke only five words a day to me when he lived, and those concerned
what wine should be served with supper! Marry, the man was a devil with a
bottle.* And so forth."

Garnet pressed Anne's hand to his smiling lips. "Blessed Eliza," he
whispered. He doubted that the lord Cecil would have been taken in by
the sillies, but Eliza, it seemed, had been given a less formidable interro-
gator. He thanked God she was free.

Still, Eliza's guilt in this plot troubled him. Like Catesby, she had
frustrated all his attempts to sound her on her knowledge of the plan,
and to counsel her. In this effort he had failed, despite his promise to
Anne.

He looked at his friend, soberly now, hoping to convey all this to
her through his eyes. She grew quiet as well, returning his gaze. It was

perilous to speak of anything here. "Our . . . other friends?" he asked cautiously.

She moistened her lips and spoke in the faintest of whispers. "Catesby and Percy were shot dead."

"God rest them!"

"The rest are taken or — "

"The *rest?*"

"Of those who plotted," she said quickly. "But many of the innocent have been harried and questioned, and it goes on."

He raised a hand. "No names."

"No. Some escaped. The little carpenter has crossed the water to France. And — "

Heavy footfalls sounded in the corridor outside. She turned her head quickly. "Five minutes," a guard said brusquely through the partly-opened door.

Henry gripped her hands desperately. "Pray with me, dear friend."

"I had come for that."

Garnet began in English, fearing Latin might land Anne in trouble. *"For though I should walk in the midst of the shadow of death, I will fear no evils, for thou art with me."* They spoke together. *"Thy rod and thy staff, they have comforted me."*

The guard stood in the doorway. He granted them their psalm. After a moment or two, the guard took his cap off, and bowed his head. When he heard them fall silent, he said gently, "Come. Out with you now, lady."

The pair of them rose, holding one another's hands. Anne lightly kissed Henry's cheek, knelt to pick up her lantern, and walked quickly to the door. There she turned and stood still for a moment. "Bless you, Father!" she said with fierce ardor. Then she was gone.

He heard her quick steps retreating down the passageway. The guard shut the door.

Henry closed his eyes and sank back on the pallet. He would lift his sour cross, he now knew, with no last rites, and no confessor to grant him penance for his sins.

Chapter 39

May 3, 1606. The Feast of the Cross.

They were hanged one by one at the western end of Parliament Place, so that heaven's thwarting of their plot might be visually signified. Even at Essex's beheading there had not been seen such a crowd. The people overflowed into the streets outside. Children stood on barrels behind their parents. Above, men and women peered from windows to watch the spectacle of God's justice.

Young Everard Digby was the first to mount the scaffold. Mary Digby watched him unblinking, hidden within the murmuring mob. His eyes traveled, seeking desperately, until they lighted on hers. She stood straight, pressed by the hot festival crowd. When their eyes met she smiled lovingly, gripping the hands of Anne and Eliza Vaux, who stood on either side of her. Mary Digby had braved the horror for this one shared glance, to hearten her husband. Her twins and her infant son had not been left home, for they had no home now. The Digby manor in Buckinghamshire had been plundered and burned, their estate confiscated by the Crown. The children were with friends at Harrowden, which against all probabilities — and some said all justice — had been left in Eliza's possession.

Mary Digby's children would not see what she saw and what she would see, sleeping and waking, each day of her life to come. This was the body of her beloved cut down from the rope while it still breathed and then sliced apart, and his heart held up by the executioner, while that swordsman announced to all that this was the heart of a traitor.

The same was then done in terrible succession to Gawain and Bors Wintour, Ambrose Rookwood, Robert Keyes, Guido Fawkes, and young Tom Bates — Bates, who found he would hang with gentlemen after all, in a grim leveling. Save those who'd died at Holbeach House, Francis Tresham and the blind John Grant were the luckiest ones. Having failed to buy his way out of this scandal, Tresham had taken ill in the Tower and perished there. Grant had died in jail too, from the festering of his burns.

The crowd was howling. More than once the three women wondered if their lives had ended and they now stood in Hell. Yet without flinching or falling Eliza and Anne Vaux and Mary Digby watched the men die. The women held no rosaries, only each other's hands, as they stood and prayed.

From a window in Westminster Palace, King James watched as well, looking pale and unhappy. He schooled himself to the lesson. Surely papists were the devil's servants, the beggars who threw rocks when not given alms, and every kindness done to them was answered with a treason. His dear wife Anna's superstitions notwithstanding, the papists could not be endured. New laws must be drawn up to bar them from office, higher fines levied . . . .

By James's sides, as was proper, sat his sons, now aged twelve and four, there to serve as witnesses to the just destruction of those who would have killed them. As the third traitor's heart was held up, young Henry turned and vomited on a servant. Little Charles had been yawning at the long and ghastly spectacle, which he thought was not real but some new masque made for his father's entertainment. His interest was revived by the sight and sound of his brother's retching. He stared at Prince Henry raptly, fingering the chain of pretty beads the big knight at the Christmas Revels had given him sixteen months before. The chain had broken, but he still carried it everywhere.

And now Father Garnet stood high on the scaffold, searching everywhere for Anne's eyes. When he found them he hardly knew them for their swollenness. Yet there she was, standing with Eliza Vaux and Mary Digby. He looked at her hard for a moment, extracting her last blessing, before the shifting sea of people hid her face from view. Then he chided himself, knowing he did her no good seeking her comfort thus, as though she were wife to him, as though she were what she was, the earthly love of his life. He had told her a hundred times his spouse was otherwhere. He would look down no longer. Setting his gaze on the sky, he felt an arrow of joy pierce his heart at the thought of the coming union. He stripped off his clothes to his shirt. His animal body shook with fear and cold. He must suffer with his body. But his body was not himself.

He had determined that at the least, whatever confessions they'd wrung from him, or thought they had, he would not recite the lines they'd scripted for him: lines that said, falsely, that he recanted the counterfeit faith of the Catholic Church. When pressed to do so by the lord who stood next to him on the scaffold, he shook his head. "I die a true and perfect Catholic!" he said, as loudly as he could, to jeers from the mob. *"Truly spoken, papist!"* *"Aye, and you do!"* He raised his voice. "And a priest after the order of Melchisedec!" Some in the crowd quieted at that, looking frightened and unsure.

Garnet put his head in the noose.

Time slowed for him. The visions came, like prophecies, or hopes.

There was dear Father Quindle, riding hard through the mountains of Wales, then stowing away at Milford Haven on a ship bound for Calais, and finally wending his way through the Papal States, wearing the borrowed traveling cloak of a generous French nobleman. Quindle, crossing a whole continent, and finally finding Garnet's lost letter to the pope, and buying it from the under-secretary who'd pocketed it, thinking a Catholic uprising in England would be interesting, viewed from afar.

Now a wedding, twenty-two years hence! Edward Vaux, Eliza's son, now in his forties, is bending to kiss his new bride. She is a matronly woman, plump with the passage of years, but still unmistakably his beloved Elizabeth Howard, who six months ago buried her old first husband, Lord Knollys. Leaving the church, his shining eyes young in a middle-aged face, Edward Vaux pats the shoulder of his stepson, whom, in Christian generosity, he has adopted — and who looks miraculously like him.

And back again, and off to the west, at this very moment in 1606, Thomas Percy's widow Martha is racing the sun, riding fast from Northumbria on a stolen horse, carrying jewels, her daughter, and her newborn son. Martha's dark hair has come loose from its bands, and streams behind her in a way her husband would have thought unseemly, so wanton it was, and so wild. But she doesn't care who sees it. She spurs the horse, feeling the weight of the babe she has strapped to her breast. Martha wants only to save her children, herself, and her money. She halts at an inn in Chester, just short of the Welsh border. There, in that town, in quick time, she makes shift to divest herself of both the dangerous name of Percy and her maiden name, Wright, vowing she'll marry a prosperous Protestant, what e'er he be. And here, in the end, is Martha's choice:

a wizened and amiable widower, a talkative Chester tavern host, who finds her congenial in speech and well-suited to warm his old bones, and so, welcomes her and her boy and girl.

Now a wonder! Years later, here is Martha's second child, the infant grown, the long-awaited son her Thomas fathered but never knew. He is a Percy by nature, but never by faith. Since his Chester christening, the boy has borne the Puritan name of Ark-of-the-Covenant Buckmaster. At eighteen he travels to London to earn his fortune. He concludes that his road to success runs through the Inns of Court, and studies law. In decades to come, he preaches most eloquently in the House of Commons, hard by where Garnet now stands, as England erupts in open war and the Protestants, at last, fight each other. At forty-two, Buckmaster zealously champions the Puritan cause and argues the need, yea, the *duty* of a Christian commonwealth to cast down the king it has made an idol like the golden calf of the Israelites, yea, to bring that king to the chopping block, that only God might rule their island! And this idol king, now brought to the block, is not pale, retching Prince Henry — Henry, spared death by powderblast, but felled by typhus at eighteen. It is Prince Henry's brother, laughing little Charles, who as a man not only possesses, like all Stuarts, the mind of an absolute monarch, but finds himself oddly drawn to the papist ceremonies the Puritans despise. There before the grandchildren of the Londoners who mocked Garnet, on the very scaffold where a gunpowder priest once shivered in the English wind, King Charles the First kneels, grasping some beads he has carried always since he was three. He breathes a Latin prayer, then surrenders his neck to the axe.

All these visions crowd Garnet's mind in the seconds before he hangs, gladly dead, from the gallows. And in the moment the rope tightens around his neck, in his ecstasy he perceives something more. He sees that the Church will be broken until the end of time, but that God in his mercy is whole. He sees that the Christ he now figures died for King James as well as for the powdermen, and for the hooded man who sharpens his sword at the base of the scaffold. Christ died for these no less than for himself, Henry Garnet, priest of England. *There is a kingdom deeper than Rome,* he thinks as he drops.

Acknowledgments

Thanks to all those who have helped me with this book, which was long in the making. Thanks to Heather Addison, Chuck Bentley, Meg Dupuis, the late Carolyn French, Katherine Joslin, Mustafa Mirzeler, Chris Nagle, Eve Salisbury, Amy Silver, Michèle Sterlin, Amanda Tiffany, and Nick Witschi for their sympathetic reading and support, and to Western Michigan University for assisting my research with a FRACAA grant. My talented editor, Sharonah Fredrick, saw the story I meant to tell and helped me bring it into the light. I am especially grateful to James Shapiro for the generous gift of his reading time and expert counsel regarding things Jacobean, and to my husband Tom Lucking, whose enthusiasm and shrewd advice persuaded me to stick with the novel and make it better.

CPSIA information can be obtained
at www.ICGtesting.com
Printed in the USA
LVOW04s1558250416

485219LV00020B/730/P